MW00479913

THE WEIRD TALES OF
CONAN
THE BARBARIAN

ROBERT E. HOWARD

DOVER PUBLICATIONS, INC.
Mineola, New York

Bibliographical Note

This Dover edition, first published in 2016, is an unabridged republication of the text of the following five stories by Robert E. Howard: "The Devil in Iron," originally published in *Weird Tales* magazine, in August 1934; "The People of the Black Circle," originally published in *Weird Tales* magazine, in September 1934; "Beyond the Black River," originally published in *Weird Tales* magazine, in May–June 1935; "Red Nails," originally published in serial form in *Weird Tales* magazine, in July, August-September, and October 1936; and "The Hour of the Dragon," originally published in serial form in *Weird Tales* magazine, December 1935 through April 1936.

Library of Congress Cataloging-in-Publication Data

Names: Howard, Robert E. (Robert Ervin), 1906–1936, author.
Title: The weird tales of Conan the Barbarian / Robert E. Howard.
Description: Dover edition. | Mineola, New York : Dover Publications, 2016.
Identifiers: LCCN 2015047541 | ISBN 9780486794884 (softcover) |
    ISBN 0486794881 (softcover)
Subjects: LCSH: Conan (Fictitious character)—Fiction. | BISAC: FICTION /
    Fantasy / General. | GSAFD: Fantasy fiction.
Classification: LCC PS3515.O842 A6 2016 | DDC 813/.52—dc23 LC
record available at http://lccn.loc.gov/2015047541

Manufactured in the United States by RR Donnelley
79488101   2016
www.doverpublications.com

Contents

Contents

The Devil in Iron

1

The fisherman loosened his knife in its scabbard. The gesture was instinctive, for what he feared was nothing a knife could slay, not even the saw-edged crescent blade of the Yuetshi that could disembowel a man with an upward stroke. Neither man nor beast threatened him in the solitude which brooded over the castellated isle of Xapur.

He had climbed the cliffs, passed through the jungle that bordered them, and now stood surrounded by evidences of a vanished state. Broken columns glimmered among the trees, the straggling lines of crumbling walls meandered off into the shadows, and under his feet were broad paves, cracked and bowed by roots growing beneath.

The fisherman was typical of his race, that strange people whose origin is lost in the gray dawn of the past, and who have dwelt in their rude fishing huts along the southern shore of the Sea of Vilayet since time immemorial. He was broadly built, with long, apish arms and a mighty chest, but with lean loins and thin, bandy legs. His face was broad, his forehead low and retreating, his hair thick and tangled. A belt for a knife and a rag for a loin cloth were all he wore in the way of clothing.

That he was where he was proved that he was less dully incurious than most of his people. Men seldom visited Xapur. It was uninhabited, all but forgotten, merely one among the myriad isles which dotted the great inland sea. Men called it Xapur, the Fortified, because of its ruins, remnants of some prehistoric kingdom, lost and forgotten before the conquering Hyborians had ridden southward. None knew who reared those stones, though dim legends lingered amond the Yuetshi which half intelligibly suggested a connection of immeasurable antiquity between the fishers and the unknown island kingdom.

But it had been a thousand years since any Yuetshi had understood the import of these tales; they repeated them now as a meaningless formula, a gibberish framed to their lips by custom. No Yuetshi had come to Xapur for a century. The adjacent coast of the mainland was uninhabited, a reedy marsh given over to the grim beasts that haunted it. The fisher's village lay some distance to the south, on the mainland.

A storm had blown his frail fishing craft far from his accustomed haunts and wrecked it in a night of flaring lightning and roaring waters on the towering cliffs of the isle. Now, in the dawn, the sky shone blue and clear; the rising sun made jewels of the dripping leaves. He had climbed the cliffs to which he had clung through the night because, in the midst of the storm, he had seen an appalling lance of lightning fork out of the black heavens, and the concussion of its stroke, which had shaken the whole island, had been accompanied by a cataclysmic crash that he doubted could have resulted from a riven tree.

A dull curiosity had caused him to investigate; and now he had found what he sought, and an animal-like uneasiness possessed him, a sense of lurking peril.

Among the trees reared a broken domelike structure, built of gigantic blocks of the peculiar ironlike green stone found only on the islands of Vilayet. It seemed incredible that human hands could have shaped and placed them, and certainly it was beyond human power to have overthrown the structure they formed. But the thunderbolt had splintered the ton-heavy blocks like so much glass, reduced others to green dust, and ripped away the whole arch of the dome.

The fisherman climbed over the debris and peered in, and what he saw brought a grunt from him. Within the ruined dome, surrounded by stone dust and bits of broken masonry, lay a man on a golden block. He was clad in a sort of skirt and a shagreen girdle. His black hair, which fell in a square mane to his massive shoulders, was confined about his temples by a narrow gold band. On his bare, muscular breast lay a curious dagger with a jeweled pommel, a shagreen-bound hilt, and a broad, crescent blade. It was much like the knife the fisherman wore at his hip, but it lacked the serrated edge and was made with infinitely greater skill.

The fisherman lusted for the weapon. The man, of course, was dead; had been dead for many centuries. This dome was his tomb. The fisherman did not wonder by what art the ancients had preserved the body in such a vivid likeness of life, which kept the muscular limbs full and unshrunken, the dark flesh vital. The dull brain of the Yuetshi had room only for his desire for the knife with its delicate, waving lines along the dully gleaming blade.

Scrambling down into the dome, he lifted the weapon from the man's breast. As he did so, a strange and terrible thing came to pass. The muscular, dark hands knotted convulsively, the lids flared open, revealing great, dark, magnetic eyes, whose stare struck the startled fisherman like a physical blow. He recoiled, dropping the jeweled dagger in his peturbation. The man on the dais heaved up to a sitting position, and the fisherman gaped at the full extent of his size, thus revealed. His narrowed eyes held the Yuetshi, and in those slitted orbs he read neither friendliness nor gratitude; he saw only a fire as alien and hostile as that which burns in the eyes of a tiger.

Suddenly the man rose and towered above him, menace in his every aspect. There was no room in the fisherman's dull brain for fear, at least for such fear as might grip a man who has just seen the fundamental laws of nature defied. As the great hands fell to his shoulders, he drew his saw-edged knife and struck upward with the same motion. The blade splintered against the stranger's corded belly as against a steel column, and then the fisherman's thick neck broke like a rotten twig in the giant hands.

2

Jehungir Aagha, lord of Khawarizm and keeper of the costal border, scanned once more the ornate parchment scroll with its peacock seal and laughed shortly and sardonically.

"Well?" bluntly demanded his counsellor Ghaznavi.

Jehungir shrugged his shoulders. He was a handsome man, with the merciless pride of birth and accomplishment.

"The king grows short of patience," he said. "In his own hand he complains bitterly of what he calls my failure to guard the frontier. By Tarim, if I cannot deal a blow to these robbers of the steppes, Khawarizm may own a new lord."

Ghaznavi tugged his gray-shot beard in meditation. Yezdigerd, king of Turan, was the mightiest monarch in the world. In his palace in the great port city of Aghrapur was heaped the plunder of empires. His fleets of purple-sailed war galleys had made Vilayet an Hyrkanian lake. The dark-skinned people of Zamora paid him tribute, as did the eastern provinces of Koth. The Shemites bowed to his rule as far west as Shushan. His armies ravaged the borders of Stygia in the south and the snowy lands of the Hyperboreans in the north. His riders bore torch and sword westward into Brythunia and Ophir and Corinthia, even to the borders of Nemedia. His gilt-helmeted swordsmen had trampled hosts under their horses' hoofs, and walled cities went up in flames at his command. In the glutted slave markets of Aghrapur, Sultanapur, Khawarizm, Shahpur, and Khorusun, women were sold for three small silver coins—blonde Brythunians, tawny Stygians, dark-haired Zamorians, ebon Kushites, olive-skinned Shemites.

Yet, while his swift horsemen overthrew armies far from his frontiers, at his very borders an audacious foe plucked his beard with a red-dripping and smoke-stained hand.

On the broad steppes between the Sea of Vilayet and the borders of the easternmost Hyborian kingdoms, a new race had sprung up in the past half-century, formed originally of fleeing criminals, broken men, escaped slaves, and deserting soldiers. They were men of many crimes and countries, some born on the steppes, some fleeing from the kingdoms in the West. They were called kozak, which means wastrel.

Dwelling on the wild, open steppes, owning no law but their own peculiar code, they had become a people capable even of defying the Grand Monarch. Ceaselessly they raided the Turanian frontier, retiring in the steppes when defeated; with the pirates of Vilayet, men of much the same breed, they harried the coast, preying off the merchant ships which plied between the Hyrkanian ports.

"How am I to crush these wolves?" demanded Jehungir. "If I follow them into the steppes, I run the risk either of being cut off and destroyed, or of having them elude me entirely and burn the city in my absence. Of late they have been more daring than ever."

"That is because of the new chief who has risen among them," answered Ghaznavi. "You know whom I mean."

"Aye!" replied Jehungir feelingly. "It is that devil Conan; he is even wilder than the kozaks, yet he is crafty as a mountain lion."

"It is more through wild animal instinct than through intelligence," answered Ghaznavi. "The other kozaks are at least descendants of civilized men. He is a barbarian. But to dispose of him would be to deal them a crippling blow."

"But how?" demanded Jehungir. "He has repeatedly cut his way out of spots that seemed certain death for him. And, instinct or cunning, he has avoided or escaped every trap set for him."

"For every beast and for every man there is a trap he will not escape," quoth Ghaznavi. "When we have parleyed with the kozaks for the ransom of captives, I have observed this man Conan. He has a keen relish for women and strong drink. Have your captive Octavia fetched here."

Jehungir clapped his hands, and an impressive Kushite eunuch, an image of shining ebony in silken pantaloons, bowed before him and went to do his bidding. Presently he returned, leading by the wrist a tall, handsome girl, whose yellow hair, clear eyes, and fair skin identified her as a pure-blooded member of her race. Her scanty silk tunic, girded at the waist, displayed the marvelous contours of her magnificent figure. Her fine eyes flashed with resentment and her red lips were sulky, but submission had been taught her during her captivity. She stood with hanging head before her master until he motioned her to a seat on the divan beside him. Then he looked inquiringly at Ghaznavi.

"We must lure Conan away from the kozaks," said the counsellor abruptly. "Their war camp is at present pitched somewhere on the lower reaches of the Zaporoska River—which, as you well know, is a wilderness of reeds, a swampy jungle in which our last expedition was cut to pieces by those masterless devils."

"I am not likely to forget that," said Jehungir wryly.

"There is an uninhabited island near the mainland," said Ghaznavi, "known as Xapur, the Fortified, because of some ancient ruins upon it. There is a peculiarity about it which makes it perfect for our purpose. It has no shoreline but rises sheer out of the sea in cliffs a hundred and fifty feet tall. Not even an ape could negotiate them. The only place where a man can go up or down is a narrow path on the western side that has the appearance of a worn stair, carved into the solid rock of the cliffs.

"If we could trap Conan on that island, alone, we could hunt him down at our leisure, with bows, as men hunt a lion."

"As well wish for the moon," said Jehungir impatiently. "Shall we send him a messenger, bidding him climb the cliffs and await our coming?"

"In effect, yes!" Seeing Jehungir's look of amazement, Ghaznavi continued: "We will ask for a parley with the kozaks in regard to prisoners, at the edge of the steppes by Fort Ghori. As usual, we will go with a force and encamp outside the castle. They will come, with an equal force, and the parley will go forward with the usual distrust and suspicion. But this time we will take with us, as if by casual chance, your beautiful captive." Octavia changed color and listened with intensified interest as the counsellor nodded toward her. "She will use all her wiles to attract Conan's attention. That should not be difficult. To that wild reaver, she should appear a dazzling vision of loveliness. Her vitality and substantial figure should appeal to him more vividly than would one of the doll-like beauties of your seraglio."

Octavia sprang up, her white fists clenched, her eyes blazing and her figure quivering with outraged anger.

"You would force me to play the trollop with this barbarian?" she exclaimed. "I will not! I am no market-block slut to smirk and ogle at a steppes robber. I am the daughter of a Nemedian lord—"

"You were of the Nemedian nobility before my riders carried you off," returned Jehungir cynically. "Now you are merely a slave who will do as she is bid."

"I will not!" she raged.

"On the contrary," rejoined Jehungir with studied cruelty, "you will. I like Ghaznavi's plan. Continue, prince among counsellors."

"Conan will probably wish to buy her. You will refuse to sell her, of course, or to exchange her for Hyrkanian prisoners. He may then try to steal her, or take her by force—though I do not think even he would break the parley truce. Anyway, we must be prepared for whatever he might attempt.

"Then, shortly after the parley, before he has time to forget all about her, we will send a messenger to him, under a flag of truce, accusing him of stealing the girl and demanding her return. He may kill the messenger, but at least he will think that she has escaped.

"Then we will send a spy—a Yuetishi fisherman will do—to the kozak camp, who will tell Conan that Octavia is hiding on Xapur. If I know my man, he will go straight to that place."

"But we do not know that he will go alone," Jehungir argued.

"Does a man take a band of warriors with him, when going to a rendezvous with a woman he desires?" retorted Ghaznavi. "The chances are all that he will go alone. But we will take care of the other alternative. We will not await him on the island, where we might be trapped ourselves, but among the reeds of a marshy point, which juts out to within a thousand yards of Xapur. If he brings a large force, we'll beat a retreat and think up another plot. If he comes alone or with a small party, we will have him. Depend upon it, he will come, remembering your charming slave's smiles and meaning glances."

"I will never descend to such shame!" Octavia was wild with fury and humiliation. "I will die first!"

"You will not die, my rebellious beauty," said Jehungir, "but you will be subjected to a very painful and humiliating experience."

He clapped his hands, and Octavia palled. This time it was not the Kushite who entered, but a Shemite, a heavily muscled man of medium height with a short, curled, blue-black beard.

"Here is work for you, Gilzan," said Jehungir. "Take this fool, and play with her awhile. Yet be careful not to spoil her beauty."

With an inarticulate grunt the Shemite seized Octavia's wrist, and at the grasp of his iron fingers, all the defiance went out of her. With a piteous cry she tore away and threw herself on her knees before her implacable master, sobbing incoherently for mercy. Jehungir dismissed the disappointed torturer with a gesture, and said to Ghaznavi: "If your plan succeeds, I will fill your lap with gold."

3

In the darkness before dawn, an unaccustomed sound disturbed the solitude that slumbered over the reedy marshes and the misty waters of the coast. It was not a drowsy waterfowl nor a waking beast. It was a human who struggled through the thick reeds, which were taller than a man's head.

It was a woman, had there been anyone to see, tall, and yellow-haired, her splendid limbs molded by her draggled tunic. Octavia had escaped in good earnest, every outraged fiber of her still tingling from her experience in a captivity that had become unendurable.

Jehungir's mastery of her had been bad enough; but with deliberate fiendishness Jehungir had given her to a nobleman whose name was a byword for degeneracy even in Khawarizm.

Octavia's resilient flesh crawled and quivered at her memories. Desperation had nerved her climb from Jelal Khan's castle on a rope made of strips from torn tapestries, and chance had led her to a picketed horse. She had ridden all night, and dawn found her with a foundered steed on the swampy shores of the sea. Quivering with the abhorence of being dragged back to the revolting destiny planned for her by Jelal Khan, she plunged into the morass, seeking a hiding place from the pursuit she expected. When the reeds grew thinner around her and the water rose about her thighs, she saw the dim loom of an island ahead of her. A broad span of water lay between, but she did not hesitate. She waded out until the low waves were lapping about her waist; then she struck out strongly, swimming with a vigor that promised unusual endurance.

As she neared the island, she saw that it rose sheer from the water in castlelike cliffs. She reached them at last but found neither ledge to stand on below the water, nor to cling to above. She swam on, following the curve of the cliffs, the strain of her long flight beginning to weight her limbs. Her hands fluttered along the sheer stone, and suddenly they found a depression. With a sobbing gasp of relief, she pulled herself out of the water and clung there, a dripping white goddess in the dim starlight.

She had come upon what seemed to be steps carved in the cliff. Up them she went, flattening herself against the stone as she caught a faint clack of muffled oars. She strained her eyes and thought she made out a vague bulk moving toward the reedy point she had just quitted. But it was too far away for her to be sure in the darkness, and presently the faint sound ceased and she continued her climb. If it were her pursuers, she knew of no better course than to hide on the island. She knew that most of the islands off that marshy coast were uninhabited. This might be a pirate's lair, but even pirates would be preferable to the beast she had escaped.

A vagrant thought crossed her mind as she climbed, in which she mentally compared her former master with the kozak chief with whom—by compulsion—she had shamefully flirted in the pavillions of the camp by Fort Ghori, where the Hyrkanian lords had parleyed with the warriors of the steppes. His burning gaze had frightened and humiliated her, but his cleanly elemental fierceness set him above Jelal Khan, a monster such as only an overly opulent civilization can produce.

She scrambled up over the cliff edge and looked timidly at the dense shadows which confronted her. The trees grew close to the cliffs, presenting a solid mass of blackness. Something whirred above her head and she cowered, even though realizing it was only a bat.

She did not like the looks of those ebony shadows, but she set her teeth and went toward them, trying not to think of snakes. Her bare feet made no sound in the spongy loam under the trees.

Once among them, the darkness closed frighteningly about her. She had not taken a dozen steps when she was no longer able to look back and see the cliffs and the sea beyond. A few steps more and she became hopelessly confused and lost her sense of direction. Through the tangled branches not even a star peered. She groped and floundered on, blindly, and then came to a sudden halt.

Somewhere ahead there began the rhythmical booming of a drum. It was not such a sound as she would have expected to hear in that time and place. Then she forgot it as she was aware of a presence near her. She could not see, but she knew that something was standing beside her in the darkness.

With a stifled cry she shrank back, and as she did so, something that even in her panic she recognized as a human arm curved about her waist. She screamed and threw all her supple young strength into a wild lunge for freedom, but her captor caught her up like a child, crushing her frantic resistance with ease. The silence with which her frenzied pleas and protests were received added to her terror as she felt herself being carried through the darkness toward the distant drum, which still pulsed and muttered.

4

As the first tinge of dawn reddened the sea, a small boat with a solitary occupant approached the cliffs. The man in the boat was a picturesque figure. A crimson scarf was knotted about his head; his wide silk breeches, of flaming hue, were upheld by a broad sash, which likewise supported a scimitar in a shagreen scabbard. His gilt-worked leather boots suggested the horseman rather than the seaman, but he handled his boat with skill. Through his widely open white silk shirt showed his broad, muscular breast, burned brown by the sun.

The muscles of his heavy, bronzed arms rippled as he pulled the oars with an almost feline ease of motion. A fierce vitality that was evident in each feature and motion set him apart from the common men; yet his expression was neither savage nor somber, though the smoldering blue eyes hinted at ferocity easily wakened. This was Conan, who had wandered into the armed camps of the kozaks with no other possession than his wits and his sword, and who had carved his way to leadership among them.

He paddled to the carven stair as one familiar with his environs and moored the boat to a projection of the rock. Then he went up the worn steps without hesitation. He was keenly alert, not because he consciously suspected hidden danger, but because alertness was a part of him, whetted by the wild existence he followed.

What Ghaznavi had considered animal intuition or some sixth sense was merely the razor-edged faculties and savage wit of the barbarian. Conan had no instinct to tell him that men were watching him from a covert among the reeds of the mainland.

As he climbed the cliff, one of these men breathed deeply and stealthily lifted a bow. Jehungir caught his wrist and hissed an oath into his ear. "Fool! Will you betray us? Don't you realize he is out of range? Let him get upon the island. He will go looking for the girl. We will stay here awhile. He may have sensed our presence or guessed our plot. He may have warriors hidden somewhere. We will wait. In an hour, if nothing suspicious occurs, we'll row up to the foot of the stair and wait him there. If he does not return in a reasonable time, some of us will go upon the island and hunt him down. But I do not wish to do that if it can be helped. Some of us are sure to die if we have to go into the bush after him. I had rather catch him with arrows from a safe distance."

Meanwhile, the unsuspecting kozak had plunged into a forest. He went silently in his soft leather boots, his gaze sifting every shadow in eagerness to catch sight of the splendid, tawny-haired beauty of whom he had dreamed ever since he had seen her in the pavilion of Jehungir Agha by Fort Ghori. He would have desired her even if she had displayed repugnance toward him. But her cryptic smiles and glances had fired his blood, and with all the lawless violence which was his heritage he desired that white-skinned, golden-haired woman of civilization.

He had been on Xapur before. Less than a month ago, he had held a secret conclave here with a pirate crew. He knew that he was approaching a point where he could see the mysterious ruins which gave the island its name, and he wondered if he could find the girl hiding among them. Even with the thought, he stopped as though struck dead.

Ahead of him, among the trees, rose something that his reason told him was not possible. It was a great dark green wall, with towers rearing beyond the battlements.

Conan stood paralyzed in the disruption of the faculties which demoralizes anyone who is confronted by an impossible negation of sanity. He doubted neither his sight nor his reason, but something was monstrously out of joint. Less than a month ago, only broken ruins had showed among the trees. What human hands could rear such a mammoth pile as now met his eyes, in the few weeks which had elapsed? Besides, the buccaneers who roamed Vilyet ceaselessly would have learned of any work going on on such stupendous scale and would have informed the kozaks.

There was no explaining this thing, but it was so. he was on Xapur, and that fantastic heap of towering masonry was on Xapur, and all was madness and paradox; yet it was all true.

He wheeled to race back through the jungle, down the carven stair and across the blue waters to the distant camp at the mouth of the Zaporoska. In that moment of unreasoning panic, even the thought of halting so near the inland sea was repugnant. He would leave it behind him, would quit the armed camps and the steppes and put a thousand miles between him and the blue, mysterious East where the most basic laws of nature could be set at naught, by what diabolism he could not guess.

For an instant, the future fate of kingdoms that hinged on this gay-clad barbarian hung in the balance. It was a small thing that tipped the scales—merely a shred of silk hanging on a bush that caught his uneasy glance. He leaned to it, his nostrils expanding, his nerves quivering to a subtle stimulant. On that bit of torn cloth, so faint that it was less with his physical faculties than by some obscure instinctive sense that he recognized it, lingered the tantalizing perfume that he connected with the sweet, firm flesh of the woman he had seen in Jehugir's pavilion. The fisherman had not lied, then; she was here! Then in the soil he saw a single track in the loam, the track of a bare foot, long and slender, but a man's, not a woman's, and sunk deeper than was natural. The conclusion was obvious; the man who made that track was carrying a burden, and what should it be but the girl the kozak was seeking?

He stood silently facing the dark towers that loomed through the trees, his eyes slits of blue balefire. Desire for the yellow-haired woman vied with a sullen, primordial rage at whoever had taken her. His human passion fought down his ultra-human fears, and dropping into the stalking crouch of a hunting panther, he glided toward the walls, taking advantage of the dense foliage to escape detection from the battlements.

As he approached, he saw that the walls were composed of the same green stone that had formed the ruins, and he was haunted by a vague sense of familiarity. It was as if he looked upon something he had never before seen but had dreamed of or pictured mentally. At last he recognized the sensation. The walls and towers followed the plan of the ruins. It was as if the crumbling lines had grown back into the structures they originally were.

No sound disturbed the morning quiet as Conan stole to the foot of the wall, which rose sheer from the luxuriant growth. On the southern reaches of the inland sea, the vegetation was almost tropical. He saw no one on the battlements, heard no sounds within. He saw a massive gate a short distance to his left and had no reason to suppose that it was not locked and guarded. But he believed that the woman he sought was somewhere beyond that wall, and the course he took was characteristically reckless.

Above him, vine-festooned branches reached out toward the battlements. He went up a great tree like a cat, and reaching a point above the parapet, he gripped a thick limb with both hands, swung back and forth at arm's length until he had gained momentum, and then let go and catapulted through the air, landing catlike on the battlements. Crouching there, he stared down into the streets of a city.

The circumference of the wall was not great, but the number of green stone buildings it contained was surprising. They were three or four stories in height, mainly flat-roofed, reflecting a fine architectural style. The streets converged like the spokes of a wheel into an octagon-shaped court in the centre of the town, which gave upon a lofty edifice, which, with its domes and towers, dominated the whole city. He saw no one moving in the streets or looking out of the windows, though the sun was already coming up. The silence that reigned there might have been that of a dead and deserted city. A narrow stone stair ascended the wall near him; down this he went.

Houses shouldered so closely to the wall that halfway down the stair, he found himself within arm's length of a window and halted to peer in. There were no bars, and the silk curtains were caught back with satin cords. He looked into a chamber whose walls were hidden by dark velvet tapestries. The floor was covered with thick rugs, and there were benches of polished ebony and an ivory dais heaped with furs.

He was about to continue his descent, when he heard the sound of someone approaching in the street below. Before the unknown person could round a corner and see him on the stair, he stepped quickly across the intervening space and dropped lightly into the room, drawing his scimitar. He stood for an instant statue-like; then, as nothing happened, he was moving across the rugs toward an arched doorway, when a hanging was drawn aside, revealing a cushioned alcove from which a slender, dark-haired girl regarded him with languid eyes.

Conan glared at her tensely, expecting her momentarily to start screaming. But she merely smothered a yawn with a dainty hand, rose from the alcove, and leaned negligently against the hanging which she held with one hand.

She was undoubtedly a member of a white race, though her skin was very dark. Her square-cut hair was black as midnight, her only garment a wisp of silk about her supple hips.

Presently she spoke, but the tongue was unfamiliar to him, and he shook his head. She yawned again, stretched lithely and, without any show of fear or surprise, shifted to a language he did understand, a dialect of Yuetshi which sounded strangely archaic.

"Are you looking for someone?" she asked, as indifferently as if the invasion of her chamber by an armed stranger were the most common thing imaginable.

"Who are you?" he demanded.

"I am Yateli," she answered languidly. "I must have feasted late last night, I am so sleepy now. Who are you?"

"I am Conan, a hetman among the kozaks," he answered, watching her narrowly. He believed her attitude to be a pose and expected her to try to escape from the chamber or rouse the house. But, though a velvet rope that might be a signal cord hung near her, she did not reach for it.

"Conan," she repeated drowsily. "You are not a Dagonian. I suppose you are a mercenary. Have you cut the heads off many Yuetshi?"

"I do not war on water rats!" he snorted.

"But they are very terrible," she murmured. "I remember when they were our slaves. But they revolted and burned and slew. Only the magic of Khosatral Khel has kept them from the walls—" she paused, a puzzled look struggling with the sleepiness of her expression. "I forgot," she muttered. "They did climb the walls, last night. There was shouting and fire, and the people calling in vain on Khosatral." She shook her head as if to clear it. "But that cannot be," she murmured, "because I am alive, and I thought I was dead. Oh, to the devil with it!"

She came across the chamber, and taking Conan's hand, drew him to the dais. He yielded in bewilderment and uncertainty. The girl smiled at him like a sleepy child; her long silky lashes drooped over dusky, clouded eyes. She ran her fingers through his thick black locks as if to assure herself of his reality.

"It was a dream," she yawned. "Perhaps it's all a dream. I feel like a dream now. I don't care. I can't remember something—I have forgotten—there is something I cannot understand, but I grow so sleepy when I try to think. Anyway, it doesn't matter."

"What do you mean?" he asked uneasily. "You said they climbed the walls last night? Who?"

"The Yuetshi. I thought so, anyway. A cloud of smoke hid everything, but a naked, bloodstained devil caught me by the throat and drove his knife into my breast. Oh, it hurt! But it was a dream, because see, there is no scar." She idly inspected her smooth bosom, and then sank upon Conan's lap and passed her supple arms about his massive neck. "I cannot remember," she murmured, nestling her dark head against his mighty breast. "Everything is dim and misty. It does not matter. You are no dream. You are strong. Let us live while we can. Love me!"

He cradled the girl's glossy head in the bend of his heavy arm and kissed her full red lips with unfeigned relish.

"You are strong," she repeated, her voice waning. "Love me—love—" The sleepy murmur faded away; the dusky eyes closed, the long lashes drooping over the sensuous cheeks; the supple body relaxed in Conan's arms.

He scowled down at her. She seemed to partake of the illusion that haunted this whole city, but the firm resilience of her limbs under his questing fingers convinced him that he had a living human girl in his arms, and not the shadow of a dream. No less disturbed, he hastily laid her on the furs upon the dais. Her sleep was too deep to be natural. He decided that she must be an addict of some drug, perhaps like the black lotus of Xuthal.

Then he found something else to make him wonder. Among the furs on the dais was a gorgeous spotted skin, whose predominant hue was golden. It was not a clever copy, but the skin of an actual beast. And that beast, Conan knew, had been extinct for at least a thousand years; it was the great golden leopard which figures so prominently in Hyborian legendry, and which the ancient artists delighted to portray in pigments and marble.

Shaking his head in bewilderment, Conan passed through the archway into a winding corridor. Silence hung over the house, but outside he heard a sound which his keen ears recognized as something ascending the stair on the wall from which he had entered the building. An instant later he was startled to hear something land with a soft but weighty thud on the floor of the chamber he had just quitted. Turning quickly away, he hurried along the twisting hallway until something on the floor before him brought him to a halt.

It was a human figure, which lay half in the hall and half in an opening that obviously was normally concealed by a door, which was a duplicate of the panels of the wall. It was a man, dark and lean, clad only in a silk loincloth, with a shaven head and cruel features, and he lay as if death had struck him just as he was emerging from the panel. Conan bent above him, seeking the cause of his death, and discovered him to be merely sunk in the same deep sleep as the girl in the chamber.

But why should he select such a place for his slumbers? While meditating on the matter, Conan was galvanized by a sound behind him. Something was moving up the corridor in his direction. A quick glance down it showed that it ended in a great door, which might be locked.

Conan jerked the supine body out of the panel entrance and stepped through, pulling the panel shut after him. A click told him it was locked in place. Standing in utter darkness, he heard a shuffling tread halt just outside the door, and a faint chill trickled along his spine. That was no human step, nor that of any beast he had ever encountered.

There was an instant of silence, then a faint creak of wood and metal. Putting out his hand he felt the door straining and bending inward, as if a great weight were being steadily borne against it from the outside. As he reached for his sword, this ceased and he heard a strange, slobbering mouthing that prickled the short hairs on his scalp. Scimitar in hand, he began backing away, and his heels felt steps, down which he nearly tumbled. He was in a narrow staircase leading downward.

He groped his way down in the blackness, feeling for, but not finding, some other opening in the walls. Just as he decided that he was no longer in the house, but deep in the earth under it, the steps ceased in a level tunnel.

5

Along the dark, silent tunnel Conan groped, momentarily dreading a fall into some unseen pit; but at last his feet struck steps again, and he went up them until he came to a door on which his fumbling fingers found a metal catch. He came out into a dim and lofty room of enormous proportions. Fantastic columns marched about the mottled walls, upholding a ceiling, which, at once translucent and dusky, seemed like a cloudy midnight sky, giving an illusion of impossible height. If any light filtered in from the outside, it was curiously altered.

In a brooding twilight, Conan moved across the bare green floor. The great room was circular, pierced on one side by the great, bronze valves of a giant door. Opposite this, on a dais against the wall, up to which led broad curving steps, there stood a throne of copper, and when Conan saw what was coiled on this throne, he retreated hastily, lifting his scimitar.

Then, as the thing did not move, he scanned it more closely and presently mounted the glass steps and stared down at it. It was a gigantic snake, apparently carved of some jadelike substance. Each scale stood out as distinctly as in real life, and the iridescent colors were vividly reproduced. The great wedge-shaped head was half submerged in the folds of its trunk; so neither the eyes nor jaws were visible. Recognition stirred in his mind. The snake was evidently meant to represent one of those grim monsters of the marsh, which in past ages had haunted the reedy edges of Vilayet's southern shores. But, like the golden leopard, they had been extinct for hundreds of years. Conan had seen rude images of them, in miniature, among the idol huts of the Yuetshi, and there was a description of them in the Book of Skelos, which drew on prehistoric sources.

Conan admired the scaly torso, thick as his thigh and obviously of great length, and he reached out and laid a curious hand on the thing. And as he did so, his heart nearly stopped. An icy chill congealed the blood in his veins and lifted the short hair on his scalp. Under his hand there was not the smooth, brittle surface of glass or metal or stone, but the yielding, fibrous mass of a living thing. He felt cold, sluggish life flowing under his fingers.

His hand jerked back in instinctive repulsion. Sword shaking in his grasp, horror and revulsion and fear almost choking him, he backed away and down the glass steps with painful care, glaring in awful fascination at the grisly thing that slumbered on the copper throne. It did not move.

He reached the bronze door and tried it, with his heart in his teeth, sweating with fear that he should find himself locked in with that slimy horror. But the valves yielded to his touch, and he glided though and closed them behind him.

He found himself in a wide hallway with lofty, tapestried walls, where the light was the same twilight gloom. It made distant objects indistinct, and that made him uneasy, rousing thoughts of serpents gliding unseen through the dimness. A door at the other end seemed miles away in the illusive light. Nearer at hand, the tapestry hung in such a way as to suggest an opening behind it, and lifting it cautiously he discovered a narrow stair leading up.

While he hesitated he heard, in the great room he had just left, the same shuffling tread he had heard outside the locked panel. Had he been followed through the tunnel? He went up the stair hastily, dropping the tapestry in place behind him.

Emerging presently into a twisting corridor, he took the first doorway he came to. He had a twofold purpose in his apparently aimless prowling; to escape from the building and its mysteries, and to find the Nemedian girl who, he felt, was imprisoned somewhere in this palace, temple, or whatever it was. He believed it was the great domed edifice at the center of the city, and it was likely that here dwelt the ruler of the town, to whom a captive woman would doubtless be brought.

He found himself in a chamber, not another corridor, and was about to retrace his steps, when he heard a voice which came from behind one of the walls. There was no door in that wall, but he leaned close and heard distinctly. And an icy chill crawled slowly along his spine. The tongue was Nemedian, but the voice was not human. There was a terrifying resonance about it, like a bell tolling at midnight.

"There was no life in the Abyss, save that which was incorporated in me," it tolled. "Nor was there light, nor motion, nor any sound. Only the urge behind and beyond life guided and impelled me on my upward journey, blind, insensate, inexorable. Through ages upon ages, and the changeless strata of darkness I climbed—"

Ensorcelled by that belling resonance, Conan crouched forgetful of all else, until its hypnotic power caused a strange replacement of faculties and perception, and sound created the illusion of sight. Conan was no longer aware of the voice, save as far-off rhythmical waves of sound. Transported beyond his age and his own individuality, he was seeing the transmutation of the being men called Khosatral Khel which crawled up from Night and the Abyss ages ago to clothe itself in the substance of the material universe.

But human flesh was too frail, too paltry to hold the terrific essence that was Khosatral Khel. So he stood up in the shape and aspect of a man, but his flesh was not flesh; nor the bone, bone; nor blood, blood. He became a blasphemy against all nature, for he caused to live and think and act a basic substance that before had never known the pulse and stir of animate being.

He stalked through the world as a god, for no earthly weapon could harm him, and to him a century was like an hour. In his wanderings he came upon a primitive people inhabiting the island of Dagonia, and it pleased him to give this race culture and civilization, and by his aid they built the city of Dagon and they abode there and worshipped him. Strange and grisly were his servants, called from the dark corners of the planet where grim survivals of forgotten ages yet lurked. His house in Dagon was connected with every other house by tunnels through which his shaven-headed priests bore victims for the sacrifice.

But after many ages, a fierce and brutish people appeared on the shores of the sea. They called themselves Yuetshi, and after a fierce battle were defeated and enslaved, and for nearly a generation they died on the altars of Khosatral.

His sorcery kept them in bonds. Then their priest, a strange, gaunt man of unknown race, plunged into the wilderness, and when he returned he bore a knife that was of no earthly substance. It was forged of a meteor, which flashed through the sky like a flaming arrow and fell in a far valley. The slaves rose. Their saw-edged crescents cut down the men of Dagon like sheep, and against that unearthly knife the magic of Khosatral was impotent. While carnage and slaughter bellowed through the red smoke that choked the streets, the grimmest act of that grim drama was played in the cryptic dome behind the great daised chamber with its copper throne and its walls mottled like the skin of serpents.

From that dome, the Yuetshi priest emerged alone. He had not slain his foe, because he wished to hold the threat of his loosing over the heads of his own rebellious subjects. He had left Khosatral lying upon the golden dais with the mystic knife across his breast for a spell to hold him senseless and inanimate until doomsday.

But the ages passed and the priest died, the towers of deserted Dagon crumbled, the tales became dim, and the Yuetshi were reduced by plagues and famines and war to scattered remnants, dwelling in squalor along the seashore.

Only the cryptic dome resisted the rot of time, until a chance thunderbolt and the curiosity of a fisherman lifted from the breast of the god the magic knife and broke the spell. Khosatral Khel rose and lived and waxed mighty once more. It pleased him to restore the city as it was in the days before its fall. By his necromancy he lifted the towers from the dust of forgotten millenia, and the folk which had been dust for ages moved in life again.

But folk who have tasted of death are only partly alive. In the dark corners of their souls and minds, death still lurks unconquered. By night the people of Dagon moved and loved, hated and feasted, and remembered the fall of Dagon and their own slaughter only as a dim dream; they moved in an enchanted mist of illusion, feeling the strangeness of their existence but not inquiring the reasons therefor. With the coming of day, they sank into deep sleep, to be roused again only by the coming of night, which is akin to death.

All this rolled in a terrible panorama before Conan's consciousness as he crouched beside the tapestried wall. His reason staggered. All certainty and sanity were swept away, leaving a shadowy universe through which stole hooded figures of grisly potentialities. Through the belling

of the voice, which was like a tolling of triumph over the ordered laws
of a sane planet, a human sound anchored Conan's mind from its flight
through spheres of madness. It was the hysterical sobbing of a woman.
Involuntarily he sprung up.

6

Jehungir Agha waited with growing impatience in his boat among the
reeds. More than an hour passed, and Conan had not reappeared.
Doubtless he was still searching the island for the girl he thought to be
hidden there. But another surmise occurred to the Agha. Suppose the
hetman had left his warriors near by, and that they should grow suspicious and come to investigate his long absence? Jehungir spoke to the
oarsmen, and the long boat slid from among the reeds and glided
toward the carven stairs.

Leaving half a dozen men in the boat, he took the rest, ten mighty
archers of Khawarizm, in spired helmets and tiger-skin cloaks. Like
hunters invading the retreat of the lion, they stole forward under the
trees, arrows on strings. Silence reigned over the forest except when a
great green thing that might have been a parrot swirled over their heads
with a low thunder of broad wings and then sped off through the trees.
With a sudden gesture, Jehungir halted his party, and they stared
incredulously at the towers that showed through the verdure in the
distance.

"Tarim!" muttered Jehungir. "The pirates have rebuilt the ruins!
Doubtless Conan is there. We must investigate this. A fortified town
this close to the mainland!—Come!"

With renewed caution, they glided through the trees. The game had
altered; from pursuers and hunters they had become spies.

And as they crept through the tangled growth, the man they sought
was in peril more deadly than their filigreed arrows.

Conan realized with a crawling of his skin that beyond the wall the
belling voice had ceased. He stood motionless as a statue, his gaze fixed
on a curtained door through which he knew that a culminating horror
would presently appear.

It was dim and misty in the chamber, and Conan's hair began to lift
on his scalp as he looked. He saw a head and a pair of gigantic shoulders
grow out of the twilight doom. There was no sound of footsteps, but
the great dusky form grew more distinct until Conan recognized the
figure of a man. He was clad in sandals, a skirt, and a broad shagreen

girdle. His square-cut mane was confined by a circle of gold. Conan stared at the sweep of the monstrous shoulders, the breadth of swelling breast, the bands and ridges and clusters of muscles on torso and limbs. The face was without weakness and without mercy. The eyes were balls of dark fire. And Conan knew that this was Khosatral Khel, the ancient from the Abyss, the god of Dagonia.

No word was spoken. No word was necessary. Khosatral spread his great arms, and Conan, crouching beneath them, slashed at the giant's belly. Then he bounded back, eyes blazing with surprise. The keen edge had rung on the mighty body as on an anvil, rebounding without cutting. Then Khosatral came upon him in an irrestible surge.

There was a fleeting concussion, a fierce writhing and intertwining of limbs and bodies, and then Conan sprang clear, every thew quivering from the violence of his efforts; blood started where the grazing fingers had torn the skin. In that instant of contact, he had experienced the ultimate madness of blasphemed nature; no human flesh had bruised his, but metal animated and sentient; it was a body of living iron which opposed his.

Khosatral loomed above the warrior in the gloom. Once let those great fingers lock and they would not loosen until the human body hung limp in their grasp. In that twilit chamber it was as if a man fought with a dream-monster in a nightmare.

Flinging down his useless sword, Conan caught up a heavy bench and hurled it with all his power. It was such a missile as few men could even lift. On Khosatral's mighty breast it smashed into shreds and splinters. It did not even shake the giant on his braced legs. His face lost something of its human aspect, a nimbus of fire played about his awesome head, and like a moving tower he came on.

With a desperate wrench Conan ripped a whole section of tapestry from the wall and whirling it, with a muscular effort greater than that required for throwing the bench, he flung it over the giant's head. For an instant Khosatral floundered, smothered and blinded by the clinging stuff that resisted his strength as wood or steel could not have done, and in that instant Conan caught up his scimitar and shot out into the corridor. Without checking his speed, he hurled himself through the door of the adjoining chamber, slammed the door, and shot the bolt.

Then as he wheeled, he stopped short, all the blood in him seeming to surge to his head. Crouching on a heap of silk cushions, golden hair streaming over her naked shoulders, eyes blank with terror, was the woman for whom he had dared so much. He almost forgot the horror at his heels until a splintering crash behind him brought him to his senses. He caught up the girl and sprang for the opposite door. She was too helpless with fright either to resist or to aid him. A faint whimper was the only sound of which she seemed capable.

Conan wasted no time trying the door. A shattering stroke of his scimitar hewed the lock asunder, and as he sprang through to the stair that loomed beyond it, he saw the head and shoulders of Khosatral crash through the other door. The colossus was splintering the massive panels as if they were of cardboard.

Conan raced up the stair, carrying the big girl over one shoulder as easily as if she had been a child. Where he was going he had no idea, but the stair ended at the door of a round, domed chamber. Khosatral was coming up the stair behind them, silently as a wind of death, and as swiftly.

The chamber's walls were of solid steel, and so was the door. Conan shut it and dropped in place the great bars with which it was furnished. The thought struck him that this was Khosatral's chamber, where he locked himself in to sleep securely from the monsters he had loosed from the Pits to do his bidding.

Hardly were the bolts in place when the great door shook and trembled to the giant's assault. Conan shrugged his shoulders. This was the end of the trail. There was no other door in the chamber, nor any window. Air, and the strange misty light, evidently came from interstices in the dome. He tested the nicked edge of his scimitar, quite cool now that he was at bay. He had done his volcanic best to escape; when the giant came crashing through that door, he would explode in another savage onslaught with the useless sword, not because he expected it to do any good, but because it was his nature to die fighting. For the moment there was no course of action to take, and his calmness was not forced or feigned.

The gaze he turned on his fair companion was as admiring and intense as if he had a hundred years to live. He had dumped her unceremoniously on the floor when he turned to close the door, and she had risen to her knees, mechanically arranging her streaming locks and her scanty garment. Conan's fierce eyes glowed with approval as they devoured her thick golden hair, her clear, wide eyes, her milky skin, sleek with exuberant health, the firm swell of her breasts, the contours of her splendid hips.

A low cry escaped her as the door shook and a bolt gave way with a groan.

Conan did not look around. He knew the door would hold a little while longer.

"They told me you had escaped," he said. "A Yuetshi fisher told me you were hiding here. What is your name?"

"Octavia," she gasped mechanically. Then words came in a rush. She caught at him with desperate fingers. "Oh Mitra! what nightmare is this? The people—the dark-skinned people—one of them caught me in the forest and brought me here. They carried me to—to that—that thing. He told me—he said—am I mad? Is this a dream?"

He glanced at the door which bulged inward as if from the impact of a battering-ram.

"No," he said; "it's no dream. That hinge is giving way. Strange that a devil has to break down a door like a common man; but after all, his strength itself is a diabolism."

"Can you not kill him?" she panted. "You are strong."

Conan was too honest to lie to her. "If a mortal man could kill him, he'd be dead now," he answered. "I nicked my blade on his belly."

Her eyes dulled. "Then you must die, and I must—oh Mitra!" she screamed in sudden frenzy, and Conan caught her hands, fearing that she would harm herself. "He told me what he was going to do to me!" she panted. "Kill me! Kill me with your sword before he bursts the door!"

Conan looked at her and shook his head.

"I'll do what I can," he said. "That won't be much, but it'll give you a chance to get past him down the stair. Then run for the cliffs. I have a boat tied at the foot of the steps. If you can get out of the palace, you may escape him yet. The people of this city are all asleep."

She dropped her head in her hands. Conan took up his scimitar and moved over to stand before the echoing door. One watching him would not have realized that he was waiting for a death he regarded as inevitable. His eyes smoldered more vividly; his muscular hand knotted harder on his hilt; that was all.

The hinges had given under the giant's terrible assault, and the door rocked crazily, held only by the bolts. And these solid steel bars were buckling, bending, bulging out of their sockets. Conan watched in an almost impersonal fascination, envying the monster his inhuman strength.

Then, without warning, the bombardment ceased. In the stillness, Conan heard other noises on the landing outside—the beat of wings, and a muttering voice that was like the whining of wind through midnight branches. Then presently there was silence, but there was a new feel in the air. Only the whetted instincts of barbarism could have sensed it, but Conan knew, without seeing or hearing him leave, that the master of Dagon no longer stood outside the door.

He glared through a crack that had been started in the steel of the portal. The landing was empty. He drew the warped bolts and cautiously pulled aside the sagging door. Khosatral was not on the stair, but far below he heard the clang of a metal door. He did not know whether the giant was plotting new deviltries or had been summoned away by that muttering voice, but he wasted no time in conjectures.

He called to Octavia, and the new note in his voice brought her up to her feet and to his side almost without her conscious volition.

"What is it?" she gasped.

"Don't stop to talk!" He caught her wrist. "Come on!" The chance for action had transformed him; his eyes blazed, his voice crackled. "The knife!" he muttered, while almost dragging the girl down the stair in his fierce haste. "The magic Yuetshi blade! He left it in the dome! I——" his voice died suddenly as a clear mental picture sprang up before him. That dome adjoined the great room where stood the copper throne—sweat started out on his body. The only way to that dome was through that room with the copper throne and the foul thing that slumbered in it.

But he did not hesitate. Swiftly they descended the stair, crossed the chamber, descended the next stair, and came into the great dim hall with its mysterious hangings. They had seen no sign of the colossus. Halting before the great bronze-valved door, Conan caught Octavia by her shoulders and shook her in his intensity.

"Listen!" he snapped. "I'm going into the room and fasten the door. Stand here and listen; if Khosatral comes, call to me. If you hear me cry out for you to go, run as though the Devil were on your heels—which he probably will be. Make for that door at the other end of the hall, because I'll be past helping you. I'm going for the Yuetshi knife!"

Before she could voice the protest her lips were framing, he had slid through the valves and shut them behind him. He lowered the bolt cautiously, not noticing that it could be worked from the outside. In the dim twilight his gaze sought that grim copper throne; yes, the scaly brute was still there, filling the throne with its loathsome coils. He saw a door behind the throne and knew that it led into the dome. But to reach it he must mount the dais, a few feet from the throne itself.

A wind blowing across the green floor would have made more noise than Conan's slinking feet. Eyes glued on the sleeping reptile he reached the dais and mounted the glass steps. The snake had not moved. He was reaching for the door...

The bolt on the bronze portal clanged and Conan stifled an awful oath as he saw Octavia come into the room. She stared about, uncertain in the deeper gloom, and he stood frozen, not daring to shout a warning. Then she saw his shadowy figure and ran toward the dais, crying: "I want to go with you! I'm afraid to stay alone—oh!" She threw up her hands with a terrible scream as for the first time she saw the occupant of the throne. The wedge-shaped head had lifted from its coils and thrust out toward her on a yard of shining neck.

Then with a smooth, flowing motion, it began to ooze from the throne, coil by coil, its ugly head bobbing in the direction of the paralyzed girl.

Conan cleared the space between him and the throne with a desperate bound, his scimitar swinging with all his power. And with such blinding speed did the serpent move that it whipped about and met him in full midair, lapping his limbs and body with half a dozen coils. His half-checked stroke fell futilely as he crashed down on the dais, gashing the scaly trunk but not severing it.

Then he was writhing on the glass steps with fold after slimy fold knotting about him, twisting, crushing, killing him. His right arm was still free, but he could get no purchase to strike a killing blow, and he knew one blow must suffice. With a groaning convulsion of muscular expansion that bulged his veins almost to bursting on his temples and tied his muscles in quivering, tortured knots, he heaved up on his feet, lifting almost the full weight of that forty-foot devil.

An instant he reeled on wide-braced legs, feeling his ribs caving in on his vitals and his sight growing dark, while his scimitar gleamed above his head. Then it fell, shearing through the scales and flesh and vertebrae. And where there had been one huge, writhing cable, now there were horribly two, lashing and flopping in the death throes. Conan staggered away from their blind strokes. He was sick and dizzy, and blood oozed from his nose. Groping in a dark mist he clutched Octavia and shook her until she gasped for breath.

"Next time I tell you to stay somewhere," he gasped, "you stay!"

He was too dizzy even to know whether she replied. Taking her wrist like a truant schoolgirl, he led her around the hideous stumps that still loomed and knotted on the floor. Somewhere, in the distance, he thought he heard men yelling, but his ears were still roaring so that he could not be sure.

The door gave to his efforts. If Khosatral had placed the snake there to guard the thing he feared, evidently he considered it ample precaution. Conan half expected some other monstrosity to leap at him with the opening of the door, but in the dimmer light he saw only the vague sweep of the arch above, a dully gleaming block of gold, and a half-moon glimmer on the stone.

With a gasp of gratification, he scooped it up and did not linger for further exploration. He turned and fled across the room and down the great hall toward the distant door that he felt led to the outer air. He was correct. A few minutes later he emerged into the silent streets, half carrying, half guiding his companion. There was no one to be seen, but beyond the western wall there sounded cries and moaning wails that made Octavia tremble. He led her to the southwestern wall and without difficulty found a stone stair that mounted the rampart. He had appropriated a thick tapestry rope in the great hall, and now, having reached the parapet, he looped the soft, strong cord about the girl's hips and lowered her to the earth. Then, making one end fast to a merlon, he slid down after her. There was but one way of escape from the island—the stair on the western cliffs. In that direction he hurried, swinging wide around the spot from which had come the cries and the sound of terrible blows.

Octavia sensed that grim peril lurked in those leafy fastnesses. Her breath came pantingly and she pressed close to her protector. But the forest was silent now, and they saw no shape of menace until they emerged from the trees and glimpsed a figure standing on the edge of the cliffs.

Jehungir Agha had escaped the doom that had overtaken his warriors when an iron giant sallied suddenly from the gate and battered and crushed them into bits of shredded flesh and splintered bone. When he saw the swords of his archers break on that manlike juggernaut, he had known it was no human foe they faced, and he had fled, hiding in the deep woods until the sounds of slaughter ceased. Then he crept back to the stair, but his boatmen were not waiting for him.

They had heard the screams, and presently, waiting nervously, had seen, on the cliff above them, a blood-smeared monster waving gigantic arms in awful triumph. They had waited for no more. When Jehungir came upon the cliffs, they were just vanishing among the reeds beyond earshot. Khosatral was gone—had either returned to the city or was prowling the forest in search of the man who had escaped him outside the walls.

Jehungir was just preparing to descend the stairs and depart in Conan's boat, when he saw the hetman and the girl emerge from the trees. The experience which had congealed his blood and almost blasted his reason had not altered Jehungir's intentions towards the kozak chief. The sight of the man he had come to kill filled him with gratification. He was astonished to see the girl he had given to Jelal Khan, but he wasted no time on her. Lifting his bow he drew the shaft to its head and loosed. Conan crouched and the arrow splintered on a tree, and Conan laughed.

"Dog!" he taunted. "You can't hit me! I was not born to die on Hyrkanian steel! Try again, pig of Turan!"

Jehungir did not try again. That was his last arrow. He drew his scimitar and advanced, confident in his spired helmet and close-meshed mail. Conan met him halfway in a blinding whirl of swords. The curved blades ground together, sprang apart, circled in glittering arcs that blurred the sight which tried to follow them. Octavia, watching, did not see the stroke, but she heard its chopping impact and saw Jehungir fall, blood spurting from his side where the Cimmerian's steel had sundered his mail and bitten to his spine.

But Octavia's scream was not caused by the death of her former master. With a crash of bending boughs, Khosatral Khel was upon them. The girl could not flee; a moaning cry escaped her as her knees gave way and pitched her groveling to the sward.

Conan, stooping above the body of the Agha, made no move to escape. Shifting his reddened scimitar to his left hand, he drew the great half-blade of the Yuetshi. Khosatral Khel was towering above him, his arms lifted like mauls, but as the blade caught the sheen of the sun, the giant gave back suddenly.

But Conan's blood was up. He rushed in, slashing with the crescent blade. And it did not splinter. Under its edge, the dusky metal of Khosatral's body gave way like common flesh beneath a cleaver. From the deep gash flowed a strange ichor, and Khosatral cried out like the dirging of a great bell. His terrible arms flailed down, but Conan, quicker than the archers who had died beneath those awful flails, avoided their strokes and struck again and yet again. Khosatral reeled and tottered; his cries were awful to hear, as if metal were given a tongue of pain, as if iron shrieked and bellowed under torment.

Then, wheeling away, he staggered into the forest; he reeled in his gait, crashed through bushes, and caromed off trees. Yet though Conan followed him with the speed of hot passion, the walls and towers of Dagon loomed through the trees before the man came with dagger-reach of the giant.

Then Khosatral turned again, flailing the air with desperate blows, but Conan, fired to beserk fury, was not to be denied. As a panther strikes down a bull moose at bay, so he plunged under the bludgeoning arms and drove the crescent blade to the hilt under the spot where a human's heart would be.

Khosatral reeled and fell. In the shape of a man he reeled, but it was not the shape of a man that struck the loam. Where there had been the likeness of a human face, there was no face at all, and the metal limbs melted and changed... Conan, who had not shrunk from Khosatral living, recoiled blenching for Khosatral dead, for he had witnessed an awful transmutation; in his dying throes Khosatral Khel had become again the thing that had crawled up from the Abyss millennia gone. Gagging with intolerable repugnance, Conan turned to flee the sight; and he was suddenly aware that the pinnacles of Dagon no longer glimmered through the trees. They had faded like smoke—the battlements, the crenellated towers, the great bronze gates, the velvets, the gold, the ivory, and the dark-haired women, and the men with their shaven skulls. With the passing of the inhuman intellect which had given them rebirth, they had faded back into the dust which they had been for ages uncounted. Only the stumps of broken columns rose above crumbling walls and broken paves and shattered dome. Conan again looked upon the ruins of Xapur as he remembered them.

The wild hetman stood like a statue for a space, dimly grasping something of the cosmic tragedy of the fitful ephemera called mankind and the hooded shapes of darkness which prey upon it. Then as he heard his voice called in accents of fear, he started, as one awakening from a dream, glanced again at the thing on the ground, shuddered and turned away toward the cliffs and the girl that waited there.

She was peering fearfully under the trees, and she greeted him with a half-stifled cry of relief. He had shaken off the dim monstrous visions which had momentarily haunted him, and was his exuberant self again.

"Where is he?" she shuddered.

"Gone back to Hell whence he crawled," he replied cheerfully. "Why didn't you climb the stair and make your escape in my boat?"

"I wouldn't desert—" she began, then changed her mind, and amended rather sulkily, "I have nowhere to go. The Hyrkanians would enslave me again, and the pirates would—"

"What of the kozaks?" he suggested.

"Are they better than the pirates?" she asked scornfully. Conan's admiration increased to see how well she had recovered her poise after having endured such frantic terror. Her arrogance amused him.

"You seemed to think so in the camp by Ghori," he answered. "You were free enough with your smiles then."

Her red lips curled in disdain. "Do you think I was enamored of you? Do you dream that I would have shamed myself before an ale-guzzling, meat-gorging barbarian unless I had to? My master—whose body lies there—forced me to do as I did."

"Oh!" Conan seemed rather crestfallen. Then he laughed with undiminished zest. "No matter. You belong to me now. Give me a kiss."

"You dare ask—" she began angrily, when she felt herself snatched off her feet and crushed to the hetman's muscular breast. She fought him fiercely, with all the supple strength of her magnificent youth, but he only laughed exuberantly, drunk with the possession of this splendid creature writhing in his arms.

He crushed her struggles easily, drinking the nectar of her lips with all the unrestrained passion that was his, until the arms that strained against them melted and twined convulsively about his massive neck. Then he laughed down into the clear eyes, and said: "Why should not a chief of the Free People be preferable to a city-bred dog of Turan?"

She shook back her tawny locks, still tingling in every nerve from the fire of his kisses. She did not loosen her arms from his neck. "Do you deem yourself an Agha's equal?" she challenged.

He laughed and strode with her in his arms toward the stair. "You shall judge," he boasted. "I'll burn Khawarizm for a torch to light your way to my tent."

THE END

The People of the Black Circle

1 Death Strikes a King

The king of Vendhya was dying. Through the hot, stifling night the temple gongs boomed and the conchs roared. Their clamor was a faint echo in the gold-domed chamber where Bunda Chand struggled on the velvet-cushioned dais. Beads of sweat glistened on his dark skin; his fingers twisted the gold-worked fabric beneath him. He was young; no spear had touched him, no poison lurked in his wine. But his veins stood out like blue cords on his temples, and his eyes dilated with the nearness of death. Trembling slave-girls knelt at the foot of the dais, and leaning down to him, watching him with passionate intensity, was his sister, the Devi Yasmina. With her was the *wazim*, a noble grown old in the royal court.

She threw up her head in a gusty gesture of wrath and despair as the thunder of the distant drums reached her ears.

"The priests and their clamor!" she exclaimed. "They are no wiser than the leeches who are helpless! Nay, he dies and none can say why. He is dying now—and I stand here helpless, who would burn the whole city and spill the blood of thousands to save him."

"Not a man of Ayodhya but would die in his place, if it might be, Devi," answered the *wazam*. "This poison—"

"I tell you it is not poison!" she cried. "Since his birth he has been guarded so closely that the cleverest poisoners of the East could not reach him. Five skulls bleaching on the Tower of the Kites can testify to attempts which were made—and which failed. As you well know, there are ten men and ten women whose sole duty is to taste his food and wine, and fifty armed warriors guard his chamber as they guard it now. No, it is not poison; it is sorcery—black, ghastly magic—"

She ceased as the king spoke; his livid lips did not move, and there was no recognition in his glassy eyes. But his voice rose in an eery call, indistinct and far away, as if called to her from beyond vast, wind-blown gulfs.

"Yasmina! Yasmina! My sister, where are you? I can not find you. All is darkness, and the roaring of great winds!"

29

"Brother!" cried Yasmina, catching his limp hand in a convulsive grasp. "I am here! Do you not know me—"

Her voice died at the utter vacancy of his face. A low confused moan waned from his mouth. The slave-girls at the foot of the dais whimpered with fear, and Yasmina beat her breast in anguish.

★ ★ ★

In another part of the city a man stood in a latticed balcony overlooking a long street in which torches tossed luridly, smokily revealing upturned dark faces and the whites of gleaming eyes. A long-drawn wailing rose from the multitude.

The man shrugged his broad shoulders and turned back into the arabesque chamber. He was a tall man, compactly built, and richly clad.

"The king is not yet dead, but the dirge is sounded," he said to another man who sat cross-legged on a mat in a corner. This man was clad in a brown camel-hair robe and sandals, and a green turban was on his head. His expression was tranquil, his gaze impersonal.

"The people know he will never see another dawn," this man answered.

The first speaker favored him with a long, searching stare.

"What I can not understand," he said, "is why I have had to wait so long for your masters to strike. If they have slain the king now, why could they not have slain him months ago?"

"Even the arts you call sorcery are governed by cosmic laws," answered the man in the green turban. "The stars direct these actions, as in other affairs. Not even my masters can alter the stars. Not until the heavens were in the proper order could they perform this necromancy." With a long, stained fingernail he mapped the constellations on the marble-tiled floor. "The slant of the moon presaged evil for the king of Vendhya; the stars are in turmoil, the Serpent in the House of the Elephant. During such juxtaposition, the invisible guardians are removed from the spirit of Bhunda Chand. A path is opened in the unseen realms, and once a point of contact was established, mighty powers were put in play along that path."

"Point of contact?" inquired the other. "Do you mean that lock of Bhunda Chand's hair?"

"Yes. All discarded portions of the human body still remain part of it, attached to it by intangible connections. The priests of Asura have a dim inkling of this truth, and so all nail trimmings, hair and other waste products of the persons of the royal family are carefully reduced to ashes and the ashes hidden. But at the urgent entreaty of the princess of Khosala, who loved Bhunda Chand vainly, he gave her a lock of his long black hair as a token of remembrance. When my masters decided upon his doom, the lock, in its golden, jewel-encrusted case, was stolen from under her pillow while she slept, and another substituted, so like the first that she never knew the difference. Then the genuine lock travelled by camel-caravan up the long, long road to Peshkhauri, thence up the Zhaibar Pass, until it reached the hands of those for whom it was intended."

"Only a lock of hair," murmured the nobleman.

"By which a soul is drawn from its body and across gulfs of echoing space," returned the man on the mat.

The nobleman studied him curiously.

"I do not know if you are a man or a demon, Khemsa," he said at last. "Few of us are what we seem. I, whom the Kshatriyas know as Kerim Shah, a prince from Iranistan, am no greater a masquerader than most men. They are all traitors in one way or another, and half of them know not whom they serve. There at least I have no doubts; for I serve King Yezdigerd of Turan."

"And I the Black Seers of Yimsha," said Khemsa; "and my masters are greater than yours, for they have accomplished by their arts what Yezdigerd could not with a hundred thousand swords."

★ ★ ★

Outside, the moan of the tortured thousands shuddered up to the stars which crusted the sweating Vendhyan night, and the conchs bellowed like oxen in pain.

In the gardens of the palace the torches glinted on polished helmets and curved swords and gold-chased corselets. All the noble-born fighting-men of Ayodhya were gathered in the great palace or about it, and at each broad-arched gate and door fifty archers stood on guard, with bows in their hands. But Death stalked through the royal palace and none could stay his ghostly tread.

On the dais under the golden dome the king cried out again, racked by awful paroxysms. Again his voice came faintly and far away, and again the Devi bent to him, trembling with a fear that was darker than the terror of death.

"Yasmina!" Again that far, weirdly dreeing cry, from realms immeasurable. "Aid me! I am far from my mortal house! Wizards have drawn my soul through the wind-blown darkness. They seek to snap the silver cord that binds me to my dying body. They cluster around me; their hands are taloned, their eyes are red like flame burning in darkness. *Aie*, save me, my sister! Their fingers sear me like fire! They would slay my body and damn my soul! What is this they bring before me?—*Aie!*"

★ ★ ★

At the terror in his hopeless cry Yasmina screamed uncontrollably and threw herself bodily upon him in the abandon of her anguish. He was torn by a terrible convulsion; foam flew from his contorted lips and his writhing fingers left their marks on the girl's shoulders. But the glassy blankness passed from his eyes like smoke blown from a fire, and he looked up at his sister with recognition.

"Brother!" she sobbed. "Brother—"

"Swift!" he gasped, and his weakening voice was rational. "I know now what brings me to the pyre. I have been on a far journey and I understand. I have been ensorcelled by the wizards of the Himelians. They drew my soul out of my body and far away, into a stone room. There they strove to break the silver cord of life, and thrust my soul into the body of a foul night-weird their sorcery summoned up from hell. Ah! I feel their pull upon me now! Your cry and the grip of your fingers brought me back, but I am going fast. My soul clings to my body, but its hold weakens. Quick—kill me, before they can trap my soul for ever!"

"I cannot!" she wailed, smiting her naked breasts.

"Swiftly, I command you!" There was the old imperious note in his failing whisper. "You have never disobeyed me—obey my last command! Send my soul clean to Asura! Haste, lest you damn me to spend eternity as a filthy gaunt of darkness. Strike, I command you! *Strike!*"

Sobbing wildly, Yasmina plucked a jeweled dagger from her girdle and plunged it to the hilt in his breast. He stiffened and then went limp, a grim smile curving his dead lips. Yasmina hurled herself face-down on the rush-covered floor, beating the reeds with her clenched hands. Outside, the gongs and conchs brayed and thundered and the priests gashed themselves with copper knives.

2 A Barbarian from the Hills

Chunder Shan, governor of Peshkhauri, laid down his golden pen and carefully scanned that which he had written on parchment that bore his official seal. He had ruled Peshkhauri so long only because he weighed his every word, spoken or written. Danger breeds caution, and only a wary man lives long in that wild country where the hot Vendhyan plains meet the crags of the Himelians. An hour's ride westward or northward and one crossed the border and was among the Hills where men lived by the law of the knife.

The governor was alone in his chamber, seated at his ornately carven table of inlaid ebony. Through the wide window, open for the coolness, he could see a square of the blue Himelian night, dotted with great white stars. An adjacent parapet was a shadowy line, and further crenelles and embrasures were barely hinted at in the dim starlight. The governor's fortress was strong, and situated outside the walls of the city it guarded. The breeze that stirred the tapestries on the wall brought faint noises from the streets of Peshkhauri—occasional snatches of wailing song, or the thrum of a cithern.

The governor read what he had written, slowly, with his open hand shading his eyes from the bronze butterlamp, his lips moving. Absently, as he read, he heard the drum of horses' hoofs outside the barbican, the sharp staccato of the guards' challenge. He did not heed, intent upon his letter. It was addressed to the *wazam* of Vendhya, at the royal court of Ayodhya, and it stated, after the customary salutations:

"Let it be known to your excellency that I have faithfully carried out your excellency's instructions. The seven tribesmen are well guarded in their prison, and I have repeatedly sent word into the hills that their chief come in person to bargain for their release. But he has made no move, except to send word that unless they are freed he will burn Peshkhauri and cover his saddle with my hide, begging your excellency's indulgence. This he is quite capable of attempting, and I have tripled the numbers of the lance guards. The man is not a native of Ghulistan. I cannot with certainty predict his next move. But since it is the wish of the Devi—"

He was out of his ivory chair and on his feet facing the arched door, all in one instant. He snatched at the curved sword lying in its ornate scabbard on the table, and then checked the movement.

It was a woman who had entered unannounced, a woman whose gossamer robes did not conceal the rich garments beneath them any more than they concealed the suppleness and beauty of her tall, slender figure. A filmy veil fell below her breasts, supported by a flowing head-dress bound about with a triple gold braid and adorned with a golden crescent. Her dark eyes regarded the astonished governor over the veil, and then with an imperious gesture of her white hand, she uncovered her face.

"Devi!" The governor dropped to his knees before her, surprize and confusion somewhat spoiling the stateliness of his obeisance. With a gesture she motioned him to rise, and he hastened to lead her to the ivory chair, all the while bowing level with his girdle. But his first words were of reproof.

"Your Majesty! This was most unwise! The border is unsettled. Raids from the hills are incessant. You came with a large attendance?"

"An ample retinue followed me to Peshkhauri," she answered. "I lodged my people there and came on to the fort with my maid, Gitara."

Chunder Shan groaned in horror.

"Devi! You do not understand the peril. An hour's ride from this spot the hills swarm with barbarians who make a profession of murder and rapine. Women have been stolen and men stabbed between the fort and the city. Peshkhauri is not like your southern provinces—"

"But I am here, and unharmed," she interrupted with a trace of impatience. "I showed my signet ring to the guard at the gate, and to the one outside your door, and they admitted me unannounced, not knowing me, but supposing me to be a secret courier from Ayodhya. Let us not now waste time.

"You have received no word from the chief of the barbarians?"

"None save threats and curses, Devi. He is wary and suspicious. He deems it a trap, and perhaps he is not to be blamed. The Kshatriyas have not always kept their promises to the hill people."

"He must be brought to terms!" broke in Yasmina, the knuckles of her clenched hands showing white.

"I do not understand." The governor shook his head. "When I chanced to capture these seven hill-men, I reported their capture to the *wazam*, as is the custom, and then, before I could hang them, there came an order to hold them and communicate with their chief. This I did, but the man holds aloof, as I have said. These men are of the tribe of Afghulis, but he is a foreigner from the west, and he is called Conan. I have threatened to hang them tomorrow at dawn, if he does not come."

"Good!" exclaimed the Devi. "You have done well. And I will tell you why I have given these orders. My brother—" she faltered, choking, and the governor bowed his head, with the customary gesture of respect for a departed sovereign.

"The king of Vendhya was destroyed by magic," she said at last. "I have devoted my life to the destruction of his murderers. As he died he gave me a clue, and I have followed it. I have read the Book of Skelos, and talked with nameless hermits in the caves below Jhelai. I learned how, and by whom, he was destroyed. His enemies were the Black Seers of Mount Yimsha."

"Asura!" whispered Chunder Shan, paling.

Her eyes knifed him through. "Do you fear them?"

"Who does not, Your Majesty?" he replied. "They are black devils, haunting the uninhabited hills beyond the Zhaibar. But the sages say that they seldom interfere in the lives of mortal men."

"Why they slew my brother I do not know," she answered. "But I have sworn on the altar of Asura to destroy them! And I need the aid of a man beyond the border. A Kshatriya army, unaided, would never reach Yimsha."

"Aye," muttered Chunder Shan. "You speak the truth there. It would be fight every step of the way, with hairy hill-men hurling down boulders from every height, and rushing us with their long knives in every valley. The Turanians fought their way through the Himelians once, but how many returned to Khurusun? Few of those who escaped the swords of the Kshatriyas, after the king, your brother, defeated their host on the Jhumda River, ever saw Secunderam again."

"And so I must control men across the border," she said, "men who know the way to Mount Yimsha—"

"But the tribes fear the Black Seers and shun the unholy mountain," broke in the governor.

"Does the chief, Conan, fear them?" she asked.

"Well, as to that," muttered the governor, "I doubt if there is anything that devil fears."

"So I have been told. Therefore he is the man I must deal with. He wishes the release of his seven men. Very well; their ransom shall be the heads of the Black Seers!" Her voice thrummed with hate as she uttered the last words, and her hands clenched at her sides. She looked an image of incarnate passion as she stood there with her head thrown high and her bosom heaving.

Again the governor knelt, for part of his wisdom was the knowledge that a woman in such an emotional tempest is as perilous as a blind cobra to any about her.

"It shall be as you wish, Your Majesty." Then as she presented a calmer aspect, he rose and ventured to drop a word of warning. "I can not predict what the chief Conan's action will be. The tribesmen are always turbulent, and I have reason to believe that emissaries from the Turanians are stirring them up to raid our borders. As your majesty knows, the Turanians have established themselves in Secunderam and other northern cities, though the hill tribes remain unconquered. King Yezdigerd has long looked southward with greedy lust and perhaps is seeking to gain by treachery what he could not win by force of arms. I have thought that Conan might well be one of his spies."

"We shall see," she answered. "If he loves his followers, he will be at the gates at dawn, to parley. I shall spend the night in the fortress. I came in disguise to Peshkhauri, and lodged my retinue at an inn instead of the palace. Besides my people, only yourself knows of my presence here."

"I shall escort you to your quarters, Your Majesty," said the governor, and as they emerged from the doorway, he beckoned the warrior on guard there, and the man fell in behind them, spear held at salute.

The maid waited, veiled like her mistress, outside the door, and the group traversed a wide, winding corridor, lighted by smoky torches, and reached the quarters reserved for visiting notables— generals and viceroys, mostly; none of the royal family had ever honored the fortress before. Chunder Shan had a perturbed feeling that the suite was not suitable to such an exalted personage as the Devi, and though she sought to make him feel at ease in her presence, he was glad when she dismissed him and he bowed himself out. All the menials of the fort had been summoned to serve his royal guest— though he did not divulge her identity—and he stationed a squad of spearmen before her doors, among them the warrior who had guarded his own chamber. In his preoccupation he forgot to replace the man.

The governor had not been long gone from her when Yasmina suddenly remembered something else which she had wished to discuss with him, but had forgotten until that moment. It concerned the past actions of one Kerim Shah, a nobleman from Iranistan, who had dwelt for a while in Peshkhauri before coming on to the court at Ayodhya. A vague suspicion concerning the man had been stirred by a glimpse of him in Peshkhauri that night. She wondered if he had followed her from Ayodhya. Being a truly remarkable Devi, she did not summon the governor to her again, but hurried out into the corridor alone, and hastened toward his chamber.

★ ★ ★

Chunder Shan, entering his chamber, closed the door and went to his table. There he took the letter he had been writing and tore it to bits. Scarcely had he finished when he heard something drop softly onto the parapet adjacent to the window. He looked up to see a figure loom briefly against the stars, and then a man dropped lightly into the room. The light glinted on a long sheen of steel in his hand.

"Shhhh!" he warned. "Don't make a noise, or I'll send the devil a henchman!"

The governor checked his motion toward the sword on the table. He was within reach of the yard-long Zhaibar knife that glittered in the intruder's fist, and he knew the desperate quickness of a hillman.

The invader was a tall man, at once strong and supple. He was dressed like a hillman, but his dark features and blazing blue eyes did not match his garb. Chunder Shan had never seen a man like him; he was not an Easterner, but some barbarian from the West. But his aspect was as untamed and formidable as any of the hairy tribesmen who haunt the hills of Ghulistan.

"You come like a thief in the night," commented the governor, recovering some of his composure, although he remembered that there was no guard within call. Still, the hillman could not know that.

"I climbed a bastion," snarled the intruder. "A guard thrust his head over the battlement in time for me to rap it with my knife-hilt."

"You are Conan?"

"Who else? You sent word into the hills that you wished for me to come and parley with you. Well, by Crom, I've come! Keep away from that table or I'll gut you."

"I merely wish to seat myself," answered the governor, carefully sinking into the ivory chair, which he wheeled away from the table. Conan moved restlessly before him, glancing suspiciously at the door, thumbing the razor edge of his three-foot knife. He did not walk like an Afghuli, and was bluntly direct where the East is subtle.

"You have seven of my men," he said abruptly. "You refused the ransom I offered. What the devil do you want?"

"Let us discuss terms," answered Chunder Shan cautiously.

"Terms?" There was a timbre of dangerous anger in his voice. "What do you mean? Haven't I offered you gold?"

Chunder Shan laughed.

"Gold? There is more gold in Peshkhauri than you ever saw."

"You're a liar," retorted Conan. "I've seen the *suk* of the goldsmiths in Khurusun."

"Well, more than an Afghuli ever saw," amended Chunder Shan. "And it is but a drop of all the treasure of Vendhya. Why should we desire gold? It would be more to our advantage to hang these seven thieves."

Conan ripped out a sulfurous oath and the long blade quivered in his grip as the muscles rose in ridges on his brown arm.

"I'll split your head like a ripe melon!"

A wild blue flame flickered in the hillman's eyes, but Chunder Shan shrugged his shoulders, though keeping an eye on the keen steel.

"You can kill me easily, and probably escape over the wall afterward. But that would not save the seven tribesmen. My men would surely hang them. And these men are headmen among the Afghulis."

"I know it," snarled Conan. "The tribe is baying like wolves at my heels because I have not procured their release. Tell me in plain words what you want, because, by Crom! if there's no other way, I'll raise a horde and lead it to the very gates of Peshkhauri!"

Looking at the man as he stood squarely, knife in fist and eyes glaring, Chunder Shan did not doubt that he was capable of it. The governor did not believe any hill-horde could take Peshkhauri, but he did not wish a devastated countryside.

"There is a mission you must perform," he said, choosing his words with as much care as if they had been razors. "There—"

Conan had sprung back, wheeling to face the door at the same instant, lips asnarl. His barbarian ears had caught the quick tread of soft slippers outside the door. The next instant the door was thrown open and a slim, silk-robed form entered hastily, pulling the door shut—then stopping short at sight of the hillman.

Chunder Shan sprang up, his heart jumping into his mouth.

"Devi!" he cried involuntarily, losing his head momentarily in his fright.

"Devi!" It was like an explosive echo from the hillman's lips. Chunder Shan saw recognition and intent flame up in the fierce blue eyes.

The governor shouted desperately and caught at his sword, but the hillman moved with the devastating speed of a hurricane. He sprang, knocked the governor sprawling with a savage blow of his knife-hilt, swept up the astounded Devi in one brawny arm and leaped for the window. Chunder Shan, struggling frantically to his feet, saw the man poise an instant on the sill in a flutter of silken skirts and white limbs that was his royal captive, and heard his fierce, exultant snarl: *"Now dare to hang my men!"* and then Conan leaped to the parapet and was gone. A wild scream floated back to the governor's ears.

"Guard! *Guard!"* screamed the governor, struggling up and running drunkenly to the door. He tore it open and reeled into the hall. His shouts re-echoed along the corridors, and warriors came running, gaping to see the governor holding his broken head, from which the blood streamed.

"Turn out the lancers!" he roared. "There has been an abduction!" Even in his frenzy he had enough sense left to withhold the full truth. He stopped short as he heard a sudden drum of hoofs outside, a frantic scream and a wild yell of barbaric exultation.

Followed by the bewildered guardsmen, the governor raced for the stair. In the courtyard of the fort a force of lancers stood by saddled steeds, ready to ride at an instant's notice. Chunder Shan led his squadron flying after the fugitive, though his head swam so he had to hold with both hands to the saddle. He did not divulge the identity of the victim, but said merely that the noblewoman who had borne the royal signet-ring had been carried away by the chief of the Afghulis. The abductor was out of sight and hearing, but they knew the path he would strike—the road that runs straight to the mouth of the Zhaibar. There was no moon; peasant huts rose dimly in the star-light. Behind them fell away the grim bastion of the fort, and the towers of Peshkhauri. Ahead of them loomed the black walls of the Himelians.

3 Khemsa Uses Magic

In the confusion that reigned in the fortress while the guard was being turned out, no one noticed that the girl who had accompanied the Devi slipped out the great arched gate and vanished in the darkness. She ran straight for the city, her garments tucked high. She did not follow the open road, but cut straight through fields and over slopes, avoiding fences and leaping irrigation ditches as surely as if it were broad daylight, and as easily as if she were a trained masculine runner. The hoof-drum of the guardsmen had faded away up the hill before she reached the city wall. She did not go to the great gate, beneath whose arch men leaned on spears and craned their necks into the darkness, discussing the unwonted activity about the fortress. She skirted the wall until she reached a certain point where the spire of the tower was visible above the battlements. Then she placed her hands to her mouth and voiced a low weird call that carried strangely.

Almost instantly a head appeared at an embrasure and a rope came wriggling down the wall. She seized it, placed a foot in the loop at the end, and waved her arm. Then quickly and smoothly she was drawn up the sheer stone curtain. An instant later she scrambled over the merlons and stood up on a flat roof which covered a house that was built against the wall. There was an open trap there, and a man in a camel-hair robe who silently coiled the rope, not showing in any way the strain of hauling a full-grown woman up a forty-foot wall.

"Where is Kerim Shah?" she gasped, panting after her long run.

"Asleep in the house below. You have news?"

"Conan has stolen the Devi out of the fortress and carried her away into the hills!" She blurted out her news in a rush, the words stumbling over one another.

Khemsa showed no emotion, but merely nodded his turbaned head. "Kerim Shah will be glad to hear that," he said.

"Wait!" The girl threw her supple arms about his neck. She was panting hard, but not only from exertion. Her eyes blazed like black jewels in the starlight. Her upturned face was close to Khemsa's, but though he submitted to her embrace, he did not return it.

"Do not tell the Hyrkanian!" she panted. "Let us use this knowledge ourselves! The governor has gone into the hills with his riders, but he might as well chase a ghost. He has not told anyone that it was the Devi who was kidnapped. None in Peshkhauri or the fort knows it except us."

"But what good does it do us?" the man expostulated. "My masters sent me with Kerim Shah to aid him in every way—"

"Aid yourself!" she cried fiercely. "Shake off your yoke!"

"You mean—disobey my masters?" he gasped, and she felt his whole body turn cold under her arms.

"Aye!" she shook him in the fury of her emotion. "You too are a magician! Why will you be a slave, using your powers only to elevate others? Use your arts for yourself!"

"That is forbidden!" He was shaking as if with an ague. "I am not one of the Black Circle. Only by the command of the masters do I dare to use the knowledge they have taught me."

"But you *can* use it!" she argued passionately. "Do as I beg you! Of course Conan has taken the Devi to hold as hostage against the seven tribesmen in the governor's prison. Destroy them, so Chunder Shan can not use them to buy back the Devi. Then let us go into the mountains and take her from the Afghulis. They can not stand against your sorcery with their knives. The treasure of the Vendhyan kings will be ours as ransom—and then when we have it in our hands, we can trick them, and sell her to the king of Turan. We shall have wealth beyond our maddest dreams. With it we can buy warriors. We will take Khorbhul, oust the Turanians from the hills, and send our hosts southward; become king and queen of an empire!"

Khemsa too was panting, shaking like a leaf in her grasp; his face showed gray in the starlight, beaded with great drops of perspiration.

"I love you!" she cried fiercely, writhing her body against his, almost strangling him in her wild embrace, shaking him in her abandon. "I will make a king of you! For love of you I betrayed my mistress; for love of me betray your masters! Why fear the Black Seers? By your love for me you have broken one of their laws already! Break the rest! You are as strong as they!"

A man of ice could not have withstood the searing heat of her passion and fury. With an inarticulate cry he crushed her to him, bending her backward and showering gasping kisses on her eyes, face and lips.

"I'll do it!" His voice was thick with laboring emotions. He staggered like a drunken man. "The arts they have taught me shall work for me, not for my masters. We shall be rulers of the world—of the world—"

"Come then!" Twisting lithely out of his embrace, she seized his hand and led him toward the trap-door. "First we must make sure that the governor does not exchange those seven Afghulis for the Devi."

He moved like a man in a daze, until they had descended a ladder and she paused in the chamber below. Kerim Shah lay on a couch motionless, an arm across his face as though to shield his sleeping eyes from the soft light of a brass lamp. She plucked Khemsa's arm and made a quick gesture across her own throat. Khemsa lifted his hand; then his expression changed and he drew away.

"I have eaten his salt," he muttered. "Besides, he can not interfere with us."

He led the girl through a door that opened on a winding stair. After their soft tread had faded into silence, the man on the couch sat up. Kerim Shah wiped the sweat from his face. A knife-thrust he did not dread, but he feared Khemsa as a man fears a poisonous reptile.

"People who plot on roofs should remember to lower their voices," he muttered. "But as Khemsa has turned against his masters, and as he was my only contact between them, I can count on their aid no longer. From now on I play the game in my own way."

Rising to his feet he went quickly to a table, drew pen and parchment from his girdle and scribbled a few succinct lines.

"To Khosru Khan, governor of Secunderam: the Cimmerian Conan has carried the Devi Yasmina to the villages of the Afghulis. It is an opportunity to get the Devi into our hands, as the king has so long desired. Send three thousand horsemen at once. I will meet them in the valley of Gurashah with native guides."

And he signed it with a name that was not in the least like Kerim Shah.

Then from a golden cage he drew forth a carrier pigeon, to whose leg he made fast the parchment, rolled into a tiny cylinder and secured with gold wire. Then he went quickly to a casement and tossed the bird into the night. It wavered on fluttering wings, balanced, and was gone like a flitting shadow. Catching up helmet, sword and cloak, Kerim Shah hurried out of the chamber and down the winding stair.

★ ★ ★

The prison quarters of Peshkhauri were separated from the rest of the city by a massive wall, in which was set a single iron-bound door under an arch. Over the arch burned a lurid red cresset, and beside the door squatted a warrior with spear and shield.

This warrior, leaning on his spear, and yawning from time to time, started suddenly to his feet. He had not thought he had dozed, but a man was standing before him, a man he had not heard approach. The man wore a camel-hair robe and a green turban. In the flickering light of the cresset his features were shadowy, but a pair of lambent eyes shone surprizingly in the lurid glow.

"Who comes?" demanded the warrior, presenting his spear. "Who are you?"

The stranger did not seem perturbed, though the spear-point touched his bosom. His eyes held the warrior's with strange intensity. "What are you obliged to do?" he asked, strangely. "To guard the gate!" The warrior spoke thickly and mechanically; he stood rigid as a statue, his eyes slowly glazing. "You lie! You are obliged to obey me! You have looked into my eyes, and your soul is no longer your own. Open that door!"

Stiffly, with the wooden features of an image, the guard wheeled about, drew a great key from his girdle, turned it in the massive lock and swung open the door. Then he stood at attention, his unseeing stare straight ahead of him.

A woman glided from the shadows and laid an eager hand on the mesmerist's arm.

"Bid him fetch us horses, Khemsa," she whispered.

"No need of that," answered the Rakhsha. Lifting his voice slightly he spoke to the guardsman. "I have no more use for you. Kill yourself!"

Like a man in a trance the warrior thrust the butt of his spear against the base of the wall, and placed the keen head against his body, just below the ribs. Then slowly, stolidly, he leaned against it with all his weight, so that it transfixed his body and came out between his shoulders. Sliding down the shaft he lay still, the spear jutting above him its full length, like a horrible stalk growing out of his back.

The girl stared down at him in morbid fascination, until Khemsa took her arm and led her through the gate. Torches lighted a narrow space between the outer wall and a lower inner one, in which were arched doors at regular intervals. A warrior paced this enclosure, and when the gate opened he came sauntering up, so secure in his knowledge of the prison's strength that he was not suspicious until Khemsa and the girl emerged from the archway. Then it was too late. The Rakhsha did not waste time in hypnotism, though his action savored of magic to the girl. The guard lowered his spear threateningly, opening his mouth to shout an alarm that would bring spearmen swarming out of the guardrooms at either end of the alleyway. Khemsa flicked the spear aside with his left hand, as a man might flick a straw, and his right flashed out and back, seeming gently to caress the warrior's neck in passing. And the guard pitched on his face without a sound, his head lolling on a broken neck.

Khemsa did not glance at him, but went straight to one of the arched doors and placed his open hand against the heavy bronze lock. With a rending shudder the portal buckled inward. As the girl followed him through, she saw that the thick teakwood hung in splinters, the bronze bolts were bent and twisted from their sockets, and the great hinges broken and disjointed. A thousand-pound battering-ram with forty men to swing it could have shattered the barrier no more completely. Khemsa was drunk with freedom and the exercise of his power, glorying in his might and flinging his strength about as a young giant exercises his thews with unnecessary vigor in the exultant pride of his prowess.

The broken door let them into a small courtyard, lit by a cresset. Opposite the door was a wide grille of iron bars. A hairy hand was visible, gripping one of these bars, and in the darkness behind them glimmered the whites of eyes.

Khemsa stood silent for a space, gazing into the shadows from which those glimmering eyes gave back his stare with burning intensity. Then his hand went into his robe and came out again, and from his opening fingers a shimmering feather of sparkling dust sifted to the flags. Instantly a flare of green fire lighted the enclosure. In the brief glare the forms of seven men, standing motionless behind the bars, were limned in vivid detail; tall, hairy men in ragged hill-men's garments. They did not speak, but in their eyes blazed the fear of death, and their hairy fingers gripped the bars.

The fire died out but the glow remained, a quivering ball of lambent green that pulsed and shimmered on the flags before Khemsa's feet. The wide gaze of the tribesmen was fixed upon it. It wavered, elongated; it turned into a luminous greensmoke spiraling upward. It twisted and writhed like a great shadowy serpent, then broadened and billowed out in shining folds and whirls. It grew to a cloud moving silently over the flags—straight toward the grille. The men watched its coming with dilated eyes; the bars quivered with the grip of their desperate fingers. Bearded lips parted but no sound came forth. The green cloud rolled on the bars and blotted them from sight; like a fog it oozed through the grille and hid the men within. From the enveloping folds came a strangled gasp, as of a man plunged suddenly under the surface of water. That was all.

Khemsa touched the girl's arm, as she stood with parted lips and dilated eyes. Mechanically she turned away with him, looking back over her shoulder. Already the mist was thinning; close to the bars she saw a pair of sandalled feet, the toes turned upward—she glimpsed the indistinct outlines of seven still, prostrate shapes.

"And now for a steed swifter than the fastest horse ever bred in a mortal stable," Khemsa was saying. "We will be in Afghulistan before dawn."

4 An Encounter in the Pass

Yasmina Devi could never clearly remember the details of her abduction. The unexpectedness and violence stunned her; she had only a confused impression of a whirl of happenings—the terrifying grip of a mighty arm, the blazing eyes of her abductor, and his hot breath burning on her flesh. The leap through the window to the parapet, the mad race across battlements and roofs when the fear of falling froze her, the reckless descent of a rope bound to a merlon—he went down almost at a run, his captive folded limply over his brawny shoulder—all this was a befuddled tangle in the Devi's mind. She retained a more vivid memory of him running fleetly into the shadows of the trees, carrying her like a child, and vaulting into the saddle of a fierce Bhalkhana stallion which reared and snorted. Then there was a sensation of flying, and the racing hoofs were striking sparks of fire from the flinty road as the stallion swept up the slopes.

As the girl's mind cleared, her first sensations were furious rage and shame. She was appalled. The rulers of the golden kingdoms south of the Himelians were considered little short of divine; and she was the Devi of Vendhya! Fright was submerged in regal wrath. She cried out furiously and began struggling. She, Yasmina, to be carried on the saddlebow of a hill chief, like a common wench of the market-place! He merely hardened his massive thews slightly against her writhings, and for the first time in her life she experienced the coercion of superior physical strength. His arms felt like iron about her slender limbs. He glanced down at her and grinned hugely. His teeth glimmered whitely in the starlight. The reins lay loose on the stallion's flowing mane, and every thew and fiber of the great beast strained as he hurtled along the boulder-strewn trail. But Conan sat easily, almost carelessly, in the saddle, riding like a centaur.

"You hill-bred dog!" she panted, quivering with the impact of shame, anger, and the realization of helplessness. "You dare—you *dare*! Your life shall pay for this! Where are you taking me?"

"To the villages of Afghulistan," he answered, casting a glance over his shoulder.

Behind them, beyond the slopes they had traversed, torches were tossing on the walls of the fortress, and he glimpsed a flare of light that meant the great gate had been opened. And he laughed, a deep-throated boom gusty as the hill wind.

"The governor has sent his riders after us," he laughed. "By Crom, we will lead him a merry chase! What do you think, Devi—will they pay seven lives for a Kshatriya princess?"

"They will send an army to hang you and your spawn of devils," she promised him with conviction.

He laughed gustily and shifted her to a more comfortable position in his arms. But she took this as a fresh outrage, and renewed her vain struggle, until she saw that her efforts were only amusing him. Besides, her light silken garments, floating on the wind, were being outrageously disarranged by her struggles. She concluded that a scornful submission was the better part of dignity, and lapsed into a smoldering quiescence.

She felt even her anger being submerged by awe as they entered the mouth of the Pass, lowering like a black well mouth in the blacker walls that rose like colossal ramparts to bar their way. It was as if a gigantic knife had cut the Zhaibar out of walls of solid rock. On either hand sheer slopes pitched up for thousands of feet, and the mouth of the Pass was dark as hate. Even Conan could not see with any accuracy, but he knew the road, even by night. And knowing that armed men were racing through the starlight after him, he did not check the stallion's speed. The great brute was not yet showing fatigue. He thundered along the road that followed the valley bed, labored up a slope, swept along a low ridge where treacherous shale on either hand lurked for the unwary, and came upon a trail that followed the lap of the left-hand wall.

Not even Conan could spy, in that darkness, an ambush set by Zhaibar tribesmen. As they swept past the black mouth of a gorge that opened into the Pass, a javelin swished through the air and thudded home behind the stallion's straining shoulder. The great beast let out his life in a shuddering sob and stumbled, going headlong in mid-stride. But Conan had recognized the flight and stroke of the javelin, and he acted with spring-steel quickness.

As the horse fell he leaped clear, holding the girl aloft to guard her from striking boulders. He lit on his feet like a cat, thrust her into a cleft of rock, and wheeled toward the outer darkness, drawing his knife.

Yasmina, confused by the rapidity of events, not quite sure just what had happened, saw a vague shape rush out of the darkness, bare feet slapping softly on the rock, ragged garments whipping on the wind of his haste. She glimpsed the flicker of steel, heard the lightning crack of stroke, parry and counter-stroke, and the crunch of bone as Conan's long knife split the other's skull.

Conan sprang back, crouching in the shelter of the rocks. Out in the night men were moving and a stentorian voice roared: "What, you dogs! Do you flinch? In, curse you, and take them!"

Conan started, peered into the darkness and lifted his voice.

"Yar Afzal! Is it you?"

There sounded a startled imprecation, and the voice called warily.

"Conan? Is it you, Conan?"

"Aye!" the Cimmerian laughed. "Come forth, you old war-dog. I've slain one of your men."

There was movement among the rocks, a light flared dimly, and then a flame appeared and came bobbing toward him, and as it approached, a fierce bearded countenance grew out of the darkness. The man who carried it held it high, thrust forward, and craned his neck to peer among the boulders it lighted; the other hand gripped a great curved tulwar. Conan stepped forward, sheathing his knife, and the other roared a greeting.

"Aye, it is Conan! Come out of your rocks, dogs! It is Conan!"

Others pressed into the wavering circle of light—wild, ragged, bearded men, with eyes like wolves, and long blades in their fists. They did not see Yasmina, for she was hidden by Conan's massive body. But peeping from her covert, she knew icy fear for the first time that night. These men were more like wolves than human beings.

"What are you hunting in the Zhaibar by night, Yar Afzal?" Conan demanded of the burly chief, who grinned like a bearded ghoul.

"Who knows what might come up the Pass after dark? We Wazulis are night-hawks. But what of you, Conan?"

"I have a prisoner," answered the Cimmerian. And moving aside he disclosed the cowering girl. Reaching a long arm into the crevice he drew her trembling forth.

Her imperious bearing was gone. She stared timidly at the ring of bearded faces that hemmed her in, and was grateful for the strong arm that clasped her possessively. The torch was thrust close to her, and there was a sucking intake of breath about the ring.

"She is my captive," Conan warned, glancing pointedly at the feet of the man he had slain, just visible within the ring of light. "I was taking her to Afghulistan, but now you have slain my horse, and the Kshatriyas are close behind me."

"Come with us to my village," suggested Yar Afzal. "We have horses hidden in the gorge. They can never follow us in the darkness. They are close behind you, you say?"

"So close that I hear now the clink of their hoofs on the flint," answered Conan grimly.

Instantly there was movement; the torch was dashed out and the ragged shapes melted like phantoms into the darkness. Conan swept up the Devi in his arms, and she did not resist. The rocky ground hurt her slim feet in their soft slippers and she felt very small and helpless in that brutish, primordial blackness among those colossal, nighted crags.

Feeling her shiver in the wind that moaned down the defiles, Conan jerked a ragged cloak from its owner's shoulders and wrapped it about her. He also hissed a warning in her ear, ordering her to make no sound. She did not hear the distant clink of shod hoofs on rock that warned the keen-eared hill-men; but she was far too frightened to disobey, in any event.

She could see nothing but a few faint stars far above, but she knew by the deepening darkness when they entered the gorge mouth. There was a stir about them, the uneasy movement of horses. A few muttered words, and Conan mounted the horse of the man he had killed, lifting the girl up in front of him. Like phantoms except for the click of their hoofs, the band swept away up the shadowy gorge. Behind them on the trail they left the dead horse and the dead man, which were found less than half an hour later by the riders from the fortress, who recognized the man as a Wazuli and drew their own conclusions accordingly.

Yasmina, snuggled warmly in her captor's arms, grew drowsy in spite of herself. The motion of the horse, though it was uneven, uphill and down, yet possessed a certain rhythm which combined with weariness and emotional exhaustion to force sleep upon her. She had lost all sense of time or direction. They moved in soft thick darkness, in which she sometimes glimpsed vaguely gigantic walls sweeping up like black ramparts, or great crags shouldering the stars; at times she sensed echoing depths beneath them, or felt the wind of dizzy heights blowing cold about her. Gradually these things faded into a dreamy unwakefulness in which the clink of hoofs and the creak of saddles were like the irrelevant sounds in a dream.

She was vaguely aware when the motion ceased and she was lifted down and carried a few steps. Then she was laid down on something soft and rustling, and something—a folded coat perhaps—was thrust under her head, and the cloak in which she was wrapped was carefully tucked about her. She heard Yar Afzal laugh.

"A rare prize, Conan; fit mate for a chief of the Afghulis."

"Not for me," came Conan's answering rumble. "This wench will buy the lives of my seven headmen, blast their souls."

That was the last she heard as she sank into dreamless slumber.

She slept while armed men rode through the dark hills, and the fate of kingdoms hung in the balance. Through the shadowy gorges and defiles that night there rang the hoofs of galloping horses, and the star-light glimmered on helmets and curved blades, until the ghoulish shapes that haunt the crags stared into the darkness from ravine and boulder and wondered what things were afoot.

A band of these sat gaunt horses in the black pitmouth of a gorge as the hurrying hoofs swept past. Their leader, a well-built man in a hel-met and gilt-braided cloak, held up his hand warningly, until the riders had sped on. Then he laughed softly.

"They must have lost the trail! Or else they have found that Conan has already reached the Afghuli villages. It will take many riders to smoke out that hive. There will be squadrons riding up the Zhaibar by dawn."

"If there is fighting in the hills there will be looting," muttered a voice behind him, in the dialect of the Irakzai.

"There will be looting," answered the man with the helmet. "But first it is our business to reach the valley of Gurashah and await the riders that will be galloping southward from Secunderam before daylight."

He lifted his reins and rode out of the defile, his men falling in behind him—thirty ragged phantoms in the starlight.

5 The Black Stallion

The sun was well up when Yasmina awoke. She did not start and stare blankly, wondering where she was. She awoke with full knowledge of all that had occurred. Her supple limbs were stiff from her long ride, and her firm flesh seemed to feel the contact of the muscular arm that had borne her so far.

She was lying on a sheepskin covering a pallet of leaves on a hard-beaten dirt floor. A folded sheepskin coat was under her head, and she was wrapped in a ragged cloak. She was in a large room, the walls of which were crudely but strongly built of uncut rocks, plastered with sun-baked mud. Heavy beams supported a roof of the same kind, in which showed a trap-door up to which led a ladder. There were no windows in the thick walls, only loop-holes. There was one door, a sturdy bronze affair that must have been looted from some Vendhyan border tower. Opposite it was a wide opening in the wall, with no door, but several strong wooden bars in place. Beyond them Yasmina saw a magnificent black stallion munching a pile of dried grass. The building was fort, dwelling-place and stable in one.

At the other end of the room a girl in the vest and baggy trousers of a hill-woman squatted beside a small fire, cooking strips of meat on an iron grid laid over blocks of stone. There was a sooty cleft in the wall a few feet from the floor, and some of the smoke found its way out there. The rest floated in blue wisps about the room.

The hill-girl glanced at Yasmina over her shoulder, displaying a bold, handsome face, and then continued her cooking. Voices boomed outside; then the door was kicked open, and Conan strode in. He looked more enormous than ever with the morning sunlight behind him, and Yasmina noted some details that had escaped her the night before. His garments were clean and not ragged. The broad Bakhariot girdle that supported his knife in its ornamented scabbard would have matched the robes of a prince, and there was a glint of fine Turanian mail under his shirt.

"Your captive is awake, Conan," said the Wazuli girl, and he grunted, strode up to the fire and swept the strips of mutton off into a stone dish.

The squatting girl laughed up at him, with some spicy jest, and he grinned wolfishly, and hooking a toe under her haunches, tumbled her sprawling onto the floor. She seemed to derive considerable amusement from this bit of rough horse-play, but Conan paid no more heed to her. Producing a great hunk of bread from somewhere, with a copper jug of wine, he carried the lot to Yasmina, who had risen from her pallet and was regarding him doubtfully.

"Rough fare for a Devi, girl, but our best," he grunted. "It will fill your belly, at least."

He set the platter on the floor, and she was suddenly aware of a ravenous hunger. Making no comment, she seated herself cross-legged on the floor, and taking the dish in her lap, she began to eat, using her fingers, which were all she had in the way of table utensils. After all, adaptability is one of the tests of true aristocracy. Conan stood looking down at her, his thumbs hooked in his girdle. He never sat cross-legged, after the Eastern fashion.

"Where am I?" she asked abruptly.

"In the hut of Yar Afzal, the chief of the Khurum Wazulis," he answered. "Afghulistan lies a good many miles farther on to the west. We'll hide here awhile. The Kshatriyas are beating up the hills for you—several of their squads have been cut up by the tribes already."

"What are you going to do?" she asked.

"Keep you until Chunder Shan is willing to trade back my seven cow-thieves," he grunted. "Women of the Wazulis are crushing ink out of shoki leaves, and after a while you can write a letter to the governor."

A touch of her old imperious wrath shook her, as she thought how maddeningly her plans had gone awry, leaving her captive of the very man she had plotted to get into her power. She flung down the dish, with the remnants of her meal, and sprang to her feet, tense with anger.

"I will not write a letter! If you do not take me back, they will hang your seven men, and a thousand more besides!"

The Wazuli girl laughed mockingly, Conan scowled, and then the door opened and Yar Afzal came swaggering in. The Wazuli chief was as tall as Conan, and of greater girth, but he looked fat and slow beside the hard compactness of the Cimmerian. He plucked his red-stained beard and stared meaningly at the Wazuli girl, and that wench rose and scurried out without delay. Then Yar Afzal turned to his guest.

"The damnable people murmur, Conan," quoth he. "They wish me to murder you and take the girl to hold for ransom. They say that any-one can tell by her garments that she is a noble lady. They say why should the Afghuli dogs profit by her, when it is the people who take the risk of guarding her?"

"Lend me your horse," said Conan. "I'll take her and go."

"Pish!" boomed Yar Afzal. "Do you think I can't handle my own people? I'll have them dancing in their shirts if they cross me! They don't love you—or any other outlander—but you saved my life once, and I will not forget. Come out, though, Conan; a scout has returned."

Conan hitched at his girdle and followed the chief outside. They closed the door after them, and Yasmina peeped through a loop-hole. She looked out on a level space before the hut. At the farther end of that space there was a cluster of mud and stone huts, and she saw naked children playing among the boulders, and the slim erect women of the hills going about their tasks.

Directly before the chiefs hut a circle of hairy, ragged men squatted, facing the door. Conan and Yar Afzal stood a few paces before the door, and between them and the ring of warriors another man sat cross-legged. This one was addressing his chief in the harsh accents of the Wazuli which Yasmina could scarcely understand, though as part of her royal education she had been taught the languages of Iranistan and the kindred tongues of Ghulistan.

"I talked with a Dagozai who saw the riders last night," said the scout. "He was lurking near when they came to the spot where we ambushed the lord Conan. He overheard their speech. Chunder Shan was with them. They found the dead horse, and one of the men recognized it as Conan's. Then they found the man Conan slew, and knew him for a Wazuli. It seemed to them that Conan had been slain and the girl taken by the Wazuli; so they turned aside from their purpose of following to Afghulistan. But they did not know from which village the dead man was come, and we had left no trail a Kshatriya could follow.

"So they rode to the nearest Wazuli village, which was the village of Jugra, and burnt it and slew many of the people. But the men of Khojur came upon them in darkness and slew some of them, and wounded the governor. So the survivors retired down the Zhaibar in the darkness before dawn, but they returned with reinforcements before sunrise, and there has been skirmishing and fighting in the hills all morning. It is said that a great army is being raised to sweep the hills about the Zhaibar. The tribes are whetting their knives and laying ambushes in every pass from here to Gurashah valley. Moreover, Kerim Shah has returned to the hills."

A grunt went around the circle, and Yasmina leaned closer to the loop-hole at the name she had begun to mistrust.

"Where went he?" demanded Yar Afzal.

"The Dagozai did not know; with him were thirty Irakzai of the lower villages. They rode into the hills and disappeared."

"These Irakzai are jackals that follow a lion for crumbs," growled Yar Afzal. "They have been lapping up the coins Kerim Shah scatters among the border tribes to buy men like horses. I like him not, for all he is our kinsman from Iranistan."

"He's not even that," said Conan. "I know him of old. He's an Hyrkanian, a spy of Yezdigerd's. If I catch him I'll hang his hide to a tamarisk."

"But the Kshatriyas!" clamored the men in the semicircle. "Are we to squat on our haunches until they smoke us out? They will learn at last in which Wazuli village the wench is held. We are not loved by the Zhaibari; they will help the Kshatriyas hunt us out."

"Let them come," grunted Yar Afzal. "We can hold the defiles against a host."

One of the men leaped up and shook his fist at Conan.

"Are we to take all the risks while he reaps the rewards?" he howled. "Are we to fight his battles for him?"

With a stride Conan reached him and bent slightly to stare full into his hairy face. The Cimmerian had not drawn his long knife, but his left hand grasped the scabbard, jutting the hilt suggestively forward.

"I ask no man to fight my battles," he said softly. "Draw your blade if you dare, you yapping dog!"

The Wazuli started back, snarling like a cat.

"Dare to touch me and here are fifty men to rend you apart!" he screeched.

"What!" roared Yar Afzal, his face purpling with wrath. His whiskers bristled, his belly swelled with his rage. "Are you chief of Khurum? Do the Wazulis take orders from Yar Afzal, or from a low-bred cur?"

The man cringed before his invincible chief, and Yar Afzal, striding up to him, seized him by the throat and choked him until his face was turning black. Then he hurled the man savagely against the ground and stood over him with his tulwar in his hand.

"Is there any who questions my authority?" he roared, and his warriors looked down sullenly as his bellicose glare swept their semicircle. Yar Afzal grunted scornfully and sheathed his weapon with a gesture that was the apex of insult. Then he kicked the fallen agitator with a concentrated vindictiveness that brought howls from his victim.

"Get down the valley to the watchers on the heights and bring word if they have seen anything," commanded Yar Afzal, and the man went, shaking with fear and grinding his teeth with fury.

Yar Afzal then seated himself ponderously on a stone, growling in his beard. Conan stood near him, legs braced apart, thumbs hooked in his girdle, narrowly watching the assembled warriors. They stared at him sullenly, not daring to brave Yar Afzal's fury, but hating the foreigner as only a hillman can hate.

"Now listen to me, you sons of nameless dogs, while I tell you what the lord Conan and I have planned to fool the Kshatriyas." The boom of Yar Afzal's bull-like voice followed the discomfited warrior as he slunk away from the assembly.

The man passed by the cluster of huts, where women who had seen his defeat laughed at him and called stinging comments, and hastened on along the trail that wound among spurs and rocks toward the valley head.

Just as he rounded the first turn that took him out of sight of the village, he stopped short, gaping stupidly. He had not believed it possible for a stranger to enter the valley of Khurum without being detected by the hawk-eyed watchers along the heights; yet a man sat cross-legged on a low ledge beside the path—a man in a camel-hair robe and a green turban.

The Wazuli's mouth gaped for a yell, and his hand leaped to his knife-hilt. But at that instant his eyes met those of the stranger and the cry died in his throat, his fingers went limp. He stood like a statue, his own eyes glazed and vacant.

For minutes the scene held motionless; then the man on the ledge drew a cryptic symbol in the dust on the rock with his forefinger. The Wazuli did not see him place anything within the compass of that emblem, but presently something gleamed there—a round, shiny black ball that looked like polished jade. The man in the green turban took this up and tossed it to the Wazuli, who mechanically caught it.

"Carry this to Yar Afzal," he said, and the Wazuli turned like an automaton and went back along the path, holding the black jade ball in his outstretched hand. He did not even turn his head to the renewed jeers of the women as he passed the huts. He did not seem to hear.

The man on the ledge gazed after him with a cryptic smile. A girl's head rose above the rim of the ledge and she looked at him with admiration and a touch of fear that had not been present the night before.

"Why did you do that?" she asked.

He ran his fingers through her dark locks caressingly.

"Are you still dizzy from your flight on the horse-of-air, that you doubt my wisdom?" he laughed. "As long as Yar Afzal lives, Conan will bide safe among the Wazuli fighting-men. Their knives are sharp, and there are many of them. What I plot will be safer, even for me, than to seek to slay him and take her from among them. It takes no wizard to predict what the Wazulis will do, and what Conan will do, when my victim hands the globe of Yezud to the chief of Khurum."

★ ★ ★

Back before the hut, Yar Afzal halted in the midst of some tirade, surprized and displeased to see the man he had sent up the valley, pushing his way through the throng.

"I bade you go to the watchers!" the chief bellowed. "You have not had time to come from them."

The other did not reply; he stood woodenly, staring vacantly into the chief's face, his palm outstretched holding the jade ball. Conan, looking over Yar Afzal's shoulder, murmured something and reached to touch the chief's arm, but as he did so, Yar Afzal, in a paroxysm of anger, struck the man with his clenched fist and felled him like an ox. As he fell, the jade sphere rolled to Yar Afzal's foot, and the chief, seeming to see it for the first time, bent and picked it up. The men, staring perplexedly at their senseless comrade, saw their chief bend, but they did not see what he picked up from the ground.

Yar Afzal straightened, glanced at the jade, and made a motion to thrust it into his girdle.

"Carry that fool to his hut," he growled. "He has the look of a lotus-eater. He returned me a blank stare. I—*aie!*"

In his right hand, moving toward his girdle, he had suddenly felt movement where movement should not be. His voice died away as he stood and glared at nothing; and inside his clenched right hand he felt the quivering of *change*, of *motion*, of *life*. He no longer held a smooth shining sphere in his fingers. And he dared not look; his tongue clove to the roof of his mouth, and he could not open his hand. His astonished warriors saw Yar Afzal's eyes distend, the color ebb from his face. Then suddenly a bellow of agony burst from his bearded lips; he swayed and fell as if struck by lightning, his right arm tossed out in front of him. Face down he lay, and from between his opening fingers crawled a spider—a hideous, black, hairy-legged monster whose body shone like black jade. The men yelled and gave back suddenly, and the creature scuttled into a crevice of the rocks and disappeared.

The warriors started up, glaring wildly, and a voice rose above their clamor, a far-carrying voice of command which came from none knew where. Afterward each man there—who still lived—denied that he had shouted, but all there heard it.

"Yar Afzal is dead! Kill the outlander!"

That shout focused their whirling minds as one. Doubt, bewilderment and fear vanished in the uproaring surge of the blood-lust. A furious yell rent the skies as the tribesmen responded instantly to the suggestion. They came headlong across the open space, cloaks flapping, eyes blazing, knives lifted.

Conan's action was as quick as theirs. As the voice shouted he sprang for the hut door. But they were closer to him than he was to the door, and with one foot on the sill he had to wheel and parry the swipe of a yard-long blade. He split the man's skull—ducked another swinging knife and gutted the wielder—felled a man with his left fist and stabbed another in the belly—and heaved back mightily against the closed door with his shoulders. Hacking blades were nicking chips out of the jambs about his ears, but the door flew open under the impact of his shoulders, and he went stumbling backward into the room. A bearded tribesman, thrusting with all his fury as Conan sprang back, overreached and pitched head-first through the doorway. Conan stopped, grasped the slack of his garments and hauled him clear, and slammed the door in the faces of the men who came surging into it. Bones snapped under the impact, and the next instant Conan slammed the bolts into place and whirled with desperate haste to meet the man who sprang from the floor and tore into action like a madman.

Yasmina cowered in a corner, staring in horror as the two men fought back and forth across the room, almost trampling her at times; the flash and clangor of their blades filled the room, and outside the mob clamored like a wolf-pack, hacking deafeningly at the bronze door with their long knives, and dashing huge rocks against it. Somebody fetched a tree trunk, and the door began to stagger under the thunderous assault. Yasmina clasped her ears, staring wildly. Violence and fury within, cataclysmic madness without. The stallion in his stall neighed and reared, thundering with his heels against the walls. He wheeled and launched his hoofs through the bars just as the tribesman, backing away from Conan's murderous swipes, stumbled against them. His spine cracked in three places like a rotten branch and he was hurled headlong against the Cimmerian, bearing him backward so that they both crashed to the beaten floor.

Yasmina cried out and ran forward; to her dazed sight it seemed that both were slain. She reached them just as Conan threw aside the corpse and rose. She caught his arm, trembling from head to foot.

"Oh, you live! I thought—I thought you were dead!"

He glanced down at her quickly, into the pale, upturned face and the wide staring dark eyes.

"Why are you trembling?" he demanded. "Why should you care if I live or die?"

A vestige of her poise returned to her, and she drew away, making a rather pitiful attempt at playing the Devi.

"You are preferable to those wolves howling without," she answered, gesturing toward the door, the stone sill of which was beginning to splinter away.

"That won't hold long," he muttered, then turned and went swiftly to the stall of the stallion.

Yasmina clenched her hands and caught her breath as she saw him tear aside the splintered bars and go into the stall with the maddened beast. The stallion reared above him, neighing terribly, hoofs lifted, eyes and teeth flashing and ears laid back, but Conan leaped and caught his mane with a display of sheer strength that seemed impossible, and dragged the beast down on his forelegs. The steed snorted and quivered, but stood still while the man bridled him and clapped on the gold-worked saddle, with the wide silver stirrups.

Wheeling the beast around in the stall, Conan called quickly to Yasmina, and the girl came, sidling nervously past the stallion's heels. Conan was working at the stone wall, talking swiftly as he worked.

"A secret door in the wall here, that not even the Wazuli know about. Yar Afzal showed it to me once when he was drunk. It opens out into the mouth of the ravine behind the hut. Ha!"

As he tugged at a projection that seemed casual, a whole section of the wall slid back on oiled iron runners. Looking through, the girl saw a narrow defile opening in a sheer stone cliff within a few feet of the hut's back wall. Then Conan sprang into the saddle and hauled her up before him. Behind them the great door groaned like a living thing and crashed in, and a yell rang to the roof as the entrance was instantly flooded with hairy faces and knives in hairy fists. And then the great stallion went through the wall like a javelin from a catapult, and thundered into the defile, running low, foam flying from the bit-rings.

That move came as an absolute surprize to the Wazulis. It was a surprize, too, to those stealing down the ravine. It happened so quickly—the hurricane-like charge of the great horse—that a man in a green turban was unable to get out of the way. He went down under the frantic hoofs, and a girl screamed. Conan got one glimpse of her as they thundered by—a slim, dark girl in silk trousers and a jeweled breast-band, flattening herself against the ravine wall. Then the black horse and his riders were gone up the gorge like the spume blown before a storm, and the men who came tumbling through the wall into the defile after them met that which changed their yells of blood-lust to shrill screams of fear and death.

6 The Mountain of the Black Seers

"Where now?" Yasmina was trying to sit erect on the rocking saddle-bow, clutching her captor. She was conscious of a recognition of shame that she should not find unpleasant the feel of his muscular flesh under her fingers.

"To Afghulistan," he answered. "It's a perilous road, but the stallion will carry us easily, unless we fall in with some of your friends, or my tribal enemies. Now that Yar Afzal is dead, those damned Wazulis will be on our heels. I'm surprized we haven't sighted them behind us already."

"Who was that man you rode down?" she asked.

"I don't know. I never saw him before. He's no Ghuli, that's certain. What the devil he was doing there is more than I can say. There was a girl with him, too."

"Yes." Her gaze was shadowed. "I can not understand that. That girl was my maid, Gitara. Do you suppose she was coming to aid me? That the man was a friend? If so, the Wazulis have captured them both."

"Well," he answered, "there's nothing we can do. If we go back, they'll skin us both. I can't understand how a girl like that could get this far into the mountains with only one man—and he a robed scholar, for that's what he looked like. There's something infernally queer in all this. That fellow Yar Afzal beat and sent away—he moved like a man walking in his sleep. I've seen the priests of Zamora perform their abominable rituals in their forbidden temples, and their victims had a stare like that man. The priests looked into their eyes and muttered incantations, and then the people became the walking dead men, with glassy eyes, doing as they were ordered.

"And then I saw what the fellow had in his hand, which Yar Afzal picked up. It was like a big black jade bead, such as the temple girls of Yezud wear when they dance before the black stone spider which is their god. Yar Afzal held it in his hand, and he didn't pick up anything else. Yet when he fell dead, a spider, like the god at Yezud, only smaller, ran out of his fingers. And then, when the Wazulis stood uncertain there, a voice cried out for them to kill me, and I know that voice didn't come from any of the warriors, nor from the women who watched by the huts. It seemed to come from *above*."

Yasmina did not reply. She glanced at the stark outlines of the mountains all about them and shuddered. Her soul shrank from their gaunt brutality. This was a grim, naked land where anything might happen. Age-old traditions invested it with shuddery horror for anyone born in the hot, luxuriant southern plains.

The sun was high, beating down with fierce heat, yet the wind that blew in fitful gusts seemed to sweep off slopes of ice. Once she heard a strange rushing above them that was not the sweep of the wind, and from the way Conan looked up, she knew it was not a common sound to him, either. She thought that a strip of the cold blue sky was momentarily blurred, as if some all but invisible object had swept between it and herself, but she could not be sure. Neither made any comment, but Conan loosened his knife in his scabbard.

They were following a faintly marked path dipping down into ravines so deep the sun never struck bottom, laboring up steep slopes where loose shale threatened to slide from beneath their feet, and following knife-edge ridges with blue-hazed echoing depths on either hand.

The sun had passed its zenith when they crossed a narrow trail winding among the crags. Conan reined the horse aside and followed it southward, going almost at right angles to their former course.

"A Galzai village is at one end of this trail," he explained. "Their women follow it to a well, for water. You need new garments."

Glancing down at her filmy attire, Yasmina agreed with him. Her cloth-of-gold slippers were in tatters, her robes and silken under-garments torn to shreds that scarcely held together decently. Garments meant for the streets of Peshkhauri were scarcely appropriate for the crags of the Himelians.

Coming to a crook in the trail, Conan dismounted, helped Yasmina down and waited. Presently he nodded, though she heard nothing.

"A woman coming along the trail," he remarked. In sudden panic she clutched his arm.

"You will not—not kill her?"

"I don't kill women ordinarily," he grunted; "though some of the hill-women are she-wolves. No," he grinned as at a huge jest. "By Crom, I'll *pay* for her clothes! How is that?" He displayed a large handful of gold coins, and replaced all but the largest. She nodded, much relieved. It was perhaps natural for men to slay and die; her flesh crawled at the thought of watching the butchery of a woman.

Presently a woman appeared around the crook of the trail—a tall, slim Galzai girl, straight as a young sapling, bearing a great empty gourd. She stopped short and the gourd fell from her hands when she saw them; she wavered as though to run, then realized that Conan was too close to her to allow her to escape, and so stood still, staring at them with a mixed expression of fear and curiosity.

Conan displayed the gold coin.

"If you will give this woman your garments," he said, "I will give you this money."

The response was instant. The girl smiled broadly with surprize and delight, and, with the disdain of a hill-woman for prudish conventions, promptly yanked off her sleeveless embroidered vest, slipped down her wide trousers and stepped out of them, twitched off her wide-sleeved shirt, and kicked off her sandals. Bundling them all in a bunch, she proffered them to Conan, who handed them to the astonished Devi.

"Get behind that rock and put these on," he directed, further proving himself no native hillman. "Fold your robes up into a bundle and bring them to me when you come out."

"The money!" clamored the hill-girl, stretching out her hands eagerly. "The gold you promised me!"

Conan flipped the coin to her, she caught it, bit, then thrust it into her hair, bent and caught up the gourd and went on down the path, as devoid of self-consciousness as of garments. Conan waited with some impatience while the Devi, for the first time in her pampered life, dressed herself. When she stepped from behind the rock he swore in surprize, and she felt a curious rush of emotions at the unrestrained admiration burning in his fierce blue eyes. She felt shame, embarrassment, yet a stimulation of vanity she had never before experienced, and a tingling when meeting the impact of his eyes. He laid a heavy hand on her shoulder and turned her about, staring avidly at her from all angles.

"By Crom!" said he. "In those smoky, mystic robes you were aloof and cold and far off as a star! Now you are a woman of warm flesh and blood! You went behind that rock as the Devi of Vendhya; you come out as a hill-girl—though a thousand times more beautiful than any wench of the Zhaibar! You were a goddess—now you are real!"

He spanked her resoundingly, and she, recognizing this as merely another expression of admiration, did not feel outraged. It was indeed as if the changing of her garments had wrought a change in her personality. The feelings and sensations she had suppressed rose to domination in her now, as if the queenly robes she had cast off had been material shackles and inhibitions.

But Conan, in his renewed admiration, did not forget that peril lurked all about them. The farther they drew away from the region of the Zhaibar, the less likely he was to encounter any Kshatriya troops. On the other hand he had been listening all throughout their flight for sounds that would tell him the vengeful Wazulis of Khurum were on their heels.

Swinging the Devi up, he followed her into the saddle and again reined the stallion westward. The bundle of garments she had given him, he hurled over a cliff, to fall into the depths of a thousand-foot gorge.

"Why did you do that?" she asked. "Why did you not give them to the girl?"

"The riders from Peshkhauri are combing these hills," he said. "They'll be ambushed and harried at every turn, and by way of reprisal they'll destroy every village they can take. They may turn westward any time. If they found a girl wearing your garments, they'd torture her into talking, and she might put them on my trail."

"What will she do?" asked Yasmina.

"Go back to her village and tell her people that a stranger attacked her," he answered. "She'll have them on our track, all right. But she had to go on and get the water first; if she dared go back without it, they'd whip the skin off her. That gives us a long start. They'll never catch us. By nightfall we'll cross the Afghuli border."

"There are no paths or signs of human habitation in these parts," she commented. "Even for the Himelians this region seems singularly deserted. We have not seen a trail since we left the one where we met the Galzai woman."

For answer he pointed to the northwest, where she glimpsed a peak in a notch of the crags.

"Yimsha," grunted Conan. "The tribes build their villages as far from the mountain as they can."

She was instantly rigid with attention.

"Yimsha!" she whispered. "The mountain of the Black Seers!"

"So they say," he answered. "This is as near as I ever approached it. I have swung north to avoid any Kshatriya troops that might be prowling through the hills. The regular trail from Khurum to Afghulistan lies farther south. This is an ancient one, and seldom used."

She was staring intently at the distant peak. Her nails bit into her pink palms.

"How long would it take to reach Yimsha from this point?"

"All the rest of the day, and all night," he answered, and grinned. "Do you want to go there? By Crom, it's no place for an ordinary human, from what the hill-people say."

"Why do they not gather and destroy the devils that inhabit it?" she demanded.

"Wipe out wizards with swords? Anyway, they never interfere with people, unless the people interfere with them. I never saw one of them, though I've talked with men who swore they had. They say they've glimpsed people from the tower among the crags at sunset or sunrise—tall, silent men in black robes."

"Would you be afraid to attack them?"

"I?" The idea seemed a new one to him. "Why, if they imposed upon me, it would be my life or theirs. But I have nothing to do with them. I came to these mountains to raise a following of human beings, not to war with wizards."

Yasmina did not at once reply. She stared at the peak as at a human enemy, feeling all her anger and hatred stir in her bosom anew. And another feeling began to take dim shape. She had plotted to hurl against the masters of Yimsha the man in whose arms she was now carried. Perhaps there was another way, besides the method she had planned, to accomplish her purpose. She could not mistake the look that was beginning to dawn in this wild man's eyes as they rested on her. Kingdoms have fallen when a woman's slim white hands pulled the strings of destiny. Suddenly she stiffened, pointing.

"Look!"

Just visible on the distant peak there hung a cloud of peculiar aspect. It was a frosty crimson in color, veined with sparkling gold. This cloud was in motion; it rotated, and as it whirled it contracted. It dwindled to a spinning taper that flashed in the sun. And suddenly it detached itself from the snow-tipped peak, floated out over the void like a gay-hued feather, and became invisible against the cerulean sky.

"What could that have been?" asked the girl uneasily, as a shoulder of rock shut the distant mountain from view; the phenomenon had been disturbing, even in its beauty.

"The hill-men call it Yimsha's Carpet, whatever that means," answered Conan. "I've seen five hundred of them running as if the devil were at their heels, to hide themselves in caves and crags, because they saw that crimson cloud float up from the peak. What in—"

They had advanced through a narrow, knife-cut gash between turreted walls and emerged upon a broad ledge, flanked by a series of rugged slopes on one hand, and a gigantic precipice on the other. The dim trail followed this ledge, bent around a shoulder and reappeared at intervals far below, working a tedious way downward. And emerging from the cut that opened upon the ledge, the black stallion halted short, snorting. Conan urged him on impatiently, and the horse snorted and threw his head up and down, quivering and straining as if against an invisible barrier.

Conan swore and swung off, lifting Yasmina down with him. He went forward, with a hand thrown out before him as if expecting to encounter unseen resistance, but there was nothing to hinder him, though when he tried to lead the horse, it neighed shrilly and jerked back. Then Yasmina cried out, and Conan wheeled, hand starting to knife-hilt.

Neither of them had seen him come, but he stood there, with his arms folded, a man in a camel-hair robe and a green turban. Conan grunted with surprize to recognize the man the stallion had spurned in the ravine outside the Wazuli village.

"Who the devil are you?" he demanded.

The man did not answer. Conan noticed that his eyes were wide, fixed, and of a peculiar luminous quality. And those eyes held his like a magnet.

Khemsa's sorcery was based on hypnotism, as is the case with most Eastern magic. The way has been prepared for the hypnotist for untold centuries of generations who have lived and died in the firm conviction of the reality and power of hypnotism, building up, by mass thought and practise, a colossal though intangible atmosphere against which the individual, steeped in the traditions of the land, finds himself helpless.

But Conan was not a son of the East. Its traditions were meaningless to him; he was the product of an utterly alien atmosphere. Hypnotism was not even a myth in Cimmeria. The heritage that prepared a native of the East for submission to the mesmerist was not his.

He was aware of what Khemsa was trying to do to him; but he felt the impact of the man's uncanny power only as a vague impulsion, a tugging and pulling that he could shake off as a man shakes off spiderwebs from his garments.

Aware of hostility and black magic, he ripped out his long knife and lunged, as quick on his feet as a mountain lion.

But hypnotism was not all of Khemsa's magic. Yasmina, watching, did not see by what roguery of movement or illusion the man in the green turban avoided the terrible disembowelling thrust. But the keen blade whickered between side and lifted arm, and to Yasmina it seemed that Khemsa merely brushed his open palm lightly against Conan's bull-neck. But the Cimmerian went down like a slain ox.

Yet Conan was not dead; breaking his fall with his left hand, he slashed at Khemsa's legs even as he went down, and the Rakhsha avoided the scythe-like swipe only by a most unwizardly bound backward. Then Yasmina cried out sharply as she saw a woman she recognized as Gitara glide out from among the rocks and come up to the man. The greeting died in the Devi's throat as she saw the malevolence in the girl's beautiful face.

Conan was rising slowly, shaken and dazed by the cruel craft of that blow which, delivered with an art forgotten of men before Atlantis sank, would have broken like a rotten twig the neck of a lesser man. Khemsa gazed at him cautiously and a trifle uncertainly. The Rakhsha had learned the full flood of his own power when he faced at bay the knives of the maddened Wazulis in the ravine behind Khurum village; but the Cimmerian's resistance had perhaps shaken his new-found confidence a trifle. Sorcery thrives on success, not on failure.

He stepped forward, lifting his hand—then halted as if frozen, head tilted back, eyes wide open, hand raised. In spite of himself Conan followed his gaze, and so did the women—the girl cowering by the trembling stallion, and the girl beside Khemsa.

Down the mountain slopes, like a whirl of shining dust blown before the wind, a crimson, conoid cloud came dancing. Khemsa's dark face turned ashen; his hand began to tremble, then sank to his side. The girl beside him, sensing the change in him, stared at him inquiringly.

The crimson shape left the mountain slope and came down in a long arching sweep. It struck the ledge between Conan and Khemsa, and the Rakhsha gave back with a stifled cry. He backed away, pushing the girl Gitara back with groping, fending hands.

The crimson cloud balanced like a spinning top for an instant, whirling in a dazzling sheen on its point. Then without warning it was gone, vanished as a bubble vanishes when burst. There on the ledge stood four men. It was miraculous, incredible, impossible, yet it was true. They were not ghosts or phantoms. They were four tall men, with shaven, vulture-like heads, and black robes that hid their feet. Their hands were concealed by their wide sleeves. They stood in silence, their naked heads nodding slightly in unison. They were facing Khemsa, but behind them Conan felt his own blood turning to ice in his veins. Rising, he backed stealthily away, until he could feel the stallion's shoulder trembling against his back, and the Devi crept into the shelter of his arm. There was no word spoken. Silence hung like a stifling pall.

All four of the men in black robes stared at Khemsa. Their vulture-like faces were immobile, their eyes introspective and contemplative. But Khemsa shook like a man in an ague. His feet were braced on the rock, his calves straining as if in physical combat. Sweat ran in streams down his dark face. His right hand locked on something under his brown robe so desperately that the blood ebbed from that hand and left it white. His left hand fell on the shoulder of Gitara and clutched in agony like the grasp of a drowning man. She did not flinch or whimper, though his fingers dug like talons into her firm flesh.

Conan had witnessed hundreds of battles in his wild life, but never one like this, wherein four diabolical wills sought to beat down one lesser but equally devilish will that opposed them. But he only faintly sensed the monstrous quality of that hideous struggle. With his back to the wall, driven to bay by his former masters, Khemsa was fighting for his life with all the dark power, all the frightful knowledge they had taught him through long, grim years of neophytism and vassalage.

He was stronger than even he had guessed, and the free exercise of his powers in his own behalf had tapped unsuspected reservoirs of forces. And he was nerved to super-energy by frantic fear and desperation. He reeled before the merciless impact of those hypnotic eyes, but he held his ground. His features were distorted into a bestial grin of agony, and his limbs were twisted as on a rack. It was a war of souls, of frightful brains steeped in lore forbidden to men for a million years, of mentalities which had plumbed the abysses and explored the dark stars where spawn the shadows.

Yasmina understood this better than did Conan. And she dimly understood why Khemsa could withstand the concentrated impact of those four hellish wills which might have blasted into atoms the very rock on which he stood. The reason was the girl that he clutched with the strength of his despair. She was like an anchor to his staggering soul, battered by the waves of those psychic emanations. His weakness was now his strength. His love for the girl, violent and evil though it might be, was yet a tie that bound him to the rest of humanity, providing an earthly leverage for his will, a chain that his inhuman enemies could not break; at least not break through Khemsa.

They realized that before he did. And one of them turned his gaze from the Rakhsha full upon Gitara. There was no battle there. The girl shrank and wilted like a leaf in the drought. Irresistibly impelled, she tore herself from her lover's arms before he realized what was happening. Then a hideous thing came to pass. She began to back toward the precipice, facing her tormentors, her eyes wide and blank as dark gleaming glass from behind which a lamp has been blown out. Khemsa groaned and staggered toward her, falling into the trap set for him. A divided mind could not maintain the unequal battle. He was beaten, a straw in their hands. The girl went backward, walking like an automaton, and Khemsa reeled drunkenly after her, hands vainly outstretched, groaning, slobbering in his pain, his feet moving heavily like dead things.

On the very brink she paused, standing stiffly, her heels on the edge, and he fell on his knees and crawled whimpering toward her, groping for her, to drag her back from destruction. And just before his clumsy fingers touched her, one of the wizards laughed, like the sudden, bronze note of a bell in hell. The girl reeled suddenly and, consummate climax of exquisite cruelty, reason and understanding flooded back into her eyes, which flared with awful fear. She screamed, clutched wildly at her lover's straining hand, and then, unable to save herself, fell headlong with a moaning cry.

Khemsa hauled himself to the edge and stared over, haggardly, his lips working as he mumbled to himself. Then he turned and stared for a long minute at his torturers, with wide eyes that held no human light. And then with a cry that almost burst the rocks, he reeled up and came rushing toward them, a knife lifted in his hand.

One of the Rakhshas stepped forward and stamped his foot, and as he stamped, there came a rumbling that grew swiftly to a grinding roar. Where his foot struck, a crevice opened in the solid rock that widened instantly. Then, with a deafening crash, a whole section of the ledge gave way. There was a last glimpse of Khemsa, with arms wildly upflung, and then he vanished amidst the roar of the avalanche that thundered down into the abyss.

The four looked contemplatively at the ragged edge of rock that formed the new rim of the precipice, and then turned suddenly. Conan, thrown off his feet by the shudder of the mountain, was rising, lifting Yasmina. He seemed to move as slowly as his brain was working. He was befogged and stupid. He realized that there was a desperate need for him to lift the Devi on the black stallion and ride like the wind, but an unaccountable sluggishness weighted his every thought and action.

And now the wizards had turned toward him; they raised their arms, and to his horrified sight, he saw their outlines fading, dimming,

becoming hazy and nebulous, as a crimson smoke billowed around
their feet and rose about them. They were blotted out by a sudden
whirling cloud—and then he realized that he too was enveloped in a
blinding crimson mist—he heard Yasmina scream, and the stallion cried
out like a woman in pain. The Devi was torn from his arm, and as he
lashed out with his knife blindly, a terrific blow like a gust of storm
wind knocked him sprawling against a rock. Dazedly he saw a crimson
conoid cloud spinning up and over the mountain slopes. Yasmina was
gone, and so were the four men in black. Only the terrified stallion
shared the ledge with him.

7 On to Yimsha

As mists vanish before a strong wind, the cobwebs vanished from
Conan's brain. With a searing curse he leaped into the saddle and the
stallion reared neighing beneath him. He glared up the slopes, hesitated,
and then turned down the trail in the direction he had been going when
halted by Khemsa's trickery. But now he did not ride at a measured gait.
He shook loose the reins and the stallion went like a thunderbolt, as if
frantic to lose hysteria in violent physical exertion. Across the ledge and
around the crag and down the narrow trail threading the great steep they
plunged at breakneck speed. The path followed a fold of rock, winding
interminably down from tier to tier of striated escarpment, and once, far
below, Conan got a glimpse of the ruin that had fallen—a mighty pile
of broken stone and boulders at the foot of a gigantic cliff.

The valley floor was still far below him when he reached a long and
lofty ridge that led out from the slope like a natural causeway. Out
upon this he rode, with an almost sheer drop on either hand. He could
trace ahead of him the trail and made a great horseshoe back into the
river-bed at his left hand. He cursed the necessity of traversing those
miles, but it was the only way. To try to descend to the lower lap of
the trail here would be to attempt the impossible. Only a bird could get
to the river-bed with a whole neck.

So he urged on the wearying stallion, until a clink of hoofs reached
his ears, welling up from below. Pulling up short and reining to the lip
of the cliff, he stared down into the dry river-bed that wound along the
foot of the ridge. Along that gorge rode a motley throng—bearded
men on half-wild horses, five hundred strong, bristling with weapons.
And Conan shouted suddenly, leaning over the edge of the cliff, three
hundred feet above them.

At his shout they reined back, and five hundred bearded faces were tilted up towards him; a deep, clamorous roar filled the canyon. Conan did not waste words.

"I was riding for Ghor!" he roared. "I had not hoped to meet you dogs on the trail. Follow me as fast as your nags can push! I'm going to Yimsha, and—"

"Traitor!" The howl was like a dash of ice-water in his face.

"What?" He glared down at them, jolted speechless. He saw wild eyes blazing up at him, faces contorted with fury, fists brandishing blades.

"Traitor!" they roared back, wholeheartedly. "Where are the seven chiefs held captive in Peshkhauri?"

"Why, in the governor's prison, I suppose," he answered.

A bloodthirsty yell from a hundred throats answered him, with such a waving of weapons and a clamor that he could not understand what they were saying. He beat down the din with a bull-like roar, and bellowed: "What devil's play is this? Let one of you speak, so I can understand what you mean!"

A gaunt old chief elected himself to this position, shook his tulwar at Conan as a preamble, and shouted accusingly: "You would not let us go raiding Peshkhauri to rescue our brothers!"

"No, you fools!" roared the exasperated Cimmerian. "Even if you'd breached the wall, which is unlikely, they'd have hanged the prisoners before you could reach them."

"And you went alone to traffic with the governor!" yelled the Afghuli, working himself into a frothing frenzy.

"Well?"

"Where are the seven chiefs?" howled the old chief, making his tulwar into a glimmering wheel of steel about his head. "Where are they? Dead!"

"What!" Conan nearly fell off his horse in his surprise.

"Aye, dead!" five hundred bloodthirsty voices assured him.

The old chief brandished his arms and got the floor again. "They were not hanged!" he screeched. "A Wazuli in another cell saw them die! The governor sent a wizard to slay them by craft!"

"That must be a lie," said Conan. "The governor would not dare. Last night I talked with him—"

The admission was unfortunate. A yell of hate and accusation split the skies.

"Aye! You went to him alone! To betray us! It is no lie. The Wazuli escaped through the doors the wizard burst in his entry, and told the tale to our scouts whom he met in Zhaibar. They had been sent forth to search for you, when you did not return. When they heard the Wazuli's tale, they returned with all haste to Ghor, and we saddled our steeds and girt our swords!"

"And what do you fools mean to do?" demanded the Cimmerian.

"To avenge our brothers!" they howled. "Death to the Kshatriyas! Slay him, brothers, he is a traitor!"

Arrows began to rattle around him. Conan rose in his stirrups, striving to make himself heard above the tumult, and then, with a roar of mingled rage, defiance and disgust, he wheeled and galloped back up the trail. Behind him and below him the Afghulis came pelting, mouthing their rage, too furious even to remember that the only way they could reach the height whereon he rode was to traverse the riverbed in the other direction, make the broad bend and follow the twisting trail up over the ridge. When they did remember this, and turned back, their repudiated chief had almost reached the point where the ridge joined the escarpment.

At the cliff he did not take the trail by which he had descended, but turned off on another, a mere trace along a rock-fault, where the stallion scrambled for footing. He had not ridden far when the stallion snorted and shied back from something lying in the trail. Conan stared down on the travesty of a man, a broken, shredded, bloody heap that gibbered and gnashed splintered teeth.

Impelled by some obscure reason, Conan dismounted and stood looking down at the ghastly shape, knowing that he was witness of a thing miraculous and opposed to nature. The Rakhsha lifted his gory head, and his strange eyes, glazed with agony and approaching death, rested on Conan with recognition.

"Where are they?" It was a racking croak not even remotely resembling a human voice.

"Gone back to their damnable castle on Yimsha," grunted Conan. "They took the Devi with them."

"I will go!" muttered the man. "I will follow them! They killed Gitara; I will kill them—the acolytes, the Four of the Black Circle, the Master himself! Kill—kill them all!" He strove to drag his mutilated frame along the rock, but not even his indomitable will could animate that gory mass longer, where the splintered bones hung together only by torn tissue and ruptured fibre.

"Follow them!" raved Khemsa, drooling a bloody slaver. "Follow!"

"I'm going to," growled Conan. "I went to fetch my Afghulis, but they've turned on me. I'm going on to Yimsha alone. I'll have the Devi back if I have to tear down that damned mountain with my bare hands. I didn't think the governor would dare kill my headmen, when I had the Devi, but it seems he did. I'll have his head for that. She's no use to me now as a hostage, but—"

"The curse of Yizil on them!" gasped Khemsa. "Go! I am dying. Wait—take my girdle."

He tried to fumble with a mangled hand at his tatters, and Conan, understanding what he sought to convey, bent and drew from about his gory waist a girdle of curious aspect.

"Follow the golden vein through the abyss," muttered Khemsa. "Wear the girdle. I had it from a Stygian priest. It will aid you, though it failed me at last. Break the crystal globe with the four golden pomegranates. Beware of the Master's transmutations—I am going to Gitara—she is waiting for me in hell—*aie, ya Skelos yar!*" And so he died.

Conan stared down at the girdle. The hair of which it was woven was not horsehair. He was convinced that it was woven of the thick black tresses of a woman. Set in the thick mesh were tiny jewels such as he had never seen before. The buckle was strangely made, in the form of a golden serpent-head, flat, wedge-shaped and scaled with curious art. A strong shudder shook Conan as he handled it, and he turned as though to cast it over the precipice; then he hesitated, and finally buckled it about his waist, under the Bakhariot girdle. Then he mounted and pushed on.

The sun had sunk behind the crags. He climbed the trail in the vast shadow of the cliffs that was thrown out like a dark blue mantle over valleys and ridges far below. He was not far from the crest when, edging around the shoulder of a jutting crag, he heard the clink of shod hoofs ahead of him. He did not turn back. Indeed, so narrow was the path that the stallion could not have wheeled his great body upon it. He rounded the jut of the rock and came upon a portion of the path that broadened somewhat. A chorus of threatening yells broke on his ear, but his stallion pinned a terrified horse hard against the rock, and Conan caught the arm of the rider in an iron grip, checking the lifted sword in midair.

"Kerim Shah!" muttered Conan, red glints smoldering luridly in his eyes. The Turanian did not struggle; they sat their horses almost breast to breast, Conan's fingers locking the other's sword-arm. Behind Kerim Shah filed a group of lean Irakzai on gaunt horses. They glared like wolves, fingering bows and knives, but rendered uncertain because of the narrowness of the path and the perilous proximity of the abyss that yawned beneath them.

"Where is the Devi?" demanded Kerim Shah.

"What's it to you, you Hyrkanian spy?" snarled Conan.

"I know you have her," answered Kerim Shah. "I was on my way northward with some tribesmen when we were ambushed by enemies in Shalizah Pass. Many of my men were slain, and the rest of us harried through the hills like jackals. When we had beaten off our pursuers, we turned westward, toward Amir Jehun Pass, and this morning we came upon a Wazuli wandering through the hills. He was quite mad, but I learned much from his incoherent gibberings before he died. I learned that he was the sole survivor of a band which followed a chief of the Afghulis and a captive Kshatriya woman into a gorge behind Khurum village. He babbled much of a man in a green turban whom the Afghuli rode down, but who, when attacked by the Wazulis who pursued, smote them with a nameless doom that wiped them out as a gust of wind-driven fire wipes out a cluster of locusts.

"How that one man escaped, I do not know, nor did he; but I knew from his maunderings that Conan of Ghor had been in Khurum with his royal captive. And as we made our way through the hills, we over-took a naked Galzai girl bearing a gourd of water, who told us a tale of having been stripped and ravished by a giant foreigner in the garb of an Afghuli chief, who, she said, gave her garments to a Vendhyan woman who accompanied him. She said you rode westward."

Kerim Shah did not consider it necessary to explain that he had been on his way to keep his rendezvous with the expected troops from Secunderam when he found his way barred by hostile tribesmen. The road to Gurashah valley through Shalizah Pass was longer than the road that wound through Amir Jehun Pass, but the latter traversed part of the Afghuli country, which Kerim Shah had been anxious to avoid until he came with an army. Barred from the Shalizah road, however, he had turned to the forbidden route, until news that Conan had not yet reached Afghulistan with his captive had caused him to turn south-ward and push on recklessly in the hope of overtaking the Cimmerian in the hills.

"So you had better tell me where the Devi is," suggested Kerim Shah. "We outnumber you—"

"Let one of your dogs nock a shaft and I'll throw you over the cliff," Conan promised. "It wouldn't do you any good to kill me, anyhow. Five hundred Afghulis are on my trail, and if they find you've cheated them, they'll flay you alive. Anyway, I haven't got the Devi. She's in the hands of the Black Seers of Yimsha."

"Tarim!" swore Kerim Shah softly, shaken out of his poise for the first time. "Khemsa—"

"Khemsa's dead," grunted Conan. "His masters sent him to hell on a landslide. And now get out of my way. I'd be glad to kill you if I had the time, but I'm on my way to Yimsha."

"I'll go with you," said the Turanian abruptly.

Conan laughed at him. "Do you think I'd trust you, you Hyrkanian dog?"

"I don't ask you to," returned Kerim Shah. "We both want the Devi. You know my reason; King Yezdigerd desires to add her kingdom to his empire, and herself in his seraglio. And I knew you, in the days when you were a hetman of the kozak steppes; so I know your ambition is wholesale plunder. You want to loot Vendhya, and to twist out a huge ransom for Yasmina. Well, let us for the time being, without any illusion about each other, unite our forces, and try to rescue the Devi from the Seers. If we succeed, and live, we can fight it out to see who keeps her."

Conan narrowly scrutinized the other for a moment, and then nodded, releasing the Turanian's arm. "Agreed; what about your men?"

Kerim Shah turned to the silent Irakzai and spoke briefly: "This chief and I are going to Yimsha to fight the wizards. Will you go with us, or stay here to be flayed by the Afghulis who are following this man?"

They looked at him with eyes grimly fatalistic. They were doomed and they knew it—had known it ever since the singing arrows of the ambushed Dagozai had driven them back from the pass of Shalizah. The men of the lower Zhaibar had too many reeking bloodfeuds among the crag-dwellers. They were too small a band to fight their way back through the hills to the villages of the border, without the guidance of the crafty Turanian. They counted themselves as dead already, so they made the reply that only dead men would make: "We will go with thee and die on Yimsha."

"Then in Crom's name let us be gone," grunted Conan, fidgeting with impatience as he started into the blue gulfs of the deepening twilight. "My wolves were hours behind me, but we've lost a devilish lot of time."

Kerim Shah backed his steed from between the black stallion and the cliff, sheathed his sword and cautiously turned the horse. Presently the band was filing up the path as swiftly as they dared. They came out upon the crest nearly a mile east of the spot where Khemsa had halted the Cimmerian and the Devi. The path they had traversed was a perilous one, even for hill-men, and for that reason Conan had avoided it that day when carrying Yasmina, though Kerim Shah, following him, had taken it supposing the Cimmerian had done likewise. Even Conan sighed with relief when the horses scrambled up over the last rim. They moved like phantom riders through an enchanted realm of shadows. The soft creak of leather, the clink of steel marked their passing, then again the dark mountain slopes lay naked and silent in the starlight.

8 Yasmina Knows Stark Terror

Yasmina had time but for one scream when she felt herself enveloped in that crimson whirl and torn from her protector with appalling force. She screamed once, and then she had no breath to scream. She was blinded, deafened, rendered mute and eventually senseless by the terrific rushing of the air about her. There was a dazed consciousness of dizzy height and numbing speed, a confused impression of natural sensations gone mad, and then vertigo and oblivion.

A vestige of these sensations clung to her as she recovered consciousness; so she cried out and clutched wildly as though to stay a headlong and involuntary flight. Her fingers closed on soft fabric, and a relieving sense of stability pervaded her. She took cognizance of her surroundings.

She was lying on a dais covered with black velvet. This dais stood in a great, dim room whose walls were hung with dusky tapestries across which crawled dragons reproduced with repellent realism. Floating shadows merely hinted at the lofty ceiling, and gloom that lent itself to illusion lurked in the corners. There seemed to be neither windows nor doors in the walls, or else they were concealed by the nighted tapestries. Where the dim light came from, Yasmina could not determine. The great room was a realm of mysteries, or shadows, and shadowy shapes in which she could not have sworn to observe movement, yet which invaded her mind with a dim and formless terror.

But her gaze fixed itself on a tangible object. On another, smaller dais of jet, a few feet away, a man sat cross-legged, gazing contemplatively at her. His long black velvet robe, embroidered with gold thread, fell loosely about him, masking his figure. His hands were folded in his sleeves. There was a velvet cap upon his head. His face was calm, placid, not unhandsome, his eyes lambent and slightly oblique. He did not move a muscle as he sat regarding her, nor did his expression alter when he saw she was conscious.

Yasmina felt fear crawl like a trickle of ice-water down her supple spine. She lifted herself on her elbows and stared apprehensively at the stranger.

"Who are you?" she demanded. Her voice sounded brittle and inadequate.

"I am the Master of Yimsha." The tone was rich and resonant, like the mellow tones of a temple bell.

"Why did you bring me here?" she demanded.

"Were you not seeking me?"

"If you are one of the Black Seers—yes!" she answered recklessly, believing that he could read her thoughts anyway.

He laughed softly, and chills crawled up and down her spine again.

"You would turn the wild children of the hills against the Seers of Yimsha!" He smiled. "I have read it in your mind, princess. Your weak, human mind, filled with petty dreams of hate and revenge."

"You slew my brother!" A rising tide of anger was vying with her fear; her hands were clenched, her lithe body rigid. "Why did you persecute him? He never harmed you. The priests say the Seers are above meddling in human affairs. Why did you destroy the king of Vendhya?"

"How can an ordinary human understand the motives of a Seer?" returned the Master calmly. "My acolytes in the temples of Turan, who are the priests behind the priests of Tarim, urged me to bestir myself in behalf of Yezdigerd. For reasons of my own, I complied. How can I explain my mystic reasons to your puny intellect? You could not understand."

"I understand this: that my brother died!" Tears of grief and rage shook in her voice. She rose upon her knees and stared at him with wide blazing eyes, as supple and dangerous in that moment as a she-panther.

"As Yezdigerd desired," agreed the Master calmly. "For a while it was my whim to further his ambitions."

"Is Yezdigerd your vassal?" Yasmina tried to keep the timbre of her voice unaltered. She had felt her knee pressing something hard and symmetrical under a fold of velvet. Subtly she shifted her position, moving her hand under the fold.

"Is the dog that licks up the offal in the temple yard the vassal of the god?" returned the Master.

He did not seem to notice the actions she sought to dissemble. Concealed by the velvet, her fingers closed on what she knew was the golden hilt of a dagger. She bent her head to hide the light of triumph in her eyes.

"I am weary of Yezdigerd," said the Master. "I have turned to other amusements—ha!"

With a fierce cry Yasmina sprang like a jungle cat, stabbing murderously. Then she stumbled and slid to the floor, where she cowered, staring up at the man on the dais. He had not moved; his cryptic smile was unchanged. Tremblingly she lifted her hand and stared at it with dilated eyes. There was no dagger in her fingers; they grasped a stalk of golden lotus, the crushed blossoms drooping on the bruised stem.

She dropped it as if it had been a viper, and scrambled away from the proximity of her tormenter. She returned to her own dais, because that was at least more dignified for a queen than groveling on the floor at the feet of a sorcerer, and eyed him apprehensively, expecting reprisals.

But the Master made no move.

"All substance is one to him who holds the key of the cosmos," he said cryptically. "To an adept nothing is immutable. At will, steel blossoms bloom in unnamed gardens, or flower-swords flash in the moonlight."

"You are a devil," she sobbed.

"Not I!" he laughed. "I was born on this planet, long ago. Once I was a common man, nor have I lost all human attributes in the numberless eons of my adeptship. A human steeped in the dark arts is greater than a devil. I am of human origin, but I rule demons. You have seen the Lords of the Black Circle—it would blast your soul to hear from what far realm I summoned them and from what doom I guard them with ensorcelled crystal and golden serpents.

"But only I can rule them. My foolish Khemsa thought to make himself great—poor fool, bursting material doors and hurtling himself and his mistress through the air from hill to hill! Yet if he had not been destroyed his power might have grown to rival mine."

He laughed again. "And you, poor, silly thing! Plotting to send a hairy hill chief to storm Yimsha! It was such a jest that I myself could have designed, had it occurred to me, that you should fall in his hands. And I read in your childish mind an intention to seduce by your feminine wiles to attempt your purpose, anyway.

"But for all your stupidity, you are a woman fair to look upon. It is my whim to keep you for my slave."

The daughter of a thousand proud emperors gasped with shame and fury at the word.

"You dare not!"

His mocking laughter cut her like a whip across her naked shoulders.

"The king dares not trample a worm in the road? Little fool, do you not realize that your royal pride is no more than a straw blown on the wind? I, who have known the kisses of the queens of Hell! You have seen how I deal with a rebel!"

Cowed and awed, the girl crouched on the velvet-covered dais. The light grew dimmer and more phantom-like. The features of the Master became shadowy. His voice took on a newer tone of command.

"I will never yield to you!" Her voice trembled with fear but it carried a ring of resolution.

"You will yield," he answered with horrible conviction. "Fear and pain shall teach you. I will lash you with horror and agony to the last quivering ounce of your endurance, until you become as melted wax to be bent and molded in my hands as I desire. You shall know such discipline as no mortal woman ever knew, until my slightest command is to you as the unalterable will of the gods. And first, to humble your pride, you shall travel back through the lost ages, and view all the shapes that have been you. *Aie, yil la khosa!*"

At these words the shadowy room swam before Yasmina's affrighted gaze. The roots of her hair prickled her scalp, and her tongue clove to her palate. Somewhere a gong sounded a deep, ominous note. The dragons on the tapestries glowed like blue fire, and then faded out. The Master on his dais was but a shapeless shadow. The dim light gave way to soft, thick darkness, almost tangible, that pulsed with strange radiations. She could no longer see the Master. She could see nothing. She had a strange sensation that the walls and ceiling had withdrawn immensely from her.

Then somewhere in the darkness a glow began, like a firefly that rhythmically dimmed and quickened. It grew to a golden ball, and as it expanded its light grew more intense, flaming whitely. It burst suddenly, showering the darkness with white sparks that did not illumine the shadows. But like an impression left in the gloom, a faint luminance remained, and revealed a slender dusky shaft shooting up from the shadowy floor. Under the girl's dilated gaze it spread, took shape; stems and broad leaves appeared, and great black poisonous blossoms that towered above her as she cringed against the velvet. A subtle perfume pervaded the atmosphere. It was the dread figure of the black lotus that had grown up as she watched, as it grows in the haunted, forbidden jungles of Khitai. The broad leaves were murmurous with evil life. The blossoms bent toward her like sentient things, nodding serpent-like on pliant stems. Etched against soft, impenetrable darkness it loomed over her, gigantic, blackly visible in some mad way. Her brain reeled with the drugging scent and she sought to crawl from the dais. Then she clung to it as it seemed to be pitching at an impossible slant. She cried out with terror and clung to the velvet, but she felt her fingers ruthlessly torn away. There was a sensation as of all sanity and stability crumbling and vanishing. She was a quivering atom of sentiency driven through a black, roaring, icy void by a thundering wind that threatened to extinguish her feeble flicker of animate life like a candle blown out in a storm.

Then there came a period of blind impulse and movement, when the atom that was she mingled and merged with myriad other atoms of spawning life in the yeasty morass of existence, molded by formative forces until she emerged again a conscious individual, whirling down an endless spiral of lives.

In a mist of terror she relived all her former existences, recognized and was again all the bodies that had carried her ego throughout the changing ages. She bruised her feet again over the long, weary road of life that stretched out behind her into the immemorial past. Back beyond the dimmest dawns of Time she crouched shuddering in primordial jungles, hunted by slavering beasts of prey. Skin-clad, she waded thigh-deep in rice swamps, battling with squawking water-fowl for the precious grains. She labored with the oxen to drag the pointed stick through the stubborn soil, and she crouched endlessly over looms in peasant huts.

She saw walled cities burst into flame, and fled screaming before the slayers. She reeled naked and bleeding over burning sands, dragged at the slaver's stirrup, and she knew the grip of hot, fierce hands on her writhing flesh, the shame and agony of brutal lust. She screamed under the bite of the lash, and moaned on the rack; mad with terror she fought against the hands that forced her head inexorably down on the bloody block.

She knew the agonies of childbirth, and the bitterness of love betrayed. She suffered all the woes and wrongs and brutalities that man has inflicted on woman throughout the eons; and she endured all the spite and malice of women for woman. And like the flick of a fiery whip throughout was the consciousness she retained of her Devi-ship. She was all the women she had ever been, yet in her knowing she was Yasmina. This consciousness was not lost in the throes of reincarnation. At one and the same time she was a naked slave-wench groveling under the whip, and the proud Devi of Vendhya. And she suffered not only as the slave-girl suffered, but as Yasmina, to whose pride the whip was like a white-hot brand.

Life merged into life in flying chaos, each with its burden of woe and shame and agony, until she dimly heard her own voice screaming unbearably, like one long-drawn cry of suffering echoing down the ages.

Then she awakened on the velvet-covered dais in the mystic room.

In a ghostly gray light she saw again the dais and the cryptic robed figure seated upon it. The hooded head was bent, the high shoulders faintly etched against the uncertain dimness. She could make out no details clearly, but the hood, where the velvet cap had been, stirred a formless uneasiness in her. As she stared, there stole over her a nameless fear that froze her tongue to her palate—a feeling that it was not the Master who sat so silently on that black dais.

Then the figure moved and rose upright, towering above her. It stooped over her and the long arms in their wide black sleeves bent about her. She fought against them in speechless fright, surprized by their lean hardness. The hooded head bent down toward her averted face. And she screamed, and screamed again in poignant fear and loathing. Bony arms gripped her lithe body, and from that hood looked forth a countenance of death and decay—features like rotting parchment on a moldering skull.

She screamed again, and then, as those champing, grinning jaws bent toward her lips, she lost consciousness. ...

9 The Castle of the Wizards

The sun had risen over the white Himelian peaks. At the foot of a long slope a group of horsemen halted and stared upward. High above them a stone tower poised on the pitch of the mountainside. Beyond and above that gleamed the walls of a greater keep, near the line where the snow began that capped Yimsha's pinnacle. There was a touch of unreality about the whole—purple slopes pitching up to that fantastic castle, toy-like with distance, and above it the white glistening peak shouldering the cold blue.

"We'll leave the horses here," grunted Conan. "That treacherous slope is safer for a man on foot. Besides, they're done." He swung down from the black stallion which stood with wide-braced legs and drooping head. They had pushed hard throughout the night, gnawing at scraps from saddle-bags, and pausing only to give the horses the rests they had to have.

"That first tower is held by the acolytes of the Black Seers," said Conan. "Or so men say; watch-dogs for their masters—lesser sorcerers. They won't sit sucking their thumbs as we climb this slope."

Kerim Shah glanced up the mountain, then back the way they had come; they were already far up Yimsha's side, and a vast expanse of lesser peaks and crags spread out beneath them. Among these labyrinths the Turanian sought in vain for a movement of color that would betray men. Evidently the pursuing Afghulis had lost their chiefs trail in the night.

"Let us go, then." They tied the weary horses in a clump of tamarisk and without further comment turned up the slope. There was no cover. It was a naked incline, strewn with boulders not big enough to conceal a man. But they did conceal something else.

The party had not gone fifty steps when a snarling shape burst from behind a rock. It was one of the gaunt savage dogs that infested the hill villages, and its eyes glared redly, its jaws dripped foam. Conan was leading, but it did not attack him. It dashed past him and leaped at Kerim Shah. The Turanian leaped aside, and the great dog flung itself upon the Irakzai behind him. The man yelled and threw up his arm, which was torn by the brute's fangs as it bore him backward, and the next instant half a dozen tulwars were hacking at the beast. Yet not until it was literally dismembered did the hideous creature cease its efforts to seize and rend its attackers.

Kerim Shah bound up the wounded warrior's gashed arm, looked at him narrowly, and then turned away without a word. He rejoined Conan, and they renewed the climb in silence.

Presently Kerim Shah said: "Strange to find a village dog in this place."

"There's no offal here," grunted Conan.

Both turned their heads to glance back at the wounded warrior toiling after them among his companions. Sweat glistened on his dark face and his lips were drawn back from his teeth in a grimace of pain. Then both looked again at the stone tower squatting above them.

A slumberous quiet lay over the uplands. The tower showed no sign of life, nor did the strange pyramidal structure beyond it. But the men who toiled upward went with the tenseness of men walking on the edge of a crater. Kerim Shah had unslung the powerful Turanian bow that killed at five hundred paces, and the Irakzai looked to their own lighter and less lethal bows.

But they were not within bow-shot of the tower when something shot down out of the sky without warning. It passed so close to Conan that he felt the wind of rushing wings, but it was an Irakzai who staggered and fell, blood jetting from a severed jugular. A hawk with wings like burnished steel shot up again, blood dripping from the scimitar-beak, to reel against the sky as Kerim Shah's bowstring twanged. It dropped like a plummet, but no man saw where it struck the earth.

Conan bent over the victim of the attack, but the man was already dead. No one spoke; useless to comment on the fact that never before had a hawk been known to swoop on a man. Red rage began to vie with fatalistic lethargy in the wild souls of the Irakzai. Hairy fingers nocked arrows and men glared vengefully at the tower whose very silence mocked them.

But the next attack came swiftly. They all saw it—a white puffball of smoke that tumbled over the tower-rim and came drifting and rolling down the slope toward them. Others followed it. They seemed harmless, mere woolly globes of cloudy foam, but Conan stepped aside to avoid contact with the first. Behind him one of the Irakzai reached out and thrust his sword into the unstable mass. Instantly a sharp report shook the mountainside. There was a burst of blinding flame, and then the puffball had vanished, and the too-curious warrior remained only a heap of charred and blackened bones. The crisped hand still gripped the ivory sword-hilt, but the blade was gone—melted and destroyed by that awful heat. Yet men standing almost within reach of the victim had not suffered except to be dazzled and half blinded by the sudden flare.

"Steel touches it off," grunted Conan. "Look out—here they come!"

The slope above them was almost covered by the billowing spheres. Kerim Shah bent his bow and sent a shaft into the mass, and those touched by the arrow burst like bubbles in spurting flame. His men followed his example and for the next few minutes it was as if a thunderstorm raged on the mountain slope, with bolts of lightning striking and bursting in showers of flame. When the barrage ceased, only a few arrows were left in the quivers of the archers.

They pushed on grimly, over soil charred and blackened, where the naked rock had in places been turned to lava by the explosion of those diabolical bombs.

Now they were almost within arrow-flight of the silent tower, and they spread their line, nerves taut, ready for any horror that might descend upon them.

On the tower appeared a single figure, lifting a ten-foot bronze horn. Its strident bellow roared out across the echoing slopes, like the blare of trumpets on Judgment Day. And it began to be fearfully answered. The ground trembled under the feet of the invaders, and rumblings and grindings welled up from the subterranean depths.

The Irakzai screamed, reeling like drunken men on the shuddering slope, and Conan, eyes glaring, charged recklessly up the incline, knife in hand, straight at the door that showed in the tower-wall. Above him the great horn roared and bellowed in brutish mockery. And then Kerim Shah drew a shaft to his ear and loosed.

Only a Turanian could have made that shot. The bellowing of the horn ceased suddenly, and a high, thin scream shrilled in its place. The green-robed figure on the tower staggered, clutching at the long shaft which quivered in its bosom, and then pitched across the parapet. The great horn tumbled upon the battlement and hung precariously, and another robed figure rushed to seize it, shrieking in horror. Again the Turanian bow twanged, and again it was answered by a death-howl. The second acolyte, in falling, struck the horn with his elbow and knocked it clattering over the parapet to shatter on the rocks far below.

At such headlong speed had Conan covered the ground that before the clattering echoes of that fall had died away, he was hacking at the door. Warned by his savage instinct, he gave back suddenly as a tide of molten lead splashed down from above. But the next instant he was back again, attacking the panels with redoubled fury. He was galvanized by the fact that his enemies had resorted to earthly weapons. The sorcery of the acolytes was limited. Their necromantic resources might well be exhausted.

Kerim Shah was hurrying up the slope, his hill-men behind him in a straggling crescent. They loosed as they ran, their arrows splintering against the walls or arching over the parapet.

The heavy teak portal gave way beneath the Cimmerian's assault, and he peered inside warily, expecting anything. He was looking into a circular chamber from which a stair wound upward. On the opposite side of the chamber a door gaped open, revealing the outer slope—and the backs of half a dozen green-robed figures in full retreat.

Conan yelled, took a step into the tower, and then native caution jerked him back, just as a great block of stone fell crashing to the floor where his foot had been an instant before. Shouting to his followers, he raced around the tower.

The acolytes had evacuated their first line of defence. As Conan rounded the tower he saw their green robes twinkling up the mountain ahead of him. He gave chase, panting with earnest blood-lust, and behind him Kerim Shah and the Irakzai came pelting, the latter yelling like wolves at the flight of their enemies, their fatalism momentarily submerged by temporary triumph.

The tower stood on the lower edge of a narrow plateau whose upward slant was barely perceptible. A few hundred yards away this plateau ended abruptly in a chasm which had been invisible farther down the mountain. Into this chasm the acolytes apparently leaped without checking their speed. Their pursuers saw the green robes flutter and disappear over the edge.

A few moments later they themselves were standing on the brink of the mighty moat that cut them off from the castle of the Black Seers. It was a sheer-walled ravine that extended in either direction as far as they could see, apparently girdling the mountain, some four hundred yards in width and five hundred feet deep. And in it, from rim to rim, a strange, translucent mist sparkled and shimmered.

Looking down, Conan grunted. Far below him, moving across the glimmering floor, which shone like burnished silver, he saw the forms of the green-robed acolytes. Their outline was wavering and indistinct, like figures seen under deep water. They walked in single file, moving toward the opposite wall.

Kerim Shah nocked an arrow and sent it singing downward. But when it struck the mist that filled the chasm it seemed to lose momentum and direction, wandering widely from its course.

"If they went down, so can we!" grunted Conan, while Kerim Shah stared after his shaft in amazement. "I saw them last at this spot—"

Squinting down he saw something shining like a golden thread across the canyon floor far below. The acolytes seemed to be following this thread, and there suddenly came to him Khemsa's cryptic words—"Follow the golden vein!" On the brink, under his very hand as he crouched, he found it, a thin vein of sparkling gold running from an outcropping of ore to the edge and down across the silvery floor. And he found something else, which had before been invisible to him because of the peculiar refraction of the light. The gold vein followed a narrow ramp which slanted down into the ravine, fitted with niches for hand and foot hold.

"Here's where they went down," he grunted to Kerim Shah. "They're no adepts, to waft themselves through the air! We'll follow them—"

It was at that instant that the man who had been bitten by the mad dog cried out horribly and leaped at Kerim Shah, foaming and gnashing his teeth. The Turanian, quick as a cat on his feet, sprang aside and the madman pitched head-first over the brink. The others rushed to the edge and glared after him in amazement. The maniac did not fall plummet-like. He floated slowly down through the rosy haze like a man sinking in deep water. His limbs moved like a man trying to swim, and his features were purple and convulsed beyond the contortions of his madness. Far down at last on the shining floor his body settled and lay still.

"There's death in that chasm," muttered Kerim Shah, drawing back from the rosy mist that shimmered almost at his feet. "What now, Conan?"

"On!" answered the Cimmerian grimly. "Those acolytes are human; if the mist doesn't kill them, it won't kill me."

He hitched his belt, and his hands touched the girdle Khemsa had given him; he scowled, then smiled bleakly. He had forgotten that girdle; yet thrice had death passed him by to strike another victim.

The acolytes had reached the farther wall and were moving up it like great green flies. Letting himself upon the ramp, he descended warily. The rosy cloud lapped about his ankles, ascending as he lowered himself. It reached his knees, his thighs, his waist, his arm-pits. He felt as one feels a thick heavy fog on a damp night. With it lapping about his chin he hesitated, and then ducked under. Instantly his breath ceased; all air was shut off from him and he felt his ribs caving in on his vitals. With a frantic effort he heaved himself up, fighting for life. His head rose above the surface and he drank air in great gulps.

Kerim Shah leaned down toward him, spoke to him, but Conan neither heard nor heeded. Stubbornly, his mind fixed on what the dying Khemsa had told him, the Cimmerian groped for the gold vein, and found that he had moved off it in his descent. Several series of hand-holds were niched in the ramp. Placing himself directly over the thread, he began climbing down once more. The rosy mist rose about him, engulfed him. Now his head was under, but he was still drinking pure air. Above him he saw his companions staring down at him, their features blurred by the haze that shimmered over his head. He gestured for them to follow, and went down swiftly, without waiting to see whether they complied or not.

Kerim Shah sheathed his sword without comment and followed, and the Irakzai, more fearful of being left alone than of the terrors that might lurk below, scrambled after him. Each man clung to the golden thread as they saw the Cimmerian do.

Down the slanting ramp they went to the ravine floor and moved out across the shining level, treading the gold vein like rope-walkers. It was as if they walked along an invisible tunnel through which air circulated freely. They felt death pressing in on them above and on either hand, but it did not touch them.

The vein crawled up a similar ramp on the other wall up which the acolytes had disappeared, and up it they went with taut nerves, not knowing what might be waiting for them among the jutting spurs of rock that fanged the lip of the precipice.

It was the green-robed acolytes who awaited them, with knives in their hands. Perhaps they had reached the limits to which they could retreat. Perhaps the Stygian girdle about Conan's waist could have told why their necromantic spells had proven so weak and so quickly exhausted. Perhaps it was knowledge of death decreed for failure that sent them leaping from among the rocks, eyes glaring and knives glittering, resorting in their desperation to material weapons.

There among the rocky fangs on the precipice lip was no war of wizard craft. It was a whirl of blades, where real steel bit and real blood spurted, where sinewy arms dealt forthright blows that severed quivering flesh, and men went down to be trodden under foot as the fight raged over them.

One of the Irakzai bled to death among the rocks, but the acolytes were down—slashed and hacked asunder or hurled over the edge to float sluggishly down to the silver floor that shone so far below.

Then the conquerors shook blood and sweat from their eyes, and looked at one another. Conan and Kerim Shah still stood upright, and four of the Irakzai.

They stood among the rocky teeth that serrated the precipice brink, and from that spot a path wound up a gentle slope to a broad stair, consisting of half a dozen steps, a hundred feet across, cut out of a green jade-like substance. They led up to a broad stage or roofless gallery of the same polished stone, and above it rose, tier upon tier, the castle of the Black Seers. It seemed to have been carved out of the sheer stone of the mountain. The architecture was faultless, but unadorned. The many casements were barred and masked with curtains within. There was no sign of life, friendly or hostile.

They went up the path in silence, and warily as men treading the lair of a serpent. The Irakzai were dumb, like men marching to a certain doom. Even Kerim Shah was silent. Only Conan seemed unaware what a monstrous dislocating and uprooting of accepted thought and action their invasion constituted, what an unprecedented violation of tradition. He was not of the East; and he came of a breed who fought devils and wizards as promptly and matter-of-factly as they battled human foes.

He strode up the shining stairs and across the wide green gallery straight toward the great golden-bound teak door that opened upon it. He cast but a single glance upward at the higher tiers of the great pyramidal structure towering above him. He reached a hand for the bronze prong that jutted like a handle from the door—then checked himself, grinning hardly. The handle was made in the shape of a serpent, head lifted on arched neck; and Conan had a suspicion that that metal head would come to grisly life under his hand.

He struck it from the door with one blow, and its bronze clink on the glassy floor did not lessen his caution. He flipped it aside with his knife-point, and again turned to the door. Utter silence reigned over the towers. Far below them the mountain slopes fell away into a purple haze of distance. The sun glittered on snow-clad peaks on either hand. High above, a vulture hung like a black dot in the cold blue of the sky. But for it, the men before the gold-bound door were the only evidence of life, tiny figures on a green jade gallery poised on the dizzy height, with that fantastic pile of stone towering above them.

A sharp wind off the snow slashed them, whipping their tatters about. Conan's long knife splintering through the teak panels roused the startled echoes. Again and again he struck, hewing through polished wood and metal bands alike. Through the sundered ruins he glared into the interior, alert and suspicious as a wolf. He saw a broad chamber, the polished stone walls untapestried, the mosaic floor uncarpeted. Square, polished ebon stools and a stone dais formed the only furnishings. The room was empty of human life. Another door showed in the opposite wall.

"Leave a man on guard outside," grunted Conan. "I'm going in."

Kerim Shah designated a warrior for that duty, and the man fell back toward the middle of the gallery, bow in hand. Conan strode into the castle, followed by the Turanian and the three remaining Irakzai. The one outside spat, grumbled in his beard, and started suddenly as a low mocking laugh reached his ears.

He lifted his head and saw, on the tier above him, a tall, black-robed figure, naked head nodding slightly as he stared down. His whole attitude suggested mockery and malignity. Quick as a flash the Irakzai bent his bow and loosed, and the arrow streaked upward to strike full in the black-robed breast. The mocking smile did not alter. The Seer plucked out the missile and threw it back at the bowman, not as a weapon is hurled, but with a contemptuous gesture. The Irakzai dodged, instinctively throwing up his arm. His fingers closed on the revolving shaft.

Then he shrieked. In his hand the wooden shaft suddenly *writhed.* Its rigid outline became pliant, melting in his grasp. He tried to throw it from him, but it was too late. He held a living serpent in his naked hand, and already it had coiled about his wrist and its wicked wedge-shaped head darted at his muscular arm. He screamed again and his eyes became distended, his features purple. He went to his knees shaken by an awful convulsion, and then lay still.

The men inside had wheeled at his first cry. Conan took a swift stride toward the open doorway, and then halted short, baffled. To the men behind him it seemed that he strained against empty air. But though he could see nothing, there was a slick, smooth, hard surface under his hands, and he knew that a sheet of crystal had been let down in the doorway. Through it he saw the Irakzai lying motionless on the glassy gallery, an ordinary arrow sticking in his arm.

Conan lifted his knife and smote, and the watchers were dumbfounded to see his blow checked apparently in midair, with the loud clang of steel that meets an unyielding substance. He wasted no more effort. He knew that not even the legendary tulwar of Amir Khurum could shatter that invisible curtain.

In a few words he explained the matter to Kerim Shah, and the Turanian shrugged his shoulders. "Well, if our exit is barred, we must find another. In the meanwhile our way lies forward, does it not?"

With a grunt the Cimmerian turned and strode across the chamber to the opposite door, with a feeling of treading on the threshold of doom. As he lifted his knife to shatter the door, it swung silently open as if of its own accord. He strode into the great hall, flanked with tall glassy columns. A hundred feet from the door began the broad jade-green steps of a stair that tapered toward the top like the side of a pyramid. What lay beyond that stair he could not tell. But between him and its shimmering foot stood a curious altar of gleaming black jade. Four great golden serpents twined their tails about this altar and reared their wedge-shaped heads in the air, facing the four quarters of the compass like the enchanted guardians of a fabled treasure. But on the altar, between the arching necks, stood only a crystal globe filled with a cloudy smoke-like substance, in which floated four golden pomegranates.

The sight stirred some dim recollection in his mind; then Conan heeded the altar no longer, for on the lower steps of the stair stood four black-robed figures. He had not seen them come. They were simply there, tall, gaunt, their vulture-heads nodding in unison, their feet and hands hidden by their flowing garments.

One lifted his arm and the sleeve fell away revealing his hand—and it was not a hand at all. Conan halted in mid-stride, compelled against his will. He had encountered a force differing subtly from Khemsa's mesmerism, and he could not advance, though he felt it in his power to retreat if he wished. His companions had likewise halted, and they seemed even more helpless than he, unable to move in either direction.

The seer whose arm was lifted beckoned to one of the Irakzai, and the man moved toward him like one in a trance, eyes staring and fixed, blade hanging in limp fingers. As he pushed past Conan, the Cimmerian threw an arm across his breast to arrest him. Conan was so much stronger than the Irakzai that in ordinary circumstances he could have broken his spine between his hands. But now the muscular arm was brushed aside like straw and the Irakzai moved toward the stair, treading jerkily and mechanically. He reached the steps and knelt stiffly, proffering his blade and bending his head. The Seer took the sword. It flashed as he swung it up and down. The Irakzai's head tumbled from his shoulders and thudded heavily on the black marble floor. An arch of blood jetted from the severed arteries and the body slumped over and lay with arms spread wide.

Again a malformed hand lifted and beckoned, and another Irakzai stumbled stiffly to his doom. The ghastly drama was re-enacted and another headless form lay beside the first.

As the third tribesman clumped his way past Conan to his death, the Cimmerian, his veins bulging in his temples with his efforts to break past the unseen barrier that held him, was suddenly aware of allied forces, unseen, but waking into life about him. This realization came without warning, but so powerfully that he could not doubt his instinct. His left hand slid involuntarily under his Bakhariot belt and closed on the Stygian girdle. And as he gripped it he felt new strength flood his numbed limbs; the will to live was a pulsing white-hot fire, matched by the intensity of his burning rage.

The third Irakzai was a decapitated corpse, and the hideous finger was lifting again when Conan felt the bursting of the invisible barrier. A fierce, involuntary cry burst from his lips as he leaped with the explosive suddenness of pent-up ferocity. His left hand gripped the sorcerer's girdle as a drowning man grips a floating log, and the long knife was a sheen of light in his right. The men on the steps did not move. They watched calmly, cynically; if they felt surprise they did not show it. Conan did not allow himself to think what might chance when he came within knife-reach of them. His blood was pounding in his temples, a mist of crimson swam before his sight. He was afire with the urge to kill—to drive his knife deep into flesh and bone, and twist the blade in blood and entrails.

Another dozen strides would carry him to the steps where the sneering demons stood. He drew his breath deep, his fury rising redly as his charge gathered momentum. He was hurtling past the altar with its golden serpents when like a levin-flash there shot across his mind again as vividly as if spoken in his external ear, the cryptic words of Khemsa: "*Break the crystal ball!*"

His reaction was almost without his own volition. Execution followed impulse so spontaneously that the greatest sorcerer of the age would not have had time to read his mind and prevent his action. Wheeling like a cat from his headlong charge, he brought his knife crashing down upon the crystal. Instantly the air vibrated with a peal of terror, whether from the stairs, the altar, or the crystal itself he could not tell. Hisses filled his ears as the golden serpents, suddenly vibrant with hideous life, writhed and smote at him. But he was fired to the speed of a maddened tiger. A whirl of steel sheared through the hideous trunks that waved toward him, and he smote the crystal sphere again and yet again. And the globe burst with a noise like a thunderclap, raining fiery shards on the black marble, and the gold pomegranates, as if released from captivity, shot upward toward the lofty roof and were gone.

A mad screaming, bestial and ghastly, was echoing through the great hall. On the steps writhed four black-robed figures, twisting in convulsions, froth dripping from their livid mouths. Then with one frenzied crescendo of inhuman ululation they stiffened and lay still, and Conan knew that they were dead. He stared down at the altar and the crystal shards. Four headless golden serpents still coiled about the altar, but no alien life now animated the dully gleaming metal.

Kerim Shah was rising slowly from his knees, whither he had been dashed by some unseen force. He shook his head to clear the ringing from his ears.

"Did you hear that crash when you struck? It was as if a thousand crystal panels shattered all over the castle as that globe burst. Were the souls of the wizards imprisoned in those golden balls?—Ha!"

Conan wheeled as Kerim Shah drew his sword and pointed.

Another figure stood at the head of the stair. His robe, too, was black, but of richly embroidered velvet, and there was a velvet cap on his head. His face was calm, and not unhandsome.

"Who the devil are you?" demanded Conan, staring up at him, knife in hand.

"I am the Master of Yimsha!" His voice was like the chime of a temple bell, but a note of cruel mirth ran through it.

"Where is Yasmina?" demanded Kerim Shah.

The Master laughed down at him.

"What is that to you, dead man? Have you so quickly forgotten my strength, once lent to you, that you come armed against me, you poor fool? I think I will take your heart, Kerim Shah!"

He held out his hand as if to receive something, and the Turanian cried out sharply like a man in mortal agony. He reeled drunkenly, and then, with a splintering of bones, a rending of flesh and muscle and a snapping of mail-links, his breast burst outward with a shower of blood, and through the ghastly aperture something red and dripping shot through the air into the Master's outstretched hand, as a bit of steel leaps to the magnet. The Turanian slumped to the floor and lay motionless, and the Master laughed and hurled the object to fall before Conan's feet—a still-quivering human heart.

With a roar and a curse Conan charged the stair. From Khemsa's girdle he felt strength and deathless hate flow into him to combat the terrible emanation of power that met him on the steps. The air filled with a shimmering steely haze through which he plunged like a swimmer, head lowered, left arm bent about his face, knife gripped low in his right hand. His half-blinded eyes, glaring over the crook of his elbow, made out the hated shape of the Seer before and above him, the outline wavering as a reflection wavers in disturbed water.

He was racked and torn by forces beyond his comprehension, but he felt a driving power outside and beyond his own lifting him inexorably upward and onward, despite the wizard's strength and his own agony.

Now he had reached the head of the stairs, and the Master's face floated in the steely haze before him, and a strange fear shadowed the inscrutable eyes. Conan waded through the mist as through a surf, and his knife lunged upward like a live thing. The keen point ripped the Master's robe as he sprang back with a low cry. Then before Conan's gaze, the wizard vanished—simply disappeared like a burst bubble, and something long and undulating darted up one of the smaller stairs that led up to left and right from the landing.

Conan charged after it, up the left-hand stair, uncertain as to just what he had seen whip up those steps, but in a berserk mood that drowned the nausea and horror whispering at the back of his consciousness.

He plunged out into a broad corridor whose uncarpeted floor and untapestried walls were of polished jade, and something long and swift whisked down the corridor ahead of him, and into a curtained door. From within the chamber rose a scream of urgent terror. The sound lent wings to Conan's flying feet and he hurtled through the curtains and headlong into the chamber within.

A frightful scene met his glare. Yasmina cowered on the farther edge of a velvet-covered dais, screaming her loathing and horror, an arm lifted as if to ward off attack, while before her swayed the hideous head of a giant serpent, shining neck arching up from dark-gleaming coils. With a choked cry Conan threw his knife.

Instantly the monster whirled and was upon him like the rush of wind through tall grass. The long knife quivered in its neck, point and a foot of blade showing on one side, and the hilt and a hand's-breadth of steel on the other, but it only seemed to madden the giant reptile. The great head towered above the man who faced it, and then darted down, the venom-dripping jaws gaping wide. But Conan had plucked a dagger from his girdle and he stabbed upward as the head dipped down. The point tore through the lower jaw and transfixed the upper, pinning them together. The next instant the great trunk had looped itself about the Cimmerian as the snake, unable to use its fangs, employed its remaining form of attack.

Conan's left arm was pinioned among the bone-crushing folds, but his right was free. Bracing his feet to keep upright, he stretched forth his hand, gripped the hilt of the long knife jutting from the serpent's neck, and tore it free in a shower of blood. As if divining his purpose with more than bestial intelligence, the snake writhed and knotted, seeking to cast its loops about his right arm. But with the speed of light the long knife rose and fell, shearing halfway through the reptile's giant trunk.

Before he could strike again, the great pliant loops fell from him and the monster dragged itself across the floor, gushing blood from its ghastly wounds. Conan sprang after it, knife lifted, but his vicious swipe cut empty air as the serpent writhed away from him and struck its blunt nose against a paneled screen of sandalwood. One of the panels gave inward and the long, bleeding barrel whipped through it and was gone.

Conan instantly attacked the screen. A few blows rent it apart and he glared into the dim alcove beyond. No horrific shape coiled there; there was blood on the marble floor, and bloody tracks led to a cryptic arched door. Those tracks were of a man's bare feet....

"Conan!" He wheeled back into the chamber just in time to catch the Devi of Vendhya in his arms as she rushed across the room and threw herself upon him, catching him about the neck with a frantic clasp, half hysterical with terror and gratitude and relief.

His wild blood had been stirred to its uttermost by all that had passed. He caught her to him in a grasp that would have made her wince at another time, and crushed her lips with his. She made no resistance; the Devi was drowned in the elemental woman. She closed her eyes and drank in his fierce, hot, lawless kisses with all the abandon of passionate thirst. She was panting with his violence when he ceased for breath, and glared down at her lying limp in his mighty arms.

"I knew you'd come for me," she murmured. "You would not leave me in this den of devils."

At her words recollection of their environment came to him suddenly. He lifted his head and listened intently. Silence reigned over the castle of Yimsha, but it was a silence impregnated with menace. Peril crouched in every corner, leered invisibly from every hanging.

"We'd better go while we can," he muttered. "Those cuts were enough to kill any common beast—or man—but a wizard has a dozen lives. Wound one, and he writhes away like a crippled snake to soak up fresh venom from some source of sorcery."

He picked up the girl and carrying her in his arms like a child, he strode out into the gleaming jade corridor and down the stairs, nerves tautly alert for any sign or sound.

"I met the Master," she whispered, clinging to him and shuddering. "He worked his spells on me to break my will. The most awful thing was a moldering corpse which seized me in its arms—I fainted then and lay as one dead, I do not know how long. Shortly after I regained consciousness I heard sounds of strife below, and cries, and then that snake came slithering through the curtains—ah!" She shook at the memory of that horror. "I knew somehow that it was not an illusion, but a real serpent that sought my life."

"It was not a shadow, at least," answered Conan cryptically. "He knew he was beaten, and chose to slay you rather than let you be rescued."

"What do you mean, *he?*" she asked uneasily, and then shrank against him, crying out, and forgetting her question. She had seen the corpses at the foot of the stairs. Those of the Seers were not good to look at; as they lay twisted and contorted, their hands and feet were exposed to view, and at the sight Yasmina went livid and hid her face against Conan's powerful shoulder.

10 Yasmina and Conan

Conan passed through the hall quickly enough, traversed the outer chamber and approached the door that led upon the gallery. Then he saw the floor sprinkled with tiny, glittering shards. The crystal sheet that had covered the doorway had been shivered to bits, and he remembered the crash that had accompanied the shattering of the crystal globe. He believed that every piece of crystal in the castle had broken at that instant, and some dim instinct or memory of esoteric lore vaguely suggested the truth of the monstrous connection between the Lords of the Black Circle and the golden pomegranates. He felt the short hair bristle chilly at the back of his neck and put the matter hastily out of his mind.

He breathed a deep sigh of relief as he stepped out upon the green jade gallery. There was still the gorge to cross, but at least he could see the white peaks glistening in the sun, and the long slopes falling away into the distant blue hazes.

The Irakzai lay where he had fallen, an ugly blotch on the glassy smoothness. As Conan strode down the winding path, he was surprised to note the position of the sun. It had not yet passed its zenith; and yet it seemed to him that hours had passed since he plunged into the castle of the Black Seers.

He felt an urge to hasten, not a mere blind panic, but an instinct of peril growing behind his back. He said nothing to Yasmina, and she seemed content to nestle her dark head against his arching breast and find security in the clasp of his iron arms. He paused an instant on the brink of the chasm, frowning down. The haze which danced in the gorge was no longer rose-hued and sparkling. It was smoky, dim, ghostly, like the life-tide that flickered thinly in a wounded man. The thought came vaguely to Conan that the spells of magicians were more closely bound to their personal beings than were the actions of common men to the actors.

But far below, the floor shone like tarnished silver, and the gold thread sparkled undimmed. Conan shifted Yasmina across his shoulder, where she lay docilely, and began the descent. Hurriedly he descended the ramp, and hurriedly he fled across the echoing floor. He had a conviction that they were racing with time, that their chances of survival depended upon crossing that gorge of horrors before the wounded Master of the castle should regain enough power to loose some other doom upon them.

When he toiled up the farther ramp and came out upon the crest, he breathed a gusty sigh of relief and stood Yasmina upon her feet.

"You walk from here," he told her; "it's downhill all the way."

She stole a glance at the gleaming pyramid across the chasm; it reared up against the snowy slope like the citadel of silence and immemorial evil.

"Are you a magician, that you have conquered the Black Seers of Yimsha, Conan of Ghor?" she asked, as they went down the path, with his heavy arm about her supple waist.

"It was a girdle Khemsa gave me before he died," Conan answered. "Yes, I found him on the trail. It is a curious one, which I'll show you when I have time. Against some spells it was weak, but against others it was strong, and a good knife is always a hearty incantation."

"But if the girdle aided you in conquering the Master," she argued, "why did it not aid Khemsa?"

He shook his head. "Who knows? But Khemsa had been the Master's slave; perhaps that weakened its magic. He had no hold on me as he had on Khemsa. Yet I can't say that I conquered him. He retreated, but I have a feeling that we haven't seen the last of him. I want to put as many miles between us and his lair as we can."

He was further relieved to find horses tethered among the tamarisks as he had left them. He loosed them swiftly and mounted the black stallion, swinging the girl up before him. The others followed, freshened by their rest.

"And what now?" she asked. "To Afghulistan?"

"Not just now!" He grinned hardly. "Somebody—maybe the governor—killed my seven headmen. My idiotic followers think I had something to do with it, and unless I am able to convince them otherwise, they'll hunt me like a wounded jackal."

"Then what of me? If the headmen are dead, I am useless to you as a hostage. Will you slay me, to avenge them?"

He looked down at her, with eyes fiercely aglow, and laughed at the suggestion.

"Then let us ride to the border," she said. "You'll be safe from the Afghulis there—"

"Yes, on a Vendhyan gibbet."

"I am Queen of Vendhya," she reminded him with a touch of her old imperiousness. "You have saved my life. You shall be rewarded."

She did not intend it as it sounded, but he growled in his throat, ill pleased.

"Keep your bounty for your city-bred dogs, princess! If you're a queen of the plains, I'm a chief of the hills, and not one foot toward the border will I take you!"

"But you would be safe—" she began bewilderedly.

"And you'd be the Devi again," he broke in. "No, girl; I prefer you as you are now—a woman of flesh and blood, riding on my saddle-bow."

"But you can't keep me!" she cried. "You can't—"

"Watch and see!" he advised grimly.

"But I will pay you a vast ransom—"

"Devil take your ransom!" he answered roughly, his arms hardening about her supple figure. "The kingdom of Vendhya could give me nothing I desire half so much as I desire you. I took you at the risk of my neck; if your courtiers want you back, let them come up the Zhaibar and fight for you."

"But you have no followers now!" she protested. "You are hunted! How can you preserve your own life, much less mine?"

"I still have friends in the hills," he answered. "There is a chief of the Khurakzai who will keep you safely while I bicker with the Afghulis. If they will have none of me, by Crom! I will ride northward with you to the steppes of the *kozaki*. I was a hetman among the Free Companions before I rode southward. I'll make you a queen on the Zaporoska River!"

"But I can not!" she objected. "You must not hold me—"

"If the idea's so repulsive," he demanded, "why did you yield your lips to me so willingly?"

"Even a queen is human," she answered, coloring. "But because I am a queen, I must consider my kingdom. Do not carry me away into some foreign country. Come back to Vendhya with me!"

"Would you make me your king?" he asked sardonically.

"Well, there are customs—" she stammered, and he interrupted her with a hard laugh.

"Yes, civilized customs that won't let you do as you wish. You'll marry some withered old king of the plains, and I can go my way with only the memory of a few kisses snatched from your lips. Ha!"

"But I must return to my kingdom!" she repeated helplessly.

"Why?" he demanded angrily. "To chafe your rump on gold thrones, and listen to the plaudits of smirking, velvet-skirted fools? Where is the gain? Listen: I was born in the Cimmerian hills where the people are all barbarians. I have been a mercenary soldier, a corsair, a *kozak*, and a hundred other things. What king has roamed the countries, fought the battles, loved the women, and won the plunder that I have?

"I came into Ghulistan to raise a horde and plunder the kingdoms to the south—your own among them. Being chief of the Afghulis was only a start. If I can conciliate them, I'll have a dozen tribes following me within a year. But if I can't I'll ride back to the steppes and loot the Turanian borders with the *kozaki*. And you'll go with me. To the devil with your kingdom; they fended for themselves before you were born."

She lay in his arms looking up at him, and she felt a tug at her spirit, a lawless, reckless urge that matched his own and was by it called into being. But a thousand generations of sovereignship rode heavy upon her.

"I can't! I can't!" she repeated helplessly.

"You haven't any choice," he assured her. "You—what the devil!"

They had left Yimsha some miles behind them, and were riding along a high ridge that separated two deep valleys. They had just topped a steep crest where they could gaze down into the valley on their right hand. And there was a running fight in progress. A strong wind was blowing away from them, carrying the sound from their ears, but even so the clashing of steel and thunder of hoofs welled up from far below.

They saw the glint of the sun on lance-tip and spired helmet. Three thousand mailed horsemen were driving before them a ragged band of turbaned riders, who fled snarling and striking like fleeing wolves.

"Turanians," muttered Conan. "Squadrons from Secunderam. What the devil are they doing here?"

"Who are the men they pursue?" asked Yasmina. "And why do they fall back so stubbornly? They can not stand against such odds."

"Five hundred of my mad Afghulis," he growled, scowling down into the vale. "They're in a trap, and they know it."

The valley was indeed a cul-de-sac at that end. It narrowed to a high-walled gorge, opening out further into a round bowl, completely rimmed with lofty, unscalable walls.

The turbaned riders were being forced into this gorge, because there was nowhere else for them to go, and they went reluctantly, in a shower of arrows and a whirl of swords. The helmeted riders harried them, but did not press in too rashly. They knew the desperate fury of the hill tribes, and they knew too that they had their prey in a trap from which there was no escape. They had recognized the hill-men as Afghulis, and they wished to hem them in and force a surrender. They needed hostages for the purpose they had in mind.

Their emir was a man of decision and initiative. When he reached the Gurashah valley, and found neither guides nor emissary waiting for him, he pushed on, trusting to his own knowledge of the country. All the way from Secunderam there had been fighting, and tribesmen were licking their wounds in many a crag-perched village. He knew there was a good chance that neither he nor any of his helmeted spearmen would ever ride through the gates of Secunderam again, for the tribes would all be up behind him now, but he was determined to carry out his orders—which were to take Yasmina Devi from the Afghulis at all costs, and to bring her captive to Secunderam, or if confronted by impossibility, to strike off her head before he himself died.

Of all this, of course, the watchers on the ridge were not aware. But Conan fidgeted with nervousness.

"Why the devil did they get themselves trapped?" he demanded of the universe at large. "I know what they're doing in these parts—they were hunting me, the dogs! Poking into every valley—and found themselves penned in before they knew it. The poor fools! They're making a stand in the gorge, but they can't hold out for long. When the Turanians have pushed them back into the bowl, they'll slaughter them at their leisure."

The din welling up from below increased in volume and intensity. In the strait of the narrow gut, the Afghulis, fighting desperately, were for the time holding their own against the mailed riders, who could not throw their whole weight against them.

Conan scowled darkly, moved restlessly, fingering his hilt, and finally spoke bluntly: "Devi, I must go down to them. I'll find a place for you to hide until I come back to you. You spoke of your kingdom—well, I don't pretend to look on those hairy devils as my children, but after all, such as they are, they're my henchmen. A chief should never desert his followers, even if they desert him first. They think they were right in kicking me out—hell, I won't be cast off! I'm still chief of the Afghulis, and I'll prove it! I can climb down on foot into the gorge."

"But what of me?" she queried. "You carried me away forcibly from my people; now will you leave me to die in the hills alone while you go down and sacrifice yourself uselessly?"

His veins swelled with the conflict of his emotions.

"That's right," he muttered helplessly. "Crom knows what I *can* do."

She turned her head slightly, a curious expression dawning on her beautiful face. Then:

"Listen!" she cried. "Listen!"

A distant fanfare of trumpets was borne faintly to their ears. They stared into the deep valley on the left, and caught a glint of steel on the farther side. A long line of lances and polished helmets moved along the vale, gleaming in the sunlight.

"The riders of Vendhya!" she cried exultingly.

"There are thousands of them!" muttered Conan. "It has been long since a Kshatriya host has ridden this far into the hills."

"They are searching for me!" she exclaimed. "Give me your horse! I will ride to my warriors! The ridge is not so precipitous on the left, and I can reach the valley floor. I will lead my horsemen into the valley at the upper end and fall upon the Turanians! We will crush them in the vise! Quick, Conan! Will you sacrifice your men to your own desire?"

The burning hunger of the steppes and the wintry forests glared out of his eyes, but he shook his head and swung off the stallion, placing the reins in her hands.

"You win!" he grunted. "Ride like the devil!"

She wheeled away down the left-hand slope and he ran swiftly along the ridge until he reached the long ragged cleft that was the defile in which the fight raged. Down the rugged wall he scrambled like an ape, clinging to projections and crevices, to fall at last, feet first, into the mêlée that raged in the mouth of the gorge. Blades were whickering and clanging about him, horses rearing and stamping, helmet plumes nodding among turbans that were stained crimson.

As he hit, he yelled like a wolf, caught a gold-worked rein, and dodging the sweep of a scimitar, drove his long knife upward through the rider's vitals. In another instant he was in the saddle, yelling ferocious orders to the Afghulis. They stared at him stupidly for an instant; then as they saw the havoc his steel was wreaking among their enemies, they fell to their work again, accepting him without comment. In that inferno of licking blades and spurting blood there was no time to ask or answer questions.

The riders in their spired helmets and gold-worked hauberks swarmed about the gorge mouth, thrusting and slashing, and the narrow defile was packed and jammed with horses and men, the warriors crushed breast to breast, stabbing with shortened blades, slashing murderously when there was an instant's room to swing a sword. When a man went down he did not get up from beneath the stamping, swirling hoofs. Weight and sheer strength counted heavily there, and the chief of the Afghulis did the work of ten. At such times accustomed habits sway men strongly, and the warriors, who were used to seeing Conan in their vanguard, were heartened mightily, despite their distrust of him.

But superior numbers counted too. The pressure of the men behind forced the horsemen of Turan deeper and deeper into the gorge, in the teeth of the flickering tulwars. Foot by foot the Afghulis were shoved back, leaving the defile-floor carpeted with dead, on which the riders trampled. As he hacked and smote like a man possessed, Conan had time for some chilling doubts—would Yasmina keep her word? She had but to join her warriors, turn southward and leave him and his band to perish.

But at last, after what seemed centuries of desperate battling, in the valley outside there rose another sound above the clash of steel and yells of slaughter. And then with a burst of trumpets that shook the walls, and rushing thunder of hoofs, five thousand riders of Vendhya smote the hosts of Secunderam.

That stroke split the Turanian squadrons asunder, shattered, tore and rent them and scattered their fragments all over the valley. In an instant the surge had ebbed back out of the gorge; there was a chaotic, confused swirl of fighting, horsemen wheeling and smiting singly and in clusters, and then the emir went down with a Kshatriya lance through his breast, and the riders in their spired helmets turned their horses down the valley, spurring like mad and seeking to slash a way through the swarms which had come upon them from the rear. As they scattered in flight, the conquerors scattered in pursuit, and all across the valley floor, and up on the slopes near the mouth and over the crests streamed the fugitives and the pursuers. The Afghulis, those left to ride, rushed out of the gorge and joined in the harrying of their foes, accepting the unexpected alliance as unquestioningly as they had accepted the return of their repudiated chief.

The sun was sinking toward the distant crags when Conan, his garments hacked to tatters and the mail under them reeking and clotted with blood, his knife dripping and crusted to the hilt, strode over the corpses to where Yasmina Devi sat her horse among her nobles on the crest of the ridge, near a lofty precipice.

"You kept your word, Devi!" he roared. "By Crom, though, I had some bad seconds down in that gorge—*look out!*"

Down from the sky swooped a vulture of tremendous size with a thunder of wings that knocked men sprawling from their horses.

The scimitar-like beak was slashing for the Devi's soft neck, but Conan was quicker—a short run, a tigerish leap, the savage thrust of a dripping knife, and the vulture voiced a horribly human cry, pitched sideways and went tumbling down the cliffs to the rocks and river a thousand feet below. As it dropped, its black wings thrashing the air, it took on the semblance, not of a bird, but of a black-robed human body that fell, arms in wide black sleeves thrown abroad.

Conan turned to Yasmina, his red knife still in his hand, his blue eyes smoldering, blood oozing from wounds on his thickly muscled arms and thighs.

"You are the Devi again," he said, grinning fiercely at the gold-clasped gossamer robe she had donned over her hill-girl attire, and awed not at all by the imposing array of chivalry about him. "I have you to thank for the lives of some three hundred and fifty of my rogues, who are at least convinced that I didn't betray them. You have put my hands on the reins of conquest again."

"I still owe you my ransom," she said, her dark eyes glowing as they swept over him. "Ten thousand pieces of gold I will pay you—"

He made a savage, impatient gesture, shook the blood from his knife and thrust it back in its scabbard, wiping his hands on his mail.

"I will collect your ransom in my own way, at my own time," he said. "I will collect it in your palace at Ayodhya, and I will come with fifty thousand men to see that the scales are fair."

She laughed, gathering her reins into her hands. "And I will meet you on the shores of the Jhumda with a hundred thousand!"

His eyes shone with fierce appreciation and admiration, and stepping back, he lifted his hand with a gesture that was like the assumption of kingship, indicating that her road was clear before her.

THE END

Beyond the Black River

1 Conan Loses His Ax

The stillness of the forest trail was so primeval that the tread of a soft-booted foot was a startling disturbance. At least it seemed so to the ears of the wayfarer, though he was moving along the path with the caution that must be practised by any man who ventures beyond Thunder River. He was a young man of medium height, with an open countenance and a mop of tousled tawny hair unconfined by cap or helmet. His garb was common enough for that country—a coarse tunic, belted at the waist, short leather breeches beneath, and soft buckskin boots that came short of the knee. A knife-hilt jutted from one boot-top. The broad leather belt supported a short, heavy sword and a buckskin pouch. There was no perturbation in the wide eyes that scanned the green walls which fringed the trail. Though not tall, he was well built, and the arms that the short wide sleeves of the tunic left bare were thick with corded muscle.

He tramped imperturbably along, although the last settler's cabin lay miles behind him, and each step was carrying him nearer the grim peril that hung like a brooding shadow over the ancient forest.

He was not making as much noise as it seemed to him, though he well knew that the faint tread of his booted feet would be like a tocsin of alarm to the fierce ears that might be lurking in the treacherous green fastness. His careless attitude was not genuine; his eyes and ears were keenly alert, especially his ears, for no gaze could penetrate the leafy tangle for more than a few feet in either direction.

But it was instinct more than any warning by the external senses which brought him up suddenly, his hand on his hilt. He stood stock-still in the middle of the trail, unconsciously holding his breath, wondering what he had heard, and wondering if indeed he had heard anything. The silence seemed absolute. Not a squirrel chattered or bird chirped. Then his gaze fixed itself on a mass of bushes beside the trail a few yards ahead of him. There was no breeze, yet he had seen a branch quiver. The short hairs on his scalp prickled, and he stood for an instant undecided, certain that a move in either direction would bring death streaking at him from the bushes.

A heavy chopping crunch sounded behind the leaves. The bushes were shaken violently, and simultaneously with the sound, an arrow arched erratically from among them and vanished among the trees along the trail. The wayfarer glimpsed its flight as he sprang frantically to cover.

Crouching behind a thick stem, his sword quivering in his fingers, he saw the bushes part, and a tall figure stepped leisurely into the trail. The traveler stared in surprise. The stranger was clad like himself in regard to boots and breeks, though the latter were of silk instead of leather. But he wore a sleeveless hauberk of dark mesh-mail in place of a tunic, and a helmet perched on his black mane. That helmet held the other's gaze; it was without a crest, but adorned by short bull's horns. No civilized hand ever forged that head-piece. Nor was the face below it that of a civilized man: dark, scarred, with smoldering blue eyes, it was a face untamed as the primordial forest which formed its background. The man held a broadsword in his right hand, and the edge was smeared with crimson.

"Come on out," he called, in an accent unfamiliar to the wayfarer. "All's safe now. There was only one of the dogs. Come on out."

The other emerged dubiously and stared at the stranger. He felt curiously helpless and futile as he gazed on the proportions of the forest man—the massive iron-clad breast, and the arm that bore the reddened sword, burned dark by the sun and ridged and corded with muscles. He moved with the dangerous ease of a panther; he was too fiercely supple to be a product of civilization, even of that fringe of civilization which composed the outer frontiers.

Turning, he stepped back to the bushes and pulled them apart. Still not certain just what had happened, the wayfarer from the east advanced and stared down into the bushes. A man lay there, a short, dark, thickly-muscled man, naked except for a loin-cloth, a necklace of human teeth and a brass armlet. A short sword was thrust into the girdle of the loin-cloth, and one hand still gripped a heavy black bow. The man had long black hair; that was about all the wayfarer could tell about his head, for his features were a mask of blood and brains. His skull had been split to the teeth.

"A Pict, by the gods!" exclaimed the wayfarer.

The burning blue eyes turned upon him.

"Are you surprised?"

"Why, they told me at Velitrium and again at the settlers' cabins along the road, that these devils sometimes sneaked across the border, but I didn't expect to meet one this far in the interior."

"You're only four miles east of Black River," the stranger informed him. "They've been shot within a mile of Velitrium. No settler between Thunder River and Fort Tuscelan is really safe. I picked up this dog's trail three miles south of the fort this morning, and I've been following him ever since. I came up behind him just as he was drawing an arrow on you. Another instant and there'd have been a stranger in Hell. But I spoiled his aim for him."

The wayfarer was staring wide-eyed at the larger man, dumfounded by the realization that the man had actually tracked down one of the forest-devils and slain him unsuspected. That implied woodsmanship of a quality undreamed, even for Conajohara.

"You are one of the fort's garrison?" he asked.

"I'm no soldier. I draw the pay and rations of an officer of the line, but I do my work in the woods. Valannus knows I'm of more use ranging along the river than cooped up in the fort."

Casually the slayer shoved the body deeper into the thickets with his foot, pulled the bushes together and turned away down the trail. The other followed him.

"My name is Balthus," he offered. "I was at Velitrium last night. I haven't decided whether I'll take up a hide of land, or enter fort service."

"The best land near Thunder River is already taken," grunted the slayer. "Plenty of good land between Scalp Creek—you crossed it a few miles back—and the fort, but that's getting too devilish close to the river. The Picts steal over to burn and murder—as that one did. They don't always come singly. Some day they'll try to sweep the settlers out of Conajohara. And they may succeed—probably will succeed. This colonization business is mad, anyway. There's plenty of good land east of the Bossonian marches. If the Aquilonians would cut up some of the big estates of their barons, and plant wheat where now only deer are hunted, they wouldn't have to cross the border and take the land of the Picts away from them."

"That's queer talk from a man in the service of the Governor of Conajohara," objected Balthus.

"It's nothing to me," the other retorted. "I'm a mercenary. I sell my sword to the highest bidder. I never planted wheat and never will, so long as there are other harvests to be reaped with the sword. But you

Hyborians have expanded as far as you'll be allowed to expand. You've crossed the marches, burned a few villages, exterminated a few clans and pushed back the frontier to Black River; but I doubt if you'll even be able to hold what you've conquered, and you'll never push the frontier any further westward. Your idiotic king doesn't understand conditions here. He won't send you enough reinforcements, and there are not enough settlers to withstand the shock of a concerted attack from across the river."

"But the Picts are divided into small clans," persisted Balthus. "they'll never unite. We can whip any single clan."

"Or any three or four clans," admitted the slayer. "But some day a man will rise and unite thirty or forty clans, just as was done among the Cimmerians, when the Gundermen tried to push the border northward, years ago. They tried to colonize the southern marches of Cimmeria: destroyed a few small clans, built a fort-town, Venarium— you've heard the tale."

"So I have indeed," replied Balthus, wincing. The memory of that red disaster was a black blot in the chronicles of a proud and war-like people. "My uncle was at Venarium when the Cimmerians swarmed over the walls. He was one of the few who escaped that slaughter. I've heard him tell the tale, many a time. The barbarians swept out of the hills in a ravening horde, without warning, and stormed Venarium with such fury none could stand before them. Men, women and children were butchered. Venarium was reduced to a mass of charred ruins, as it is to this day. The Aquilonians were driven back across the marches, and have never since tried to colonize the Cimmerian country. But you speak of Venarium familiarly. Perhaps you were there?"

"I was," grunted the other. "I was one of the horde that swarmed over the walls. I hadn't yet seen fifteen snows, but already my name was repeated about the council fires."

Balthus involuntarily recoiled, staring. It seemed incredible that the man walking tranquilly at his side should have been one of those screeching, blood-mad devils that had poured over the walls of Venarium on that long-gone day to make her streets run crimson.

"Then you, too, are a barbarian!" he exclaimed involuntarily.

The other nodded, without taking offence.

"I am Conan, a Cimmerian."

"I've heard of you." Fresh interest quickened Balthus' gaze. No wonder the Pict had fallen victim to his own sort of subtlety. The Cimmerians were barbarians as ferocious as the Picts, and much more intelligent. Evidently Conan had spent much time among civilized men, though that contact had obviously not softened him, nor weakened any of his primitive instincts. Balthus' apprehension turned to admiration as he marked the easy cat-like stride, the effortless silence with which the Cimmerian moved along the trail. The oiled links of his armor did not clink, and Balthus knew Conan could glide through the deepest thicket or most tangled copse as noiselessly as any naked Pict that ever lived.

"You're not a Gunderman?" It was more assertion than question.

Balthus shook his head. "I'm from the Tauran."

"I've seen good woodsmen from the Tauran. But the Bossonians have sheltered you Aquilonians from the outer wildernesses for too many centuries. You need hardening."

That was true; the Bossonian marches, with their fortified villages filled with determined bowmen, had long served Aquilonia as a buffer against the outlying barbarians. Now among the settlers beyond Thunder River there was growing up a breed of forest men capable of meeting the barbarians at their own game, but their numbers were still scanty. Most of the frontiersmen were like Balthus—more of the settler than the woodsman type.

The sun had not set, but it was no longer in sight, hidden as it was behind the dense forest wall. The shadows were lengthening, deepening back in the woods as the companions strode on down the trail.

"It will be dark before we reach the fort," commented Conan casually; then: "Listen!"

He stopped short, half crouching, sword ready, transformed into a savage figure of suspicion and menace, poised to spring and rend. Balthus had heard it too—a wild scream that broke at its highest note. It was the cry of a man in dire fear or agony.

Conan was off in an instant, racing down the trail, each stride widening the distance between him and his straining companion. Balthus puffed a curse. Among the settlements of the Tauran he was accounted a good runner, but Conan was leaving him behind with maddening ease. Then Balthus forgot his exasperation as his ears were outraged by the most frightful cry he had ever heard. It was not human, this one; it was a demoniacal caterwauling of hideous triumph that seemed to exult over fallen humanity and find echo in black gulfs beyond human ken.

Balthus faltered in his stride, and clammy sweat beaded his flesh. But Conan did not hesitate; he darted around a bend in the trail and disappeared, and Balthus, panicky at finding himself alone with that awful scream still shuddering through the forest in grisly echoes, put on an extra burst of speed and plunged after him.

The Aquilonian slid to a stumbling halt, almost colliding with the Cimmerian who stood in the trail over a crumpled body. But Conan was not looking at the corpse which lay there in the crimson-soaked dust. He was glaring into the deep woods on either side of the trail.

Balthus muttered a horrified oath. It was the body of a man which lay there in the trail, a short, fat man, clad in the gilt-worked boots and (despite the heat) the ermine-trimmed tunic of a wealthy merchant. His fat, pale face was set in a stare of frozen horror; his thick throat had been slashed from ear to ear as if by a razor-sharp blade. The short sword still in its scabbard seemed to indicate that he had been struck down without a chance to fight for his life.

"A Pict?" Balthus whispered, as he turned to peer into the deepening shadows of the forest.

Conan shook his head and straightened to scowl down at the dead man.

"A forest devil. This is the fifth, by Crom!"

"What do you mean?"

"Did you ever hear of a Pictish wizard called Zogar Sag?"

Balthus shook his head uneasily.

"He dwells in Gwawela, the nearest village across the river. Three months ago he hid beside this road and stole a string of pack-mules from a pack-train bound for the fort—drugged their drivers, somehow. The mules belonged to this man"—Conan casually indicated the corpse with his foot—"Tiberias, a merchant of Velitrium. They were loaded with ale-kegs, and old Zogar stopped to guzzle before he got across the river. A woodsman named Soractus trailed him, and led Valannus and three soldiers to where he lay dead drunk in a thicket. At the importunities of Tiberias, Valannus threw Zogar Sag into a cell, which is the worst insult you can give a Pict. He managed to kill his guard and escape, and sent back word that he meant to kill Tiberias and the five men who captured him in a way that would make Aquilonians shudder for centuries to come.

"Well, Soractus and the soldiers are dead. Soractus was killed on the river, the soldiers in the very shadow of the fort. And now Tiberias is dead. No Pict killed any of them. Each victim—except Tiberias, as you see—lacked his head—which no doubt is now ornamenting the altar of Zogar Sag's particular god."

"How do you know they weren't killed by the Picts?" demanded Balthus.

Conan pointed to the corpse of the merchant.

"You think that was done with a knife or a sword? Look closer and you'll see that only a talon could have made a gash like that. The flesh is ripped, not cut."

"Perhaps a panther—" began Balthus, without conviction.

Conan shook his head impatiently.

"A man from the Tauran couldn't mistake the mark of a panther's claws. No. It's a forest devil summoned by Zogar Sag to carry out his revenge. Tiberias was a fool to start for Velitrium alone, and so close to dusk. But each one of the victims seemed to be smitten with madness just before doom overtook him. Look here; the signs are plain enough. Tiberias came riding along the trail on his mule, maybe with a bundle of choice otter pelts behind his saddle to sell in Velitrium, and the thing sprang on him from behind that bush. See where the branches are crushed down.

"Tiberias gave one scream, and then his throat was torn open and he was selling his otter skins in Hell. The mule ran away into the woods. Listen! Even now you can hear him thrashing about under the trees. The demon didn't have time to take Tiberias" head; it took fright as we came up."

"As you came up," amended Balthus. "It must not be a very terrible creature if it flees from one armed man. But how do you know it was not a Pict with some kind of a hook that rips instead of slicing? Did you see it?"

"Tiberias was an armed man," grunted Conan. "If Zogar Sag can bring demons to aid him, he can tell them which men to kill and which to let alone. No, I didn't see it. I only saw the bushes shake as it left the trail. But if you want further proof, look here!"

The slayer had stepped into the pool of blood in which the dead man sprawled. Under the bushes at the edge of the path there was a footprint, made in blood on the hard loam.

"Did a man make that?" demanded Conan.

Balthus felt his scalp prickle. Neither man nor any beast that he had ever seen could have left that strange, monstrous three-toed print, that was curiously combined of the bird and the reptile, yet a true type of neither. He spread his fingers above the print, careful not to touch it, and grunted explosively. He could not span the mark.

"What is it?" he whispered. "I never saw a beast that left a spoor like that."

"Nor any other sane man," answered Conan grimly. "It's a swamp demon—they're thick as bats in the swamps beyond Black River. You can hear them howling like damned souls when the wind blows strong from the south on hot nights."

"What shall we do?" asked the Aquilonian, peering uneasily into the deep blue shadows. The frozen fear on the dead countenance haunted him. He wondered what hideous head the wretch had seen thrust grinning from among the leaves to chill his blood with terror.

"No use to try to follow a demon," grunted Conan, drawing a short woodsman's ax from his girdle. "I tried tracking him after he killed Soractus. I lost his trail within a dozen steps. He might have grown himself wings and flown away, or sunk down through the earth to Hell. I don't know. I'm not going after the mule, either. It'll either wander back to the fort, or to some settler's cabin."

As he spoke Conan was busy at the edge of the trail with his ax. With a few strokes he cut a pair of saplings nine or ten feet long, and denuded them of their branches. Then he cut a length from a serpent-like vine that crawled among the bushes near by, and making one end fast to one of the poles, a couple of feet from the end, whipped the vine over the other sapling and interlaced it back and forth. In a few moments he had a crude but strong litter.

"The demon isn't going to get Tiberias' head if I can help it," he growled. "We'll carry the body into the fort. It isn't more than three miles. I never liked the fat fool, but we can't have Pictish devils making so cursed free with white men's heads."

The Picts were a white race, though swarthy, but the border men never spoke of them as such.

Balthus took the rear end of the litter, onto which Conan unceremoniously dumped the unfortunate merchant, and they moved on down the trail as swiftly as possible. Conan made no more noise laden with their grim burden than he had made when unencumbered. He had made a loop with the merchant's belt at the end of the poles, and was carrying his share of the load with one hand, while the other gripped his naked broadsword, and his restless gaze roved the sinister walls about them. The shadows were thickening. A darkening blue mist blurred the outlines of the foliage. The forest deepened in the twilight, became a blue haunt of mystery sheltering unguessed things.

They had covered more than a mile, and the muscles in Balthus' sturdy arms were beginning to ache a little, when a cry rang shuddering from the woods whose blue shadows were deepening into purple. Conan started convulsively, and Balthus almost let go the poles.

"A woman!" cried the younger man. "Great Mitra, a woman cried out then!"

"A settler's wife straying in the woods," snarled Conan, setting down his end of the litter. "Looking for a cow, probably, and—stay here!"

He dived like a hunting wolf into the leafy wall. Balthus' hair bristled.

"Stay here alone with this corpse and a devil hiding in the woods?" he yelped. "I'm coming with you!"

And suiting action to words, he plunged after the Cimmerian. Conan glanced back at him, but made no objection, though he did not moderate his pace to accommodate the shorter legs of his companion. Balthus wasted his wind in swearing as the Cimmerian drew away from him again, like a phantom between the trees, and then Conan burst into a dim glade and halted crouching, lips snarling, sword lifted.

"What are we stopping for?" panted Balthus, dashing the sweat out of his eyes and gripping his short sword.

"That scream came from this glade, or near by," answered Conan. "I don't mistake the location of sounds, even in the woods. But where—"

Abruptly the sound rang out again—behind them; in the direction of the trail they had just quitted. It rose piercingly and pitifully, the cry of a woman in frantic terror—and then, shockingly, it changed to a yell of mocking laughter that might have burst from the lips of a fiend of lower Hell.

"What in Mitra's name—" Balthus' face was a pale blur in the gloom.

With a scorching oath Conan wheeled and dashed back the way he had come, and the Aquilonian stumbled bewilderedly after him. He blundered into the Cimmerian as the latter stopped dead, and rebounded from his brawny shoulders as though from an iron statue. Gasping from the impact, he heard Conan's breath hiss through his teeth. The Cimmerian seemed frozen in his tracks.

Looking over his shoulder, Balthus felt his hair stand up stiffly. Something was moving through the deep bushes that fringed the trail—something that neither walked nor flew, but seemed to glide like a serpent. But it was not a serpent. Its outlines were indistinct, but it was taller than a man, and not very bulky. It gave off a glimmer of weird light, like a faint blue flame. Indeed, the eery fire was the only tangible thing about it. It might have been an embodied flame moving with reason and purpose through the blackening woods.

Conan snarled a savage curse and hurled his ax with ferocious will. But the thing glided on without altering its course. Indeed it was only a few instants' fleeting glimpse they had of it—a tall, shadowy thing of misty flame floating through the thickets. Then it was gone, and the forest crouched in breathless stillness.

With a snarl Conan plunged through the intervening foliage and into the trail. His profanity, as Balthus floundered after him, was lurid and impassioned. The Cimmerian was standing over the litter on which lay the body of Tiberias. And that body no longer possessed a head.

"Tricked us with its damnable caterwauling!" raved Conan, swinging his great sword about his head in his wrath. "I might have known! I might have guessed a trick! Now there'll be five heads to decorate Zogar's altar."

"But what thing is it that can cry like a woman and laugh like a devil, and shines like witch-fire as it glides through the trees?" gasped Balthus, mopping the sweat from his pale face.

"A swamp devil," responded Conan morosely. "Grab those poles. We'll take in the body, anyway. At least our load's a bit lighter."

With which grim philosophy he gripped the leathery loop and stalked down the trail.

2 The Wizard of Gwawela

Fort Tuscelan stood on the eastern bank of Black River, the tides of which washed the foot of the stockade. The latter was of logs, as were all the buildings within, including the donjon (to dignify it by that appellation), in which were the governor's quarters, overlooking the stockade and the sullen river. Beyond that river lay a huge forest, which approached jungle-like density along the spongy shores. Men paced the runways along the log parapet day and night, watching that dense green wall. Seldom a menacing figure appeared, but the sentries knew that they too were watched, fiercely, hungrily, with the mercilessness of ancient hate. The forest beyond the river might seem desolate and vacant of life to the ignorant eye, but life teemed there, not alone of bird and beast and reptile, but also of men, the fiercest of all the hunting beasts.

There, at the fort, civilization ended. Fort Tuscelan was the last outpost of a civilized world; it represented the westernmost thrust of the dominant Hyborian races. Beyond the river the primitive still reigned in shadowy forests, brush-thatched huts where hung the grinning skulls of men, and mud-walled enclosures where fires flickered and drums rumbled, and spears were whetted in the hands of dark, silent men with tangled black hair and the eyes of serpents. Those eyes often glared through the bushes at the fort across the river. Once dark-skinned men had built their huts where that fort stood; yes, and their huts had risen where now stood the fields and log cabins of fair-haired settlers, back beyond Velitrium, that raw, turbulent frontier town on the banks of Thunder River, to the shores of that other river that bounds the Bossonian marches. Traders had come, and priests of Mitra who walked with bare feet and empty hands, and died horribly, most of them; but soldiers had followed, and men with axes in their hands and women and children in ox-drawn wains. Back to Thunder River, and still back, beyond Black River, the aborigines had been pushed, with slaughter and massacre. But the dark-skinned people did not forget that once Conajohara had been theirs.

The guard inside the eastern gate bawled a challenge. Through a barred aperture torchlight flickered, glinting on a steel headpiece and suspicious eyes beneath it.

"Open the gate," snorted Conan. "You see it's I, don't you?"

Military discipline put his teeth on edge.

The gate swung inward and Conan and his companion passed through. Balthus noted that the gate was flanked by a tower on each side, the summits of which rose above the stockade. He saw loopholes for arrows.

The guardsmen grunted as they saw the burden borne between the men. Their pikes jangled against each other as they thrust shut the gate, chin on shoulder, and Conan asked testily: "Have you never seen a headless body before?"

The face of the soldiers were pallid in the torchlight.

"That's Tiberias," blurted one. "I recognize that fur-trimmed tunic. Valerius here owes me five lunas. I told him Tiberias had heard the loon call when he rode through the gate on his mule, with his glassy stare. I wagered he'd come back without his head."

Conan grunted enigmatically, motioned Balthus to ease the litter to the ground, and then strode off toward the governor's quarters, with the Aquilonian at his heels. The tousle-headed youth stared about him eagerly and curiously, noting the rows of barracks along the walls, the stables, the tiny merchants' stalls, the towering blockhouse, and the other buildings, with the open square in the middle where the soldiers drilled, and where, now, fires danced and men off duty lounged. These were now hurrying to join the morbid crowd gathered about the litter at the gate. The rangy figures of Aquilonian pikemen and forest runners mingled with the shorter, stockier forms of Bossonian archers.

He was not greatly surprised that the governor received them himself. Autocratic society with its rigid caste laws lay east of the marches. Valannus was still a young man, well knit, with a finely chiseled countenance already carved into sober cast by toil and responsibility.

"You left the fort before daybreak, I was told," he said to Conan. "I had begun to fear that the Picts had caught you at last."

"When they smoke my head the whole river will know it," grunted Conan. "They'll hear Pictish women wailing their dead as far as Velitrium—I was on a lone scout. I couldn't sleep. I kept hearing drums talking across the river."

"They talk each night," reminded the governor, his fine eyes shadowed, as he stared closely at Conan. He had learned the unwisdom of discounting wild men's instincts.

"There was a difference last night," growled Conan. "There has been ever since Zogar Sag got back across the river."

"We should either have given him presents and sent him home, or else hanged him," sighed the governor. "You advised that, but—"

"But it's hard for you Hyborians to learn the ways of the outlands," said Conan. "Well, it can't be helped now, but there'll be no peace on the border so long as Zogar lives and remembers the cell he sweated in. I was following a warrior who slipped over to put a few white notches on his bow. After I split his head I fell in with this lad whose name is Balthus and who's come from the Tauran to help hold the frontier."

Valannus approvingly eyed the young man's frank countenance and strongly-knit frame.

"I am glad to welcome you, young sir. I wish more of your people would come. We need men used to forest life. Many of our soldiers and some of our settlers are from the eastern provinces and know nothing of woodcraft, or even of agricultural life."

"Not many of that breed this side of Velitrium," grunted Conan. "That town's full of them, though. But listen, Valannus, we found Tiberias dead on the trail." And in a few words he related the grisly affair.

Valannus paled. "I did not know he had left the fort. He must have been mad!"

"He was," answered Conan. "Like the other four; each one, when his time came, went mad and rushed into the woods to meet his death like a hare running down the throat of a python. Something called to them from the deeps of the forest, something the men call a loon, for lack of a better name, but only the doomed ones could hear it. Zogar Sag has made a magic that Aquilonian civilization can't overcome."

To this thrust Valannus made no reply; he wiped his brow with a shaky hand.

"Do the soldiers know of this?"

"We left the body by the eastern gate."

"You should have concealed the fact, hidden the corpse somewhere in the woods. The soldiers are nervous enough already."

"They'd have found it out some way. If I'd hidden the body, it would have been returned to the fort as the corpse of Soractus was— tied up outside the gate for the men to find in the morning."

Valannus shuddered. Turning, he walked to a casement and stared silently out over the river, black and shiny under the glint of the stars. Beyond the river the jungle rose like an ebony wall. The distant screech of a panther broke the stillness. The night pressed in, blurring the sounds of the soldiers outside the blockhouse, dimming the fires. A wind whispered through the black branches, rippling the dusky water. On its wings came a low, rhythmic pulsing, sinister as the pad of a leopard's foot.

"After all," said Valannus, as if speaking his thoughts aloud, "what do we know—what does anyone know—of the things that jungle may hide? We have dim rumors of great swamps and rivers, and a forest that stretches on and on over everlasting plains and hills to end at last on the shores of the western ocean. But what things lie between this river and that ocean we dare not even guess. No white man has ever plunged deep into that fastness and returned alive to tell us what he found. We are wise in our civilized knowledge, but our knowledge extends just so far—to the western bank of that ancient river! Who knows what shapes earthly and unearthly may lurk beyond the dim circle of light our knowledge has cast?

"Who knows what gods are worshipped under the shadows of that heathen forest, or what devils crawl out of the black ooze of the swamps? Who can be sure that all the inhabitants of that black country are natural? Zogar Sag—a sage of the eastern cities would sneer at his primitive magic-making as the mummery of a fakir; yet he has driven mad and killed five men in a manner no man can explain. I wonder if he himself is wholly human."

"If I can get within ax-throwing distance of him I'll settle that question," growled Conan, helping himself to the governor's wine and pushing a glass toward Balthus, who took it hesitatingly, and with an uncertain glance toward Valannus.

The governor turned toward Conan and stared at him thoughtfully.

"The soldiers, who do not believe in ghosts or devils," he said, "are almost in a panic of fear. You, who believe in ghosts, ghouls, goblins, and all manner of uncanny things, do not seem to fear any of the things in which you believe."

"There's nothing in the universe cold steel won't cut," answered Conan. "I threw my ax at the demon, and he took no hurt, but I might have missed, in the dusk, or a branch deflected its flight. I'm not going out of my way looking for devils; but I wouldn't step out of my path to let one go by."

Valannus lifted his head and met Conan's gaze squarely.

"Conan, more depends on you than you realize. You know the weakness of this province—a slender wedge thrust into the untamed wilderness. You know that the lives of all the people west of the marches depend on this fort. Were it to fall, red axes would be splintering the gates of Velitrium before a horseman could cross the marches. His majesty, or his majesty's advisers, have ignored my plea that more troops be sent to hold the frontier. They know nothing of border conditions, and are averse to expending any more money in this direction. The fate of the frontier depends upon the men who now hold it.

"You know that most of the army which conquered Conajohara has been withdrawn. You know the force left is inadequate, especially since that devil Zogar Sag managed to poison our water supply, and forty men died in one day. Many of the others are sick, or have been bitten by serpents or mauled by wild beasts which seem to swarm in increasing numbers in the vicinity of the fort. The soldiers believe Zogar's boast that he could summon the forest beasts to slay his enemies.

"I have three hundred pikemen, four hundred Bossonian archers, and perhaps fifty men who, like yourself, are skilled in woodcraft. They are worth ten times their number of soldiers, but there are so few of them. Frankly, Conan, my situation is becoming precarious. The soldiers whisper of desertion; they are low-spirited, believing Zogar Sag has loosed devils on us. They fear the black plague with which he threatened us—the terrible black death of the swamplands. When I see a sick soldier I sweat with fear of seeing him turn black and shrivel and die before my eyes.

"Conan, if the plague is loosed upon us, the soldiers will desert in a body! The border will be left unguarded and nothing will check the sweep of the dark-skinned hordes to the very gates of Velitrium— maybe beyond! If we can not hold the fort, how can they hold the town?

"Conan, Zogar Sag must die, if we are to hold Conajohara. You have penetrated the unknown deeper than any other man in the fort; you know where Gwawela stands, and something of the forest trails across the river. Will you take a band of men tonight and endeavour to kill or capture him? Oh, I know it's mad. There isn't more than one chance in a thousand that any of you will come back alive. But if we don't get him, it's death for us all. You can take as many men as you wish."

"A dozen men are better for a job like that than a regiment," answered Conan. "Five hundred men couldn't fight their way to Gwawela and back, but a dozen might slip in and out again. Let me pick my men. I don't want any soldiers."

"Let me go!" eagerly exclaimed Balthus. "I've hunted deer all my life on the Tauran."

"All right. Valannus, we'll eat at the stall where the foresters gather, and I'll pick my men. We'll start within an hour, drop down the river in a boat to a point below the village and then steal upon it through the woods. If we live, we should be back by daybreak."

3 The Crawlers in the Dark

The river was a vague trace between walls of ebony. The paddles that propelled the long boat creeping along in the dense shadow of the eastern bank dipped softly into the water, making no more noise than the beak of a heron. The broad shoulders of the man in front of Balthus were a blur in the dense gloom. He knew that not even the keen eyes of the man who knelt in the prow would discern anything more than a few feet ahead of them. Conan was feeling his way by instinct and an intensive familiarity with the river.

No one spoke. Balthus had had a good look at his companions in the fort before they slipped out of the stockade and down the bank into the waiting canoe. They were of a new breed growing up in the world on the raw edge of the frontier—men whom grim necessity had taught woodcraft. Aquilonians of the western provinces to a man, they had many points in common. They dressed alike—in buckskin boots, leathern breeks and deerskin shirts, with broad girdles that held axes and short swords; and they were all gaunt and scarred and hard-eyed; sinewy and taciturn.

They were wild men, of a sort, yet there was still a wide gulf between them and the Cimmerian. They were sons of civilization, reverted to a semi-barbarism. He was a barbarian of a thousand generations of barbarians. They had acquired stealth and craft, but he had been born to these things. He excelled them even in lithe economy of motion. They were wolves, but he was a tiger.

Balthus admired them and their leader and felt a pulse of pride that he was admitted into their company. He was proud that his paddle made no more noise than did theirs. In that respect at least he was their equal, though woodcraft learned in hunts on the Tauran could never equal that ground into the souls of men on the savage border.

Below the fort the river made a wide bend. The lights of the outpost were quickly lost, but the canoe held on its way for nearly a mile, avoiding snags and floating logs with almost uncanny precision.

Then a low grunt from their leader, and they swung its head about and glided toward the opposite shore. Emerging from the black shadows of the brush that fringed the bank and coming into the open of the midstream created a peculiar illusion of rash exposure. But the stars gave little light, and Balthus knew that unless one were watching for it, it would be all but impossible for the keenest eye to make out the shadowy shape of the canoe crossing the river.

They swung in under the overhanging bushes of the western shore and Balthus groped for and found a projecting root which he grasped. No word was spoken. All instructions had been given before the scouting-party left the fort. As silently as a great panther Conan slid over the side and vanished in the bushes. Equally noiseless, nine men followed him. To Balthus, grasping the root with his paddle across his knee, it seemed incredible that ten men should thus fade into the tangled forest without a sound.

He settled himself to wait. No word passed between him and the other man who had been left with him. Somewhere, a mile or so to the northwest, Zogar Sag's village stood girdled with thick woods. Balthus understood his orders; he and his companion were to wait for the return of the raiding-party. If Conan and his men had not returned by the first tinge of dawn, they were to race back up the river to the fort and report that the forest had again taken its immemorial toll of the invading race. The silence was oppressive. No sound came from the black woods, invisible beyond the ebony masses that were the overhanging bushes. Balthus no longer heard the drums. They had been silent for hours. He kept blinking, unconsciously trying to see through the deep gloom. The dank night-smells of the river and the damp forest oppressed him. Somewhere, near by, there was a sound as if a big fish had flopped and splashed the water. Balthus thought it must have leaped so close to the canoe that it had struck the side, for a slight quiver vibrated the craft. The boat's stern began to swing, slightly away from the shore. The man behind him must have let go of the projection he was gripping. Balthus twisted his head to hiss a warning, and could just make out the figure of his companion, a slightly blacker bulk in the blackness.

The man did not reply. Wondering if he had fallen asleep, Balthus reached out and grasped his shoulder. To his amazement, the man crumpled under his touch and slumped down in the canoe. Twisting his body half about, Balthus groped for him, his heart shooting into his throat. His fumbling fingers slid over the man's throat—only the youth's convulsive clenching of his jaws choked back the cry that rose to his lips. His fingers encountered a gaping, oozing wound—his companion's throat had been cut from ear to ear.

In that instant of horror and panic Balthus started up—and then a muscular arm out of the darkness locked fiercely about his throat, strangling his yell. The canoe rocked wildly. Balthus' knife was in his hand, though he did not remember jerking it out of his boot, and he stabbed fiercely and blindly. He felt the blade sink deep, and a fiendish yell rang in his ear, a yell that was horribly answered. The darkness seemed to come to life about him. A bestial clamor rose on all sides, and other arms grappled him. Borne under a mass of hurtling bodies the canoe rolled sidewise, but before he went under with it, something cracked against Balthus' head and the night was briefly illuminated by a blinding burst of fire before it gave way to a blackness where not even stars shone.

4 The Beasts of Zogar Sag

Fires dazzled Balthus again as he slowly recovered his senses. He blinked, shook his head. Their glare hurt his eyes. A confused medley of sound rose about him, growing more distinct as his senses cleared.

He lifted his head and stared stupidly about him. Black figures hemmed him in, etched against crimson tongues of flame.

Memory and understanding came in a rush. He was bound upright to a post in an open space, ringed by fierce and terrible figures. Beyond that ring fires burned, tended by naked, dark-skinned women. Beyond the fires he saw huts of mud and wattle, thatched with brush. Beyond the huts there was a stockade with a broad gate. But he saw these things only incidentally. Even the cryptic dark women with their curious coiffures were noted by him only absently. His full attention was fixed in awful fascination on the men who stood glaring at him.

Short men, broad-shouldered, deep-chested, lean-hipped, they were naked except for scanty loin-clouts. The firelight brought out the play of their swelling muscles in bold relief. Their dark faces were immobile, but their narrow eyes glittered with the fire that burns in the eyes of a stalking tiger. Their tangled manes were bound back with bands of copper. Swords and axes were in their hands. Crude bandages banded the limbs of some, and smears of blood were dried on their dark skins. There had been fighting, recent and deadly.

His eyes wavered away from the steady glare of his captors, and he repressed a cry of horror. A few feet away there rose a low, hideous pyramid: it was built of gory human heads. Dead eyes glared glassily up at the black sky. Numbly he recognized the countenances which were turned toward him. They were the heads of the men who had followed Conan into the forest. He could not tell if the Cimmerian's head were among them. Only a few faces were visible to him. It looked to him as if there must be ten or eleven heads at least. A deadly sickness assailed him. He fought a desire to retch. Beyond the heads lay the bodies of half a dozen Picts, and he was aware of a fierce exultation at the sight. The forest runners had taken toll, at least.

Twisting his head away from the ghastly spectacle, he became aware that another post stood near him—a stake painted black as was the one to which he was bound. A man sagged in his bonds there, naked except for his leathern breeks, whom Balthus recognized as one of Conan's woodsmen. Blood trickled from his mouth, oozed sluggishly from a gash in his side. Lifting his head as he licked his livid lips, he muttered, making himself heard with difficulty above the fiendish clamor of the Picts: "So they got you, too!"

"Sneaked up in the water and cut the other fellow's throat," groaned Balthus. "We never heard them till they were on us. Mitra, how can anything move so silently?"

"They're devils," mumbled the frontiersman. "They must have been watching us from the time we left midstream. We walked into a trap. Arrows from all sides were ripping into us before we knew it. Most of us dropped at the first fire. Three or four broke through the bushes and came to hand-grips. But there were too many. Conan might have gotten away. I haven't seen his head. Been better for you and me if they'd killed us outright. I can't blame Conan. Ordinarily we'd have gotten to the village without being discovered. They don't keep spies on the river bank as far down as we landed. We must have stumbled into a big party coming up the river from the south. Some devilment is up. Too many Picts here. These aren't all Gwaweli; men from the western tribes here and from up and down the river."

Balthus stared at the ferocious shapes. Little as he knew of Pictish ways, he was aware that the number of men clustered about them was out of proportion to the size of the village. There were not enough huts to have accommodated them all. Then he noticed that there was a difference in the barbaric tribal designs painted on their faces and breasts.

"Some kind of devilment," muttered the forest runner. "They might have gathered here to watch Zogar's magic-making. He'll make some rare magic with our carcasses. Well, a border-man doesn't expect to die in bed. But I wish we'd gone out along with the rest."

The wolfish howling of the Picts rose in volume and exultation, and from a movement in their ranks, an eager surging and crowding, Balthus deduced that someone of importance was coming. Twisting his head about, he saw that the stakes were set before a long building, larger than the other huts, decorated by human skulls dangling from the eaves. Through the door of that structure now danced a fantastic figure.

"Zogar!" muttered the woodsman, his bloody countenance set in wolfish lines as he unconsciously strained at his cords. Balthus saw a lean figure of middle height, almost hidden in ostrich plumes set on a harness of leather and copper. From amidst the plumes peered a hideous and malevolent face. The plumes puzzled Balthus. He knew their source lay half the width of a world to the south. They fluttered and rustled evilly as the shaman leaped and cavorted.

With fantastic bounds and prancings he entered the ring and whirled before his bound and silent captives. With another man it would have seemed ridiculous—a foolish savage prancing meaninglessly in a whirl of feathers. But that ferocious face glaring out from the billowing mass gave the scene a grim significance. No man with a face like that could seem ridiculous or like anything except the devil he was.

Suddenly he froze to statuesque stillness; the plumes rippled once and sank about him. The howling warriors fell silent. Zogar Sag stood erect and motionless, and he seemed to increase in height—to grow and expand. Balthus experienced the illusion that the Pict was towering above him, staring contemptuously down from a great height, though he knew the shaman was not as tall as himself. He shook off the illusion with difficulty.

The shaman was talking now, a harsh, guttural intonation that yet carried the hiss of a cobra. He thrust his head on his long neck toward the wounded man on the stake; his eyes shone red as blood in the firelight. The frontiersman spat full in his face.

With a fiendish howl Zogar bounded convulsively into the air, and the warriors gave tongue to a yell that shuddered up to the stars. They rushed toward the man on the stake, but the shaman beat them back. A snarled command sent men running to the gate. They hurled it open, turned and raced back to the circle. The ring of men split, divided with desperate haste to right and left. Balthus saw the women and naked children scurrying to the huts. They peeked out of doors and windows. A broad lane was left to the open gate, beyond which loomed the black forest, crowding sullenly in upon the clearing, unlighted by the fires.

A tense silence reigned as Zogar Sag turned toward the forest, raised on his tiptoes and sent a weird inhuman call shuddering out into the night. Somewhere, far out in the black forest, a deeper cry answered him. Balthus shuddered. From the timbre of that cry he knew it never came from a human throat. He remembered what Valannus had said—that Zogar boasted that he could summon wild beasts to do his bidding. The woodsman was livid beneath his mask of blood. He licked his lips spasmodically.

The village held its breath. Zogar Sag stood still as a statue, his plumes trembling faintly about him. But suddenly the gate was no longer empty.

A shuddering gasp swept over the village and men crowded hastily back, jamming one another between the huts. Balthus felt the short hair stir on his scalp. The creature that stood in the gate was like the embodiment of nightmare legend. Its color was of a curious pale quality which made it seem ghostly and unreal in the dim light. But there was nothing unreal about the low-hung savage head, and the great curved fangs that glistened in the firelight. On noiseless padded feet it approached like a phantom out of the past. It was a survival of an older, grimmer age, the ogre of many an ancient legend—a saber-tooth tiger. No Hyborian hunter had looked upon one of those primordial brutes for centuries. Immemorial myths lent the creatures a supernatural quality, induced by their ghostly color and their fiendish ferocity.

The beast that glided toward the men on the stakes was longer and heavier than a common, striped tiger, almost as bulky as a bear. Its shoulders and forelegs were so massive and mightily muscled as to give it a curiously top-heavy look, though its hind-quarters were more powerful than that of a lion. Its jaws were massive, but its head was brutishly shaped. Its brain capacity was small. It had room for no instincts except those of destruction. It was a freak of carnivorous development, evolution run amuck in a horror of fangs and talons.

This was the monstrosity Zogar Sag had summoned out of the forest. Balthus no longer doubted the actuality of the shaman's magic. Only the black arts could establish a domination over that tiny-brained, mighty-thewed monster. Like a whisper at the back of his consciousness rose the vague memory of the name of an ancient god of darkness and primordial fear, to whom once both men and beasts bowed and whose children—men whispered—still lurked in dark corners of the world. New horror tinged the glare he fixed on Zogar Sag.

The monster moved past the heap of bodies and the pile of gory heads without appearing to notice them. He was no scavenger. He hunted only the living, in a life dedicated solely to slaughter. An awful hunger burned greenly in the wide, unwinking eyes; the hunger not alone of belly-emptiness, but the lust of death-dealing. His gaping jaws slavered. The shaman stepped back; his hand waved toward the woodsman.

The great cat sank into a crouch, and Balthus numbly remembered tales of its appalling ferocity: of how it would spring upon an elephant and drive its sword-like fangs so deeply into the titan's skull that they could never be withdrawn, but would keep it nailed to its victim, to die by starvation. The shaman cried out shrilly, and with an ear-shattering roar the monster sprang.

Balthus had never dreamed of such a spring, such a hurtling of incarnated destruction embodied in that giant bulk of iron thews and ripping talons. Full on the woodsman's breast it struck, and the stake splintered and snapped at the base, crashing to the earth under the impact. Then the saber-tooth was gliding toward the gate, half dragging, half carrying a hideous crimson hulk that only faintly resembled a man. Balthus glared almost paralysed, his brain refusing to credit what his eyes had seen.

In that leap the great beast had not only broken off the stake, it had ripped the mangled body of its victim from the post to which it was bound. The huge talons in that instant of contact had disemboweled and partially dismembered the man, and the giant fangs had torn away the whole top of his head, shearing through the skull as easily as through flesh. Stout rawhide thongs had given way like paper; where the thongs had held, flesh and bones had not. Balthus retched suddenly. He had hunted bears and panthers, but he had never dreamed the beast lived which could make such a red ruin of a human frame in the flicker of an instant.

The saber-tooth vanished through the gate, and a few moments later a deep roar sounded through the forest, receding in the distance. But the Picts still shrank back against the huts, and the shaman still stood facing the gate that was like a black opening to let in the night.

Cold sweat burst suddenly out on Balthus' skin. What new horror would come through that gate to make carrion-meat of his body? Sick panic assailed him and he strained futilely at his thongs. The night pressed in very black and horrible outside the firelight. The fires themselves glowed lurid as the fires of Hell. He felt the eyes of the Picts upon him— hundreds of hungry, cruel eyes that reflected the lust of souls utterly without humanity as he knew it. They no longer seemed men; they were devils of this black jungle, as inhuman as the creatures to which the fiend in the nodding plumes screamed through the darkness.

Zogar sent another call shuddering through the night, and it was utterly unlike the first cry. There was a hideous sibilance in it—Balthus turned cold at the implication. If a serpent could hiss that loud, it would make just such a sound.

This time there was no answer—only a period of breathless silence in which the pound of Balthus' heart strangled him; and then there sounded a swishing outside the gate, a dry rustling that sent chills down Balthus' spine. Again the firelit gate held a hideous occupant.

Again Balthus recognized the monster from ancient legends. He saw and knew the ancient and evil serpent which swayed there, its wedge-shaped head, huge as that of a horse, as high as a tall man's head, and its palely gleaming barrel rippling out behind it. A forked tongue darted in and out, and the firelight glittered on bared fangs.

Balthus became incapable of emotion. The horror of his fate para-lysed him. That was the reptile that the ancients called Ghost Snake, the pale, abominable terror that of old glided into huts by night to devour whole families. Like the python it crushed its victim, but unlike other constrictors its fangs bore venom that carried madness and death. It too had long been considered extinct. But Valannus had spoken truly. No white man knew what shapes haunted the great forests beyond Black River.

It came on silently rippling over the ground, its hideous head on the same level, its neck curving back slightly for the stroke. Balthus gazed with glazed, hypnotized stare into that loathesome gullet down which he would soon be engulfed, and he was aware of no sensation except a vague nausea.

And then something that glinted in the firelight streaked from the shadows of the huts, and the great reptile whipped about and went into instant convulsions. As in a dream Balthus saw a short throwing-spear transfixing the mighty neck, just below the gaping jaws; the shaft protruded from one side, the steel head from the other.

Knotting and looping hideously, the maddened reptile rolled into the circle of men who strove back from him. The spear had not severed its spine, but merely transfixed its great neck muscles. Its furiously lashing tail mowed down a dozen men and its jaws snapped convulsively, splashing others with venom that burned like liquid fire. Howling, cursing, screaming, frantic, they scattered before it, knocking each other down in their flight, trampling the fallen, bursting through the huts. The giant snake rolled into a fire, scattering sparks and brands, and the pain lashed it to more frenzied efforts. A hut wall buckled under the ram-like impact of its flailing tail, disgorging howling people.

Men stampeded through the fires, knocking the logs right and left. The flames sprang up, then sank. A reddish dim glow was all that lighted that nightmare scene where the giant reptile whipped and rolled, and men clawed and shrieked in frantic flight.

Balthus felt something jerk at his wrists, and then, miraculously, he was free, and a strong hand dragged him behind the post. Dazedly he saw Conan, felt the forest man's iron grip on his arm.

There was blood on the Cimmerian's mail, dried blood on the sword in his right hand; he loomed dim and gigantic in the shadowy light.

"Come on! Before they get over their panic!"

Balthus felt the haft of an ax shoved into his hand. Zogar Sag had disappeared. Conan dragged Balthus after him until the youth's numb brain awoke, and his legs began to move of their own accord. Then Conan released him and ran into the building where the skulls hung.

Balthus followed him. He got a glimpse of a grim stone altar, faintly lighted by the glow outside; five human heads grinned on that altar, and there was a grisly familiarity about the features of the freshest; it was the head of the merchant Tiberias. Behind the altar was an idol, dim, indistinct, bestial, yet vaguely man-like in outline. Then fresh horror choked Balthus as the shape heaved up suddenly with a rattle of chains, lifting long misshapen arms in the gloom.

Conan's sword flailed down, crunching through flesh and bone, and then the Cimmerian was dragging Balthus around the altar, past a huddled shaggy bulk on the floor, to a door at the back of the long hut. Through this they burst, out into the enclosure again. But a few yards beyond them loomed the stockade.

It was dark behind the altar-hut. The mad stampede of the Picts had not carried them in that direction. At the wall Conan halted, gripped Balthus and heaved him at arm's length into the air as he might have lifted a child. Balthus grasped the points of the upright logs set in the sun-dried mud and scrambled up on them, ignoring the havoc done his skin. He lowered a hand to the Cimmerian, when around a corner of the altar-hut sprang a fleeing Pict. He halted short, glimpsing the man on the wall in the faint glow of the fires. Conan hurled his ax with deadly aim, but the warrior's mouth was already open for a yell of warning, and it rang loud above the din, cut short as he dropped with a shattered skull.

Blinding terror had not submerged all ingrained instincts. As that wild yell rose above the clamor, there was an instant's lull, and then a hundred throats bayed ferocious answer and warriors came leaping to repel the attack presaged by the warning.

Conan leaped high, caught, not Balthus' hand but his arm near the shoulder, and swung himself up. Balthus set his teeth against the strain, and then the Cimmerian was on the wall beside him, and the fugitives dropped down on the other side.

5 The Children of Jhebbal Sag

"Which way is the river?" Balthus was confused.

"We don't dare try for the river now," grunted Conan. "The woods between the village and the river are swarming with warriors. Come on! We'll head in the last direction they'll expect us to go—west!"

Looking back as they entered the thick growth, Balthus beheld the wall dotted with black heads as the savages peered over. The Picts were bewildered. They had not gained the wall in time to see the fugitives take cover. They had rushed to the wall expecting to repel an attack in force. They had seen the body of the dead warrior. But no enemy was in sight. Balthus realized that they did not yet know their prisoner had escaped. From other sounds he believed that the warriors, directed by the shrill voice of Zogar Sag, were destroying the wounded serpent with arrows. The monster was out of the shaman's control. A moment later the quality of the yells was altered. Screeches of rage rose in the night.

Conan laughed grimly. He was leading Balthus along a narrow trail that ran west under the black branches, stepping as swiftly and surely as if he trod a well-lighted thoroughfare. Balthus stumbled after him, guiding himself by feeling the dense wall on either hand.

"They'll be after us now. Zogar's discovered you're gone, and he knows my head wasn't in the pile before the altar-hut. The dog! If I'd had another spear I'd have thrown it through him before I struck the snake. Keep to the trail. They can't track us by torchlight, and there are a score of paths leading from the village. They'll follow those leading to the river first—throw a cordon of warriors for miles along the bank, expecting us to try to break through. We won't take to the woods until we have to. We can make better time on this trail. Now buckle down to it and run as you never ran before."

"They got over their panic cursed quick!" panted Balthus, complying with a fresh burst of speed.

"They're not afraid of anything, very long," grunted Conan.

For a space nothing was said between them. The fugitives devoted all their attention to covering distance. They were plunging deeper and deeper into the wilderness and getting farther away from civilization at every step, but Balthus did not question Conan's wisdom. The Cimmerian presently took time to grunt: "When we're far enough away from the village we'll swing back to the river in a big circle. No other village within miles of Gwawela. All the Picts are gathered in that vicinity. We'll circle wide around them. They can't track us until daylight. They'll pick up our path then, but before dawn we'll leave the trail and take to the woods."

They plunged on. The yells died out behind them. Balthus' breath was whistling through his teeth. He felt a pain in his side, and running became torture. He blundered against the bushes on each side of the trail. Conan pulled up suddenly, turned and stared back down the dim path.

Somewhere the moon was rising, a dim white glow amidst a tangle of branches.

"Shall we take to the woods?" panted Balthus.

"Give me your ax," murmured Conan softly. "Something is close behind us."

"Then we'd better leave the trail!" exclaimed Balthus.

Conan shook his head and drew his companion into a dense thicket. The moon rose higher, making a dim light in the path.

"We can't fight the whole tribe!" whispered Balthus.

"No human being could have found our trail so quickly, or followed us so swiftly," muttered Conan. "Keep silent."

There followed a tense silence in which Balthus felt that his heart could be heard pounding for miles away. Then abruptly, without a sound to announce its coming, a savage head appeared in the dim path. Balthus' heart jumped into his throat; at first glance he feared to look upon the awful head of the saber-tooth. But this head was smaller, more narrow; it was a leopard which stood there, snarling silently and glaring down the trail. What wind there was was blowing toward the hiding men, concealing their scent. The beast lowered his head and snuffed the trail, then moved forward uncertainly. A chill played down Balthus' spine. The brute was undoubtedly trailing them.

And it was suspicious. It lifted its head, its eyes glowing like balls of fire, and growled low in its throat. And at that instant Conan hurled the ax.

All the weight of arm and shoulder was behind the throw, and the ax was a streak of silver in the dim moon. Almost before he realized what had happened, Balthus saw the leopard rolling on the ground in its death-throes, the handle of the ax standing up from its head. The head of the weapon had split its narrow skull.

Conan bounded from the bushes, wrenched his ax free and dragged the limp body in among the trees, concealing it from the casual glance.

"Now let's go, and go fast!" he grunted, leading the way southward, away from the trail. "There'll be warriors coming after that cat. As soon as he got his wits back Zogar sent him after us. The Picts would follow him, but he'd leave them far behind. He'd circle the village until he hit our trail and then come after us like a streak. They couldn't keep up with him, but they'll have an idea as to our general direction. They'd follow, listening for his cry. Well, they won't hear that, but they'll find the blood on the trail, and look around and find the body in the brush. They'll pick up our spoor there, if they can. Walk with care."

He avoided clinging briars and low-hanging branches effortlessly, gliding between trees without touching the stems and always planting his feet in the places calculated to show least evidence of his passing; but with Balthus it was slower, more laborious work.

No sound came from behind them. They had covered more than a mile when Balthus said: "Does Zogar Sag catch leopard-cubs and train them for bloodhounds?"

Conan shook his head. "That was a leopard he called out of the woods."

"But," Balthus persisted, "if he can order the beasts to do his bidding, why doesn't he rouse them all and have them after us? The forest is full of leopards; why send only one after us?"

Conan did not reply for a space, and when he did it was with a curious reticence.

"He can't command all the animals. Only such as remember Jhebbal Sag."

"Jhebbal Sag?" Balthus repeated the ancient name hesitantly. He had never heard it spoken more than three or four times in his whole life.

"Once all living things worshiped him. That was long ago, when beasts and men spoke one language. Men have forgotten him; even the beasts forget. Only a few remember. The men who remember Jhebbal Sag and the beasts who remember are brothers and speak the same tongue."

Balthus did not reply; he had strained at a Pictish stake and seen the nighted jungle give up its fanged horrors at a shaman's call.

"Civilized men laugh," said Conan. "But not one can tell me how Zogar Sag can call pythons and tigers and leopards out of the wilderness and make them do his bidding. They would say it is a lie, if they dared. That's the way with civilized men. When they can't explain something by their half-baked science, they refuse to believe it."

The people on the Tauran were closer to the primitive than most Aquilonians; superstitions persisted, whose sources were lost in antiquity. And Balthus had seen that which still prickled his flesh. He could not refute the monstrous thing which Conan's words implied.

"I've heard that there's an ancient grove sacred to Jhebbal Sag somewhere in this forest," said Conan. "I don't know. I've never seen it. But more beasts remember in this country than any I've ever seen."

"Then others will be on our trail?"

"They are now," was Conan's disquieting answer. "Zogar would never leave our tracking to one beast alone."

"What are we to do, then?" asked Balthus uneasily, grasping his ax as he stared at the gloomy arches above him. His flesh crawled with the momentary expectation of ripping talons and fangs leaping from the shadows.

"Wait!"

Conan turned, squatted and with his knife began scratching a curious symbol in the mold. Stooping to look at it over his shoulder, Balthus felt a crawling of the flesh along his spine, he knew not why. He felt no wind against his face, but there was a rustling of leaves above them and a weird moaning swept ghostily through the branches. Conan glanced up inscrutably, then rose and stood staring somberly down at the symbol he had drawn.

"What is it?" whispered Balthus. It looked archaic and meaningless to him. He supposed that it was his ignorance of artistry which prevented his identifying it as one of the conventional designs of some prevailing culture. But had he been the most erudite artist in the world, he would have been no nearer the solution.

"I saw it carved in the rock of a cave no human had visited for a million years," muttered Conan, "in the uninhabited mountains beyond the Sea of Vilayet, half a world away from this spot. Later I saw a black witch-finder of Kush scratch it in the sand of a nameless river. He told me part of its meaning—it's sacred to Jhebbal Sag and the creatures which worship him. Watch!"

They drew back among the dense foliage some yards away and waited in tense silence. To the east drums muttered and somewhere to north and west other drums answered. Balthus shivered, though he knew long miles of black forest separated him from the grim beaters of those drums whose dull pulsing was a sinister overture that set the dark stage for bloody drama.

Balthus found himself holding his breath. Then with a slight shaking of the leaves, the bushes parted and a magnificent panther came into view. The moonlight dappling through the leaves shone on its glossy coat rippling with the play of the great muscles beneath it.

With its head held low it glided toward them. It was smelling out their trail. Then it halted as if frozen, its muzzle almost touching the symbol cut in the mold. For a long space it crouched motionless; it flattened its long body and laid its head on the ground before the mark. And Balthus felt the short hairs stir on his scalp. For the attitude of the great carnivore was one of awe and adoration.

Then the panther rose and backed away carefully, belly almost to the ground. With his hind-quarters among the bushes he wheeled as if in sudden panic and was gone like a flash of dappled light.

Balthus mopped his brow with a trembling hand and glanced at Conan.

The barbarian's eyes were smoldering with fires that never lit the eyes of men bred to the ideas of civilization. In that instant he was all wild, and had forgotten the man at his side. In his burning gaze Balthus glimpsed and vaguely recognized pristine images and half-embodied memories, shadows from Life's dawn, forgotten and repudiated by sophisticated races—ancient, primeval fantasms unnamed and nameless.

Then the deeper fires were masked and Conan was silently leading the way deeper into the forest.

"We've no more to fear from the beasts," he said after a while, "but we've left a sign for men to read. They won't follow our trail very easily, and until they find that symbol they won't know for sure we've turned south. Even then it won't be easy to smell us out without the beasts to aid them. But the woods south of the trail will be full of warriors looking for us. If we keep moving after daylight, we'll be sure to run into some of them. As soon as we find a good place we'll hide and wait until another night to swing back and make the river. We've got to warn Valannus, but it won't help him any if we get ourselves killed."

"Warn Valannus?"

"Hell, the woods along the river are swarming with Picts! That's why they got us. Zogar's brewing war-magic; no mere raid this time. He's done something no Pict has done in my memory—united as many as fifteen or sixteen clans. His magic did it; they'll follow a wizard farther than they will a war-chief. You saw the mob in the village; and there were hundreds hiding along the river bank that you didn't see. More coming, from the farther villages. He'll have at least three thousand fighting-men. I lay in the bushes and heard their talk as they went past. They mean to attack the fort; when, I don't know, but Zogar doesn't dare delay long. He's gathered them and whipped them into a frenzy. If he doesn't lead them into battle quickly, they'll fall to quarreling with one another. They're like blood-mad tigers.

"I don't know whether they can take the fort or not. Anyway, we've got to get back across the river and give the warning. The settlers on the Velitrium road must either get into the fort or back to Velitrium.

While the Picts are besieging the fort, war-parties will range the road far to the east—might even cross Thunder River and raid the thickly settled country behind Velitrium."

As he talked he was leading the way deeper and deeper into the ancient wilderness. Presently he grunted with satisfaction. They had reached a spot where the underbrush was more scattered, and an out-cropping of stone was visible, wandering off southward. Balthus felt more secure as they followed it. Not even a Pict could trail them over naked rock.

"How did you get away?" he asked presently.

Conan tapped his mail-shirt and helmet.

"If more borderers would wear harness there'd be fewer skulls hang-ing on the altar-huts. But most men make noise if they wear armor. They were waiting on each side of the path, without moving. And when a Pict stands motionless, the very beasts of the forest pass him without seeing him. They'd seen us crossing the river and got in their places. If they'd gone into ambush after we left the bank, I'd have had some hint of it. But they were waiting, and not even a leaf trembled. The devil himself couldn't have suspected anything. The first suspicion I had was when I heard a shaft rasp against a bow as it was pulled back. I dropped and yelled for the men behind me to drop, but they were too slow, taken by surprise like that.

"Most of them fell at the first volley that raked us from both sides. Some of the arrows crossed the trail and struck Picts on the other side. I heard them howl." He grinned with vicious satisfaction. "Such of us as were left plunged into the woods and closed with them. When I saw the others were all down or taken, I broke through and outfooted the painted devils through the darkness. They were all around me. I ran and crawled and sneaked, and sometimes I lay on my belly under the bushes while they passed me on all sides.

"I tried for the shore and found it lined with them, waiting for just such a move. But I'd have cut my way through and taken a chance on swimming, only I heard the drums pounding in the village and knew they'd taken somebody alive.

"They were all so engrossed in Zogar's magic that I was able to climb the wall behind the altar-hut. There was a warrior supposed to be watching at that point, but he was squatting behind the hut and peering around the corner at the ceremony. I came up behind him and broke his neck with my hands before he knew what was happening. It was his spear I threw into the snake, and that's his ax you're carrying."

"But what was that—that thing you killed in the altar-hut?" asked Balthus, with a shiver at the memory of the dim-seen horror.

"One of Zogar's gods. One of Jhebbal's children that didn't remember and had to be kept chained to the altar. A bull ape. The Picts think they're sacred to the Hairy One who lives on the moon—the gorilla-god of Gullah. "It's getting light. Here's a good place to hide until we see how close they're on our trail. Probably have to wait until night to break back to the river."

A low hill pitched upward, girdled and covered with thick trees and bushes. Near the crest Conan slid into a tangle of jutting rocks, crowned by dense bushes. Lying among them they could see the jungle below without being seen. It was a good place to hide or defend.

Balthus did not believe that even a Pict could have trailed them over the rocky ground for the past four or five miles, but he was afraid of the beasts that obeyed Zogar Sag. His faith in the curious symbol wavered a little now. But Conan had dismissed the possibility of beasts tracking them.

A ghostly whiteness spread through the dense branches; the patches of sky visible altered in hue, grew from pink to blue. Balthus felt the gnawing of hunger, though he had slaked his thirst at a stream they had skirted. There was complete silence, except for an occasional chirp of a bird. The drums were no longer to be heard. Balthus' thoughts reverted to the grim scene before the altar-hut.

"Those were ostrich plumes Zogar Sag wore," he said. "I've seen them on the helmets of knights who rode from the East to visit the barons of the marches. There are no ostriches in this forest, are there?"

"They came from Kush," answered Conan. "West of here, many marches, lies the seashore. Ships from Zingara occasionally come and trade weapons and ornaments and wine to the coastal tribes for skins and copper ore and gold dust. Sometimes they trade ostrich plumes they got from the Stygians, who in turn got them from the black tribes of Kush, which lies south of Stygia. The Pictish shamans place great store by them. But there's much risk in such trade. The Picts are too likely to try to seize the ship. And the coast is dangerous to ships. I've sailed along it when I was with the pirates of the Barachan Isles, which lie southwest of Zingara."

Balthus looked at his companion with admiration.

"I knew you hadn't spent your life on this frontier. You've mentioned several far places. You've traveled widely?"

"I've roamed far; farther than any other man of my race ever wandered. I've seen all the great cities of the Hyborians, the Shemites, the Stygians and the Hyrkanians. I've roamed in the unknown countries south of the black kingdoms of Kush, and east of the Sea of Vilayet. I've been a mercenary captain, a corsair, a kozak, a penniless vagabond, a general—hell, I've been everything except a king, and I may be that, before I die." The fancy pleased him, and he grinned hardly. Then he shrugged his shoulders and stretched his mighty figure on the rocks. "This is as good life as any. I don't know how long I'll stay on the frontier; a week, a month, a year. I have a roving foot. But it's as well on the border as anywhere."

Balthus set himself to watch the forest below them. Momentarily he expected to see fierce painted faces thrust through the leaves. But as the hours passed no stealthy footfall disturbed the brooding quiet. Balthus believed the Picts had missed their trail and given up the chase. Conan grew restless.

"We should have sighted parties scouring the woods for us. If they've quit the chase, it's because they're after bigger game. They may be gathering to cross the river and storm the fort."

"Would they come this far south if they lost the trail?"

"They've lost the trail, all right; otherwise they'd have been on our necks before now. Under ordinary circumstances they'd scour the woods for miles in every direction. Some of them should have passed within sight of this hill. They must be preparing to cross the river. We've got to take a chance and make for the river."

Creeping down the rocks Balthus felt his flesh crawl between his shoulders as he momentarily expected a withering blast of arrows from the green masses about them. He feared that the Picts had discovered them and were lying about in ambush. But Conan was convinced no enemies were near, and the Cimmerian was right.

"We're miles to the south of the village," grunted Conan. "We'll hit straight through for the river. I don't know how far down the river they've spread. We'll hope to hit it below them."

With haste that seemed reckless to Balthus they hurried eastward. The woods seemed empty of life. Conan believed that all the Picts were gathered in the vicinity of Gwawela, if indeed, they had not already crossed the river. He did not believe they would cross in the daytime, however.

"Some woodsman would be sure to see them and give the alarm. They'll cross above and below the fort, out of sight of the sentries.

Then others will get in canoes and make straight across for the river wall. As soon as they attack, those hidden in the woods on the east shore will assail the fort from the other sides. They've tried that before, and got the guts shot and hacked out of them. But this time they've got enough men to make a real onslaught of it."

They pushed on without pausing, though Balthus gazed longingly at the squirrels flitting among the branches, which he could have brought down with a cast of his ax. With a sigh he drew up his broad belt. The everlasting silence and gloom of the primitive forest was beginning to depress him. He found himself thinking of the open groves and sun-dappled meadows of the Tauran, of the bluff cheer of his father's steep-thatched, diamond-paned house, of the fat cows browsing through the deep, lush grass, and the hearty fellowship of the brawny, bare-armed plowmen and herdsmen.

He felt lonely, in spite of his companion. Conan was as much a part of this wilderness as Balthus was alien to it. The Cimmerian might have spent years among the great cities of the world; he might have walked with the rulers of civilization; he might even achieve his wild whim some day and rule as king of a civilized nation; stranger things had happened. But he was no less a barbarian. He was concerned only with the naked fundamentals of life. The warm intimacies of small, kindly things, the sentiments and delicious trivialities that make up so much of civilized men's lives were meaningless to him. A wolf was no less a wolf because a whim of chance caused him to run with the watchdogs. Bloodshed and violence and savagery were the natural elements of the life Conan knew; he could not, and would never, understand the little things that are so dear to civilized men and women.

The shadows were lengthening when they reached the river and peered through the masking bushes. They could see up and down the river for about a mile each way. The sullen stream lay bare and empty. Conan scowled across at the other shore.

"We've got to take another chance here. We've got to swim the river. We don't know whether they've crossed or not. The woods over there may be alive with them. We've got to risk it. We're about six miles south of Gwawela."

He wheeled and ducked as a bow-string twanged. Something like a white flash of light streaked through the bushes. Balthus knew it was an arrow. Then with a tigerish bound Conan was through the bushes. Balthus caught the gleam of steel as he whirled his sword, and heard a death scream. The next instant he had broken through the bushes after the Cimmerian.

A Pict with a shattered skull lay face-down on the ground, his fingers spasmodically clawing at the grass. Half a dozen others were swarming about Conan, swords and axes lifted. They had cast away their bows, useless at such deadly close quarters. Their lower jaws were painted white, contrasting vividly with their dark faces, and the designs on their muscular breasts differed from any Balthus had ever seen.

One of them hurled his ax at Balthus and rushed after it with lifted knife. Balthus ducked and then caught the wrist that drove the knife licking at his throat. They went to the ground together, rolling over and over. The Pict was like a wild beast, his muscles hard as steel strings.

Balthus was striving to maintain his hold on the wild man's wrist and bring his own ax into play, but so fast and furious was the struggle that each attempt to strike was blocked. The Pict was wrenching furiously to free his knife hand, was clutching at Balthus' ax, and driving his knees at the youth's groin. Suddenly he attempted to shift his knife to his free hand, and in that instant Balthus, struggling up on one knee, split the painted head with a desperate blow of his ax.

He sprang up and glared wildly about for his companion, expecting to see him overwhelmed by numbers. Then he realized the full strength and ferocity of the Cimmerian. Conan bestrode two of his attackers, shorn half asunder by that terrible broadsword. As Balthus looked he saw the Cimmerian beat down a thrusting shortsword, avoid the stroke of an ax with a cat-like sidewise spring which brought him within arm's length of a squat savage stooping for a bow. Before the Pict could straighten, the red sword flailed down and clove him from shoulder to mid-breastbone, where the blade stuck. The remaining warriors rushed in, one from either side. Balthus hurled his ax with an accuracy that reduced the attackers to one, and Conan, abandoning his efforts to free his sword, wheeled and met the remaining Pict with his bare hands. The stocky warrior, a head shorter than his tall enemy, leaped in, striking with his ax, at the same time stabbing murderously with his knife. The knife broke on the Cimmerian's mail, and the ax checked in mid-air as Conan's fingers locked like iron on the descending arm. A bone snapped loudly, and Balthus saw the Pict wince and falter. The next instant he was swept off his feet, lifted high above the Cimmerian's head—he writhed in midair for an instant, kicking and thrashing, and then was dashed headlong to the earth with such force that he rebounded, and then lay still, his limp posture telling of splintered limbs and a broken spine.

"Come on!" Conan wrenched his sword free and snatched up an ax. "Grab a bow and a handful of arrows, and hurry! We've got to trust to our heels again. That yell was heard. They'll be here in no time. If we tried to swim now, they'd feather us with arrows before we reached midstream!"

6 Red Axes of the Border

Conan did not plunge deeply into the forest. A few hundred yards from the river, he altered his slanting course and ran parallel with it. Balthus recognized a grim determination not to be hunted away from the river which they must cross if they were to warn the men in the fort. Behind them rose more loudly the yells of the forest men. Balthus believed the Picts had reached the glade where the bodies of the slain men lay. Then further yells seemed to indicate that the savages were streaming into the woods in pursuit. They had left a trail any Pict could follow.

Conan increased his speed, and Balthus grimly set his teeth and kept on his heels, though he felt he might collapse any time. It seemed centuries since he had eaten last. He kept going more by an effort of will than anything else. His blood was pounding so furiously in his eardrums that he was not aware when the yells died out behind them.

Conan halted suddenly. Balthus leaned against a tree and panted.

"They've quit!" grunted the Cimmerian, scowling.

"Sneaking—up—on—us!" gasped Balthus.

Conan shook his head.

"A short chase like this they'd yell every step of the way. No. They've gone back. I thought I heard somebody yelling behind them a few seconds before the noise began to get dimmer. They've been recalled. And that's good for us, but damned bad for the men in the fort. It means the warriors are being summoned out of the woods for the attack. These men we ran into were warriors from a tribe down the river. They were undoubtedly headed for Gwawela to join in the assault on the fort. Damn it, we're farther away than ever, now. We've got to get across the river."

Turning east he hurried through the thickets with no attempt at concealment. Balthus followed him, for the first time feeling the sting of lacerations on his breast and shoulder where the Pict's savage teeth had scored him. He was pushing through the thick bushes that fringed the bank when Conan pulled him back. Then he heard a rhythmic splashing, and peering through the leaves, saw a dugout canoe coming up the river, its single occupant paddling hard against the current. He was a strongly built Pict with a white heron feather thrust in a copper band that confined his square-cut mane.

"That's a Gwawela man," muttered Conan. "Emissary from Zogar. White plume shows that. He's carried a peace talk to the tribes down the river and now he's trying to get back and take a hand in the slaughter."

The lone ambassador was now almost even with their hiding-place, and suddenly Balthus almost jumped out of his skin. At his very ear had sounded the harsh gutturals of a Pict. Then he realized that Conan had called to the paddler in his own tongue. The man started, scanned the bushes and called back something, then cast a startled glance across the river, bent low and sent the canoe shooting in toward the western bank. Not understanding, Balthus saw Conan take from his hand the bow he had picked up in the glade, and notch an arrow.

The Pict had run his canoe in close to the shore, and staring up into the bushes, called out something. His answer came in the twang of the bow-string, the streaking flight of the arrow that sank to the feathers in his broad breast. With a choking gasp he slumped sidewise and rolled into the shallow water. In an instant Conan was down the bank and wading into the water to grasp the drifting canoe. Balthus stumbled after him and somewhat dazedly crawled into the canoe. Conan scrambled in, seized the paddle and sent the craft shooting toward the eastern shore. Balthus noted with envious admiration the play of the great muscles beneath the sun-burnt skin. The Cimmerian seemed an iron man, who never knew fatigue.

"What did you say to the Pict?" asked Balthus.

"Told him to pull into shore; said there was a white forest runner on the bank who was trying to get a shot at him."

"That doesn't seem fair," Balthus objected. "He thought a friend was speaking to him. You mimicked a Pict perfectly—"

"We needed his boat," grunted Conan, not pausing in his exertions. "Only way to lure him to the bank. Which is worse—to betray a Pict who'd enjoy skinning us both alive, or betray the men across the river whose lives depend on our getting over?"

Balthus mulled over this delicate ethical question for a moment, then shrugged his shoulder and asked: "How far are we from the fort?"

Conan pointed to a creek which flowed into Black River from the east, a few hundred yards below them.

"That's South Creek; it's ten miles from its mouth to the fort. It's the southern boundary of Conajohara. Marshes miles wide south of it. No danger of a raid from across them. Nine miles above the fort North Creek forms the other boundary. Marshes beyond that, too. That's why an attack must come from the west, across Black River. Conajohara's just like a spear, with a point nineteen miles wide, thrust into the Pictish wilderness."

"Why don't we keep to the canoe and make the trip by water?"

"Because, considering the current we've got to brace, and the bends in the river, we can go faster afoot. Besides, remember Gwawela is south of the fort; if the Picts are crossing the river we'd run right into them."

★ ★ ★

Dusk was gathering as they stepped upon the eastern bank. Without pause Conan pushed on northward, at a pace that made Balthus' sturdy legs ache.

"Valannus wanted a fort built at the mouths of North and South Creeks," grunted the Cimmerian. "Then the river could be patrolled constantly. But the Government wouldn't do it.

"Soft-bellied fools sitting on velvet cushions with naked girls offering them iced wine on their knees—I know the breed. They can't see any farther than their palace wall. Diplomacy—hell! They'd fight Picts with theories of territorial expansion. Valannus and men like him have to obey the orders of a set of damned fools. They'll never grab any more Pictish land, any more than they'll ever rebuild Venarium. The time may come when they'll see the barbarians swarming over the walls of the Eastern cities!"

A week before, Balthus would have laughed at any such preposterous suggestion. Now he made no reply. He had seen the unconquerable ferocity of the men who dwelt beyond the frontiers.

He shivered, casting glances at the sullen river, just visible through the bushes, at the arches of the trees which crowded close to its banks. He kept remembering that the Picts might have crossed the river and be lying in ambush between them and the fort. It was fast growing dark.

A slight sound ahead of them jumped his heart into his throat, and Conan's sword gleamed in the air. He lowered it when a dog, a great, gaunt, scarred beast, slunk out of the bushes and stood staring at them.

"That dog belonged to a settler who tried to build his cabin on the bank of the river a few miles south of the fort," grunted Conan. "The Picts slipped over and killed him, of course, and burned his cabin. We found him dead among the embers, and the dog lying senseless among three Picts he'd killed. He was almost cut to pieces. We took him to the fort and dressed his wounds, but after he recovered he took to the woods and turned wild.—What now, Slasher, are you hunting the men who killed your master?"

The massive head swung from side to side and the eyes glowed greenly. He did not growl or bark. Silently as a phantom he slid in behind them.

"Let him come," muttered Conan. "He can smell the devils before we can see them."

Balthus smiled and laid his hand caressingly on the dog's head. The lips involuntarily writhed back to display the gleaming fangs; then the great beast bent his head sheepishly, and his tail moved with jerky uncertainty, as if the owner had almost forgotten the emotions of friendliness. Balthus mentally compared the great gaunt hard body with the fat sleek hounds tumbling vociferously over one another in his father's kennel yard. He sighed. The frontier was no less hard for beasts than for men. This dog had almost forgotten the meaning of kindness and friendliness.

Slasher glided ahead, and Conan let him take the lead. The last tinge of dusk faded into stark darkness. The miles fell away under their steady feet. Slasher seemed voiceless. Suddenly he halted, tense, ears lifted. An instant later the men heard it—a demoniac yelling up the river ahead of them, faint as a whisper.

Conan swore like a madman.

"They've attacked the fort! We're too late! Come on!"

He increased his pace, trusting to the dog to smell out ambushes ahead. In a flood of tense excitement Balthus forgot his hunger and weariness. The yells grew louder as they advanced, and above the devilish screaming they could hear the deep shouts of the soldiers. Just as Balthus began to fear they would run into the savages who seemed to be howling just ahead of them, Conan swung away from the river in a wide semicircle that carried them to a low rise from which they could look over the forest. They saw the fort, lighted with torches thrust over the parapets on long poles. These cast a flickering, uncertain light over the clearing, and in that light they saw throngs of naked, painted figures along the fringe of the clearing. The river swarmed with canoes. The Picts had the fort completely surrounded.

An incessant hail of arrows rained against the stockade from the woods and the river. The deep twanging of the bow-strings rose above the howling. Yelling like wolves, several hundred naked warriors with axes in their hands ran from under the trees and raced toward the eastern gate. They were within a hundred and fifty yards of their objective when a withering blast of arrows from the wall littered the ground with corpses and sent the survivors fleeing back to the trees. The men in the canoes rushed their boats toward the river-wall, and were met by another shower of clothyard shafts and a volley from the small ballistae mounted on towers on that side of the stockade. Stones and logs whirled through the air and splintered and sank half a dozen canoes, killing their occupants, and the other boats drew back out of range. A deep roar of triumph rose from the walls of the fort, answered by bestial howling from all quarters.

"Shall we try to break through?" asked Balthus, trembling with eagerness.

Conan shook his head. He stood with his arms folded, his head slightly bent, a somber and brooding figure.

"The fort's doomed. The Picts are blood-mad, and won't stop until they're all killed. And there are too many of them for the men in the fort to kill. We couldn't break through, and if we did, we could do nothing but die with Valannus."

"There's nothing we can do but save our own hides, then?"

"Yes. We've got to warn the settlers. Do you know why the Picts are not trying to burn the fort with fire-arrows? Because they don't want a flame that might warn the people to the east. They plan to stamp out the fort, and then sweep east before anyone knows of its fall. They may cross Thunder River and take Velitrium before the people know what's happened. At least they'll destroy every living thing between the fort and Thunder River.

"We've failed to warn the fort, and I see now it would have done no good if we had succeeded. The fort's too poorly manned. A few more charges and the Picts will be over the walls and breaking down the gates. But we can start the settlers toward Velitrium. Come on! We're outside the circle the Picts have thrown around the fort. We'll keep clear of it."

They swung out in a wide arc, hearing the rising and falling of the volume of the yells, marking each charge and repulse. The men in the fort were holding their own; but the shrieks of the Picts did not diminish in savagery. They vibrated with a timbre that held assurance of ultimate victory.

Before Balthus realized they were close to it, they broke into the road leading east.

"Now run!" grunted Conan. Balthus set his teeth. It was nineteen miles to Velitrium, a good five to Scalp Creek beyond which began the settlements. It seemed to the Aquilonian that they had been fighting and running for centuries. But the nervous excitement that rioted through his blood stimulated him to Herculean efforts.

Slasher ran ahead of them, his head to the ground, snarling low, the first sound they had heard from him.

"Picts ahead of us!" snarled Conan, dropping to one knee and scanning the ground in the starlight. He shook his head, baffled. "I can't tell how many. Probably only a small party. Some that couldn't wait to take the fort. They've gone ahead to butcher the settlers in their beds! Come on!"

Ahead of them presently they saw a small blaze through the trees, and heard a wild and ferocious chanting. The trail bent there, and leaving it, they cut across the bend, through the thickets. A few moments later they were looking on a hideous sight. An ox-wain stood in the road piled with meager household furnishings; it was burning; the oxen lay near with their throats cut. A man and a woman lay in the road, stripped and mutilated. Five Picts were dancing about them with fantastic leaps and bounds, waving bloody axes; one of them brandished the woman's red-smeared gown.

At the sight a red haze swam before Balthus. Lifting his bow he lined the prancing figure, black against the fire, and loosed. The slayer leaped convulsively and fell dead with the arrow through his heart. Then the two white men and the dog were upon the startled survivors. Conan was animated merely by his fighting spirit and an old, old racial hate, but Balthus was afire with wrath.

He met the first Pict to oppose him with a ferocious swipe that split the painted skull, and sprang over his falling body to grapple with the others. But Conan had already killed one of the two he had chosen, and the leap of the Aquilonian was a second late. The warrior was down with the long sword through him even as Balthus' ax was lifted. Turning toward the remaining Pict, Balthus saw Slasher rise from his victim, his great jaws dripping blood.

Balthus said nothing as he looked down at the pitiful forms in the road beside the burning wain. Both were young, the woman little more than a girl. By some whim of chance the Picts had left her face unmarred, and even in the agonies of an awful death it was beautiful.

But her soft young body had been hideously slashed with many knives—a mist clouded Balthus' eyes and he swallowed chokingly. The tragedy momentarily overcame him. He felt like falling upon the ground and weeping and biting the earth.

"Some young couple just hitting out on their own," Conan was saying as he wiped his sword unemotionally. "On their way to the fort when the Picts met them. Maybe the boy was going to enter the service; maybe take up land on the river. Well, that's what will happen to every man, woman and child this side of Thunder River if we don't get them into Velitrium in a hurry."

Balthus" knees trembled as he followed Conan. But there was no hint of weakness in the long easy stride of the Cimmerian. There was a kinship between him and the great gaunt brute that glided beside him. Slasher no longer growled with his head to the trail. The way was clear before them. The yelling on the river came faintly to them, but Balthus believed the fort was still holding. Conan halted suddenly, with an oath.

He showed Balthus a trail that led north from the road. It was an old trail, partly grown with new young growth, and this growth had recently been broken down. Balthus realized this fact more by feel than sight, though Conan seemed to see like a cat in the dark. The Cimmerian showed him where broad wagon tracks turned off the main trail, deeply indented in the forest mold.

"Settlers going to the licks after salt," he grunted. "They're at the edges of the marsh, about nine miles from here. Blast it! They'll be cut off and butchered to a man! Listen! One man can warn the people on the road. Go ahead and wake them up and herd them into Velitrium. I'll go and get the men gathering the salt. They'll be camped by the licks. We won't come back to the road. We'll head straight through the woods."

With no further comment Conan turned off the trail and hurried down the dim path, and Balthus, after staring after him for a few moments, set out along the road. The dog had remained with him, and glided softly at his heels. When Balthus had gone a few rods he heard the animal growl. Whirling, he glared back the way he had come, and was startled to see a vague ghostly glow vanishing into the forest in the direction Conan had taken. Slasher rumbled deep in his throat, his hackles stiff and his eyes balls of green fire. Balthus remembered the grim apparition that had taken the head of the merchant Tiberias not far from that spot, and he hesitated. The thing must be following

Conan. But the giant Cimmerian had repeatedly demonstrated his ability to take care of himself, and Balthus felt his duty lay toward the helpless settlers who slumbered in the path of the red hurricane. The horror of the fiery phantom was overshadowed by the horror of those limp, violated bodies beside the burning ox-wain.

He hurried down the road, crossed Scalp Creek and came in sight of the first settler's cabin—a long, low structure of ax-hewn logs. In an instant he was pounding on the door. A sleepy voice inquired his pleasure.

"Get up! The Picts are over the river!"

That brought instant response. A low cry echoed his words and then the door was thrown open by a woman in a scanty shift. Her hair hung over her bare shoulders in disorder; she held a candle in one hand and an ax in the other. Her face was colorless, her eyes wide with terror.

"Come in!" she begged. "We'll hold the cabin."

"No. We must make for Velitrium. The fort can't hold them back. It may have fallen already. Don't stop to dress. Get your children and come on."

"But my man's gone with the others after salt!" she wailed, wringing her hands. Behind her peered three tousled youngsters, blinking and bewildered.

"Conan's gone after them. He'll fetch them through safe. We must hurry up the road to warn the other cabins."

Relief flooded her countenance.

"Mitra be thanked!" she cried. "If the Cimmerian's gone after them, they're safe if mortal man can save them!"

In a whirlwind of activity she snatched up the smallest child and herded the others through the door ahead of her. Balthus took the candle and ground it out under his heel. He listened an instant. No sound came up the dark road.

"Have you got a horse?"

"In the stable," she groaned. "Oh, hurry!"

He pushed her aside as she fumbled with shaking hands at the bars. He led the horse out and lifted the children on its back, telling them to hold to its mane and to one another. They stared at him seriously, making no outcry. The woman took the horse's halter and set out up the road. She still gripped her ax and Balthus knew that if cornered she would fight with the desperate courage of a she-panther.

He held behind, listening. He was oppressed by the belief that the fort had been stormed and taken; that the dark-skinned hordes were already streaming up the road toward Velitrium, drunken on slaughter and mad for blood. They would come with the speed of starving wolves.

Presently they saw another cabin looming ahead. The woman started to shriek a warning, but Balthus stopped her. He hurried to the door and knocked. A woman's voice answered him. He repeated his warning, and soon the cabin disgorged its occupants—an old woman, two young women and four children. Like the other woman's husband, their men had gone to the salt licks the day before, unsuspecting of any danger. One of the young women seemed dazed, the other prone to hysteria. But the old woman, a stern old veteran of the frontier, quieted them harshly; she helped Balthus get out the two horses that were stabled in a pen behind the cabin and put the children on them. Balthus urged that she herself mount with them, but she shook her head and made one of the younger women ride.

"She's with child," grunted the old woman. "I can walk—and fight, too, if it comes to that."

As they set out, one of the women said: "A young couple passed along the road about dusk; we advised them to spend the night at our cabin, but they were anxious to make the fort tonight. Did—did—".

"They met the Picts," answered Balthus briefly, and the woman sobbed in horror.

They were scarcely out of sight of the cabin when some distance behind them quavered a long high-pitched yell.

"A wolf!" exclaimed one of the women.

"A painted wolf with an ax in his hand," muttered Balthus. "Go! Rouse the other settlers along the road and take them with you. I'll scout along behind."

Without a word the old woman herded her charges ahead of her. As they faded into the darkness, Balthus could see the pale ovals that were the faces of the children twisted back over their shoulders to stare toward him. He remembered his own people on the Tauran and a moment's giddy sickness swam over him. With momentary weakness he groaned and sank down in the road; his muscular arm fell over Slasher's massive neck and he felt the dog's warm moist tongue touch his face.

He lifted his head and grinned with a painful effort.

"Come on, boy," he mumbled, rising. "We've got work to do."

A red glow suddenly became evident through the trees. The Picts had fired the last hut. He grinned. How Zogar Sag would froth if he knew his warriors had let their destructive natures get the better of them. The fire would warn the people farther up the road. They would be awake and alert when the fugitives reached them. But his face grew grim. The women were traveling slowly, on foot and on the over-loaded horses. The swift-footed Picts would run them down within a mile, unless—he took his position behind a tangle of fallen logs beside the trail. The road west of him was lighted by the burning cabin, and when the Picts came he saw them first—black furtive figures etched against the distant glare.

Drawing a shaft to the head, he loosed and one of the figures crumpled. The rest melted into the woods on either side of the road. Slasher whimpered with the killing lust beside him. Suddenly a figure appeared on the fringe of the trail, under the trees, and began gliding toward the fallen timbers. Balthus' bow-string twanged and the Pict yelped, staggered and fell into the shadows with the arrow through his thigh. Slasher cleared the timbers with a bound and leaped into the bushes. They were violently shaken and then the dog slunk back to Balthus' side, his jaws crimson.

No more appeared in the trail; Balthus began to fear they were stealing past his position through the woods, and when he heard a faint sound to his left he loosed blindly. He cursed as he heard the shaft splinter against a tree, but Slasher glided away as silently as a phantom, and presently Balthus heard a thrashing and a gurgling; then Slasher came like a ghost through the bushes, snuggling his great, crimson-stained head against Balthus' arm. Blood oozed from a gash in his shoulder, but the sounds in the wood had ceased for ever.

The men lurking on the edges of the road evidently sensed the fate of their companion, and decided that an open charge was preferable to being dragged down in the dark by a devil-beast they could neither see nor hear. Perhaps they realized that only one man lay behind the logs. They came with a sudden rush, breaking cover from both sides of the trail. Three dropped with arrows through them—and the remaining pair hesitated. One turned and ran back down the road, but the other lunged over the breastwork, his eyes and teeth gleaming in the dim light, his ax lifted. Balthus' foot slipped as he sprang up, but the slip saved his life. The descending ax shaved a lock of hair from his head, and the Pict rolled down the logs from the force of his wasted blow. Before he could regain his feet Slasher tore his throat out.

Then followed a tense period of waiting, in which time Balthus wondered if the man who had fled had been the only survivor of the party. Obviously it had been a small band that had either left the fighting at the fort, or was scouting ahead of the main body. Each moment that passed increased the chances for safety of the women and children hurrying toward Velitrium.

Then without warning a shower of arrows whistled over his retreat. A wild howling rose from the woods along the trail. Either the survivor had gone after aid, or another party had joined the first. The burning cabin still smoldered, lending a little light. Then they were after him, gliding through the trees beside the trail. He shot three arrows and threw the bow away. As if sensing his plight, they came on, not yelling now, but in deadly silence except for a swift pad of many feet.

He fiercely hugged the head of the great dog growling at his side, muttered: "All right, boy, give 'em hell!" and sprang to his feet, drawing his ax. Then the dark figures flooded over the breastworks and closed in a storm of flailing axes, stabbing knives and ripping fangs.

7 The Devil in the Fire

When Conan turned from the Velitrium road he expected a run of some nine miles and set himself to the task. But he had not gone four when he heard the sounds of a party of men ahead of him. From the noise they were making in their progress he knew they were not Picts. He hailed them.

"Who's there?" challenged a harsh voice. "Stand where you are until we know you, or you'll get an arrow through you."

"You couldn't hit an elephant in this darkness," answered Conan impatiently. "Come on, fool; it's I—Conan. The Picts are over the river."

"We suspected as much," answered the leader of the men, as they strode forward—tall, rangy men, stern-faced, with bows in their hands. "One of our party wounded an antelope and tracked it nearly to Black River. He heard them yelling down the river and ran back to our camp. We left the salt and the wagons, turned the oxen loose and came as swiftly as we could. If the Picts are besieging the fort, war-parties will be ranging up the road toward our cabins."

"Your families are safe," grunted Conan. "My companion went ahead to take them to Velitrium. If we go back to the main road we may run into the whole horde. We'll strike southeast, through the timber. Go ahead. I'll scout behind."

A few moments later the whole band was hurrying southeastward. Conan followed more slowly, keeping just within ear-shot. He cursed the noise they were making; that many Picts or Cimmerians would have moved through the woods with no more noise than the wind makes as it blows through the black branches.

He had just crossed a small glade when he wheeled answering the conviction of his primitive instincts that he was being followed. Standing motionless among the bushes he heard the sounds of the retreating settlers fade away. Then a voice called faintly back along the way he had come: "Conan! Conan! Wait for me, Conan!"

"Balthus!" he swore bewilderedly. Cautiously he called: "Here I am."

"Wait for me, Conan!" the voice came more distinctly.

Conan moved out of the shadows, scowling. "What the devil are you doing here?—Crom!"

He half crouched, the flesh prickling along his spine. It was not Balthus who was emerging from the other side of the glade. A weird glow burned through the trees. It moved toward him, shimmering weirdly—a green witch-fire that moved with purpose and intent.

It halted some feet away and Conan glared at it, trying to distinguish its fire-misted outlines. The quivering flame had a solid core; the flame was but a green garment that masked some animate and evil entity; but the Cimmerian was unable to make out its shape or likeness. Then, shockingly, a voice spoke to him from amidst the fiery column.

"Why do you stand like a sheep waiting for the butcher, Conan?"

The voice was human but carried strange vibrations that were not human.

"Sheep?" Conan's wrath got the best of his momentary awe. "Do you think I'm afraid of a damned Pictish swamp devil? A friend called me."

"I called in his voice," answered the other. "The men you follow belong to my brother; I would not rob his knife of their blood. But you are mine. Oh, fool, you have come from the far gray hills of Cimmeria to meet your doom in the forests of Conajohara."

"You've had your chance at me before now," snorted Conan. "Why didn't you kill me then, if you could?"

"My brother had not painted a skull black for you and hurled it into the fire that burns for ever on Gullah's black altar. He had not whispered your name to the black ghosts that haunt the uplands of the Dark Land. But a bat has flown over the Mountains of the Dead and drawn your image in blood on the white tiger's hide that hangs before the long hut where sleep the Four Brothers of the Night. The great serpents coil about their feet and the stars burn like fireflies in their hair."

"Why have the gods of darkness doomed me to death?" growled Conan. Something—a hand, foot or talon, he could not tell which, thrust out from the fire and marked swiftly on the mold. A symbol blazed there, marked with fire, and faded, but not before he recognized it. "You dared make the sign which only a priest of Jhebbal Sag dare make. Thunder rumbled through the black Mountain of the Dead and the altar-hut of Gullah was thrown down by a wind from the Gulf of Ghosts. The loon which is messenger to the Four Brothers of the Night flew swiftly and whispered your name in my ear. Your race is won. You are a dead man already. Your head will hang in the altar-hut of my brother. Your body will be eaten by the black-winged, sharp-beaked Children of Jhil."

"Who the devil is your brother?" demanded Conan. His sword was naked in his hand, and he was subtly loosening the ax in his belt.

"Zogar Sag; a child of Jhebbal Sag who still visits his sacred groves at times. A woman of Gwawela slept in a grove holy to Jhebbal Sag. Her babe was Zogar Sag. I too am a son of Jhebbal Sag, out of a fire-being from a far realm. Zogar Sag summoned me out of the Misty Lands. With incantations and sorcery and his own blood he materialized me in the flesh of his own planet. We are one, tied together by invisible threads. His thoughts are my thoughts; if he is struck, I am bruised. If I am cut, he bleeds. But I have talked enough. Soon your ghost will talk with the ghosts of the Dark Land, and they will tell you of the old gods which are not dead, but sleep in the outer abysses, and from time to time awake."

"I'd like to see what you look like," muttered Conan, working his ax free, "you who leave a track like a bird, who burn like a flame and yet speak with a human voice."

"You shall see," answered the voice from the flame, "see, and carry the knowledge with you into the Dark Land."

The flames leaped and sank, dwindling and dimming. A face began to take shadowy form. At first Conan thought it was Zogar Sag himself who stood wrapped in green fire. But the face was higher than his own and there was a demoniac aspect about it—Conan had noted various abnormalities about Zogar Sag's features—an obliqueness of the eyes, a sharpness of the ears, a wolfish thinness of the lips; these peculiarities were exaggerated in the apparition which swayed before him. The eyes were red as coals of living fire.

More details came into view: a slender torso, covered with snaky scales, which was yet man-like in shape, with man-like arms, from the waist upward; below, long crane-like legs ended in splay, three-toed feet like those of some huge bird. Along the monstrous limbs the blue fire fluttered and ran. He saw it as through a glistening mist.

Then suddenly it was towering over him, though he had not seen it move toward him. A long arm, which for the first time he noticed was armed with curving, sickle-like talons, swung high and swept down at his neck. With a fierce cry he broke the spell and bounded aside, hurling his ax. The demon avoided the cast with an unbelievably quick movement of its narrow head and was on him again with a hissing rush of leaping flames.

But fear had fought for it when it slew its other victims, and Conan was not afraid. He knew that any being clothed in material flesh can be slain by material weapons, however grisly its form may be.

One flailing talon-armed limb knocked his helmet from his head. A little lower and it would have decapitated him. But fierce joy surged through him as his savagely driven sword sank deep in the monster's groin. He bounded backward from a flailing stroke, tearing his sword free as he leaped. The talons raked his breast, ripping through mail-links as if they had been cloth. But his return spring was like that of a starving wolf. He was inside the lashing arms and driving his sword deep in the monster's belly—felt the arms lock about him and the talons ripping the mail from his back as they sought his vitals—he was lapped and dazzled by blue flame that was chill as ice—then he had torn fiercely away from the weakening arms and his sword cut the air in a tremendous swipe.

The demon staggered and fell sprawling sidewise, its head hanging only by a shred of flesh. The fires that veiled it leaped fiercely upward, now red as gushing blood, hiding the figure from view. A scent of burning flesh filled Conan's nostrils. Shaking the blood and sweat from his eyes, he wheeled and ran staggering through the woods. Blood trickled down his limbs. Somewhere, miles to the south, he saw the faint glow of flames that might mark a burning cabin. Behind him, toward the road, rose a distant howling that spurred him to greater efforts.

8 Conajohara No More

There had been fighting on Thunder River; fierce fighting before the walls of Velitrium; ax and torch had been piled up and down the bank, and many a settler's cabin lay in ashes before the painted horde was rolled back.

A strange quiet followed the storm, in which people gathered and talked in hushed voices, and men with red-stained bandages drank their ale silently in the taverns along the river bank.

There, to Conan the Cimmerian, moodily quaffing from a great wine-glass, came a gaunt forester with a bandage about his head and his arm in a sling. He was the one survivor of Fort Tuscelan.

"You went with the soldiers to the ruins of the fort?"

Conan nodded.

"I wasn't able," murmured the other. "There was no fighting?"

"The Picts had fallen back across the Black River. Something must have broken their nerve, though only the devil who made them knows what."

The woodsman glanced at his bandaged arm and sighed.

"They say there were no bodies worth disposing of."

Conan shook his head. "Ashes. The Picts had piled them in the fort and set fire to the fort before they crossed the river. Their own dead and the men of Valannus."

"Valannus was killed among the last—in the hand-to-hand fighting when they broke the barriers. They tried to take him alive, but he made them kill him. They took ten of the rest of us prisoners when we were so weak from fighting we could fight no more. They butchered nine of us then and there. It was when Zogar Sag died that I got my chance to break free and run for it."

"Zogar Sag's dead?" ejaculated Conan.

"Aye. I saw him die. That's why the Picts didn't press the fight against Velitrium as fiercely as they did against the fort. It was strange. He took no wounds in battle. He was dancing among the slain, waving an ax with which he'd just brained the last of my comrades. He came at me, howling like a wolf—and then he staggered and dropped the ax, and began to reel in a circle screaming as I never heard a man or beast scream before. He fell between me and the fire they'd built to roast me, gagging and frothing at the mouth, and all at once he went rigid and the Picts shouted that he was dead. It was during the confusion that I slipped my cords and ran for the woods."

"I saw him lying in the firelight. No weapon had touched him. Yet there were red marks like the wounds of a sword in the groin, belly and neck—the last as if his head had been almost severed from his body. What do you make of that?"

Conan made no reply, and the forester, aware of the reticence of barbarians on certain matters, continued: "He lived by magic, and somehow, he died by magic. It was the mystery of his death that took the heart out of the Picts. Not a man who saw it was in the fighting before Velitrium. They hurried back across Black River. Those that struck Thunder River were warriors who had come on before Zogar Sag died. They were not enough to take the city by themselves.

"I came along the road, behind their main force, and I know none followed me from the fort. I sneaked through their lines and got into the town. You brought the settlers through all right, but their women and children got into Velitrium just ahead of those painted devils. If the youth Balthus and old Slasher hadn't held them up awhile, they'd have butchered every woman and child in Conajohara. I passed the place where Balthus and the dog made their last stand. They were lying amid a heap of dead Picts—I counted seven, brained by his ax, or disemboweled by the dog's fangs, and there were others in the road with arrows sticking in them. Gods, what a fight that must have been!"

"He was a man," said Conan. "I drink to his shade, and to the shade of the dog, who knew no fear." He quaffed part of the wine, then emptied the rest upon the floor, with a curious heathen gesture, and smashed the goblet. "The heads of ten Picts shall pay for his, and seven heads for the dog, who was a better warrior than many a man."

And the forester, staring into the moody, smoldering blue eyes, knew the barbaric oath would be kept.

"They'll not rebuild the fort?"

"No; Conajohara is lost to Aquilonia. The frontier has been pushed back. Thunder River will be the new border."

The woodsman sighed and stared at his calloused hand, worn from contact with ax-haft and sword-hilt. Conan reached his long arm for the wine-jug. The forester stared at him, comparing him with the men about them, the men who had died along the lost river, comparing him with those other wild men over that river. Conan did not seem aware of his gaze.

"Barbarism is the natural state of mankind," the borderer said, still staring somberly at the Cimmerian. "Civilization is unnatural. It is a whim of circumstance. And barbarism must always ultimately triumph."

THE END

Red Nails

One of the strangest stories ever written—the tale of a barbarian adventurer, a woman pirate, and a weird roofed city inhabited by the most peculiar race of men ever spawned

1 The Skull on the Crag

The woman on the horse reined in her weary steed. It stood with its legs wide-braced, its head drooping, as if it found even the weight of the gold-tasseled, red-leather bridle too heavy. The woman drew a booted foot out of the silver stirrup and swung down from the gilt-worked saddle. She made the reins fast to the fork of a sapling, and turned about, hands on her hips, to survey her surroundings.

They were not inviting. Giant trees hemmed in the small pool where her horse had just drunk. Clumps of undergrowth limited the vision that quested under the somber twilight of the lofty arches formed by intertwining branches. The woman shivered with a twitch of her magnificent shoulders, and then cursed.

She was tall, full-bosomed and large-limbed, with compact shoulders. Her whole figure reflected an unusual strength, without detracting from the femininity of her appearance. She was all woman, in spite of her bearing and her garments. The latter were incongruous, in view of her present environs. Instead of a skirt she wore short, wide-legged silk breeches, which ceased a hand's breadth short of her knees, and were upheld by a wide silken sash worn as a girdle. Flaring-topped boots of soft leather came almost to her knees, and a low-necked, wide-collared, wide-sleeved silk shirt completed her costume. On one shapely hip she wore a straight double-edged sword, and on the other a long dirk. Her unruly golden hair, cut square at her shoulders, was confined by a band of crimson satin.

Against the background of somber, primitive forest she posed with an unconscious picturesqueness, bizarre and out of place. She should have been posed against a background of sea-clouds, painted masts and wheeling gulls. There was the color of the sea in her wide eyes. And that was as it should have been, because this was Valeria of the Red

Brotherhood, whose deeds are celebrated in song and ballad wherever seafarers gather.

She strove to pierce the sullen green roof of the arched branches and see the sky which presumably lay about it, but presently gave it up with a muttered oath.

Leaving her horse tied she strode off toward the east, glancing back toward the pool from time to time in order to fix her route in her mind. The silence of the forest depressed her. No birds sang in the lofty boughs, nor did any rustling in the bushes indicate the presence of any small animals. For leagues she had traveled in a realm of brooding stillness, broken only by the sounds of her own flight.

She had slaked her thirst at the pool, but she felt the gnawings of hunger and began looking about for some of the fruit on which she had sustained herself since exhausting the food she had brought in her saddle-bags.

Ahead of her, presently, she saw an outcropping of dark, flint-like rock that sloped upward into what looked like a rugged crag rising among the trees. Its summit was lost to view amidst a cloud of encircling leaves. Perhaps its peak rose above the tree-tops, and from it she could see what lay beyond—if, indeed, anything lay beyond but more of this apparently illimitable forest through which she had ridden for so many days.

A narrow ridge formed a natural ramp that led up the steep face of the crag. After she had ascended some fifty feet she came to the belt of leaves that surrounded the rock. The trunks of the trees did not crowd close to the crag, but the ends of their lower branches extended about it, veiling it with their foliage. She groped on in leafy obscurity, not able to see either above or below her; but presently she glimpsed blue sky, and a moment later came out in the clear, hot sunlight and saw the forest roof stretching away under her feet.

She was standing on a broad shelf which was about even with the tree-tops, and from it rose a spire-like jut that was the ultimate peak of the crag she had climbed. But something else caught her attention at the moment. Her foot had struck something in the litter of blown dead leaves which carpeted the shelf. She kicked them aside and looked down on the skeleton of a man. She ran an experienced eye over the bleached frame, but saw no broken bones nor any sign of violence. The man must have died a natural death; though why he should have climbed a tall crag to die she could not imagine.

★ ★ ★

She scrambled up to the summit of the spire and looked toward the horizons. The forest roof—which looked like a floor from her vantage-point—was just as impenetrable as from below. She could not even see the pool by which she had left her horse. She glanced northward, in the direction from which she had come. She saw only the rolling green ocean stretching away and away, with only a vague blue line in the distance to hint of the hill-range she had crossed days before, to plunge into this leafy waste.

West and east the view was the same; though the blue hill-line was lacking in those directions. But when she turned her eyes southward she stiffened and caught her breath. A mile away in that direction the forest thinned out and ceased abruptly, giving way to a cactus-dotted plain. And in the midst of that plain rose the walls and towers of a city. Valeria swore in amazement. This passed belief. She would not have been surprised to sight human habitations of another sort—the bee-hive-shaped huts of the black people, or the cliff-dwellings of the mysterious brown race which legends declared inhabited some country of this unexplored region. But it was a startling experience to come upon a walled city here so many long weeks' march from the nearest outposts of any sort of civilization.

Her hands tiring from clinging to the spire-like pinnacle, she let herself down on the shelf, frowning in indecision. She had come far—from the camp of the mercenaries by the border town of Sukhmet amidst the level grasslands, where desperate adventurers of many races guard the Stygian frontier against the raids that come up like a red wave from Darfar. Her flight had been blind, into a country of which she was wholly ignorant. And now she wavered between an urge to ride directly to that city in the plain, and the instinct of caution which prompted her to skirt it widely and continue her solitary flight.

Her thoughts were scattered by the rustling of the leaves below her. She wheeled cat-like, snatched at her sword; and then she froze motionless, staring wide-eyed at the man before her.

He was almost a giant in stature, muscles rippling smoothly under his skin which the sun had burned brown. His garb was similar to hers, except that he wore a broad leather belt instead of a girdle. Broadsword and poniard hung from this belt.

"Conan, the Cimmerian!" ejaculated the woman. "What are *you* doing on my trail?"

He grinned hardly, and his fierce blue eyes burned with a light any woman could understand as they ran over her magnificent figure, lingering on the swell of her splendid breasts beneath the light shirt, and the clear white flesh displayed between breeches and boot-tops.

"Don't you know?" he laughed. "Haven't I made my admiration for you plain ever since I first saw you?"

"A stallion could have made it no plainer," she answered disdainfully. "But I never expected to encounter you so far from the ale-barrels and meat-pots of Sukhmet. Did you really follow me from Zarallo's camp, or were you whipped forth for a rogue?"

He laughed at her insolence and flexed his mighty biceps.

"You know Zarallo didn't have enough knaves to whip me out of camp," he grinned. "Of course I followed you. Lucky thing for you, too, wench! When you knifed that Stygian officer, you forfeited Zarallo's favor and protection, and you outlawed yourself with the Stygians."

"I know it," she replied sullenly. "But what else could I do? You know what my provocation was."

"Sure," he agreed. "If I'd been there, I'd have knifed him myself. But if a woman must live in the war-camps of men, she can expect such things."

Valeria stamped her booted foot and swore.

"Why won't men let me live a man's life?"

"That's obvious!" Again his eager eyes devoured her. "But you were wise to run away. The Stygians would have had you skinned. That officer's brother followed you; faster than you thought, I don't doubt. He wasn't far behind you when I caught up with him. His horse was better than yours. He'd have caught you and cut your throat within a few more miles."

"Well?" she demanded.

"Well what?" He seemed puzzled.

"What of the Stygian?"

"Why, what do you suppose?" he returned impatiently. "I killed him, of course, and left his carcass for the vultures. That delayed me, though, and I almost lost your trail when you crossed the rocky spurs of the hills. Otherwise I'd have caught up with you long ago."

"And now you think you'll drag me back to Zarallo's camp?" she sneered.

"Don't talk like a fool," he grunted. "Come, girl, don't be such a spitfire. I'm not like that Stygian you knifed, and you know it."

"A penniless vagabond," she taunted.

He laughed at her.

"What do you call yourself? You haven't enough money to buy a new seat for your breeches. Your disdain doesn't deceive me. You know I've commanded bigger ships and more men than you ever did in your life. As for being penniless—what rover isn't, most of the time? I've squandered enough gold in the sea-ports of the world to fill a galleon. You know that, too."

"Where are the fine ships and the bold lads you commanded, now?" she sneered.

"At the bottom of the sea, mostly," he replied cheerfully. "The Zingarans sank my last ship off the Shemite shore—that's why I joined Zarallo's Free Companions. But I saw I'd been stung when we marched to the Darfar border. The pay was poor and the wine was sour, and I don't like black women. And that's the only kind that came to our camp at Sukhmet—rings in their noses and their teeth filed—bah! Why did you join Zarallo? Sukhmet's a long way from salt water."

"Red Ortho wanted to make me his mistress," she answered sullenly. "I jumped overboard one night and swam ashore when we were anchored off the Kushite coast. Off Zabhela, it was. There a Shemite trader told me that Zarallo had brought his Free Companies south to guard the Darfar border. No better employment offered. I joined an east-bound caravan and eventually came to Sukhmet."

★ ★ ★

"It was madness to plunge southward as you did," commented Conan, "but it was wise, too, for Zarallo's patrols never thought to look for you in this direction. Only the brother of the man you killed happened to strike your trail."

"And now what do you intend doing?" she demanded.

"Turn west," he answered. "I've been this far south, but not this far east. Many days' traveling to the west will bring us to the open savannas, where the black tribes graze their cattle. I have friends among them. We'll get to the coast and find a ship. I'm sick of the jungle."

"Then be on your way," she advised. "I have other plans."

"Don't be a fool!" He showed irritation for the first time. "You can't keep on wandering through this forest."

"I can if I choose."

"But what do you intend doing?"

"That's none of your affair," she snapped.

"Yes, it is," he answered calmly. "Do you think I've followed you this far, to turn around and ride off empty-handed? Be sensible, wench. I'm not going to harm you."

He stepped toward her, and she sprang back, whipping out her sword.

"Keep back, you barbarian dog! I'll spit you like a roast pig!"

He halted, reluctantly, and demanded: "Do you want me to take that toy away from you and spank you with it?"

"Words! Nothing but words!" she mocked, lights like the gleam of the sun on blue water dancing in her reckless eyes.

He knew it was the truth. No living man could disarm Valeria of the Brotherhood with his bare hands. He scowled, his sensations a tangle of conflicting emotions. He was angry, yet he was amused and filled with admiration for her spirit. He burned with eagerness to seize that splendid figure and crush it in his iron arms, yet he greatly desired not to hurt the girl. He was torn between a desire to shake her soundly, and a desire to caress her. He knew if he came any nearer her sword would be sheathed in his heart. He had seen Valeria kill too many men in border forays and tavern brawls to have any illusions about her. He knew she was as quick and ferocious as a tigress. He could draw his broadsword and disarm her, beat the blade out of her hand, but the thought of drawing a sword on a woman, even without intent of injury, was extremely repugnant to him.

"Blast your soul, you hussy!" he exclaimed in exasperation. "I'm going to take off your—"

He started toward her, his angry passion making him reckless, and she poised herself for a deadly thrust. Then came a startling interruption to a scene at once ludicrous and perilous.

"*What's that?*"

It was Valeria who exclaimed, but they both started violently, and Conan wheeled like a cat, his great sword flashing into his hand. Back in the forest had burst forth an appalling medley of screams—the screams of horses in terror and agony. Mingled with their screams there came the snap of splintering bones.

"Lions are slaying the horses!" cried Valeria.

"Lions, nothing!" snorted Conan, his eyes blazing. "Did you hear a lion roar? Neither did I! Listen at those bones snap—not even a lion could make that much noise killing a horse."

★ ★ ★

He hurried down the natural ramp and she followed, their personal feud forgotten in the adventurers' instinct to unite against common peril. The screams had ceased when they worked their way downward through the green veil of leaves that brushed the rock.

"I found your horse tied by the pool back there," he muttered, treading so noiselessly that she no longer wondered how he had surprised her on the crag. "I tied mine beside it and followed the tracks of your boots. Watch, now!"

They had emerged from the belt of leaves, and stared down into the lower reaches of the forest. Above them the green roof spread its dusky canopy. Below them the sunlight filtered in just enough to make a jade-tinted twilight. The giant trunks of trees less than a hundred yards away looked dim and ghostly.

"The horses should be beyond that thicket, over there," whispered Conan, and his voice might have been a breeze moving through the branches. "Listen!"

Valeria had already heard, and a chill crept through her veins; so she unconsciously laid her white hand on her companion's muscular brown arm. From beyond the thicket came the noisy crunching of bones and the loud rending of flesh, together with the grinding, slobbering sounds of a horrible feast.

"Lions wouldn't make that noise," whispered Conan. "Something's eating our horses, but it's not a lion—Crom!"

The noise stopped suddenly, and Conan swore softly. A suddenly risen breeze was blowing from them directly toward the spot where the unseen slayer was hidden.

"Here it comes!" muttered Conan, half lifting his sword.

The thicket was violently agitated, and Valeria clutched Conan's arm hard. Ignorant of jungle-lore, she yet knew that no animal she had ever seen could have shaken the tall brush like that.

"It must be as big as an elephant," muttered Conan, echoing her thought. "What the devil—" His voice trailed away in stunned silence.

Through the thicket was thrust a head of nightmare and lunacy. Grinning jaws bared rows of dripping yellow tusks; above the yawning mouth wrinkled a saurian-like snout. Huge eyes, like those of a python a thousand times magnified, stared unwinkingly at the petrified humans clinging to the rock above it. Blood smeared the scaly, flabby lips and dripped from the huge mouth.

The head, bigger than that of a crocodile, was further extended on a long scaled neck on which stood up rows of serrated spikes, and after it, crushing down the briars and saplings, waddled the body of a titan, a gigantic, barrel-bellied torso on absurdly short legs. The whitish belly almost raked the ground, while the serrated back-bone rose higher than Conan could have reached on tiptoe. A long spiked tail, like that of a gargantuan scorpion, trailed out behind.

"Back up the crag, quick!" snapped Conan, thrusting the girl behind him. "I don't think he can climb, but he can stand on his hind-legs and reach us—"

With a snapping and rending of bushes and saplings the monster came hurtling through the thickets, and they fled up the rock before him like leaves blown before a wind. As Valeria plunged into the leafy screen a backward glance showed her the titan rearing up fearsomely on his massive hind-legs, even as Conan had predicted. The sight sent panic racing through her. As he reared, the beast seemed more gigantic than ever; his snouted head towered among the trees. Then Conan's iron hand closed on her wrist and she was jerked headlong into the blinding welter of the leaves, and out again into the hot sunshine above, just as the monster fell forward with his front feet on the crag with an impact that made the rock vibrate.

★ ★ ★

Behind the fugitives the huge head crashed through the twigs, and they looked down for a horrifying instant at the nightmare visage framed among the green leaves, eyes flaming, jaws gaping. Then the giant tusks clashed together futilely, and after that the head was withdrawn, vanishing from their sight as if it had sunk in a pool.

Peering down through broken branches that scraped the rock, they saw it squatting on its haunches at the foot of the crag, staring unblinkingly up at them.

Valeria shuddered.

"How long do you suppose he'll crouch there?"

Conan kicked the skull on the leaf-strewn shelf.

"That fellow must have climbed up here to escape him, or one like him. He must have died of starvation. There are no bones broken. That thing must be a dragon, such as the black people speak of in their legends. If so, it won't leave here until we're both dead."

Valeria looked at him blankly, her resentment forgotten. She fought down a surging of panic. She had proved her reckless courage a thousand times in wild battles on sea and land, on the blood-slippery decks of burning war-ships, in the storming of walled cities, and on the trampled sandy beaches where the desperate men of the Red Brotherhood bathed their knives in one another's blood in their fights for leadership. But the prospect now confronting her congealed her blood. A cutlas-stroke in the heat of battle was nothing; but to sit idle and helpless on a bare rock until she perished of starvation, besieged by a monstrous survival of an elder age—the thought sent panic throbbing through her brain.

"He must leave to eat and drink," she said helplessly.

"He won't have to go far to do either," Conan pointed out. "He's just gorged on horse-meat, and like a real snake, he can go for a long time without eating or drinking again. But he doesn't sleep after eating, like a real snake, it seems. Anyway, he can't climb this crag."

Conan spoke imperturbably. He was a barbarian, and the terrible patience of the wilderness and its children was as much a part of him as his lusts and rages. He could endure a situation like this with a coolness impossible to a civilized person.

"Can't we get into the trees and get away, traveling like apes through the branches?" she asked desperately.

He shook his head. "I thought of that. The branches that touch the crag down there are too light. They'd break with our weight. Besides, I have an idea that devil could tear up any tree around here by its roots."

"Well, are we going to sit here on our rumps until we starve, like that?" she cried furiously, kicking the skull clattering across the ledge. "I won't do it! I'll go down there and cut his damned head off—"

Conan had seated himself on a rocky projection at the foot of the spire. He looked up with a glint of admiration at her blazing eyes and tense, quivering figure, but, realizing that she was in just the mood for any madness, he let none of his admiration sound in his voice.

"Sit down," he grunted, catching her by her wrist and pulling her down on his knee. She was too surprised to resist as he took her sword from her hand and shoved it back in its sheath. "Sit still and calm down. You'd only break your steel on his scales. He'd gobble you up at one gulp, or smash you like an egg with that spiked tail of his. We'll get out of this jam some way, but we shan't do it by getting chewed up and swallowed."

She made no reply, nor did she seek to repulse his arm from about her waist. She was frightened, and the sensation was new to Valeria of the Red Brotherhood. So she sat on her companion's—or captor's—knee with a docility that would have amazed Zarallo, who had anathematized her as a she-devil out of hell's seraglio.

Conan played idly with her curly yellow locks, seemingly intent only upon his conquest. Neither the skeleton at his feet nor the monster crouching below disturbed his mind or dulled the edge of his interest.

The girl's restless eyes, roving the leaves below them, discovered splashes of color among the green. It was fruit, large, darkly crimson globes suspended from the boughs of a tree whose broad leaves were a peculiarly rich and vivid green. She became aware of both thirst and hunger, though thirst had not assailed her until she knew she could not descend from the crag to find food and water.

"We need not starve," she said. "There is fruit we can reach."

Conan glanced where she pointed.

"If we ate that we wouldn't need the bite of a dragon," he grunted. "That's what the black people of Kush call the Apples of Derketa. Derketa is the Queen of the Dead. Drink a little of the juice, or spill it on your flesh, and you'd be dead before you could tumble to the foot of this crag."

"Oh!"

She lapsed into dismayed silence. There seemed no way out of their predicament, she reflected gloomily. She saw no way of escape, and Conan seemed to be concerned only with her supple waist and curly tresses. If he was trying to formulate a plan of escape, he did not show it.

"If you'll take your hands off me long enough to climb up on that peak," she said presently, "you'll see something that will surprise you."

He cast her a questioning glance, then obeyed with a shrug of his massive shoulders. Clinging to the spire-like pinnacle, he stared out over the forest roof.

★ ★ ★

He stood a long moment in silence, posed like a bronze statue on the rock.

"It's a walled city, right enough," he muttered presently. "Was that where you were going, when you tried to send me off alone to the coast?"

"I saw it before you came. I knew nothing of it when I left Sukhmet."

"Who'd have thought to find a city here? I don't believe the Stygians ever penetrated this far. Could black people build a city like that? I see no herds on the plain, no signs of cultivation, or people moving about."

"How could you hope to see all that, at this distance?" she demanded. He shrugged his shoulders and dropped down on the shelf. "Well, the folk of the city can't help us just now. And they might not, if they could. The people of the Black Countries are generally hostile to strangers. Probably stick us full of spears—"

He stopped short and stood silent, as if he had forgotten what he was saying, frowning down at the crimson spheres gleaming among the leaves.

"Spears!" he muttered. "What a blasted fool I am not to have thought of that before! That shows what a pretty woman does to a man's mind."

"What are you talking about?" she inquired.

Without answering her question, he descended to the belt of leaves and looked down through them. The great brute squatted below, watching the crag with the frightful patience of the reptile folk. So might one of his breed have glared up at their troglodyte ancestors, treed on a high-flung rock, in the dim dawn ages. Conan cursed him without heat, and began cutting branches, reaching out and severing them as far from the end as he could reach. The agitation of the leaves made the monster restless. He rose from his haunches and lashed his hideous tail, snapping off saplings as if they had been toothpicks. Conan watched him warily from the corner of his eye, and just as Valeria believed the dragon was about to hurl himself up the crag again, the Cimmerian drew back and climbed up to the ledge with the branches he had cut. There were three of these, slender shafts about seven feet long, but not larger than his thumb. He had also cut several strands of tough, thin vine.

"Branches too light for spear-hafts, and creepers no thicker than cords," he remarked, indicating the foliage about the crag. "It won't hold our weight—but there's strength in union. That's what the Aquilonian renegades used to tell us Cimmerians when they came into the hills to raise an army to invade their own country. But we always fight by clans and tribes."

"What the devil has that got to do with those sticks?" she demanded.

"You wait and see."

Gathering the sticks in a compact bundle, he wedged his poniard hilt between them at one end. Then with the vines he bound them together, and when he had completed his task, he had a spear of no small strength, with a sturdy shaft seven feet in length.

"What good will that do?" she demanded. "You told me that a blade couldn't pierce his scales—"

"He hasn't got scales all over him," answered Conan. "There's more than one way of skinning a panther."

Moving down to the edge of the leaves, he reached the spear up and carefully thrust the blade through one of the Apples of Derketa, drawing aside to avoid the darkly purple drops that dripped from the pierced fruit. Presently he withdrew the blade and showed her the blue steel stained a dull purplish crimson.

"I don't know whether it will do the job or not," quoth he. "There's enough poison there to kill an elephant, but—well, we'll see."

★ ★ ★

Valeria was close behind him as he let himself down among the leaves. Cautiously holding the poisoned pike away from him, he thrust his head through the branches and addressed the monster.

"What are you waiting down there for, you misbegotten offspring of questionable parents?" was one of his more printable queries. "Stick your ugly head up here again, you long-necked brute—or do you want me to come down there and kick you loose from your illegitimate spine?"

There was more of it—some of it couched in eloquence that made Valeria stare, in spite of her profane education among the seafarers. And it had its effect on the monster. Just as the incessant yapping of a dog worries and enrages more constitutionally silent animals, so the clamorous voice of a man rouses fear in some bestial bosoms and insane rage in others. Suddenly and with appalling quickness, the mastodonic brute reared up on its mighty hind legs and elongated its neck and body in a furious effort to reach this vociferous pigmy whose clamor was disturbing the primeval silence of its ancient realm.

But Conan had judged his distance with precision. Some five feet below him the mighty head crashed terribly but futilely through the leaves. And as the monstrous mouth gaped like that of a great snake, Conan drove his spear into the red angle of the jaw-bone hinge. He struck downward with all the strength of both arms, driving the long poniard blade to the hilt in flesh, sinew and bone.

Instantly the jaws clashed convulsively together, severing the triple-pieced shaft and almost precipitating Conan from his perch. He would have fallen but for the girl behind him, who caught his sword-belt in a desperate grasp. He clutched at a rocky projection, and grinned his thanks back at her.

Down on the ground the monster was wallowing like a dog with pepper in its eyes. He shook his head from side to side, pawed at it, and opened his mouth repeatedly to its widest extent. Presently he got a huge front foot on the stump of the shaft and managed to tear the blade out. Then he threw up his head, jaws wide and spouting blood, and glared up at the crag with such concentrated and intelligent fury that Valeria trembled and drew her sword. The scales along his back and flanks turned from rusty brown to a dull lurid red. Most horribly the monster's silence was broken. The sounds that issued from his blood-streaming jaws did not sound like anything that could have been produced by an earthly creation.

With harsh, grating roars, the dragon hurled himself at the crag that was the citadel of his enemies. Again and again his mighty head crashed upward through the branches, snapping vainly on empty air. He hurled his full ponderous weight against the rock until it vibrated from base to crest. And rearing upright he gripped it with his front legs like a man and tried to tear it up by the roots, as if it had been a tree.

This exhibition of primordial fury chilled the blood in Valeria's veins, but Conan was too close to the primitive himself to feel anything but a comprehending interest. To the barbarian, no such gulf existed between himself and other men, and the animals, as existed in the conception of Valeria. The monster below them, to Conan, was merely a form of life differing from himself mainly in physical shape. He attributed to it characteristics similar to his own, and saw in its wrath a counterpart of his rages, in its roars and bellowings merely reptilian equivalents to the curses he had bestowed upon it. Feeling a kinship with all wild things, even dragons, it was impossible for him to experience the sick horror which assailed Valeria at the sight of the brute's ferocity.

He sat watching it tranquilly, and pointed out the various changes that were taking place in its voice and actions.

"The poison's taking hold," he said with conviction.

"I don't believe it." To Valeria it seemed preposterous to suppose that anything, however lethal, could have any effect on that mountain of muscle and fury.

"There's pain in his voice," declared Conan. "First he was merely angry because of the stinging in his jaw. Now he feels the bite of the poison. Look! He's staggering. He'll be blind in a few more minutes. What did I tell you?"

For suddenly the dragon had lurched about and went crashing off through the bushes.

"Is he running away?" inquired Valeria uneasily.

"He's making for the pool!" Conan sprang up, galvanized into swift activity. "The poison makes him thirsty. Come on! He'll be blind in a few moments, but he can smell his way back to the foot of the crag, and if our scent's here still, he'll sit there until he dies. And others of his kind may come at his cries. Let's go!"

"Down there?" Valeria was aghast.

"Sure! We'll make for the city! They may cut our heads off there, but it's our only chance. We may run into a thousand more dragons on the way, but it's sure death to stay here. If we wait until he dies, we may have a dozen more to deal with. After me, in a hurry!"

He went down the ramp as swiftly as an ape, pausing only to aid his less agile companion, who, until she saw the Cimmerian climb, had fancied herself the equal of any man in the rigging of a ship or on the sheer face of a cliff.

★ ★ ★

They descended into the gloom below the branches and slid to the ground silently, though Valeria felt as if the pounding of her heart must surely be heard from far away. A noisy gurgling and lapping beyond the dense thicket indicated that the dragon was drinking at the pool.

"As soon as his belly is full he'll be back," muttered Conan. "It may take hours for the poison to kill him—if it does at all."

Somewhere beyond the forest the sun was sinking to the horizon. The forest was a misty twilight place of black shadows and dim vistas. Conan gripped Valeria's wrist and glided away from the foot of the crag. He made less noise than a breeze blowing among the tree-trunks, but Valeria felt as if her soft boots were betraying their flight to all the forest.

"I don't think he can follow a trail," muttered Conan. "But if a wind blew our body-scent to him, he could smell us out."

"Mitra grant that the wind blow not!" Valeria breathed.

Her face was a pallid oval in the gloom. She gripped her sword in her free hand, but the feel of the shagreen-bound hilt inspired only a feeling of helplessness in her.

They were still some distance from the edge of the forest when they heard a snapping and crashing behind them. Valeria bit her lip to check a cry.

"He's on our trail!" she whispered fiercely.

Conan shook his head.

"He didn't smell us at the rock, and he's blundering about through the forest trying to pick up our scent. Come on! It's the city or nothing now! He could tear down any tree we'd climb. If only the wind stays down—"

They stole on until the trees began to thin out ahead of them. Behind them the forest was a black impenetrable ocean of shadows. The ominous crackling still sounded behind them, as the dragon blundered in his erratic course.

"There's the plain ahead," breathed Valeria. "A little more and we'll—"

"Crom!" swore Conan.

"Mitra!" whispered Valeria.

Out of the south a wind had sprung up.

It blew over them directly into the black forest behind them. Instantly a horrible roar shook the woods. The aimless snapping and crackling of the bushes changed to a sustained crashing as the dragon came like a hurricane straight toward the spot from which the scent of his enemies was wafted.

"Run!" snarled Conan, his eyes blazing like those of a trapped wolf. "It's all we can do!"

Sailor's boots are not made for sprinting, and the life of a pirate does not train one for a runner. Within a hundred yards Valeria was panting and reeling in her gait, and behind them the crashing gave way to a rolling thunder as the monster broke out of the thickets and into the more open ground.

Conan's iron arm about the woman's waist half lifted her; her feet scarcely touched the earth as she was borne along at a speed she could never have attained herself. If he could keep out of the beast's way for a bit, perhaps that betraying wind would shift—but the wind held, and a quick glance over his shoulder showed Conan that the monster was almost upon them, coming like a war-galley in front of a hurricane. He thrust Valeria from him with a force that sent her reeling a dozen feet to fall in a crumpled heap at the foot of the nearest tree, and the Cimmerian wheeled in the path of the thundering titan.

Convinced that his death was upon him, the Cimmerian acted according to his instinct, and hurled himself full at the awful face that was bearing down on him. He leaped, slashing like a wildcat, felt his sword cut deep into the scales that sheathed the mighty snout—and then a terrific impact knocked him rolling and tumbling for fifty feet with all the wind and half the life battered out of him.

How the stunned Cimmerian regained his feet, not even he could have ever told. But the only thought that filled his brain was of the woman lying dazed and helpless almost in the path of the hurtling fiend, and before the breath came whistling back into his gullet he was standing over her with his sword in his hand.

She lay where he had thrown her, but she was struggling to a sitting posture. Neither tearing tusks nor trampling feet had touched her. It had been a shoulder or front leg that struck Conan, and the blind monster rushed on, forgetting the victims whose scent it had been following, in the sudden agony of its death throes. Headlong on its course it thundered until its low-hung head crashed into a gigantic tree in its path. The impact tore the tree up by the roots and must have dashed the brains from the misshapen skull. Tree and monster fell together, and the dazed humans saw the branches and leaves shaken by the convulsions of the creature they covered—and then grow quiet.

Conan lifted Valeria to her feet and together they started away at a reeling run. A few moments later they emerged into the still twilight of the treeless plain.

★ ★ ★

Conan paused an instant and glanced back at the ebon fastness behind them. Not a leaf stirred, nor a bird chirped. It stood as silent as it must have stood before Man was created.

"Come on," muttered Conan, taking his companion's hand. "It's touch and go now. If more dragons come out of the woods after us—"

He did not have to finish the sentence.

The city looked very far away across the plain, farther than it had looked from the crag. Valeria's heart hammered until she felt as if it would strangle her. At every step she expected to hear the crashing of the bushes and see another colossal nightmare bearing down upon them. But nothing disturbed the silence of the thickets.

With the first mile between them and the woods, Valeria breathed more easily. Her buoyant self-confidence began to thaw out again. The sun had set and darkness was gathering over the plain, lightened a little by the stars that made stunted ghosts out of the cactus growths.

"No cattle, no plowed fields," muttered Conan. "How do these people live?"

"Perhaps the cattle are in pens for the night," suggested Valeria, "and the fields and grazing-pastures are on the other side of the city."

"Maybe," he grunted. "I didn't see any from the crag, though."

The moon came up behind the city, etching walls and towers blackly in the yellow glow. Valeria shivered. Black against the moon the strange city had a somber, sinister look.

Perhaps something of the same feeling occurred to Conan, for he stopped, glanced about him, and grunted: "We stop here. No use coming to their gates in the night. They probably wouldn't let us in. Besides, we need rest, and we don't know how they'll receive us. A few hours' sleep will put us in better shape to fight or run."

He led the way to a bed of cactus which grew in a circle—a phenomenon common to the southern desert. With his sword he chopped an opening, and motioned Valeria to enter.

"We'll be safe from snakes here, anyhow."

She glanced fearfully back toward the black line that indicated the forest some six miles away.

"Suppose a dragon comes out of the woods?"

"We'll keep watch," he answered, though he made no suggestion as to what they would do in such an event. He was staring at the city, a few miles away. Not a light shone from spire or tower. A great black mass of mystery, it reared cryptically against the moonlit sky.

"Lie down and sleep. I'll keep the first watch."

She hesitated, glancing at him uncertainly, but he sat down cross-legged in the opening, facing toward the plain, his sword across his knees, his back to her. Without further comment she lay down on the sand inside the spiky circle.

"Wake me when the moon is at its zenith," she directed.

He did not reply nor look toward her. Her last impression, as she sank into slumber, was of his muscular figure, immobile as a statue hewn out of bronze, outlined against the low-hanging stars.

2 By the Blaze of the Fire-Jewels

Valeria awoke with a start, to the realization that a gray dawn was stealing over the plain.

She sat up, rubbing her eyes. Conan squatted beside the cactus, cutting off the thick pears and dexterously twitching out the spikes.

"You didn't awake me," she accused. "You let me sleep all night!"

"You were tired," he answered. "Your posterior must have been sore, too, after that long ride. You pirates aren't used to horseback."

"What about yourself?" she retorted.

"I was a *kozak* before I was a pirate," he answered. "They live in the saddle. I snatch naps like a panther watching beside the trail for a deer to come by. My ears keep watch while my eyes sleep."

And indeed the giant barbarian seemed as much refreshed as if he had slept the whole night on a golden bed. Having removed the thorns, and peeled off the tough skin, he handed the girl a thick, juicy cactus leaf.

"Skin your teeth in that pear. It's food and drink to a desert man. I was a chief of the Zuagirs once—desert men who live by plundering the caravans."

"Is there anything you haven't been?" inquired the girl, half in derision and half in fascination.

"I've never been king of an Hyborian kingdom," he grinned, taking an enormous mouthful of cactus. "But I've dreamed of being even that. I may be too, some day. Why shouldn't I?"

She shook her head in wonder at his calm audacity, and fell to devouring her pear. She found it not unpleasing to the palate, and full of cool and thirst-satisfying juice. Finishing his meal, Conan wiped his hands in the sand, rose, ran his fingers through his thick black mane, hitched at his sword-belt and said:

"Well, let's go. If the people in that city are going to cut our throats they may as well do it now, before the heat of the day begins."

His grim humor was unconscious, but Valeria reflected that it might be prophetic. She too hitched her sword-belt as she rose. Her terrors of the night were past. The roaring dragons of the distant forest were like a dim dream. There was a swagger in her stride as she moved off beside the Cimmerian. Whatever perils lay ahead of them, their foes would be men. And Valeria of the Red Brotherhood had never seen the face of the man she feared.

Conan glanced down at her as she strode along beside him with her swinging stride that matched his own.

"You walk more like a hillman than a sailor," he said. "You must be an Aquilonian. The suns of Darfar never burnt your white skin brown. Many a princess would envy you."

"I am from Aquilonia," she replied. His compliments no longer irritated her. His evident admiration pleased her. For another man to have kept her watch while she slept would have angered her; she had always fiercely resented any man's attempting to shield or protect her because of her sex. But she found a secret pleasure in the fact that this man had done so. And he had not taken advantage of her fright and the weakness resulting from it. After all, she reflected, her companion was no common man.

★ ★ ★

The sun rose behind the city, turning the towers to a sinister crimson.

"Black last night against the moon," grunted Conan, his eyes clouding with the abysmal superstition of the barbarian. "Blood-red as a threat of blood against the sun this dawn. I do not like this city."

But they went on, and as they went Conan pointed out the fact that no road ran to the city from the north.

"No cattle have trampled the plain on this side of the city," said he. "No plowshare has touched the earth for years, maybe centuries. But look: once this plain was cultivated."

Valeria saw the ancient irrigation ditches he indicated, half filled in places, and overgrown with cactus. She frowned with perplexity as her eyes swept over the plain that stretched on all sides of the city to the forest edge, which marched in a vast, dim ring. Vision did not extend beyond that ring.

She looked uneasily at the city. No helmets or spear-heads gleamed on battlements, no trumpets sounded, no challenge rang from the towers. A silence as absolute as that of the forest brooded over the walls and minarets.

The sun was high above the eastern horizon when they stood before the great gate in the northern wall, in the shadow of the lofty rampart. Rust flecked the iron bracings of the mighty bronze portal. Spiderwebs glistened thickly on hinge and sill and bolted panel.

"It hasn't been opened for years!" exclaimed Valeria.

"A dead city," grunted Conan. "That's why the ditches were broken and the plain untouched."

"But who built it? Who dwelt here? Where did they go? Why did they abandon it?"

"Who can say? Maybe an exiled clan of Stygians built it. Maybe not. It doesn't look like Stygian architecture. Maybe the people were wiped out by enemies, or a plague exterminated them."

"In that case their treasures may still be gathering dust and cobwebs in there," suggested Valeria, the acquisitive instincts of her profession waking in her; prodded, too, by feminine curiosity. "Can we open the gate? Let's go in and explore a bit."

Conan eyed the heavy portal dubiously, but placed his massive shoulder against it and thrust with all the power of his muscular calves and thighs. With a rasping screech of rusty hinges the gate moved ponderously inward, and Conan straightened and drew his sword. Valeria stared over his shoulder, and made a sound indicative of surprise.

They were not looking into an open street or court as one would have expected. The opened gate, or door, gave directly into a long, broad hall which ran away and away until its vista grew indistinct in the distance. It was of heroic proportions, and the floor of a curious red stone, cut in square tiles, that seemed to smolder as if with the reflection of flames. The walls were of a shiny green material.

"Jade, or I'm a Shemite!" swore Conan.

"Not in such quantity!" protested Valeria.

"I've looted enough from the Khitan caravans to know what I'm talking about," he asserted. "That's jade!"

The vaulted ceiling was of lapis lazuli, adorned with clusters of great green stones that gleamed with a poisonous radiance.

"Green fire-stones," growled Conan. "That's what the people of Punt call them. They're supposed to be the petrified eyes of those prehistoric snakes the ancients called Golden Serpents. They glow like a cat's eyes in the dark. At night this hall would be lighted by them, but it would be a hellishly weird illumination. Let's look around. We might find a cache of jewels."

"Shut the door," advised Valeria. "I'd hate to have to outrun a dragon down this hall."

Conan grinned, and replied: "I don't believe the dragons ever leave the forest."

But he complied, and pointed out the broken bolt on the inner side.

"I thought I heard something snap when I shoved against it. That bolt's freshly broken. Rust has eaten nearly through it. If the people ran away, why should it have been bolted on the inside?"

"They undoubtedly left by another door," suggested Valeria.

She wondered how many centuries had passed since the light of outer day had filtered into that great hall through the open door. Sunlight was finding its way somehow into the hall, and they quickly saw the source. High up in the vaulted ceiling skylights were set in slot-like openings—translucent sheets of some crystalline substance. In the splotches of shadow between them, the green jewels winked like the eyes of angry cats. Beneath their feet the dully lurid floor smoldered with changing hues and colors of flame. It was like treading the floors of hell with evil stars blinking overhead.

Three balustraded galleries ran along on each side of the hall, one above the other.

"A four-storied house," grunted Conan, "and this hall extends to the roof. It's long as a street. I seem to see a door at the other end."

Valeria shrugged her white shoulders.

"Your eyes are better than mine, then, though I'm accounted sharp-eyed among the sea-rovers."

★ ★ ★

They turned into an open door at random, and traversed a series of empty chambers, floored like the hall, and with walls of the same green jade, or of marble or ivory or chalcedony, adorned with friezes of bronze, gold or silver. In the ceilings the green fire-gems were set, and their light was as ghostly and illusive as Conan had predicted. Under the witch-fire glow the intruders moved like specters.

Some of the chambers lacked this illumination, and their doorways showed black as the mouth of the Pit. These Conan and Valeria avoided, keeping always to the lighted chambers.

Cobwebs hung in the corners, but there was no perceptible accumulation of dust on the floor, or on the tables and seats of marble, jade or carnelian which occupied the chambers. Here and there were rugs of that silk known as Khitan which is practically indestructible. Nowhere did they find any windows, or doors opening into streets or courts. Each door merely opened into another chamber or hall.

"Why don't we come to a street?" grumbled Valeria. "This place or whatever we're in must be as big as the king of Turan's seraglio."

"They must not have perished of plague," said Conan, meditating upon the mystery of the empty city. "Otherwise we'd find skeletons. Maybe it became haunted, and everybody got up and left. Maybe—"

"Maybe, hell!" broke in Valeria rudely. "We'll never know. Look at these friezes. They portray men. What race do they belong to?"

Conan scanned them and shook his head.

"I never saw people exactly like them. But there's the smack of the East about them—Vendhya, maybe, or Kosala."

"Were you a king in Kosala?" she asked, masking her keen curiosity with derision.

"No. But I was a war-chief of the Afghulis who live in the Himelian mountains above the borders of Vendhya. These people favor the Kosalans. But why should Kosalans be building a city this far to west?"

The figures portrayed were those of slender, olive-skinned men and women, with finely chiseled, exotic features. They wore filmy robes and many delicate jeweled ornaments, and were depicted mostly in attitudes of feasting, dancing or love-making.

"Easterners, all right," grunted Conan, "but from where I don't know. They must have lived a disgustingly peaceful life, though, or they'd have scenes of wars and fights. Let's go up that stair."

It was an ivory spiral that wound up from the chamber in which they were standing. They mounted three flights and came into a broad chamber on the fourth floor, which seemed to be the highest tier in the building. Skylights in the ceiling illuminated the room, in which light the fire-gems winked pallidly. Glancing through the doors they saw, except on one side, a series of similarly lighted chambers. This other door opened upon a balustraded gallery that overhung a hall much smaller than the one they had recently explored on the lower floor.

"Hell!" Valeria sat down disgustedly on a jade bench. "The people who deserted this city must have taken all their treasures with them. I'm tired of wandering through these bare rooms at random."

"All these upper chambers seem to be lighted," said Conan. "I wish we could find a window that overlooked the city. Let's have a look through that door over there."

"You have a look," advised Valeria. "I'm going to sit here and rest my feet."

★ ★ ★

Conan disappeared through the door opposite that one opening upon the gallery, and Valeria leaned back with her hands clasped behind her head, and thrust her booted legs out in front of her. These silent rooms and halls with their gleaming green clusters of ornaments and burning crimson floors were beginning to depress her. She wished they could find their way out of the maze into which they had wandered and emerge into a street. She wondered idly what furtive, dark feet had glided over those flaming floors in past centuries, how many deeds of cruelty and mystery those winking ceiling-gems had blazed down upon.

It was a faint noise that brought her out of her reflections. She was on her feet with her sword in her hand before she realized what had disturbed her. Conan had not returned, and she knew it was not he that she had heard.

The sound had come from somewhere beyond the door that opened on to the gallery. Soundlessly in her soft leather boots she glided through it, crept across the balcony and peered down between the heavy balustrades.

A man was stealing along the hall.

The sight of a human being in this supposedly deserted city was a startling shock. Crouching down behind the stone balusters, with every nerve tingling, Valeria glared down at the stealthy figure.

The man in no way resembled the figures depicted on the friezes. He was slightly above middle height, very dark, though not negroid. He was naked but for a scanty silk clout that only partly covered his muscular hips, and a leather girdle, a hand's breadth broad, about his lean waist. His long black hair hung in lank strands about his shoulders, giving him a wild appearance. He was gaunt, but knots and cords of muscles stood out on his arms and legs, without that fleshy padding that presents a pleasing symmetry of contour. He was built with an economy that was almost repellent.

Yet it was not so much his physical appearance as his attitude that impressed the woman who watched him. He slunk along, stooped in a semi-crouch, his head turning from side to side. He grasped a wide-tipped blade in his right hand, and she saw it shake with the intensity of the emotion that gripped him. He was afraid, trembling in the grip of some dire terror. When he turned his head she caught the blaze of wild eyes among the lank strands of black hair.

He did not see her. On tiptoe he glided across the hall and vanished through an open door. A moment later she heard a choking cry, and then silence fell again.

Consumed with curiosity, Valeria glided along the gallery until she came to a door above the one through which the man had passed. It opened into another, smaller gallery that encircled a large chamber.

This chamber was on the third floor, and its ceiling was not so high as that of the hall. It was lighted only by the fire-stones, and their weird green glow left the spaces under the balcony in shadows.

Valeria's eyes widened. The man she had seen was still in the chamber.

He lay face down on a dark crimson carpet in the middle of the room. His body was limp, his arms spread wide. His curved sword lay near him.

She wondered why he should lie there so motionless. Then her eyes narrowed as she stared down at the rug on which he lay. Beneath and about him the fabric showed a slightly different color, a deeper, brighter crimson.

Shivering slightly, she crouched down closer behind the balustrade, intently scanning the shadows under the overhanging gallery. They gave up no secret.

Suddenly another figure entered the grim drama. He was a man similar to the first, and he came in by a door opposite that which gave upon the hall.

His eyes glared at the sight of the man on the floor, and he spoke something in a staccato voice that sounded like "Chicmec!" The other did not move.

The man stepped quickly across the floor, bent, gripped the fallen man's shoulder and turned him over. A choking cry escaped him as the head fell back limply, disclosing a throat that had been severed from ear to ear.

The man let the corpse fall back upon the blood-stained carpet, and sprang to his feet, shaking like a wind-blown leaf. His face was an ashy mask of fear. But with one knee flexed for flight, he froze suddenly, became as immobile as an image, staring across the chamber with dilated eyes.

In the shadows beneath the balcony a ghostly light began to glow and grow, a light that was not part of the fire-stone gleam. Valeria felt her hair stir as she watched it; for, dimly visible in the throbbing radiance, there floated a human skull, and it was from this skull—human yet appallingly misshapen—that the spectral light seemed to emanate. It hung there like a disembodied head, conjured out of night and the shadows, growing more and more distinct; human, and yet not human as she knew humanity.

The man stood motionless, an embodiment of paralyzed horror, staring fixedly at the apparition. The thing moved out from the wall and a grotesque shadow moved with it. Slowly the shadow became visible as a man-like figure whose naked torso and limbs shone whitely, with the hue of bleached bones. The bare skull on its shoulders grinned eyelessly, in the midst of its unholy nimbus, and the man confronting it seemed unable to take his eyes from it. He stood still, his sword dangling from nerveless fingers, on his face the expression of a man bound by the spells of a mesmerist.

★ ★ ★

Valeria realized that it was not fear alone that paralyzed him. Some hellish quality of that throbbing glow had robbed him of his power to think and act. She herself, safely above the scene, felt the subtle impact of a nameless emanation that was a threat to sanity.

The horror swept toward its victim and he moved at last, but only to drop his sword and sink to his knees, covering his eyes with his hands. Dumbly he awaited the stroke of the blade that now gleamed in the apparition's hand as it reared above him like Death triumphant over mankind.

Valeria acted according to the first impulse of her wayward nature. With one tigerish movement she was over the balustrade and dropping to the floor behind the awful shape. It wheeled at the thud of her soft boots on the floor, but even as it turned, her keen blade lashed down, and a fierce exultation swept her as she felt the edge cleave solid flesh and mortal bone.

The apparition cried out gurglingly and went down, severed through shoulder, breast-bone and spine, and as it fell the burning skull rolled clear, revealing a lank mop of black hair and a dark face twisted in the convulsions of death. Beneath the horrific masquerade there was a human being, a man similar to the one kneeling supinely on the floor.

The latter looked up at the sound of the blow and the cry, and now he glared in wild-eyed amazement at the white-skinned woman who stood over the corpse with a dripping sword in her hand.

He staggered up, yammering as if the sight had almost unseated his reason. She was amazed to realize that she understood him. He was gibbering in the Stygian tongue, though in a dialect unfamiliar to her.

"Who are you? Whence come you? What do you in Xuchotl?" Then rushing on, without waiting for her to reply: "But you are a friend—goddess or devil, it makes no difference! You have slain the Burning Skull! It was but a man beneath it, after all! We deemed it a demon *they* conjured up out of the catacombs! *Listen!*"

He stopped short in his ravings and stiffened, straining his ears with painful intensity. The girl heard nothing.

"We must hasten!" he whispered. "*They* are west of the Great Hall! They may be all around us here! They may be creeping upon us even now!"

He seized her wrist in a convulsive grasp she found hard to break.
"Whom do you mean by "they"?" she demanded.

He stared at her uncomprehendingly for an instant, as if he found her
ignorance hard to understand.

"They?" he stammered vaguely. "Why—why, the people of Xotalanc!
The clan of the man you slew. They who dwell by the eastern gate."

"You mean to say this city is inhabited?" she exclaimed.

"Aye! Aye!" He was writhing in the impatience of apprehension.
"Come away! Come quick! We must return to Tecuhltli!"

"Where is that?" she demanded.

"The quarter by the western gate!" He had her wrist again and was
pulling her toward the door through which he had first come. Great
beads of perspiration dripped from his dark forehead, and his eyes
blazed with terror.

"Wait a minute!" she growled, flinging off his hand. "Keep your
hands off me, or I'll split your skull. What's all this about? Who are
you? Where would you take me?"

He took a firm grip on himself, casting glances to all sides, and began
speaking so fast his words tripped over each other.

"My name is Techotl. I am of Tecuhltli. I and this man who lies
with his throat cut came into the Halls of Science to try and ambush
some of the Xotalancas. But we became separated and I returned here
to find him with his gullet slit. The Burning Skull did it, I know, just
as he would have slain me had you not killed him. But perhaps he was
not alone. Others may be stealing from Xotalanc! The gods themselves
blench at the fate of those they take alive!"

At the thought he shook as with an ague and his dark skin grew ashy.
Valeria frowned puzzledly at him. She sensed intelligence behind this
rigmarole, but it was meaningless to her.

She turned toward the skull, which still glowed and pulsed on the
floor, and was reaching a booted toe tentatively toward it, when the
man who called himself Techotl sprang forward with a cry.

"Do not touch it! Do not even look at it! Madness and death lurk in
it. The wizards of Xotalanc understand its secret—they found it in the
catacombs, where lie the bones of terrible kings who ruled in Xuchotl
in the black centuries of the past. To gaze upon it freezes the blood and
withers the brain of a man who understands not its mystery. To touch
it causes madness and destruction."

She scowled at him uncertainly. He was not a reassuring figure, with
his lean, muscle-knotted frame, and snaky locks. In his eyes, behind the

glow of terror, lurked a weird light she had never seen in the eyes of a man wholly sane. Yet he seemed sincere in his protestations.

"Come!" he begged, reaching for her hand, and then recoiling as he remembered her warning, "You are a stranger. How you came here I do not know, but if you were a goddess or a demon, come to aid Tecuhltli, you would know all the things you have asked me. You must be from beyond the great forest, whence our ancestors came. But you are our friend, or you would not have slain my enemy. Come quickly, before the Xotalancas find us and slay us!"

From his repellent, impassioned face she glanced to the sinister skull, smoldering and glowing on the floor near the dead man. It was like a skull seen in a dream, undeniably human, yet with disturbing distortions and malformations of contour and outline. In life the wearer of that skull must have presented an alien and monstrous aspect. Life? It seemed to possess some sort of life of its own. Its jaws yawned at her and snapped together. Its radiance grew brighter, more vivid, yet the impression of nightmare grew too; it was a dream; all life was a dream—it was Techotl's urgent voice which snapped Valeria back from the dim gulfs whither she was drifting.

"Do not look at the skull! Do not look at the skull!" It was a far cry from across unreckoned voids.

Valeria shook herself like a lion shaking his mane. Her vision cleared. Techotl was chattering: "In life it housed the awful brain of a king of magicians! It holds still the life and fire of magic drawn from outer spaces!"

★ ★ ★

With a curse Valeria leaped, lithe as a panther, and the skull crashed to flaming bits under her swinging sword. Somewhere in the room, or in the void, or in the dim reaches of her consciousness, an inhuman voice cried out in pain and rage.

Techotl's hand was plucking at her arm and he was gibbering: "You have broken it! You have destroyed it! Not all the black arts of Xotalanc can rebuild it! Come away! Come away quickly, now!"

"But I can't go," she protested. "I have a friend somewhere near by—"

The flare of his eyes cut her short as he stared past her with an expression grown ghastly. She wheeled just as four men rushed through as many doors, converging on the pair in the center of the chamber.

They were like the others she had seen, the same knotted muscles bulging on otherwise gaunt limbs, the same lank blue-black hair, the same mad glare in their wide eyes. They were armed and clad like Techotl, but on the breast of each was painted a white skull.

There were no challenges or war-cries. Like blood-mad tigers the men of Xotalanc sprang at the throats of their enemies. Techotl met them with the fury of desperation, ducked the swipe of a wide-headed blade, and grappled with the wielder, and bore him to the floor where they rolled and wrestled in murderous silence.

The other three swarmed on Valeria, their weird eyes red as the eyes of mad dogs.

* * *

She killed the first who came within reach before he could strike a blow, her long straight blade splitting his skull even as his own sword lifted for a stroke. She side-stepped a thrust, even as she parried a slash. Her eyes danced and her lips smiled without mercy. Again she was Valeria of the Red Brotherhood, and the hum of her steel was like a bridal song in her ears.

Her sword darted past a blade that sought to parry, and sheathed six inches of its point in a leather-guarded midriff. The man gasped agonizedly and went to his knees, but his tall mate lunged in, in ferocious silence, raining blow on blow so furiously that Valeria had no opportunity to counter. She stepped back coolly, parrying the strokes and watching for her chance to thrust home. He could not long keep up that flailing whirlwind. His arm would tire, his wind would fail; he would weaken, falter, and then her blade would slide smoothly into his heart. A sidelong glance showed her Techotl kneeling on the breast of his antagonist and striving to break the other's hold on his wrist and to drive home a dagger.

Sweat beaded the forehead of the man facing her, and his eyes were like burning coals. Smite as he would, he could not break past nor beat down her guard. His breath came in gusty gulps, his blows began to fall erratically. She stepped back to draw him out—and felt her thighs locked in an iron grip. She had forgotten the wounded man on the floor.

Crouching on his knees, he held her with both arms locked about her legs, and his mate croaked in triumph and began working his way around to come at her from the left side. Valeria wrenched and tore savagely, but in vain. She could free herself of this clinging menace with a downward flick of her sword, but in that instant the curved blade of the tall warrior would crash through her skull. The wounded man began to worry at her bare thigh with his teeth like a wild beast. She reached down with her left hand and gripped his long hair, forcing his head back so that his white teeth and rolling eyes gleamed up at her. The tall Xotalanc cried out fiercely and leaped in, smiting with all the fury of his arm. Awkwardly she parried the stroke, and it beat the flat of her blade down on her head so that she saw sparks flash before her eyes, and staggered. Up went the sword again, with a low, beast-like cry of triumph—and then a giant form loomed behind the Xotalanc and steel flashed like a jet of blue lightning. The cry of the warrior broke short and he went down like an ox beneath the pole-ax, his brains gushing from his skull that had been split to the throat.

"Conan!" gasped Valeria. In a gust of passion she turned on the Xotalanc whose long hair she still gripped in her left hand. "Dog of hell!" Her blade swished as it cut the air in an upswinging arc with a blur in the middle, and the headless body slumped down, spurting blood. She hurled the severed head across the room.

"What the devil's going on here?" Conan bestrode the corpse of the man he had killed, broadsword in hand, glaring about him in amazement.

Techotl was rising from the twitching figure of the last Xotalanc, shaking red drops from his dagger. He was bleeding from the stab deep in the thigh. He stared at Conan with dilated eyes.

"What is all this?" Conan demanded again, not yet recovered from the stunning surprise of finding Valeria engaged in a savage battle with these fantastic figures in a city he had thought empty and uninhabited. Returning from an aimless exploration of the upper chambers to find Valeria missing from the room where he had left her, he had followed the sounds of strife that burst on his dumbfounded ears.

"Five dead dogs!" exclaimed Techotl, his flaming eyes reflecting a ghastly exultation. "Five slain! Five crimson nails for the black pillar! The gods of blood be thanked!"

He lifted quivering hands on high, and then, with the face of a fiend, he spat on the corpses and stamped on their faces, dancing in his ghoulish glee. His recent allies eyed him in amazement, and Conan asked, in the Aquilonian tongue: "Who is this madman?"

Valeria shrugged her shoulders.

"He says his name's Techotl. From his babblings I gather that his people live at one end of this crazy city, and these others at the other end. Maybe we'd better go with him. He seems friendly, and it's easy to see that the other clan isn't."

★ ★ ★

Techotl had ceased his dancing and was listening again, his head tilted sidewise, dog-like, triumph struggling with fear in his repellent countenance.

"Come away, now!" he whispered. "We have done enough! Five dead dogs! My people will welcome you! They will honor you! But come! It is far to Tecuhltli. At any moment the Xotalancas may come on us in numbers too great even for your swords."

"Lead the way," grunted Conan.

Techotl instantly mounted a stair leading up to the gallery, beckoning them to follow him, which they did, moving rapidly to keep on his heels. Having reached the gallery, he plunged into a door that opened toward the west, and hurried through chamber after chamber, each lighted by skylights or green fire-jewels.

"What sort of a place can this be?" muttered Valeria under her breath.

"Crom knows!" answered Conan. "I've seen *his* kind before, though. They live on the shores of Lake Zuad, near the border of Kush. They're a sort of mongrel Stygians, mixed with another race that wandered into Stygia from the east some centuries ago and were absorbed by them. They're called Tlazitlans. I'm willing to bet it wasn't they who built this city, though."

Techotl's fear did not seem to diminish as they drew away from the chamber where the dead men lay. He kept twisting his head on his shoulder to listen for sounds of pursuit, and stared with burning intensity into every doorway they passed.

Valeria shivered in spite of herself. She feared no man. But the weird floor beneath her feet, the uncanny jewels over her head, dividing the lurking shadows among them, the stealth and terror of their guide, impressed her with a nameless apprehension, a sensation of lurking, inhuman peril.

"They may be between us and Tecuhltli!" he whispered once. "We must beware lest they be lying in wait!"

"Why don't we get out of this infernal palace, and take to the streets?" demanded Valeria.

"There are no streets in Xuchotl," he answered. "No squares nor open courts. The whole city is built like one giant palace under one great roof. The nearest approach to a street is the Great Hall which traverses the city from the north gate to the south gate. The only doors opening into the outer world are the city gates, through which no living man has passed for fifty years."

"How long have you dwelt here?" asked Conan.

"I was born in the castle of Tecuhltli thirty-five years ago. I have never set foot outside the city. For the love of the gods, let us go silently! These halls may be full of lurking devils. Olmec shall tell you all when we reach Tecuhltli."

So in silence they glided on with the green fire-stones blinking overhead and the flaming floors smoldering under their feet, and it seemed to Valeria as if they fled through hell, guided by a dark-faced, lank-haired goblin.

Yet it was Conan who halted them as they were crossing an unusually wide chamber. His wilderness-bred ears were keener even than the ears of Techotl, whetted though these were by a lifetime of warfare in those silent corridors.

"You think some of your enemies may be ahead of us, lying in ambush?"

"They prowl through these rooms at all hours," answered Techotl, "as do we. The halls and chambers between Tecuhltli and Xotalanc are a disputed region, owned by no man. We call it the Halls of Silence. Why do you ask?"

"Because men are in the chambers ahead of us," answered Conan. "I heard steel clink against stone."

Again a shaking seized Techotl, and he clenched his teeth to keep them from chattering.

"Perhaps they are your friends," suggested Valeria.

"We dare not chance it," he panted, and moved with frenzied activity. He turned aside and glided through a doorway on the left which led into a chamber from which an ivory staircase wound down into darkness.

"This leads to an unlighted corridor below us!" he hissed, great beads of perspiration standing out on his brow. "They may be lurking there, too. It may all be a trick to draw us into it. But we must take the chance that they have laid their ambush in the rooms above. Come swiftly, now!"

★ ★ ★

Softly as phantoms they descended the stair and came to the mouth of a corridor black as night. They crouched there for a moment, listening, and then melted into it. As they moved along, Valeria's flesh crawled between her shoulders in momentary expectation of a sword-thrust in the dark. But for Conan's iron fingers gripping her arm she had no physical cognizance of her companions. Neither made as much noise as a cat would have made. The darkness was absolute. One hand, outstretched, touched a wall, and occasionally she felt a door under her fingers. The hallway seemed interminable.

Suddenly they were galvanized by a sound behind them. Valeria's flesh crawled anew, for she recognized it as the soft opening of a door. Men had come into the corridor behind them. Even with the thought she stumbled over something that felt like a human skull. It rolled across the floor with an appalling clatter.

"Run!" yelped Techotl, a note of hysteria in his voice, and was away down the corridor like a flying ghost.

Again Valeria felt Conan's hand bearing her up and sweeping her along as they raced after their guide. Conan could see in the dark no better than she, but he possessed a sort of instinct that made his course unerring. Without his support and guidance she would have fallen or stumbled against the wall. Down the corridor they sped, while the swift patter of flying feet drew closer and closer, and then suddenly Techotl panted: "Here is the stair! After me, quick! Oh, quick!"

His hand came out of the dark and caught Valeria's wrist as she stumbled blindly on the steps. She felt herself half dragged, half lifted up the winding stair, while Conan released her and turned on the steps, his ears and instincts telling him their foes were hard at their backs. *And the sounds were not all those of human feet.*

Something came writhing up the steps, something that slithered and rustled and brought a chill in the air with it. Conan lashed down with his great sword and felt the blade shear through something that might have been flesh and bone, and cut deep into the stair beneath. Something touched his foot that chilled like the touch of frost, and then the darkness beneath him was disturbed by a frightful thrashing and lashing, and a man cried out in agony.

The next moment Conan was racing up the winding staircase, and through a door that stood open at the head.

Valeria and Techotl were already through, and Techotl slammed the door and shot a bolt across it—the first Conan had seen since they left the outer gate.

Then he turned and ran across the well-lighted chamber into which they had come, and as they passed through the farther door, Conan glanced back and saw the door groaning and straining under heavy pressure violently applied from the other side.

Though Techotl did not abate either his speed or his caution, he seemed more confident now. He had the air of a man who has come into familiar territory, within call of friends.

But Conan renewed his terror by asking: "What was that thing that I fought on the stair?"

"The men of Xotalanc," answered Techotl, without looking back. "I told you the halls were full of them."

"This wasn't a man," grunted Conan. "It was something that crawled, and it was as cold as ice to the touch. I think I cut it asunder. It fell back on the men who were following us, and must have killed one of them in its death throes."

Techotl's head jerked back, his face ashy again. Convulsively he quickened his pace.

"It was the Crawler! A monster *they* have brought out of the catacombs to aid them! What it is, we do not know, but we have found our people hideously slain by it. In Set's name, hasten! If they put it on our trail, it will follow us to the very doors of Tecuhltli!"

"I doubt it," grunted Conan. "That was a shrewd cut I dealt it on the stair."

"Hasten! Hasten!" groaned Techotl.

They ran through a series of green-lit chambers, traversed a broad hall, and halted before a giant bronze door.

Techotl said: "This is Tecuhltli!"

3 The People of the Feud

Techotl smote on the bronze door with his clenched hand, and then turned sidewise, so that he could watch back along the hall.

"Men have been smitten down before this door, when they thought they were safe," he said.

"Why don't they open the door?" asked Conan.

"They are looking at us through the Eye," answered Techotl. "They are puzzled at the sight of you." He lifted his voice and called: "Open the door, Xecelan! It is I, Techotl, with friends from the great world beyond the forest!—They will open," he assured his allies.

"They'd better do it in a hurry, then," said Conan grimly. "I hear something crawling along the floor beyond the hall."

Techotl went ashy again and attacked the door with his fists, scream-ing: "Open, you fools, open! The Crawler is at our heels!"

Even as he beat and shouted, the great bronze door swung noiselessly back, revealing a heavy chain across the entrance, over which spear-heads bristled and fierce countenances regarded them intently for an instant. Then the chain was dropped and Techotl grasped the arms of his friends in a nervous frenzy and fairly dragged them over the thresh-old. A glance over his shoulder just as the door was closing showed Conan the long dim vista of the hall, and dimly framed at the other end an ophidian shape that writhed slowly and painfully into view, flowing in a dull-hued length from a chamber door, its hideous blood-stained head wagging drunkenly. Then the closing door shut off the view.

Inside the square chamber into which they had come heavy bolts were drawn across the door, and the chain locked into place. The door was made to stand the battering of a siege. Four men stood on guard, of the same lank-haired, dark-skinned breed as Techotl, with spears in their hands and swords at their hips. In the wall near the door there was a complicated contrivance of mirrors which Conan guessed was the Eye Techotl had mentioned, so arranged that a narrow, crystal-paned slot in the wall could be looked through from within without being discernible from without. The four guardsmen stared at the strangers with wonder, but asked no question, nor did Techotl vouchsafe any information. He moved with easy confidence now, as if he had shed his cloak of indecision and fear the instant he crossed the threshold.

"Come!" he urged his new-found friends, but Conan glanced toward the door.

"What about those fellows who were following us? Won't they try to storm that door?"

Techotl shook his head.

"They know they cannot break down the Door of the Eagle. They will flee back to Xotalanc, with their crawling fiend. Come! I will take you to the rulers of Tecuhltli."

★   ★   ★

One of the four guards opened the door opposite the one by which they had entered, and they passed through into a hallway which, like most of the rooms on that level, was lighted by both the slot-like sky-lights and the clusters of winking fire-gems. But unlike the other rooms they had traversed, this hall showed evidences of occupation. Velvet tapestries adorned the glossy jade walls, rich rugs were on the crimson floors, and the ivory seats, benches and divans were littered with satin cushions.

The hall ended in an ornate door, before which stood no guard. Without ceremony Techotl thrust the door open and ushered his friends into a broad chamber, where some thirty dark-skinned men and women lounging on satin-covered couches sprang up with exclamations of amazement.

The men, all except one, were of the same type as Techotl, and the women were equally dark and strange-eyed, though not unbeautiful in a weird dark way. They wore sandals, golden breast-plates, and scanty silk skirts supported by gem-crusted girdles, and their black manes, cut square at their naked shoulders, were bound with silver circlets.

On a wide ivory seat on a jade dais sat a man and a woman who differed subtly from the others. He was a giant, with an enormous sweep of breast and the shoulders of a bull. Unlike the others, he was bearded, with a thick, blue-black beard which fell almost to his broad girdle. He wore a robe of purple silk which reflected changing sheens of color with his every movement, and one wide sleeve, drawn back to his elbow, revealed a forearm massive with corded muscles. The band which confined his blue-black locks was set with glittering jewels.

The woman beside him sprang to her feet with a startled exclamation as the strangers entered, and her eyes, passing over Conan, fixed themselves with burning intensity on Valeria. She was tall and lithe, by far the most beautiful woman in the room. She was clad more scantily even than the others; for instead of a skirt she wore merely a broad strip of gilt-worked purple cloth fastened to the middle of her girdle which fell below her knees. Another strip at the back of her girdle completed that part of her costume, which she wore with a cynical indifference. Her breast-plates and the circlet about her temples were adorned with gems. In her eyes alone of all the dark-skinned people there lurked no brooding gleam of madness. She spoke no word after her first exclamation; she stood tensely, her hands clenched, staring at Valeria.

The man on the ivory seat had not risen.

"Prince Olmec," spoke Techotl, bowing low, with arms outspread and the palms of his hands turned upward, "I bring allies from the world beyond the forest. In the Chamber of Tezcoti the Burning Skull slew Chicmec, my companion—"

"The Burning Skull!" It was a shuddering whisper of fear from the people of Tecuhltli.

"Aye! Then came I, and found Chicmec lying with his throat cut. Before I could flee, the Burning Skull came upon me, and when I looked upon it my blood became as ice and the marrow of my bones melted. I could neither fight nor run. I could only await the stroke. Then came this white-skinned woman and struck him down with her sword; and lo, it was only a dog of Xotalanc with white paint upon his skin and the living skull of an ancient wizard upon his head! Now that skull lies in many pieces, and the dog who wore it is a dead man!"

An indescribably fierce exultation edged the last sentence, and was echoed in the low, savage exclamations from the crowding listeners.

"But wait!" exclaimed Techotl. "There is more! While I talked with the woman, four Xotalancas came upon us! One I slew—there is the stab in my thigh to prove how desperate was the fight. Two the woman killed. But we were hard pressed when this man came into the fray and split the skull of the fourth! Aye! Five crimson nails there are to be driven into the pillar of vengeance!"

He pointed at a black column of ebony which stood behind the dais. Hundreds of red dots scarred its polished surface—the bright scarlet heads of heavy copper nails driven into the black wood.

"Five red nails for five Xotalanca lives!" exulted Techotl, and the horrible exultation in the faces of the listeners made them inhuman.

"Who are these people?" asked Olmec, and his voice was like the low, deep rumble of a distant bull. None of the people of Xuchotl spoke loudly. It was as if they had absorbed into their souls the silence of the empty halls and deserted chambers.

"I am Conan, a Cimmerian," answered the barbarian briefly. "This woman is Valeria of the Red Brotherhood, an Aquilonian pirate. We are deserters from an army on the Darfar border, far to the north, and are trying to reach the coast."

The woman on the dais spoke loudly, her words tripping in her haste.

"You can never reach the coast! There is no escape from Xuchotl! You will spend the rest of your lives in this city!"

"What do you mean?" growled Conan, clapping his hand to his hilt and stepping about so as to face both the dais and the rest of the room. "Are you telling us we're prisoners?"

"She did not mean that," interposed Olmec. "We are your friends. We would not restrain you against your will. But I fear other circumstances will make it impossible for you to leave Xuchotl."

His eyes flickered to Valeria, and he lowered them quickly.

"This woman is Tascela," he said. "She is a princess of Tecuhltli. But let food and drink be brought our guests. Doubtless they are hungry, and weary from their long travels."

He indicated an ivory table, and after an exchange of glances, the adventurers seated themselves. The Cimmerian was suspicious. His fierce blue eyes roved about the chamber, and he kept his sword close to his hand. But an invitation to eat and drink never found him backward. His eyes kept wandering to Tascela, but the princess had eyes only for his white-skinned companion.

★ ★ ★

Techotl, who had bound a strip of silk about his wounded thigh, placed himself at the table to attend to the wants of his friends, seeming to consider it a privilege and honor to see after their needs. He inspected the food and drink the others brought in gold vessels and dishes, and tasted each before he placed it before his guests. While they ate, Olmec sat in silence on his ivory seat, watching them from under his broad black brows. Tascela sat beside him, chin cupped in her hands and her elbows resting on her knees. Her dark, enigmatic eyes, burning with a mysterious light, never left Valeria's supple figure. Behind her seat a sullen handsome girl waved an ostrich-plume fan with a slow rhythm.

The food was fruit of an exotic kind unfamiliar to the wanderers, but very palatable, and the drink was a light crimson wine that carried a heady tang.

"You have come from afar," said Olmec at last. "I have read the books of our fathers. Aquilonia lies beyond the lands of the Stygians and the Shemites, beyond Argos and Zingara; and Cimmeria lies beyond Aquilonia."

"We have each a roving foot," answered Conan carelessly.

"How you won through the forest is a wonder to me," quoth Olmec. "In bygone days a thousand fighting-men scarcely were able to carve a road through its perils."

"We encountered a bench-legged monstrosity about the size of a mastodon," said Conan casually, holding out his wine goblet which Techotl filled with evident pleasure. "But when we'd killed it we had no further trouble."

The wine vessel slipped from Techotl's hand to crash on the floor. His dusky skin went ashy. Olmec started to his feet, an image of stunned amazement, and a low gasp of awe or terror breathed up from the others. Some slipped to their knees as if their legs would not support them. Only Tascela seemed not to have heard. Conan glared about him bewilderedly.

"What's the matter? What are you gaping about?"

"You—you slew the dragon-god?"

"God? I killed a dragon. Why not? It was trying to gobble us up."

"But dragons are immortal!" exclaimed Olmec. "They slay each other, but no man ever killed a dragon! The thousand fighting-men of our ancestors who fought their way to Xuchotl could not prevail against them! Their swords broke like twigs against their scales!"

"If your ancestors had thought to dip their spears in the poisonous juice of Derketa's Apples," quoth Conan, with his mouth full, "and jab them in the eyes or mouth or somewhere like that, they'd have seen that dragons are not more immortal than any other chunk of beef. The carcass lies at the edge of the trees, just within the forest. If you don't believe me, go and look for yourself."

Olmec shook his head, not in disbelief but in wonder.

"It was because of the dragons that our ancestors took refuge in Xuchotl," said he. "They dared not pass through the plain and plunge into the forest beyond. Scores of them were seized and devoured by the monsters before they could reach the city."

"Then your ancestors didn't build Xuchotl?" asked Valeria.

"It was ancient when they first came into the land. How long it had stood here, not even its degenerate inhabitants knew."

"Your people came from Lake Zuad?" questioned Conan.

"Aye. More than half a century ago a tribe of the Tlazitlans rebelled against the Stygian king, and, being defeated in battle, fled southward. For many weeks they wandered over grasslands, desert and hills, and at last they came into the great forest, a thousand fighting-men with their women and children.

"It was in the forest that the dragons fell upon them, and tore many to pieces; so the people fled in a frenzy of fear before them, and at last came into the plain and saw the city of Xuchotl in the midst of it.

"They camped before the city, not daring to leave the plain, for the night was made hideous with the noise of the battling monsters throughout the forest. They made war incessantly upon one another. Yet they came not into the plain.

"The people of the city shut their gates and shot arrows at our people from the walls. The Tlazitlans were imprisoned on the plain, as if the ring of the forest had been a great wall; for to venture into the woods would have been madness.

"That night there came secretly to their camp a slave from the city, one of their own blood, who with a band of exploring soldiers had wandered into the forest long before, when he was a young man. The dragons had devoured all his companions, but he had been taken into the city to dwell in servitude. His name was Tolkemec." A flame lighted the dark eyes at mention of the name, and some of the people muttered obscenely and spat. "He promised to open the gates to the warriors. He asked only that all captives taken be delivered into his hands.

"At dawn he opened the gates. The warriors swarmed in and the halls of Xuchotl ran red. Only a few hundred folk dwelt there, decaying remnants of a once great race. Tolkemec said they came from the east, long ago, from Old Kosala, when the ancestors of those who now dwell in Kosala came up from the south and drove forth the original inhabitants of the land. They wandered far westward and finally found this forest-girdled plain, inhabited then by a tribe of black people.

"These they enslaved and set to building a city. From the hills to the east they brought jade and marble and lapis lazuli, and gold, silver and copper. Herds of elephants provided them with ivory. When their city was completed, they slew all the black slaves. And their magicians made a terrible magic to guard the city; for by their necromantic arts they re-created the dragons which had once dwelt in this lost land, and whose monstrous bones they found in the forest. Those bones they clothed in flesh and life, and the living beasts walked the earth as they walked it when Time was young. But the wizards wove a spell that kept them in the forest and they came not into the plain.

★   ★   ★

"So for many centuries the people of Xuchotl dwelt in their city, cultivating the fertile plain, until their wise men learned how to grow fruit within the city—fruit which is not planted in soil, but obtains its nourishment out of the air—and then they let the irrigation ditches run dry, and dwelt more and more in luxurious sloth, until decay seized them. They were a dying race when our ancestors broke through the forest and came into the plain. Their wizards had died, and the people had forgot their ancient necromancy. They could fight neither by sorcery nor the sword.

"Well, our fathers slew the people of Xuchotl, all except a hundred which were given living into the hands of Tolkemec, who had been their slave; and for many days and nights the halls re-echoed to their screams under the agony of his tortures.

"So the Tlazitlans dwelt here, for a while in peace, ruled by the brothers Tecuhltli and Xotalanc, and by Tolkemec. Tolkemec took a girl of the tribe to wife, and because he had opened the gates, and because he knew many of the arts of the Xuchotlans, he shared the rule of the tribe with the brothers who had led the rebellion and the flight.

"For a few years, then, they dwelt at peace within the city, doing little but eating, drinking and making love, and raising children. There was no necessity to till the plain, for Tolkemec taught them how to cultivate the air-devouring fruits. Besides, the slaying of the Xuchotlans broke the spell that held the dragons in the forest, and they came nightly and bellowed about the gates of the city. The plain ran red with the blood of their eternal warfare, and it was then that—" He bit his tongue in the midst of the sentence, then presently continued, but Valeria and Conan felt that he had checked an admission he had considered unwise.

"Five years they dwelt in peace. Then"—Olmec's eyes rested briefly on the silent woman at his side—"Xotalanc took a woman to wife, a woman whom both Tecuhltli and old Tolkemec desired. In his madness, Tecuhltli stole her from her husband. Aye, she went willingly enough. Tolkemec, to spite Xotalanc, aided Tecuhltli. Xotalanc demanded that she be given back to him, and the council of the tribe decided that the matter should be left to the woman. She chose to remain with Tecuhltli. In wrath Xotalanc sought to take her back by force, and the retainers of the brothers came to blows in the Great Hall.

"There was much bitterness. Blood was shed on both sides. The quarrel became a feud, the feud an open war. From the welter three factions emerged—Tecuhltli, Xotalanc, and Tolkemec. Already, in the days of peace, they had divided the city between them. Tecuhltli dwelt in the western quarter of the city, Xotalanc in the eastern, and Tolkemec with his family by the southern gate.

"Anger and resentment and jealousy blossomed into bloodshed and rape and murder. Once the sword was drawn there was no turning back; for blood called for blood, and vengeance followed swift on the heels of atrocity. Tecuhltli fought with Xotalanc, and Tolkemec aided first one and then the other, betraying each faction as it fitted his purposes. Tecuhltli and his people withdrew into the quarter of the western gate, where we now sit. Xuchotl is built in the shape of an oval. Tecuhltli, which took its name from its prince, occupies the western end of the oval. The people blocked up all doors connecting the quarter with the rest of the city, except one on each floor, which could be defended easily. They went into the pits below the city and built a wall cutting off the western end of the catacombs, where lie the bodies of the ancient Xuchotlans, and of those Tlazitlans slain in the feud. They dwelt as in a besieged castle, making sorties and forays on their enemies.

"The people of Xotalanc likewise fortified the eastern quarter of the city, and Tolkemec did likewise with the quarter by the southern gate. The central part of the city was left bare and uninhabited. Those empty halls and chambers became a battleground, and a region of brooding terror.

"Tolkemec warred on both clans. He was a fiend in the form of a human, worse than Xotalanc. He knew many secrets of the city he never told the others. From the crypts of the catacombs he plundered the dead of their grisly secrets—secrets of ancient kings and wizards, long forgotten by the degenerate Xuchotlans our ancestors slew. But all his magic did not aid him the night we of Tecuhltli stormed his castle and butchered all his people. Tolkemec we tortured for many days."

His voice sank to a caressing slur, and a far-away look grew in his eyes, as if he looked back over the years to a scene which caused him intense pleasure.

"Aye, we kept the life in him until he screamed for death as for a bride. At last we took him living from the torture chamber and cast him into a dungeon for the rats to gnaw as he died. From that dungeon, somehow, he managed to escape, and dragged himself into the catacombs. There without doubt he died, for the only way out of the catacombs beneath Tecuhltli is through Tecuhltli, and he never emerged by that way. His bones were never found, and the superstitious among our people swear that his ghost haunts the crypts to this day, wailing among the bones of the dead. Twelve years ago we butchered the people of Tolkemec, but the feud raged on between Tecuhltli and Xotalanc, as it will rage until the last man, the last woman is dead.

"It was fifty years ago that Tecuhltli stole the wife of Xotalanc. Half a century the feud has endured. I was born in it. All in this chamber, except Tascela, were born in it. We expect to die in it.

"We are a dying race, even as those Xuchotlans our ancestors slew. When the feud began there were hundreds in each faction. Now we of

Tecuhltli number only these you see before you, and the men who guard the four doors: forty in all. How many Xotalancas there are we do not know, but I doubt if they are much more numerous than we. For fifteen years no children have been born to us, and we have seen none among the Xotalancas.

"We are dying, but before we die we will slay as many of the men of Xotalanc as the gods permit."

And with his weird eyes blazing, Olmec spoke long of that grisly feud, fought out in silent chambers and dim halls under the blaze of the green fire-jewels, on floors smoldering with the flames of hell and splashed with deeper crimson from severed veins. In that long butchery a whole generation had perished. Xotalanc was dead, long ago, slain in a grim battle on an ivory stair. Tecuhltli was dead, flayed alive by the maddened Xotalancas who had captured him.

Without emotion Olmec told of hideous battles fought in black corridors, of ambushes on twisting stairs, and red butcheries. With a redder, more abysmal gleam in his deep dark eyes he told of men and women flayed alive, mutilated and dismembered, of captives howling under tortures so ghastly that even the barbarous Cimmerian grunted. No wonder Techotl had trembled with the terror of capture. Yet he had gone forth to slay if he could, driven by hate that was stronger than his fear. Olmec spoke further, of dark and mysterious matters, of black magic and wizardry conjured out of the black night of the catacombs, of weird creatures invoked out of darkness for horrible allies. In these things the Xotalancas had the advantage, for it was in the eastern catacombs where lay the bones of the greatest wizards of the ancient Xuchotlans, with their immemorial secrets.

★ ★ ★

Valeria listened with morbid fascination. The feud had become a terrible elemental power driving the people of Xuchotl inexorably on to doom and extinction. It filled their whole lives. They were born in it, and they expected to die in it. They never left their barricaded castle except to steal forth into the Halls of Silence that lay between the opposing fortresses, to slay and be slain. Sometimes the raiders returned with frantic captives, or with grim tokens of victory in fight. Sometimes they did not return at all, or returned only as severed limbs cast down before the bolted bronze doors. It was a ghastly, unreal nightmare existence these people lived, shut off from the rest of the world, caught together like rabid rats in the same trap, butchering one another through the years, crouching and creeping through the sunless corridors to maim and torture and murder.

While Olmec talked, Valeria felt the blazing eyes of Tascela fixed upon her. The princess seemed not to hear what Olmec was saying. Her expression, as he narrated victories or defeats, did not mirror the wild rage or fiendish exultation that alternated on the faces of the other Tecuhltli. The feud that was an obsession to her clansmen seemed meaningless to her. Valeria found her indifferent callousness more repugnant than Olmec's naked ferocity.

"And we can never leave the city," said Olmec. "For fifty years no one has left it except those—" Again he checked himself.

"Even without the peril of the dragons," he continued, "we who were born and raised in the city would not dare leave it. We have never set foot outside the walls. We are not accustomed to the open sky and the naked sun. No; we were born in Xuchotl, and in Xuchotl we shall die."

"Well," said Conan, "with your leave we'll take our chances with the dragons. This feud is none of our business. If you'll show us to the west gate, we'll be on our way."

Tascela's hands clenched, and she started to speak, but Olmec interrupted her: "It is nearly nightfall. If you wander forth into the plain by night, you will certainly fall prey to the dragons."

"We crossed it last night, and slept in the open without seeing any," returned Conan.

Tascela smiled mirthlessly. "You dare not leave Xuchotl!"

Conan glared at her with instinctive antagonism; she was not looking at him, but at the woman opposite him.

"I think they dare," retorted Olmec. "But look you, Conan and Valeria, the gods must have sent you to us, to cast victory into the laps of the Tecuhltli! You are professional fighters—why not fight for us? We have wealth in abundance—precious jewels are as common in Xuchotl as cobblestones are in the cities of the world. Some the Xuchotlans brought with them from Kosala. Some, like the fire-stones, they found in the hills to the east. Aid us to wipe out the Xotalancas, and we will give you all the jewels you can carry."

"And will you help us destroy the dragons?" asked Valeria. "With bows and poisoned arrows thirty men could slay all the dragons in the forest."

"Aye!" replied Olmec promptly. "We have forgotten the use of the bow, in years of hand-to-hand fighting, but we can learn again."

"What do you say?" Valeria inquired of Conan.

"We're both penniless vagabonds," he grinned hardily. "I'd as soon kill Xotalancas as anybody."

"Then you agree?" exclaimed Olmec, while Techotl fairly hugged himself with delight.

"Aye. And now suppose you show us chambers where we can sleep, so we can be fresh tomorrow for the beginning of the slaying."

Olmec nodded, and waved a hand, and Techotl and a woman led the adventurers into a corridor which led through a door off to the left of the jade dais. A glance back showed Valeria Olmec sitting on his throne, chin on knotted fist, staring after them. His eyes burned with a weird flame. Tascela leaned back in her seat, whispering to the sullen-faced maid, Yasala, who leaned over her shoulder, her ear to the princess' moving lips.

★ ★ ★

The hallway was not so broad as most they had traversed, but it was long. Presently the woman halted, opened a door, and drew aside for Valeria to enter.

"Wait a minute," growled Conan. "Where do I sleep?"

Techotl pointed to a chamber across the hallway, but one door farther down. Conan hesitated, and seemed inclined to raise an objection, but Valeria smiled spitefully at him and shut the door in his face. He muttered something uncomplimentary about women in general, and strode off down the corridor after Techotl.

In the ornate chamber where he was to sleep, he glanced up at the slot-like skylights. Some were wide enough to admit the body of a slender man, supposing the glass were broken.

"Why don't the Xotalancas come over the roofs and shatter those skylights?" he asked.

"They cannot be broken," answered Techotl. "Besides, the roofs would be hard to clamber over. They are mostly spires and domes and steep ridges."

He volunteered more information about the "castle" of Tecuhltli. Like the rest of the city it contained four stories, or tiers of chambers, with towers jutting up from the roof. Each tier was named; indeed, the people of Xuchotl had a name for each chamber, hall and stair in the city, as people of more normal cities designate streets and quarters. In Tecuhltli the floors were named The Eagle's Tier, The Ape's Tier, The

Tiger's Tier and The Serpent's Tier, in the order as enumerated, The Eagle's Tier being the highest, or fourth, floor.

"Who is Tascela?" asked Conan. "Olmec's wife?"

Techotl shuddered and glanced furtively about him before answering.

"No. She is—Tascela! She was the wife of Xotalanc—the woman Tecuhltli stole, to start the feud."

"What are you talking about?" demanded Conan. "That woman is beautiful and young. Are you trying to tell me that she was a wife fifty years ago?"

"Aye! I swear it! She was a full-grown woman when the Tlazitlans journeyed from Lake Zuad. It was because the king of Stygia desired her for a concubine that Xotalanc and his brother rebelled and fled into the wilderness. She is a witch, who possesses the secret of perpetual youth."

"What's that?" asked Conan.

Techotl shuddered again.

"Ask me not! I dare not speak. It is too grisly, even for Xuchotl!"

And touching his finger to his lips, he glided from the chamber.

4 Scent of Black Lotus

Valeria unbuckled her sword-belt and laid it with the sheathed weapon on the couch where she meant to sleep. She noted that the doors were supplied with bolts, and asked where they led.

"Those lead into adjoining chambers," answered the woman, indicating the doors on right and left. "That one"—pointing to a copper-bound door opposite that which opened into the corridor—"leads to a corridor which runs to a stair that descends into the catacombs. Do not fear; naught can harm you here."

"Who spoke of fear?" snapped Valeria. "I just like to know what sort of harbor I'm dropping anchor in. No, I don't want you to sleep at the foot of my couch. I'm not accustomed to being waited on—not by women, anyway. You have my leave to go."

Alone in the room, the pirate shot the bolts on all the doors, kicked off her boots and stretched luxuriously out on the couch. She imagined Conan similarly situated across the corridor, but her feminine vanity prompted her to visualize him as scowling and muttering with chagrin as he cast himself on his solitary couch, and she grinned with gleeful malice as she prepared herself for slumber.

Outside, night had fallen. In the halls of Xuchotl the green fire-jewels blazed like the eyes of prehistoric cats. Somewhere among the dark towers a night wind moaned like a restless spirit. Through the dim passages stealthy figures began stealing, like disembodied shadows.

Valeria awoke suddenly on her couch. In the dusky emerald glow of the fire-gems she saw a shadowy figure bending over her. For a bemused instant the apparition seemed part of the dream she had been dreaming. She had seemed to lie on the couch in the chamber as she was actually lying, while over her pulsed and throbbed a gigantic black blossom so enormous that it hid the ceiling. Its exotic perfume pervaded her being, inducing a delicious, sensuous languor that was something more and less than sleep. She was sinking into scented billows of insensible bliss, when something touched her face. So supersensitive were her drugged senses, that the light touch was like a dislocating impact, jolting her rudely into full wakefulness. Then it was that she saw, not a gargantuan blossom, but a dark-skinned woman standing above her.

With the realization came anger and instant action. The woman turned lithely, but before she could run Valeria was on her feet and had caught her arm. She fought like a wildcat for an instant, and then subsided as she felt herself crushed by the superior strength of her captor. The pirate wrenched the woman around to face her, caught her chin with her free hand and forced her captive to meet her gaze. It was the sullen Yasala, Tascela's maid.

"What the devil were you doing bending over me? What's that in your hand?"

The woman made no reply, but sought to cast away the object. Valeria twisted her arm around in front of her, and the thing fell to the floor—a great black exotic blossom on a jade-green stem, large as a woman's head, to be sure, but tiny beside the exaggerated vision she had seen.

"The black lotus!" said Valeria between her teeth. "The blossom whose scent brings deep sleep. You were trying to drug me! If you hadn't accidentally touched my face with the petals, you'd have—why did you do it? What's your game?"

Yasala maintained a sulky silence, and with an oath Valeria whirled her around, forced her to her knees and twisted her arm up behind her back.

"Tell me, or I'll tear your arm out of its socket!"

Yasala squirmed in anguish as her arm was forced excruciatingly up between her shoulder-blades, but a violent shaking of her head was the only answer she made.

"Slut!" Valeria cast her from her to sprawl on the floor. The pirate glared at the prostrate figure with blazing eyes. Fear and the memory of Tascela's burning eyes stirred in her, rousing all her tigerish instincts of self-preservation. These people were decadent; any sort of perversity might be expected to be encountered among them. But Valeria sensed here something that moved behind the scenes, some secret terror fouler than common degeneracy. Fear and revulsion of this weird city swept her. These people were neither sane nor normal; she began to doubt if they were even human. Madness smoldered in the eyes of them all—all except the cruel, cryptic eyes of Tascela, which held secrets and mysteries more abysmal than madness.

She lifted her head and listened intently. The halls of Xuchotl were as silent as if it were in reality a dead city. The green jewels bathed the chamber in a nightmare glow, in which the eyes of the woman on the floor glittered eerily up at her. A thrill of panic throbbed through Valeria, driving the last vestige of mercy from her fierce soul.

"Why did you try to drug me?" she muttered, grasping the woman's black hair, and forcing her head back to glare into her sullen, long-lashed eyes. "Did Tascela send you?"

No answer. Valeria cursed venomously and slapped the woman first on one cheek and then the other. The blows resounded through the room, but Yasala made no outcry.

"Why don't you scream?" demanded Valeria savagely. "Do you fear someone will hear you? Whom do you fear? Tascela? Olmec? Conan?"

★   ★   ★

Yasala made no reply. She crouched, watching her captor with eyes baleful as those of a basilisk. Stubborn silence always fans anger. Valeria turned and tore a handful of cords from a near-by hanging.

"You sulky slut!" she said between her teeth. "I'm going to strip you stark naked and tie you across that couch and whip you until you tell me what you were doing here, and who sent you!"

Yasala made no verbal protest, nor did she offer any resistance, as Valeria carried out the first part of her threat with a fury that her captive's obstinacy only sharpened. Then for a space there was no sound in the chamber except the whistle and crackle of hard-woven silken cords on naked flesh. Yasala could not move her fast-bound hands or feet. Her body writhed and quivered under the chastisement, her head swayed from side to side in rhythm with the blows. Her teeth were sunk into her lower lip and a trickle of blood began as the punishment continued. But she did not cry out.

The pliant cords made no great sound as they encountered the quivering body of the captive; only a sharp crackling snap, but each cord left a red streak across Yasala's dark flesh. Valeria inflicted the punishment with all the strength of her war-hardened arm, with all the mercilessness acquired during a life where pain and torment were daily happenings, and with all the cynical ingenuity which only a woman displays toward a woman. Yasala suffered more, physically and mentally, than she would have suffered under a lash wielded by a man, however strong.

It was the application of this feminine cynicism which at last tamed Yasala.

A low whimper escaped from her lips, and Valeria paused, arm lifted, and raked back a damp yellow lock. "Well, are you going to talk?" she demanded. "I can keep this up all night, if necessary!"

"Mercy!" whispered the woman. "I will tell."

Valeria cut the cords from her wrists and ankles, and pulled her to her feet. Yasala sank down on the couch, half reclining on one bare hip, supporting herself on her arm, and writhing at the contact of her smarting flesh with the couch. She was trembling in every limb.

"Wine!" she begged, dry-lipped, indicating with a quivering hand a gold vessel on an ivory table. "Let me drink. I am weak with pain. Then I will tell you all."

Valeria picked up the vessel, and Yasala rose unsteadily to receive it. She took it, raised it toward her lips—then dashed the contents full into the Aquilonian's face. Valeria reeled backward, shaking and clawing the stinging liquid out of her eyes. Through a smarting mist she saw Yasala dart across the room, fling back a bolt, throw open the copper-bound door and run down the hall. The pirate was after her instantly, sword out and murder in her heart.

But Yasala had the start, and she ran with the nervous agility of a woman who has just been whipped to the point of hysterical frenzy. She rounded a corner in the corridor, yards ahead of Valeria, and when the pirate turned it, she saw only an empty hall, and at the other end a door that gaped blackly. A damp moldy scent reeked up from it, and Valeria shivered. That must be the door that led to the catacombs. Yasala had taken refuge among the dead.

Valeria advanced to the door and looked down a flight of stone steps that vanished quickly into utter blackness. Evidently it was a shaft that led straight to the pits below the city, without opening upon any of the lower floors. She shivered slightly at the thought of the thousands of corpses lying in their stone crypts down there, wrapped in their moldering cloths. She had no intention of groping her way down those stone steps. Yasala doubtless knew every turn and twist of the subterranean tunnels.

She was turning back, baffled and furious, when a sobbing cry welled up from the blackness. It seemed to come from a great depth, but human words were faintly distinguishable, and the voice was that of a woman. "Oh, help! Help, in Set's name! Ahhh!" It trailed away, and Valeria thought she caught the echo of a ghostly tittering.

Valeria felt her skin crawl. What had happened to Yasala down there in the thick blackness? There was no doubt that it had been she who had cried out. But what peril could have befallen her? Was a Xotalanca lurking down there? Olmec had assured them that the catacombs below Tecuhltli were walled off from the rest, too securely for their enemies to break through. Besides, that tittering had not sounded like a human being at all.

Valeria hurried back down the corridor, not stopping to close the door that opened on the stair. Regaining her chamber, she closed the door and shot the bolt behind her. She pulled on her boots and buckled her sword-belt about her. She was determined to make her way to Conan's room and urge him, if he still lived, to join her in an attempt to fight their way out of that city of devils.

But even as she reached the door that opened into the corridor, a long-drawn scream of agony rang through the halls, followed by the stamp of running feet and the loud clangor of swords.

5 Twenty Red Nails

Two warriors lounged in the guardroom on the floor known as the Tier of the Eagle. Their attitude was casual, though habitually alert. An attack on the great bronze door from without was always a possibility, but for many years no such assault had been attempted on either side.

"The strangers are strong allies," said one. "Olmec will move against the enemy tomorrow, I believe."

He spoke as a soldier in a war might have spoken. In the miniature world of Xuchotl each handful of feudists was an army, and the empty halls between the castles was the country over which they campaigned.

The other meditated for a space.

"Suppose with their aid we destroy Xotalanc," he said. "What then, Xatmec?"

"Why," returned Xatmec, "we will drive red nails for them all. The captives we will burn and flay and quarter."

"But afterward?" pursued the other. "After we have slain them all? Will it not seem strange, to have no foes to fight? All my life I have fought and hated the Xotalancas. With the feud ended, what is left?"

Xatmec shrugged his shoulders. His thoughts had never gone beyond the destruction of their foes. They could not go beyond that.

Suddenly both men stiffened at a noise outside the door.

"To the door, Xatmec!" hissed the last speaker. "I shall look through the Eye—".

Xatmec, sword in hand, leaned against the bronze door, straining his ear to hear through the metal. His mate looked into the mirror. He started convulsively. Men were clustered thickly outside the door; grim, dark-faced men with swords gripped in their teeth—*and their fingers thrust into their ears.* One who wore a feathered head-dress had a set of pipes which he set to his lips, and even as the Tecuhltli started to shout a warning, the pipes began to skirl.

The cry died in the guard's throat as the thin, weird piping penetrated the metal door and smote on his ears. Xatmec leaned frozen against the door, as if paralyzed in that position. His face was that of a wooden image, his expression one of horrified listening. The other guard, farther removed from the source of the sound, yet sensed the horror of what was taking place, the grisly threat that lay in that demoniac fifing. He felt the weird strains plucking like unseen fingers at the tissues of his brain, filling him with alien emotions and impulses of madness. But with a soul-tearing effort he broke the spell, and shrieked a warning in a voice he did not recognize as his own.

But even as he cried out, the music changed to an unbearable shrilling that was like a knife in the ear-drums. Xatmec screamed in sudden agony, and all the sanity went out of his face like a flame blown out in a wind. Like a madman he ripped loose the chain, tore open the door and rushed out into the hall, sword lifted before his mate could stop him. A dozen blades struck him down, and over his mangled body the

Xotalancas surged into the guardroom, with a long-drawn, blood-mad yell that sent the unwonted echoes reverberating.

His brain reeling from the shock of it all, the remaining guard leaped to meet them with goring spear. The horror of the sorcery he had just witnessed was submerged in the stunning realization that the enemy were in Tecuhltli. And as his spearhead ripped through a dark-skinned belly he knew no more, for a swinging sword crushed his skull, even as wild-eyed warriors came pouring in from the chambers behind the guardroom.

It was the yelling of men and the clanging of steel that brought Conan bounding from his couch, wide awake and broadsword in hand. In an instant he had reached the door and flung it open, and was glaring out into the corridor just as Techotl rushed up it, eyes blazing madly.

"The Xotalancas!" he screamed, in a voice hardly human, "*They are within the door!*"

Conan ran down the corridor, even as Valeria emerged from her chamber.

"What the devil is it?" she called.

"Techotl says the Xotalancas are in," he answered hurriedly. "That racket sounds like it."

★ ★ ★

With the Tecuhltli on their heels they burst into the throne room and were confronted by a scene beyond the most frantic dream of blood and fury. Twenty men and women, their black hair streaming, and the white skulls gleaming on their breasts, were locked in combat with the people of Tecuhltli. The women on both sides fought as madly as the men, and already the room and the hall beyond were strewn with corpses.

Olmec, naked but for a breech-clout, was fighting before his throne, and as the adventurers entered, Tascela ran from an inner chamber with a sword in her hand.

Xatmec and his mate were dead, so there was none to tell the Tecuhltli how their foes had found their way into their citadel. Nor was there any to say what had prompted that mad attempt. But the losses of the Xotalancas had been greater, their position more desperate, than the Tecuhltli had known. The maiming of their scaly ally, the destruction of the Burning Skull, and the news, gasped by a dying man, that mysterious white-skin allies had joined their enemies, had driven them to the frenzy of desperation and the wild determination to die dealing death to their ancient foes.

The Tecuhltli, recovering from the first stunning shock of the surprise that had swept them back into the throne room and littered the floor with their corpses, fought back with an equally desperate fury, while the door-guards from the lower floors came racing to hurl themselves into the fray. It was the death-fight of rabid wolves, blind, panting, merciless. Back and forth it surged, from door to dais, blades whickering and striking into flesh, blood spurting, feet stamping the crimson floor where redder pools were forming. Ivory tables crashed over, seats were splintered, velvet hangings torn down were stained red. It was the bloody climax of a bloody half-century, and every man there sensed it.

But the conclusion was inevitable. The Tecuhltli outnumbered the invaders almost two to one, and they were heartened by that fact and by the entrance into the mêlée of their light-skinned allies.

These crashed into the fray with the devastating effect of a hurricane plowing through a grove of saplings. In sheer strength no three Tlazitlans were a match for Conan, and in spite of his weight he was quicker on his feet than any of them. He moved through the whirling, eddying mass with the surety and destructiveness of a gray wolf amidst a pack of alley curs, and he strode over a wake of crumpled figures.

Valeria fought beside him, her lips smiling and her eyes blazing. She was stronger than the average man, and far quicker and more ferocious. Her sword was like a living thing in her hand. Where Conan beat down opposition by the sheer weight and power of his blows, breaking spears, splitting skulls and cleaving bosoms to the breast-bone, Valeria brought into action a finesse of sword-play that dazzled and bewildered her antagonists before it slew them. Again and again a warrior, heaving high his heavy blade, found her point in his jugular before he could strike. Conan, towering above the field, strode through the welter smiting right and left, but Valeria moved like an illusive phantom, constantly shifting, and thrusting and slashing as she shifted. Swords missed her again and again as the wielders flailed the empty air and died with her point in their hearts or throats, and her mocking laughter in their ears.

Neither sex nor condition was considered by the maddened combatants. The five women of the Xotalancas were down with their throats cut before Conan and Valeria entered the fray, and when a man or woman went down under the stamping feet, there was always a knife ready for the helpless throat, or a sandaled foot eager to crush the prostrate skull.

From wall to wall, from door to door rolled the waves of combat, spilling over into adjoining chambers. And presently only Tecuhltli and their white-skinned allies stood upright in the great throne room. The survivors stared bleakly and blankly at each other, like survivors after Judgment Day or the destruction of the world. On legs wide-braced, hands gripping notched and dripping swords, blood trickling down their arms, they stared at one another across the mangled corpses of friends and foes. They had no breath left to shout, but a bestial mad howling rose from their lips. It was not a human cry of triumph. It was the howling of a rabid wolf-pack stalking among the bodies of its victims.

Conan caught Valeria's arm and turned her about.

"You've got a stab in the calf of your leg," he growled.

She glanced down, for the first time aware of a stinging in the muscles of her leg. Some dying man on the floor had fleshed his dagger with his last effort.

"You look like a butcher yourself," she laughed.

He shook a red shower from his hands.

"Not mine. Oh, a scratch here and there. Nothing to bother about. But that calf ought to be bandaged."

★ ★ ★

Olmec came through the litter, looking like a ghoul with his naked massive shoulders splashed with blood, and his black beard dabbled in crimson. His eyes were red, like the reflection of flame on black water.

"We have won!" he croaked dazedly. "The feud is ended! The dogs of Xotalanc lie dead! Oh, for a captive to flay alive! Yet it is good to look upon their dead faces. Twenty dead dogs! Twenty red nails for the black column!"

"You'd best see to your wounded," grunted Conan, turning away from him. "Here, girl, let me see that leg."

"Wait a minute!" she shook him off impatiently. The fire of fighting still burned brightly in her soul. "How do we know these are all of them? These might have come on a raid of their own."

"They would not split the clan on a foray like this," said Olmec, shaking his head, and regaining some of his ordinary intelligence.

Without his purple robe the man seemed less like a prince than some repellent beast of prey. "I will stake my head upon it that we have slain them all. There were less of them than I dreamed, and they must have been desperate. But how came they in Tecuhltli?"

Tascela came forward, wiping her sword on her naked thigh, and holding in her other hand an object she had taken from the body of the feathered leader of the Xotalancas.

"The pipes of madness," she said. "A warrior tells me that Xatmec opened the door to the Xotalancas and was cut down as they stormed into the guardroom. This warrior came to the guardroom from the inner hall just in time to see it happen and to hear the last of a weird strain of music which froze his very soul. Tolkemec used to talk of these pipes, which the Xuchotlans swore were hidden somewhere in the catacombs with the bones of the ancient wizard who used them in his lifetime. Somehow the dogs of Xotalanc found them and learned their secret."

"Somebody ought to go to Xotalanc and see if any remain alive," said Conan. "I'll go if somebody will guide me."

Olmec glanced at the remnants of his people. There were only twenty left alive, and of these several lay groaning on the floor. Tascela was the only one of the Tecuhltli who had escaped without a wound. The princess was untouched, though she had fought as savagely as any.

"Who will go with Conan to Xotalanc?" asked Olmec.

Techotl limped forward. The wound in his thigh had started bleeding afresh, and he had another gash across his ribs.

"I will go!"

"No, you won't," vetoed Conan. "And you're not going either, Valeria. In a little while that leg will be getting stiff."

"I will go," volunteered a warrior, who was knotting a bandage about a slashed forearm.

"Very well, Yanath. Go with the Cimmerian. And you, too, Topal." Olmec indicated another man whose injuries were slight. "But first aid us to lift the badly wounded on these couches where we may bandage their hurts."

This was done quickly. As they stooped to pick up a woman who had been stunned by a war-club, Olmec's beard brushed Topal's ear. Conan thought the prince muttered something to the warrior, but he could not be sure. A few moments later he was leading his companions down the hall.

Conan glanced back as he went out the door, at that shambles where the dead lay on the smoldering floor, blood-stained dark limbs knotted in attitudes of fierce muscular effort, dark faces frozen in masks of hate, glassy eyes glaring up at the green fire-jewels which bathed the ghastly scene in a dusky emerald witch-light. Among the dead the living moved aimlessly, like people moving in a trance. Conan heard Olmec call a woman and direct her to bandage Valeria's leg. The pirate followed the woman into an adjoining chamber, already beginning to limp slightly.

★　★　★

Warily the two Tecuhltli led Conan along the hall beyond the bronze door, and through chamber after chamber shimmering in the green fire. They saw no one, heard no sound. After they crossed the Great Hall which bisected the city from north to south, their caution was increased by the realization of their nearness to enemy territory. But chambers and halls lay empty to their wary gaze, and they came at last along a broad dim hallway and halted before a bronze door similar to the Eagle Door of Tecuhltli. Gingerly they tried it, and it opened silently under their fingers. Awed, they stared into the green-lit chambers beyond. For fifty years no Tecuhltli had entered those halls save as a prisoner going to a hideous doom. To go to Xotalanc had been the ultimate horror that could befall a man of the western castle. The terror of it had stalked through their dreams since earliest childhood. To Yanath and Topal that bronze door was like the portal of hell.

They cringed back, unreasoning horror in their eyes, and Conan pushed past them and strode into Xotalanc.

Timidly they followed him. As each man set foot over the threshold he stared and glared wildly about him. But only their quick, hurried breathing disturbed the silence.

They had come into a square guardroom, like that behind the Eagle Door of Tecuhltli, and, similarly, a hall ran away from it to a broad chamber that was a counterpart of Olmec's throne room.

Conan glanced down the hall with its rugs and divans and hangings, and stood listening intently. He heard no noise, and the rooms had an empty feel. He did not believe there were any Xotalancas left alive in Xuchotl.

"Come on," he muttered, and started down the hall.

He had not gone far when he was aware that only Yanath was following him. He wheeled back to see Topal standing in an attitude of horror, one arm out as if to fend off some threatening peril, his distended eyes fixed with hypnotic intensity on something protruding from behind a divan.

"What the devil?" Then Conan saw what Topal was staring at, and he felt a faint twitching of the skin between his giant shoulders. A monstrous head protruded from behind the divan, a reptilian head, broad as the head of a crocodile, with down-curving fangs that projected over the lower jaw. But there was an unnatural limpness about the thing, and the hideous eyes were glazed.

Conan peered behind the couch. It was a great serpent which lay there limp in death, but such a serpent as he had never seen in his wanderings. The reek and chill of the deep black earth were about it, and its color was an indeterminable hue which changed with each new angle from which he surveyed it. A great wound in the neck showed what had caused its death.

"It is the Crawler!" whispered Yanath.

"It's the thing I slashed on the stair," grunted Conan. "After it trailed us to the Eagle Door, it dragged itself here to die. How could the Xotalancas control such a brute?"

The Tecuhltli shivered and shook their heads.

"They brought it up from the black tunnels *below* the catacombs. They discovered secrets unknown to Tecuhltli."

"Well, it's dead, and if they'd had any more of them, they'd have brought them along when they came to Tecuhltli. Come on."

They crowded close at his heels as he strode down the hall and thrust on the silver-worked door at the other end.

"If we don't find anybody on this floor," he said, "we'll descend into the lower floors. We'll explore Xotalanc from the roof to the catacombs. If Xotalanc is like Tecuhltli, all the rooms and halls in this tier will be lighted—what the devil!"

They had come into the broad throne chamber, so similar to that one in Tecuhltli. There were the same jade dais and ivory seat, the same divans, rugs and hangings on the walls. No black, red-scarred column stood behind the throne-dais, but evidences of the grim feud were not lacking.

Ranged along the wall behind the dais were rows of glass-covered shelves. And on those shelves hundreds of human heads, perfectly pre-

served, stared at the startled watchers with emotionless eyes, as they had
stared for only the gods knew how many months and years.

⋆ ⋆ ⋆

Topal muttered a curse, but Yanath stood silent, the mad light growing
in his wide eyes. Conan frowned, knowing that Tlazitlan sanity was
hung on a hair-trigger.

Suddenly Yanath pointed to the ghastly relics with a twitching
finger.

"There is my brother's head!" he murmured. "And there is my
father's younger brother! And there beyond them is my sister's eldest
son!"

Suddenly he began to weep, dry-eyed, with harsh, loud sobs that
shook his frame. He did not take his eyes from the heads. His sobs grew
shriller, changed to frightful, high-pitched laughter, and that in turn
became an unbearable screaming. Yanath was stark mad.

Conan laid a hand on his shoulder, and as if the touch had released
all the frenzy in his soul, Yanath screamed and whirled, striking at the
Cimmerian with his sword. Conan parried the blow, and Topal tried
to catch Yanath's arm. But the madman avoided him and with froth
flying from his lips, he drove his sword deep into Topal's body. Topal
sank down with a groan, and Yanath whirled for an instant like a crazy
dervish; then he ran at the shelves and began hacking at the glass with
his sword, screeching blasphemously.

Conan sprang at him from behind, trying to catch him unaware and
disarm him, but the madman wheeled and lunged at him, screaming
like a lost soul. Realizing that the warrior was hopelessly insane, the
Cimmerian side-stepped, and as the maniac went past, he swung a cut
that severed the shoulder-bone and breast, and dropped the man dead
beside his dying victim.

Conan bent over Topal, seeing that the man was at his last gasp. It was
useless to seek to stanch the blood gushing from the horrible wound.

"You're done for, Topal," grunted Conan. "Any word you want to
send to your people?"

"Bend closer," gasped Topal, and Conan complied—and an instant
later caught the man's wrist as Topal struck at his breast with a dagger.

"Crom!" swore Conan. "Are you mad, too?"

"Olmec ordered it!" gasped the dying man. "I know not why. As
we lifted the wounded upon the couches he whispered to me, bidding

me to slay you as we returned to Tecuhltli—" And with the name of his clan on his lips, Topal died.

Conan scowled down at him in puzzlement. This whole affair had an aspect of lunacy. Was Olmec mad, too? Were all the Tecuhltli madder than he had realized? With a shrug of his shoulders he strode down the hall and out of the bronze door, leaving the dead Tecuhltli lying before the staring dead eyes of their kinsmen's heads.

Conan needed no guide back through the labyrinth they had traversed. His primitive instinct of direction led him unerringly along the route they had come. He traversed it as warily as he had before, his sword in his hand, and his eyes fiercely searching each shadowed nook and corner; for it was his former allies he feared now, not the ghosts of the slain Xotalancas.

He had crossed the Great Hall and entered the chambers beyond when he heard something moving ahead of him—something which gasped and panted, and moved with a strange, floundering, scrambling noise. A moment later Conan saw a man crawling over the flaming floor toward him—a man whose progress left a broad bloody smear on the smoldering surface. It was Techotl and his eyes were already glazing; from a deep gash in his breast blood gushed steadily between the fingers of his clutching hand. With the other he clawed and hitched himself along.

"Conan," he cried chokingly, "Conan! Olmec has taken the yellow-haired woman!"

"So that's why he told Topal to kill me!" murmured Conan, dropping to his knee beside the man, who his experienced eye told him was dying. "Olmec isn't so mad as I thought."

Techotl's groping fingers plucked at Conan's arm. In the cold, loveless and altogether hideous life of the Tecuhltli his admiration and affection for the invaders from the outer world formed a warm, human oasis, constituted a tie that connected him with a more natural humanity that was totally lacking in his fellows, whose only emotions were hate, lust and the urge of sadistic cruelty.

"I sought to oppose him," gurgled Techotl, blood bubbling frothily to his lips. "But he struck me down. He thought he had slain me, but I crawled away. Ah, Set, how far I have crawled in my own blood! Beware, Conan! Olmec may have set an ambush for your return! Slay Olmec! He is a beast. Take Valeria and flee! Fear not to traverse the forest. Olmec and Tascela lied about the dragons. They slew each other years ago, all save the strongest. For a dozen years there has been only one dragon. If you have slain him, there is naught in the forest to harm you. He was the god Olmec worshipped; and Olmec fed human sacrifices to him, the very old and the very young, bound and hurled from the wall. Hasten! Olmec has taken Valeria to the Chamber of the—"

His head slumped down and he was dead before it came to rest on the floor.

★ ★ ★

Conan sprang up, his eyes like live coals. So that was Olmec's game, having first used the strangers to destroy his foes! He should have known that something of the sort would be going on in that black-bearded degenerate's mind.

The Cimmerian started toward Tecuhltli with reckless speed. Rapidly he reckoned the numbers of his former allies. Only twenty-one, counting Olmec, had survived that fiendish battle in the throne room. Three had died since, which left seventeen enemies with which to reckon. In his rage Conan felt capable of accounting for the whole clan single-handed.

But the innate craft of the wilderness rose to guide his berserk rage. He remembered Techotl's warning of an ambush. It was quite probable that the prince would make such provisions, on the chance that Topal might have failed to carry out his order. Olmec would be expecting him to return by the same route he had followed in going to Xotalanc.

Conan glanced up at a skylight under which he was passing and caught the blurred glimmer of stars. They had not yet begun to pale for dawn. The events of the night had been crowded into a comparatively short space of time.

He turned aside from his direct course and descended a winding staircase to the floor below. He did not know where the door was to be found that let into the castle on that level, but he knew he could find it. How he was to force the locks he did not know; he believed that the doors of Tecuhltli would all be locked and bolted, if for no other reason than the habits of half a century. But there was nothing else but to attempt it.

Sword in hand, he hurried noiselessly on through a maze of green-lit or shadowy rooms and halls. He knew he must be near Tecuhltli, when a sound brought him up short. He recognized it for what it was—a human being trying to cry out through a stifling gag. It came from somewhere ahead of him, and to the left. In those deathly-still chambers a small sound carried a long way.

Conan turned aside and went seeking after the sound, which continued to be repeated. Presently he was glaring through a doorway upon a weird scene. In the room into which he was looking a low rack-like frame of iron lay on the floor, and a giant figure was bound prostrate upon it. His head rested on a bed of iron spikes, which were already crimson-pointed with blood where they had pierced his scalp. A peculiar harness-like contrivance was fastened about his head, though in such a manner that the leather band did not protect his scalp from the spikes. This harness was connected by a slender chain to the mechanism that upheld a huge iron ball which was suspended above the captive's hairy breast. As long as the man could force himself to remain motionless the iron ball hung in its place. But when the pain of the iron points caused him to lift his head, the ball lurched downward a few inches. Presently his aching neck muscles would no longer support his head in its unnatural position and it would fall back on the spikes again. It was obvious that eventually the ball would crush him to a pulp, slowly and inexorably. The victim was gagged, and above the gag his great black ox-eyes rolled wildly toward the man in the doorway, who stood in silent amazement. The man on the rack was Olmec, prince of Tecuhltli.

6 The Eyes of Tascela

"Why did you bring me into this chamber to bandage my legs?" demanded Valeria. "Couldn't you have done it just as well in the throne room?"

She sat on a couch with her wounded leg extended upon it, and the Tecuhltli woman had just bound it with silk bandages. Valeria's red-stained sword lay on the couch beside her.

She frowned as she spoke. The woman had done her task silently and efficiently, but Valeria liked neither the lingering, caressing touch of her slim fingers nor the expression in her eyes.

"They have taken the rest of the wounded into the other chambers," answered the woman in the soft speech of the Tecuhltli women, which somehow did not suggest either softness or gentleness in the speakers. A little while before, Valeria had seen this same woman stab a Xotalanca woman through the breast and stamp the eyeballs out of a wounded Xotalanca man.

"They will be carrying the corpses of the dead down into the cata-combs," she added, "lest the ghosts escape into the chambers and dwell there."

"Do you believe in ghosts?" asked Valeria.

"I know the ghost of Tolkemec dwells in the catacombs," she answered with a shiver. "Once I saw it, as I crouched in a crypt among the bones of a dead queen. It passed by in the form of an ancient man with flowing white beard and locks, and luminous eyes that blazed in the darkness. It was Tolkemec; I saw him living when I was a child and he was being tortured."

Her voice sank to a fearful whisper: "Olmec laughs, but I *know* Tolkemec's ghost dwells in the catacombs! They say it is rats which gnaw the flesh from the bones of the newly dead—but ghosts eat flesh. Who knows but that—"

She glanced up quickly as a shadow fell across the couch. Valeria looked up to see Olmec gazing down at her. The prince had cleansed his hands, torso and beard of the blood that had splashed them; but he had not donned his robe, and his great dark-skinned hairless body and limbs renewed the impression of strength bestial in its nature. His deep black eyes burned with a more elemental light, and there was the suggestion of a twitching in the fingers that tugged at his thick blue-black beard.

He stared fixedly at the woman, and she rose and glided from the chamber. As she passed through the door she cast a look over her shoulder at Valeria, a glance full of cynical derision and obscene mockery.

"She has done a clumsy job," criticized the prince, coming to the divan and bending over the bandage. "Let me see—"

With a quickness amazing in one of his bulk he snatched her sword and threw it across the chamber. His next move was to catch her in his giant arms.

Quick and unexpected as the move was, she almost matched it; for even as he grabbed her, her dirk was in her hand and she stabbed mur-derously at his throat. More by luck than skill he caught her wrist, and then began a savage wrestling-match. She fought him with fists, feet, knees, teeth and nails, with all the strength of her magnificent body and all the knowledge of hand-to-hand fighting she had acquired in her years of roving and fighting on sea and land. It availed her nothing against his brute strength. She lost her dirk in the first moment of con-tact, and thereafter found herself powerless to inflict any appreciable pain on her giant attacker.

The blaze in his weird black eyes did not alter, and their expression filled her with fury, fanned by the sardonic smile that seemed carved upon his bearded lips. Those eyes and that smile contained all the cruel cynicism that seethes below the surface of a sophisticated and degenerate race, and for the first time in her life Valeria experienced fear of a man. It was like struggling against some huge elemental force; his iron arms thwarted her efforts with an ease that sent panic racing through her limbs. He seemed impervious to any pain she could indict. Only once, when she sank her white teeth savagely into his wrist so that the blood started, did he react. And that was to buffet her brutally upon the side of the head with his open hand, so that stars flashed before her eyes and her head rolled on her shoulders.

Her shirt had been torn open in the struggle, and with cynical cruelty he rasped his thick beard across her bare breasts, bringing the blood to suffuse the fair skin, and fetching a cry of pain and outraged fury from her. Her convulsive resistance was useless; she was crushed down on a couch, disarmed and panting, her eyes blazing up at him like the eyes of a trapped tigress.

A moment later he was hurrying from the chamber, carrying her in his arms. She made no resistance, but the smoldering of her eyes showed that she was unconquered in spirit, at least. She had not cried out. She knew that Conan was not within call, and it did not occur to her that any in Tecuhltli would oppose their prince. But she noticed that Olmec went stealthily, with his head on one side as if listening for sounds of pursuit, and he did not return to the throne chamber. He carried her through a door that stood opposite that through which he had entered, crossed another room and began stealing down a hall. As she became convinced that he feared some opposition to the abduction, she threw back her head and screamed at the top of her lusty voice.

She was rewarded by a slap that half stunned her, and Olmec quickened his pace to a shambling run.

But her cry had been echoed, and twisting her head about, Valeria, through the tears and stars that partly blinded her, saw Techotl limping after them.

Olmec turned with a snarl, shifting the woman to an uncomfortable and certainly undignified position under one huge arm, where he held her writhing and kicking vainly, like a child.

"Olmec!" protested Techotl. "You cannot be such a dog as to do this thing! She is Conan's woman! She helped us slay the Xotalancas, and—"

*   *   *

Without a word Olmec balled his free hand into a huge fist and stretched the wounded warrior senseless at his feet. Stooping, and hindered not at all by the struggles and imprecations of his captive, he drew Techotl's sword from its sheath and stabbed the warrior in the breast. Then casting aside the weapon he fled on along the corridor. He did not see a woman's dark face peer cautiously after him from behind a hanging. It vanished, and presently Techotl groaned and stirred, rose dazedly and staggered drunkenly away, calling Conan's name.

Olmec hurried on down the corridor, and descended a winding ivory staircase. He crossed several corridors and halted at last in a broad chamber whose doors were veiled with heavy tapestries, with one exception—a heavy bronze door similar to the Door of the Eagle on the upper floor.

He was moved to rumble, pointing to it: "That is one of the outer doors of Tecuhltli. For the first time in fifty years it is unguarded. We need not guard it now, for Xotalanc is no more."

"Thanks to Conan and me, you bloody rogue!" sneered Valeria, trembling with fury and the shame of physical coercion. "You treacherous dog! Conan will cut your throat for this!"

Olmec did not bother to voice his belief that Conan's own gullet had already been severed according to his whispered command. He was too utterly cynical to be at all interested in her thoughts or opinions. His flame-lit eyes devoured her, dwelling burningly on the generous expanses of clear white flesh exposed where her shirt and breeches had been torn in the struggle.

"Forget Conan," he said thickly. "Olmec is lord of Xuchotl. Xotalanc is no more. There will be no more fighting. We shall spend our lives in drinking and love-making. First let us drink!"

He seated himself on an ivory table and pulled her down on his knees, like a dark-skinned satyr with a white nymph in his arms. Ignoring her un-nymphlike profanity, he held her helpless with one great arm about her waist while the other reached across the table and secured a vessel of wine.

"Drink!" he commanded, forcing it to her lips, as she writhed her head away.

The liquor slopped over, stinging her lips, splashing down on her naked breasts.

"Your guest does not like your wine, Olmec," spoke a cool, sardonic voice.

Olmec stiffened; fear grew in his flaming eyes. Slowly he swung his great head about and stared at Tascela who posed negligently in the curtained doorway, one hand on her smooth hip. Valeria twisted herself about in his iron grip, and when she met the burning eyes of Tascela, a chill tingled along her supple spine. New experiences were flooding Valeria's proud soul that night. Recently she had learned to fear a man; now she knew what it was to fear a woman.

Olmec sat motionless, a gray pallor growing under his swarthy skin. Tascela brought her other hand from behind her and displayed a small gold vessel.

"I feared she would not like your wine, Olmec," purred the princess, "so I brought some of mine, some I brought with me long ago from the shores of Lake Zuad—do you understand, Olmec?"

Beads of sweat stood out suddenly on Olmec's brow. His muscles relaxed, and Valeria broke away and put the table between them. But though reason told her to dart from the room, some fascination she could not understand held her rigid, watching the scene.

Tascela came toward the seated prince with a swaying, undulating walk that was mockery in itself. Her voice was soft, slurringly caressing, but her eyes gleamed. Her slim fingers stroked his beard lightly.

"You are selfish, Olmec," she crooned, smiling. "You would keep our handsome guest to yourself, though you knew I wished to entertain her. You are much at fault, Olmec!"

The mask dropped for an instant; her eyes flashed, her face was contorted and with an appalling show of strength her hand locked convulsively in his beard and tore out a great handful. This evidence of unnatural strength was no more terrifying than the momentary baring of the hellish fury that raged under her bland exterior.

Olmec lurched up with a roar, and stood swaying like a bear, his mighty hands clenching and unclenching.

"Slut!" His booming voice filled the room. "Witch! She-devil! Tecuhltli should have slain you fifty years ago! Begone! I have endured too much from you! This white-skinned wench is mine! Get hence before I slay you!"

The princess laughed and dashed the blood-stained strands into his face. Her laughter was less merciful than the ring of flint on steel.

"Once you spoke otherwise, Olmec," she taunted. "Once, in your youth, you spoke words of love. Aye, you were my lover once, years ago, and because you loved me, you slept in my arms beneath the enchanted lotus—and thereby put into my hands the chains that enslaved you. You know you cannot withstand me. You know I have but to gaze into your eyes, with the mystic power a priest of Stygia taught me, long ago, and you are powerless. You remember the night beneath the black lotus that waved above us, stirred by no worldly breeze; you scent again the unearthly perfumes that stole and rose like a cloud about you to enslave you. You cannot fight against me. You are my slave as you were that night—as you shall be so long as you shall live, Olmec of Xuchotl!"

★   ★   ★

Her voice had sunk to a murmur like the rippling of a stream running through starlit darkness. She leaned close to the prince and spread her long tapering fingers upon his giant breast. His eyes glazed, his great hands fell limply to his sides.

With a smile of cruel malice, Tascela lifted the vessel and placed it to his lips.

"Drink!"

Mechanically the prince obeyed. And instantly the glaze passed from his eyes and they were flooded with fury, comprehension and an awful fear. His mouth gaped, but no sound issued. For an instant he reeled on buckling knees, and then fell in a sodden heap on the floor.

His fall jolted Valeria out of her paralysis. She turned and sprang toward the door, but with a movement that would have shamed a leaping panther, Tascela was before her. Valeria struck at her with her clenched fist, and all the power of her supple body behind the blow. It would have stretched a man senseless on the floor. But with a lithe twist of her torso, Tascela avoided the blow and caught the pirate's wrist. The next instant Valeria's left hand was imprisoned, and holding her wrists together with one hand, Tascela calmly bound them with a cord she drew from her girdle. Valeria thought she had tasted the ultimate in humiliation already that night, but her shame at being manhandled by Olmec was nothing to the sensations that now shook her supple frame. Valeria had always been inclined to despise the other members of her sex; and it was overwhelming to encounter another woman who could handle her like a child. She scarcely resisted at all when Tascela forced her into a chair and drawing her bound wrists down between her knees, fastened them to the chair.

Casually stepping over Olmec, Tascela walked to the bronze door and shot the bolt and threw it open, revealing a hallway without.

"Opening upon this hall," she remarked, speaking to her feminine captive for the first time, "there is a chamber which in old times was used as a torture room. When we retired into Tecuhltli, we brought most of the apparatus with us, but there was one piece too heavy to move. It is still in working order. I think it will be quite convenient now."

An understanding flame of terror rose in Olmec's eyes. Tascela strode back to him, bent and gripped him by the hair.

"He is only paralyzed temporarily," she remarked conversationally. "He can hear, think, and feel—aye, he can feel very well indeed!"

With which sinister observation she started toward the door, dragging the giant bulk with an ease that made the pirate's eyes dilate. She passed into the hall and moved down it without hesitation, presently disappearing with her captive into a chamber that opened into it, and whence shortly thereafter issued the clank of iron.

Valeria swore softly and tugged vainly, with her legs braced against the chair. The cords that confined her were apparently unbreakable.

Tascela presently returned alone; behind her a muffled groaning issued from the chamber. She closed the door but did not bolt it. Tascela was beyond the grip of habit, as she was beyond the touch of other human instincts and emotions.

Valeria sat dumbly, watching the woman in whose slim hands, the pirate realized, her destiny now rested.

Tascela grasped her yellow locks and forced back her head, looking impersonally down into her face. But the glitter in her dark eyes was not impersonal.

"I have chosen you for a great honor," she said. "You shall restore the youth of Tascela. Oh, you stare at that! My appearance is that of youth, but through my veins creeps the sluggish chill of approaching age, as I have felt it a thousand times before. I am old, so old I do not remember my childhood. But I was a girl once, and a priest of Stygia loved me, and gave me the secret of immortality and youth everlasting. He died, then—some said by poison. But I dwelt in my palace by the shores of Lake Zuad and the passing years touched me not. So at last a king of Stygia desired me, and my people rebelled and brought me to this land. Olmec called me a princess. I am not of royal blood. I am greater than a princess. I am Tascela, whose youth your own glorious youth shall restore."

Valeria's tongue clove to the roof of her mouth. She sensed here a mystery darker than the degeneracy she had anticipated.

The taller woman unbound the Aquilonian's wrists and pulled her to her feet. It was not fear of the dominant strength that lurked in the princess' limbs that made Valeria a helpless, quivering captive in her hands. It was the burning, hypnotic, terrible eyes of Tascela.

7 He Comes from the Dark

"Well, I'm a Kushite!"

Conan glared down at the man on the iron rack.

"What the devil are *you* doing on that thing?"

Incoherent sounds issued from behind the gag and Conan bent and tore it away, evoking a bellow of fear from the captive; for his action caused the iron ball to lurch down until it nearly touched the broad breast.

"Be careful, for Set's sake!" begged Olmec.

"What for?" demanded Conan. "Do you think I care what happens to you? I only wish I had time to stay here and watch that chunk of iron grind your guts out. But I'm in a hurry. Where's Valeria?"

"Loose me!" urged Olmec, "I will tell you all!"

"Tell me first."

"Never!" The prince's heavy jaws set stubbornly.

"All right." Conan seated himself on a near-by bench. "I'll find her myself, after you've been reduced to a jelly. I believe I can speed up that process by twisting my sword-point around in your ear," he added, extending the weapon experimentally.

"Wait!" Words came in a rush from the captive's ashy lips. "Tascela took her from me. I've never been anything but a puppet in Tascela's hands."

"Tascela?" snorted Conan, and spat. "Why, the filthy—"

"No, no!" panted Olmec. "It's worse than you think. Tascela is old—centuries old. She renews her life and her youth by the sacrifice of beautiful young women. That's one thing that has reduced the clan to its present state. She will draw the essence of Valeria's life into her own body, and bloom with fresh vigor and beauty."

"Are the doors locked?" asked Conan, thumbing his sword edge.

"Aye! But I know a way to get into Tecuhltli. Only Tascela and I know, and she thinks me helpless and you slain. Free me and I swear I will help you rescue Valeria. Without my help you cannot win into Tecuhltli; for even if you tortured me into revealing the secret, you couldn't work it. Let me go, and we will steal on Tascela and kill her before she can work magic—before she can fix her eyes on us. A knife thrown from behind will do the work. I should have killed her thus long ago, but I feared that without her to aid us the Xotalancas would overcome us. She needed my help, too; that's the only reason she let me live this long. Now neither needs the other, and one must die. I swear that when we have slain the witch, you and Valeria shall go free without harm. My people will obey me when Tascela is dead."

Conan stooped and cut the ropes that held the prince, and Olmec slid cautiously from under the great ball and rose, shaking his head like a bull and muttering imprecations as he fingered his lacerated scalp. Standing shoulder to shoulder the two men presented a formidable picture of primitive power. Olmec was as tall as Conan, and heavier; but there was something repellent about the Tlazitlan, something abysmal and monstrous that contrasted unfavorably with the clean-cut, compact hardness of the Cimmerian. Conan had discarded the remnants of his tattered, blood-soaked shirt, and stood with his remarkable muscular development impressively revealed. His great shoulders were as broad as those of Olmec, and more cleanly outlined, and his huge breast arched with a more impressive sweep to a hard waist that lacked the paunchy thickness of Olmec's midsection. He might have been an image of primal strength cut out of bronze. Olmec was darker, but not from the burning of the sun. If Conan was a figure out of the dawn of Time, Olmec was a shambling, somber shape from the darkness of Time's pre-dawn.

"Lead on," demanded Conan. "And keep ahead of me. I don't trust you any farther than I can throw a bull by the tail."

Olmec turned and stalked on ahead of him, one hand twitching slightly as it plucked at his matted beard.

★　★　★

Olmec did not lead Conan back to the bronze door, which the prince naturally supposed Tascela had locked, but to a certain chamber on the border of Tecuhltli.

"This secret has been guarded for half a century," he said. "Not even our own clan knew of it, and the Xotalancas never learned. Tecuhltli himself built this secret entrance, afterward slaying the slaves who did the work; for he feared that he might find himself locked out of his own kingdom some day because of the spite of Tascela, whose passion for him soon changed to hate. But she discovered the secret, and barred the hidden door against him one day as he fled back from an unsuccessful raid, and the Xotalancas took him and flayed him. But once, spying upon her, I saw her enter Tecuhltli by this route, and so learned the secret."

He pressed upon a gold ornament in the wall, and a panel swung inward, disclosing an ivory stair leading upward.

"This stair is built within the wall," said Olmec. "It leads up to a tower upon the roof, and thence other stairs wind down to the various chambers. Hasten!"

"After you, comrade!" retorted Conan satirically, swaying his broadsword as he spoke, and Olmec shrugged his shoulders and stepped onto the staircase. Conan instantly followed him, and the door shut behind them. Far above a cluster of fire-jewels made the staircase a well of dusky dragon-light.

They mounted until Conan estimated that they were above the level of the fourth floor, and then came out into a cylindrical tower, in the domed roof of which was set the bunch of fire-jewels that lighted the stair. Through gold-barred windows, set with unbreakable crystal panes, the first windows he had seen in Xuchotl, Conan got a glimpse of high ridges, domes and more towers, looming darkly against the stars. He was looking across the roofs of Xuchotl.

Olmec did not look through the windows. He hurried down one of the several stairs that wound down from the tower, and when they had descended a few feet, this stair changed into a narrow corridor that wound tortuously on for some distance. It ceased at a steep flight of steps leading downward. There Olmec paused.

Up from below, muffled, but unmistakable, welled a woman's scream, edged with fright, fury and shame. And Conan recognized Valeria's voice.

In the swift rage roused by that cry, and the amazement of wondering what peril could wring such a shriek from Valeria's reckless lips, Conan forgot Olmec. He pushed past the prince and started down the stair. Awakening instinct brought him about again, just as Olmec struck with his great mallet-like fist. The blow, fierce and silent, was aimed at the base of Conan's brain. But the Cimmerian wheeled in time to receive the buffet on the side of his neck instead. The impact would have snapped the vertebræ of a lesser man. As it was, Conan swayed backward, but even as he reeled he dropped his sword, useless at such close quarters, and grasped Olmec's extended arm, dragging the prince with him as he fell. Headlong they went down the steps together, in a revolving whirl of limbs and heads and bodies. And as they went Conan's iron fingers found and locked in Olmec's bull-throat.

The barbarian's neck and shoulder felt numb from the sledge-like impact of Olmec's huge fist, which had carried all the strength of the massive forearm, thick triceps and great shoulder. But this did not affect his ferocity to any appreciable extent. Like a bulldog he hung on grimly, shaken and battered and beaten against the steps as they rolled, until at last they struck an ivory panel-door at the bottom with such an impact that they splintered it down its full length and crashed through its ruins. But Olmec was already dead, for those iron fingers had crushed out his life and broken his neck as they fell.

★   ★   ★

Conan rose, shaking the splinters from his great shoulder, blinking blood and dust out of his eyes.

He was in the great throne room. There were fifteen people in that room besides himself. The first person he saw was Valeria. A curious black altar stood before the throne-dais. Ranged about it, seven black candles in golden candlesticks sent up oozing spirals of thick green smoke, disturbingly scented. These spirals united in a cloud near the ceiling, forming a smoky arch above the altar. On that altar lay Valeria, stark naked, her white flesh gleaming in shocking contrast to the glistening ebon stone. She was not bound. She lay at full length, her arms stretched out above her head to their fullest extent. At the head of the altar knelt a young man, holding her wrists firmly. A young woman knelt at the other end of the altar, grasping her ankles. Between them she could neither rise nor move.

Eleven men and women of Tecuhltli knelt dumbly in a semicircle, watching the scene with hot, lustful eyes.

On the ivory throne-seat Tascela lolled. Bronze bowls of incense rolled their spirals about her; the wisps of smoke curled about her naked limbs like caressing fingers. She could not sit still; she squirmed and shifted about with sensuous abandon, as if finding pleasure in the contact of the smooth ivory with her sleek flesh.

The crash of the door as it broke beneath the impact of the hurtling bodies caused no change in the scene. The kneeling men and women merely glanced incuriously at the corpse of their prince and at the man who rose from the ruins of the door, then swung their eyes greedily back to the writhing white shape on the black altar. Tascela looked insolently at him, and sprawled back on her seat, laughing mockingly.

"Slut!" Conan saw red. His hands clenched into iron hammers as he started for her. With his first step something clanged loudly and steel bit savagely into his leg. He stumbled and almost fell, checked in his headlong stride. The jaws of an iron trap had closed on his leg, with teeth that sank deep and held. Only the ridged muscles of his calf saved the bone from being splintered. The accursed thing had sprung out of the smoldering floor without warning. He saw the slots now, in the floor where the jaws had lain, perfectly camouflaged.

"Fool!" laughed Tascela. "Did you think I would not guard against your possible return? Every door in this chamber is guarded by such traps. Stand there and watch now, while I fulfill the destiny of your handsome friend! Then I will decide your own."

Conan's hand instinctively sought his belt, only to encounter an empty scabbard. His sword was on the stair behind him. His poniard was lying back in the forest, where the dragon had torn it from his jaw. The steel teeth in his leg were like burning coals, but the pain was not as savage as the fury that seethed in his soul. He was trapped, like a wolf. If he had had his sword he would have hewn off his leg and crawled across the floor to slay Tascela. Valeria's eyes rolled toward him with mute appeal, and his own helplessness sent red waves of madness surging through his brain.

Dropping on the knee of his free leg, he strove to get his fingers between the jaws of the trap, to tear them apart by sheer strength. Blood started from beneath his finger nails, but the jaws fitted close about his leg in a circle whose segments jointed perfectly, contracted until there was no space between his mangled flesh and the fanged iron. The sight of Valeria's naked body added flame to the fire of his rage.

Tascela ignored him. Rising languidly from her seat she swept the ranks of her subjects with a searching glance, and asked: "Where are Xamec, Zlanath and Tachic?"

"They did not return from the catacombs, princess," answered a man. "Like the rest of us, they bore the bodies of the slain into the crypts, but they have not returned. Perhaps the ghost of Tolkemec took them."

"Be silent, fool!" she ordered harshly. "The ghost is a myth."

She came down from her dais, playing with a thin gold-hilted dagger. Her eyes burned like nothing on the hither side of hell. She paused beside the altar and spoke in the tense stillness.

"Your life shall make me young, white woman!" she said. "I shall lean upon your bosom and place my lips over yours, and slowly—ah, slowly!—sink this blade through your heart, so that your life, fleeing your stiffening body, shall enter mine, making me bloom again with youth and with life everlasting!"

Slowly, like a serpent arching toward its victim, she bent down through the writhing smoke, closer and closer over the now motionless woman who stared up into her glowing dark eyes—eyes that grew larger and deeper, blazing like black moons in the swirling smoke.

The kneeling people gripped their hands and held their breath, tense for the bloody climax, and the only sound was Conan's fierce panting as he strove to tear his leg from the trap.

All eyes were glued on the altar and the white figure there; the crash of a thunderbolt could hardly have broken the spell, yet it was only a low cry that shattered the fixity of the scene and brought all whirling about—a low cry, yet one to make the hair stand up stiffly on the scalp. They looked, and they saw.

Framed in the door to the left of the dais stood a nightmare figure. It was a man, with a tangle of white hair and a matted white beard that fell over his breast. Rags only partly covered his gaunt frame, revealing half-naked limbs strangely unnatural in appearance. The skin was not like that of a normal human. There was a suggestion of *scaliness* about it, as if the owner had dwelt long under conditions almost antithetical to those conditions under which human life ordinarily thrives. And there was nothing at all human about the eyes that blazed from the tangle of white hair. They were great gleaming disks that stared unwinkingly, luminous, whitish, and without a hint of normal emotion or sanity. The mouth gaped, but no coherent words issued—only a high-pitched tittering.

★ ★ ★

"Tolkemec!" whispered Tascela, livid, while the others crouched in speechless horror. "No myth, then, no ghost! Set! You have dwelt for twelve years in darkness! Twelve years among the bones of the dead! What grisly food did you find? What mad travesty of life did you live, in the stark blackness of that eternal night? I see now why Xamec and Zlanath and Tachic did not return from the catacombs—and never will return. But why have you waited so long to strike? Were you seeking something, in the pits? Some secret weapon you knew was hidden there? And have you found it at last?"

That hideous tittering was Tolkemec's only reply, as he bounded into the room with a long leap that carried him over the secret trap before the door—by chance, or by some faint recollection of the ways of Xuchotl. He was not mad, as a man is mad. He had dwelt apart from humanity so long that he was no longer human. Only an unbroken thread of memory embodied in hate and the urge for vengeance had connected him with the humanity from which he had been cut off, and held him lurking near the people he hated. Only that thin string had kept him from racing and prancing off for ever into the black corridors and realms of the subterranean world he had discovered, long ago.

"You sought something hidden!" whispered Tascela, cringing back. "And you have found it! You remember the feud! After all these years of blackness, you remember!"

For in the lean hand of Tolkemec now waved a curious jade-hued wand, on the end of which glowed a knob of crimson shaped like a pomegranate. She sprang aside as he thrust it out like a spear, and a beam of crimson fire lanced from the pomegranate. It missed Tascela, but the woman holding Valeria's ankles was in the way. It smote between her shoulders. There was a sharp crackling sound and the ray of fire flashed from her bosom and struck the black altar, with a snapping of blue sparks. The woman toppled sidewise, shriveling and withering like a mummy even as she fell.

Valeria rolled from the altar on the other side, and started for the opposite wall on all fours. For hell had burst loose in the throne room of dead Olmec.

The man who had held Valeria's hands was the next to die. He turned to run, but before he had taken half a dozen steps, Tolkemec, with an agility appalling in such a frame, bounded around to a position that placed the man between him and the altar. Again the red fire-beam flashed and the Tecuhltli rolled lifeless to the floor, as the beam completed its course with a burst of blue sparks against the altar.

Then began slaughter. Screaming insanely the people rushed about the chamber, caroming from one another, stumbling and falling. And among them Tolkemec capered and pranced, dealing death. They could not escape by the doors; for apparently the metal of the portals served like the metal-veined stone altar to complete the circuit for whatever hellish power flashed like thunderbolts from the witch-wand the ancient waved in his hand. When he caught a man or a woman between him and a door or the altar, that one died instantly. He chose no special victim. He took them as they came, with his rags flapping about his wildly gyrating limbs, and the gusty echoes of his tittering sweeping the room above the screams. And bodies fell like falling leaves about the altar and at the doors. One warrior in desperation rushed at him, lifting a dagger, only to fall before he could strike. But the rest were like crazed cattle, with no thought for resistance, and no chance of escape.

The last Tecuhltli except Tascela had fallen when the princess reached the Cimmerian and the girl who had taken refuge beside him. Tascela bent and touched the floor, pressing a design upon it. Instantly the iron jaws released the bleeding limb and sank back into the floor.

"Slay him if you can!" she panted, and pressed a heavy knife into his hand. "I have no magic to withstand him!"

With a grunt he sprang before the women, not heeding his lacerated leg in the heat of the fighting-lust. Tolkemec was coming toward him, his weird eyes ablaze, but he hesitated at the gleam of the knife in Conan's hand. Then began a grim game, as Tolkemec sought to circle about Conan and get the barbarian between him and the altar or a metal door, while Conan sought to avoid this and drive home his knife. The women watched tensely, holding their breath.

There was no sound except the rustle and scrape of quick-shifting feet. Tolkemec pranced and capered no more. He realized that grimmer game confronted him than the people who had died screaming and fleeing. In the elemental blaze of the barbarian's eyes he read an intent deadly as his own. Back and forth they weaved, and when one moved the other moved as if invisible threads bound them together. But all the time Conan was getting closer and closer to his enemy. Already the coiled muscles of his thighs were beginning to flex for a spring, when Valeria cried out. For a fleeting instant a bronze door was in line with Conan's moving body. The red line leaped, searing Conan's flank as he twisted aside, and even as he shifted he hurled the knife. Old Tolkemec went down, truly slain at last, the hilt vibrating on his breast.

★ ★ ★

Tascela sprang—not toward Conan, but toward the wand where it shimmered like a live thing on the floor. But as she leaped, so did Valeria, with a dagger snatched from a dead man, and the blade, driven with all the power of the pirate's muscles, impaled the princess of Tecuhltli so that the point stood out between her breasts. Tascela screamed once and fell dead, and Valeria spurned the body with her heel as it fell.

"I had to do that much, for my own self-respect!" panted Valeria, facing Conan across the limp corpse.

"Well, this cleans up the feud," he grunted. "It's been a hell of a night! Where did these people keep their food? I'm hungry."

"You need a bandage on that leg." Valeria ripped a length of silk from a hanging and knotted it about her waist, then tore off some smaller strips which she bound efficiently about the barbarian's lacerated limb.

"I can walk on it," he assured her. "Let's begone. It's dawn, outside this infernal city. I've had enough of Xuchotl. It's well the breed exterminated itself. I don't want any of their accursed jewels. They might be haunted."

"There is enough clean loot in the world for you and me," she said, straightening to stand tall and splendid before him.

The old blaze came back in his eyes, and this time she did not resist as he caught her fiercely in his arms.

"It's a long way to the coast," she said presently, withdrawing her lips from his.

"What matter?" he laughed. "There's nothing we can't conquer. We'll have our feet on a ship's deck before the Stygians open their ports for the trading season. And then we'll show the world what plundering means!"

THE END

The Hour of the Dragon

1 O Sleeper, Awake!

The long tapers flickered, sending the black shadows wavering along the walls, and the velvet tapestries rippled. Yet there was no wind in the chamber. Four men stood about the ebony table on which lay the green sarcophagus that gleamed like carven jade. In the upraised right hand of each man a curious black candle burned with a weird greenish light. Outside was night and a lost wind moaning among the black trees.

Inside the chamber was tense silence, and the wavering of the shadows, while four pairs of eyes, burning with intensity, were fixed on the long green case across which cryptic hieroglyphics writhed, as if lent life and movement by the unsteady light. The man at the foot of the sarcophagus leaned over it and moved his candle as if he were writing with a pen, inscribing a mystic symbol in the air. Then he set down the candle in its black gold stick at the foot of the case, and, mumbling some formula unintelligible to his companions, he thrust a broad white hand into his fur-trimmed robe. When he brought it forth again it was as if he cupped in his palm a ball of living fire.

The other three drew in their breath sharply, and the dark, powerful man who stood at the head of the sarcophagus whispered: "The Heart of Ahriman!" The other lifted a quick hand for silence. Somewhere a dog began howling dolefully, and a stealthy step padded outside the barred and bolted door. But none looked aside from the mummy-case over which the man in the ermine-trimmed robe was now moving the great flaming jewel while he muttered an incantation that was old when Atlantis sank. The glare of the gem dazzled their eyes, so that they could not be sure of what they saw; but with a splintering crash, the carven lid of the sarcophagus burst outward as if from some irresistible pressure applied from within, and the four men, bending eagerly forward, saw the occupant—a huddled, withered, wizened shape, with dried brown limbs like dead wood showing through moldering bandages.

"Bring that thing back?" muttered the small dark man who stood on the right, with a short, sardonic laugh. "It is ready to crumble at a touch. We are fools—"

"Shhh!" It was an urgent hiss of command from the large man who held the jewel. Perspiration stood upon his broad white forehead and his eyes were dilated. He leaned forward, and, without touching the thing with his hand, laid on the breast of the mummy the blazing jewel. Then he drew back and watched with fierce intensity, his lips moving in soundless invocation.

It was as if a globe of living fire nickered and burned on the dead, withered bosom. And breath sucked in, hissing, through the clenched teeth of the watchers. For as they watched, an awful transmutation became apparent. The withered shape in the sarcophagus was expanding, was growing, lengthening. The bandages burst and fell into brown dust. The shriveled limbs swelled, straightened. Their dusky hue began to fade.

"By Mitra!" whispered the tall, yellow-haired man on the left. "He was not a Stygian. That part at least was true."

Again a trembling finger warned for silence. The hound outside was no longer howling. He whimpered, as with an evil dream, and then that sound, too, died away in silence, in which the yellow-haired man plainly heard the straining of the heavy door, as if something outside pushed powerfully upon it. He half turned, his hand at his sword, but the man in the ermine robe hissed an urgent warning: "Stay! Do not break the chain! And on your life do not go to the door!"

The yellow-haired man shrugged and turned back, and then he stopped short, staring. In the jade sarcophagus lay a living man: a tall, lusty man, naked, white of skin, and dark of hair and beard. He lay motionless, his eyes wide open, and blank and unknowing as a newborn babe's. On his breast the great jewel smoldered and sparkled.

The man in ermine reeled as if from some let-down of extreme tension.

"Ishtar!" he gasped. "It is Xaltotun!—and he lives! Valerius! Tarascus! Amalric! Do you see? Do you see? You doubted me—but I have not failed! We have been close to the open gates of hell this night, and the shapes of darkness have gathered close about us—aye, they followed him to the very door—but we have brought the great magician back to life."

"And damned our souls to purgatories everlasting, I doubt not," muttered the small, dark man, Tarascus.

The yellow-haired man, Valerius, laughed harshly.

"What purgatory can be worse than life itself? So we are all damned together from birth. Besides, who would not sell his miserable soul for a throne?"

"There is no intelligence in his stare, Orastes," said the large man.

"He has long been dead," answered Orastes. "He is as one newly awakened. His mind is empty after the long sleep—nay, he was dead, not sleeping. We brought his spirit back over the voids and gulfs of night and oblivion. I will speak to him."

He bent over the foot of the sarcophagus, and fixing his gaze on the wide dark eyes of the man within, he said, slowly: "Awake, Xaltotun!"

The lips of the man moved mechanically. "Xaltotun!" he repeated in a groping whisper.

"You are Xaltotun!" exclaimed Orastes, like a hypnotist driving home his suggestions. "You are Xaltotun of Python, in Acheron."

A dim flame flickered in the dark eyes.

"I was Xaltotun," he whispered. "I am dead."

"You are Xaltotun!" cried Orastes. "You are not dead! You live!"

"I am Xaltotun," came the eery whisper. "But I am dead. In my house in Khemi, in Stygia, there I died."

"And the priests who poisoned you mummified your body with their dark arts, keeping all your organs intact!" exclaimed Orastes. "But now you live again! The Heart of Ahriman has restored your life, drawn your spirit back from space and eternity."

"The Heart of Ahriman!" The flame of remembrance grew stronger. "The barbarians stole it from me!"

"He remembers," muttered Orastes. "Lift him from the case."

The others obeyed hesitantly, as if reluctant to touch the man they had re-created, and they seemed not easier in their minds when they felt firm muscular flesh, vibrant with blood and life, beneath their fingers. But they lifted him upon the table, and Orastes clothed him in a curious dark velvet robe, splashed with gold stars and crescent moons, and fastened a cloth-of-gold fillet about his temples, confining the black wavy locks that fell to his shoulders. He let them do as they would, saying nothing, not even when they set him in a carven throne-like chair with a high ebony back and wide silver arms, and feet like golden claws. He sat there motionless, and slowly intelligence grew in his dark eyes and made them deep and strange and luminous. It was as if long-sunken witch-lights floated slowly up through midnight pools of darkness.

Orastes cast a furtive glance at his companions, who stood staring in morbid fascination at their strange guest. Their iron nerves had withstood an ordeal that might have driven weaker men mad. He knew it was with no weaklings that he conspired, but men whose courage was as profound as their lawless ambitions and capacity for evil. He turned his attention to the figure in the ebon-black chair. And this one spoke at last.

"I remember," he said in a strong, resonant voice, speaking Nemedian with a curious, archaic accent. "I am Xaltotun, who was high priest of Set in Python, which was in Acheron. The Heart of Ahriman—I dreamed I had found it again—where is it?"

Orastes placed it in his hand, and he drew breath deeply as he gazed into the depths of the terrible jewel burning in his grasp.

"They stole it from me, long ago," he said. "The red heart of the night it is, strong to save or to damn. It came from afar, and from long ago. While I held it, none could stand before me. But it was stolen from me, and Acheron fell, and I fled an exile into dark Stygia. Much I remember, but much I have forgotten. I have been in a far land, across misty voids and gulfs and unlit oceans. What is the year?"

Orastes answered him. "It is the waning of the Year of the Lion, three thousand years after the fall of Acheron."

"Three thousand years!" murmured the other. "So long? Who are you?"

"I am Orastes, once a priest of Mitra. This man is Amalric, baron of Tor, in Nemedia; this other is Tarascus, younger brother of the king of Nemedia; and this tall man is Valerius, rightful heir of the throne of Aquilonia."

"Why have you given me life?" demanded Xaltotun. "What do you require of me?"

The man was now fully alive and awake, his keen eyes reflecting the working of an unclouded brain. There was no hesitation or uncertainty in his manner. He came directly to the point, as one who knows that no man gives something for nothing. Orastes met him with equal candor.

"We have opened the doors of hell this night to free your soul and return it to your body because we need your aid. We wish to place Tarascus on the throne of Nemedia, and to win for Valerius the crown of Aquilonia. With your necromancy you can aid us."

Xaltotun's mind was devious and full of unexpected slants.

"You must be deep in the arts yourself, Orastes, to have been able to restore my life. How is it that a priest of Mitra knows of the Heart of Ahriman, and the incantations of Skelos?"

"I am no longer a priest of Mitra," answered Orastes. "I was cast forth from my order because of my delving in black magic. But for Amalric there I might have been burned as a magician.

"But that left me free to pursue my studies. I journeyed in Zamora, in Vendhya, in Stygia, and among the haunted jungles of Khitai. I read the iron-bound books of Skelos, and talked with unseen creatures in deep wells, and faceless shapes in black reeking jungles. I obtained a glimpse of your sarcophagus in the demon-haunted crypts below the black giant-walled temple of Set in the hinterlands of Stygia, and I learned of the arts that would bring back life to your shriveled corpse. From moldering manuscripts I learned of the Heart of Ahriman. Then for a year I sought its hiding-place, and at last I found it."

"Then why trouble to bring me back to life?" demanded Xaltotun, with his piercing gaze fixed on the priests. "Why did you not employ the Heart to further your own power?"

"Because no man today knows the secrets of the Heart," answered Orastes. "Not even in legends live the arts by which to loose its full powers. I knew it could restore life; of its deeper secrets I am ignorant. I merely used it to bring you back to life. It is the use of your knowledge we seek. As for the Heart, you alone know its awful secrets."

Xaltotun shook his head, staring broodingly into the flaming depths.

"My necromantic knowledge is greater than the sum of all the knowledge of other men," he said; "yet I do not know the full power of the jewel. I did not invoke it in the old days; I guarded it lest it be used against me. At last it was stolen, and in the hands of a feathered shaman of the barbarians it defeated all my mighty sorcery. Then it vanished, and I was poisoned by the jealous priests of Stygia before I could learn where it was hidden."

"It was hidden in a cavern below the temple of Mitra, in Tarantia," said Orastes. "By devious ways I discovered this, after I had located your remains in Set's subterranean temple in Stygia.

"Zamorian thieves, partly protected by spells I learned from sources better left unmentioned, stole your mummy-case from under the very talons of those which guarded it in the dark, and by camel-caravan and galley and ox-wagon it came at last to this city.

"Those same thieves—or rather those of them who still lived after their frightful quest—stole the Heart of Ahriman from its haunted cavern below the temple of Mitra, and all the skill of men and the spells of sorcerers nearly failed. One man of them lived long enough to reach

me and give the jewel into my hands, before he died slavering and gibbering of what he had seen in that accursed crypt. The thieves of
Zamora are the most faithful of men to their trust. Even with my con-
jurements, none but them could have stolen the Heart from where it
has lain in demon-guarded darkness since the fall of Acheron, three
thousand years ago."

Xaltotun lifted his lionlike head and stared far off into space, as if
plumbing the lost centuries.

"Three thousand years!" he muttered. "Set! Tell me what has
chanced in the world."

"The barbarians who overthrew Acheron set up new kingdoms,"
quoted Orastes. "Where the empire had stretched now rose realms
called Aquilonia, and Nemedia, and Argos, from the tribes that founded
them. The older kingdoms of Ophir, Corinthia and western Koth,
which had been subject to the kings of Acheron, regained their independence with the fall of the empire."

"And what of the people of Acheron?" demanded Orastes. "When
I fled into Stygia, Python was in ruins, and all the great, purple-towered
cities of Acheron fouled with blood and trampled by the sandals of the
barbarians."

"In the hills small groups of folk still boast descent from Acheron,"
answered Orastes. "For the rest, the tide of my barbarian ancestors
rolled over them and wiped them out. They—my ancestors—had suffered much from the kings of Acheron."

A grim and terrible smile curled the Pythonian's lips.

"Aye! Many a barbarian, both man and woman, died screaming on
the altar under this hand. I have seen their heads piled to make a pyramid in the great square in Python when the kings returned from the
west with their spoils and naked captives."

"Aye. And when the day of reckoning came, the sword was not
spared. So Acheron ceased to be, and purple-towered Python became
a memory of forgotten days. But the younger kingdoms rose on the
imperial ruins and waxed great. And now we have brought you back
to aid us to rule these kingdoms, which, if less strange and wonderful
than Acheron of old, are yet rich and powerful, well worth fighting for.
Look!" Orastes unrolled before the stranger a map drawn cunningly on
vellum.

Xaltotun regarded it, and then shook his head, baffled.

"The very outlines of the land are changed. It is like some familiar
thing seen in a dream, fantastically distorted."

"Howbeit," answered Orastes, tracing with his forefinger, "here is Belverus, the capital of Nemedia, in which we now are. Here run the boundaries of the land of Nemedia. To the south and southeast are Ophir and Corinthia, to the east Brythunia, to the west Aquilonia."

"It is the map of a world I do not know," said Xaltotun softly, but Orastes did not miss the lurid fire of hate that flickered in his dark eyes.

"It is a map you shall help us change," answered Orastes. "It is our desire first to set Tarascus on the throne of Nemedia. We wish to accomplish this without strife, and in such a way that no suspicion will rest on Tarascus. We do not wish the land to be torn by civil wars, but to reserve all our power for the conquest of Aquilonia.

"Should King Nimed and his sons die naturally, in a plague for instance, Tarascus would mount the throne as the next heir, peacefully and unopposed."

Xaltotun nodded, without replying, and Orastes continued.

"The other task will be more difficult. We cannot set Valerius on the Aquilonian throne without a war, and that kingdom is a formidable foe. Its people are a hardy, warlike race, toughened by continual wars with the Picts, Zingarians and Cimmerians. For five hundred years Aquilonia and Nemedia have intermittently waged war, and the ultimate advantage has always lain with the Aquilonians.

"Their present king is the most renowned warrior among the western nations. He is an outlander, an adventurer who seized the crown by force during a time of civil strife, strangling King Namedides with his own hands, upon the very throne. His name is Conan, and no man can stand before him in battle.

"Valerius is now the rightful heir of the throne. He had been driven into exile by his royal kinsman, Namedides, and has been away from his native realm for years, but he is of the blood of the old dynasty, and many of the barons would secretly hail the overthrow of Conan, who is a nobody without royal or even noble blood. But the common people are loyal to him, and the nobility of the outlying provinces. Yet if his forces were overthrown in the battle that must first take place, and Conan himself slain, I think it would not be difficult to put Valerius on the throne. Indeed, with Conan slain, the only center of the government would be gone. He is not part of a dynasty, but only a lone adventurer."

"I wish that I might see this king," mused Xaltotun, glancing toward a silvery mirror which formed one of the panels of the wall. This mirror cast no reflection, but Xaltotun's expression showed that he understood its purpose, and Orastes nodded with the pride a good craftsman takes in the recognition of his accomplishments by a master of his craft.

"I will try to show him to you," he said. And seating himself before the mirror, he gazed hypnotically into its depths, where presently a dim shadow began to take shape.

It was uncanny, but those watching knew it was no more than the reflected image of Orastes' thought, embodied in that mirror as a wizard's thoughts are embodied in a magic crystal. It floated hazily, then leaped into startling clarity—a tall man, mightily shouldered and deep of chest, with a massive corded neck and heavily muscled limbs. He was clad in silk and velvet, with the royal lions of Aquilonia worked in gold upon his rich jupon, and the crown of Aquilonia shone on his square-cut black mane; but the great sword at his side seemed more natural to him than the regal accouterments. His brow was low and broad, his eyes a volcanic blue that smoldered as if with some inner fire. His dark, scarred, almost sinister face was that of a fighting-man, and his velvet garments could not conceal the hard, dangerous lines of his limbs.

"That man is no Hyborian!" exclaimed Xaltotun.

"No; he is a Cimmerian, one of those wild tribesmen who dwell in the gray hills of the north."

"I fought his ancestors of old," muttered Xaltotun. "Not even the kings of Acheron could conquer them."

"They still remain a terror to the nations of the south," answered Orastes. "He is a true son of that savage race, and has proved himself, thus far, unconquerable."

Xaltotun did not reply; he sat staring down at the pool of living fire that shimmered in his hand. Outside, the hound howled again, long and shudderingly.

2　The Black Wind Blows

The year of the dragon had birth in war and pestilence and unrest. The black plague stalked through the streets of Belverus, striking down the merchant in his stall, the serf in his kennel, the knight at his banquet board. Before it the arts of the leeches were helpless. Men said it had been sent from Hell as punishment for the sins of pride and lust. It was swift and deadly as the stroke of an adder. The victim's body turned purple and then black, and within a few minutes he sank down dying, and the stench of his own putrefaction was in his nostrils even before death wrenched his soul from his rotting body. A hot, roaring wind blew incessantly from the south, and the crops withered in the fields, the cattle sank and died in their tracks.

Men cried out on Mitra, and muttered against the king; for somehow, throughout the kingdom, the word was whispered that the king was secretly addicted to loathsome practises and foul debauches in the seclusion of his nighted palace. And then in that palace death stalked grinning on feet about which swirled the monstrous vapors of the plague. In one night the king died with his three sons, and the drums that thundered their dirge drowned the grim and ominous bells that rang from the carts that lumbered through the streets gathering up the rotting dead.

That night, just before dawn, the hot wind that had blown for weeks ceased to rustle evilly through the silken window curtains. Out of the north rose a great wind that roared among the towers, and there was cataclysmic thunder, and blinding sheets of lightning, and driving rain. But the dawn shone clean and green and clear; the scorched ground veiled itself in grass, the thirsty crops sprang up anew, and the plague was gone—its miasma swept clean out of the land by the mighty wind.

Men said the gods were satisfied because the evil king and his spawn were slain, and when his young brother Tarascus was crowned in the great coronation hall, the populace cheered until the towers rocked, acclaiming the monarch on whom the gods smiled.

Such a wave of enthusiasm and rejoicing as swept the land is frequently the signal for a war of conquest. So no one was surprized when it was announced that King Tarascus had declared the truce made by the late king with their western neighbors void, and was gathering his hosts to invade Aquilonia. His reason was candid; his motives, loudly proclaimed, gilded his actions with something of the glamour of a crusade. He espoused the cause of Valerius, "rightful heir to the throne"; he came, he proclaimed, not as an enemy of Aquilonia, but as a friend, to free the people from the tyranny of a usurper and a foreigner.

If there were cynical smiles in certain quarters, and whispers concerning the king's good friend Amalric, whose vast personal wealth seemed to be flowing into the rather depleted royal treasury, they were unheeded in the general wave of fervor and zeal of Tarascus' popularity. If any shrewd individuals suspected that Amalric was the real ruler of Nemedia, behind the scenes, they were careful not to voice such heresy. And the war went forward with enthusiasm.

The king and his allies moved westward at the head of fifty thousand men—knights in shining armor with their pennons streaming above their helmets, pikemen in steel caps and brigandines, crossbowmen in leather jerkins. They crossed the border, took a frontier castle and burned three mountain villages, and then, in the valley of the Valkia, ten miles west of the boundary line, they met the hosts of Conan, king of Aquilonia—forty-five thousand knights, archers and men-at-arms, the flower of Aquilonian strength and chivalry. Only the knights of Poitain, under Prospero, had not yet arrived, for they had far to ride up from the southwestern corner of the kingdom. Tarascus had struck without warning. His invasion had come on the heels of his proclamation, without formal declaration of war.

The two hosts confronted each other across a wide, shallow valley, with rugged cliffs, and a shallow stream winding through masses of reeds and willows down the middle of the vale. The camp followers of both hosts came down to this stream for water, and shouted insults and hurled stones across at one another. The last glints of the sun shone on the golden banner of Nemedia with the scarlet dragon, unfurled in the breeze above the pavilion of King Tarascus on an eminence near the eastern cliffs. But the shadow of the western cliffs fell like a vast purple pall across the tents and the army of Aquilonia, and upon the black banner with its golden lion that floated above King Conan's pavilion.

All night the fires flared the length of the valley, and the wind brought the call of trumpets, the clangor of arms, and the sharp challenges of the sentries who paced their horses along either edge of the willow-grown stream.

It was in the darkness before dawn that King Conan stirred on his couch, which was no more than a pile of silks and furs thrown on a dais, and awakened. He started up, crying out sharply and clutching at his sword. Pallantides, his commander, rushing in at the cry, saw his king sitting upright, his hand on his hilt, and perspiration dripping from his strangely pale face.

"Your Majesty!" exclaimed Pallantides. "Is aught amiss?"

"What of the camp?" demanded Conan. "Are the guards out?"

"Five hundred horsemen patrol the stream, Your Majesty," answered the general. "The Nemedians have not offered to move against us in the night. They wait for dawn, even as we."

"By Crom," muttered Conan. "I awoke with a feeling that doom was creeping on me in the night."

He stared up at the great golden lamp which shed a soft glow over the velvet hangings and carpets of the great tent. They were alone; not even a slave or a page slept on the carpeted floor; but Conan's eyes blazed as they were wont to blaze in the teeth of great peril, and the sword quivered in his hand. Pallantides watched him uneasily. Conan seemed to be listening.

"Listen!" hissed the king. "Did you hear it? A furtive step!"

"Seven knights guard your tent, Your Majesty," said Pallantides. "None could approach it unchallenged."

"Not outside," growled Conan. "It seemed to sound inside the tent."

Pallantides cast a swift, startled look around. The velvet hangings merged with shadows in the corners, but if there had been anyone in the pavilion besides themselves, the general would have seen him. Again he shook his head.

"There is no one here, sire. You sleep in the midst of your host."

"I have seen death strike a king in the midst of thousands," muttered Conan. "Something that walks on invisible feet and is not seen—"

"Perhaps you were dreaming, Your Majesty," said Pallantides, somewhat perturbed.

"So I was," grunted Conan. "A devilish dream it was, too. I trod again all the long, weary roads I traveled on my way to the kingship."

He fell silent, and Pallantides stared at him unspeaking. The king was an enigma to the general, as to most of his civilized subjects. Pallantides knew that Conan had walked many strange roads in his wild, eventful life, and had been many things before a twist of Fate set him on the throne of Aquilonia.

"I saw again in the battlefield whereon I was born," said Conan, resting his chin moodily on a massive fist. "I saw myself in a panther-skin loin-clout, throwing my spear at the mountain beasts. I was a mercenary swordsman again, a hetman of the kozaki who dwell along the Zaporoska River, a corsair looting the coasts of Kush, a pirate of the Barachan Isles, a chief of the Himelian hillmen. All these things I've been, and of all these things I dreamed; all the shapes that have been I passed like an endless procession, and their feet beat out a dirge in the sounding dust.

"But throughout my dreams moved strange, veiled figures and ghostly shadows, and a far-away voice mocked me. And toward the last I seemed to see myself lying on this dais in my tent, and a shape bent over me, robed and hooded. I lay unable to move, and then the hood fell away and a moldering skull grinned down at me. Then it was that I awoke."

"This is an evil dream, Your Majesty," said Pallantides, suppressing a shudder. "But no more."

Conan shook his head, more in doubt than in denial. He came of a barbaric race, and the superstitions and instincts of his heritage lurked close beneath the surface of his consciousness.

"I've dreamed many evil dreams," he said, "and most of them were meaningless. But by Crom, this was not like most dreams! I wish this battle were fought and won, for I've had a grisly premonition ever since King Nimed died in the black plague. Why did it cease when he died?"

"Men say he sinned—"

"Men are fools, as always," grunted Conan. "If the plague struck all who sinned, then by Crom there wouldn't be enough left to count the living! Why should the gods—who the priests tell me are just—slay five hundred peasants and merchants and nobles before they slew the king, if the whole pestilence were aimed at him? Were the gods smiting blindly, like swordsmen in a fog? By Mitra, if I aimed my strokes no straighter, Aquilonia would have had a new king long ago.

"No! The black plague's no common pestilence. It lurks in Stygian tombs, and is called forth into being only by wizards. I was a swordsman in Prince Almuric's army that invaded Stygia, and of his thirty thousand, fifteen thousand perished by Stygian arrows, and the rest by the black plague that rolled on us like a wind out of the south. I was the only man who lived."

"Yet only five hundred died in Nemedia," argued Pallantides.

"Whoever called it into being knew how to cut it short at will," answered Conan. "So I know there was something planned and diabolical about it. Someone called it forth, someone banished it when the work was completed—when Tarascus was safe on the throne and being hailed as the deliverer of the people from the wrath of the gods. By Crom, I sense a black, subtle brain behind all this. What of this stranger who men say gives counsel to Tarascus?"

"He wears a veil," answered Pallantides; "they say he is a foreigner; a stranger from Stygia."

"A stranger from Stygia!" repeated Conan scowling. "A stranger from Hell, more like!—Ha! What is that?"

"The trumpets of the Nemedians!" exclaimed Pallantides. "And hark, how our own blare upon their heels! Dawn is breaking, and the captains are marshaling the hosts for the onset! Mitra be with them, for many will not see the sun go down behind the crags."

"Send my squires to me!" exclaimed Conan, rising with alacrity and casting off his velvet night-garment; he seemed to have forgotten his forebodings at the prospect of action. "Go to the captains and see that all is in readiness. I will be with you as soon as I don my armor."

Many of Conan's ways were inexplicable to the civilized people he ruled, and one of them was his insistence on sleeping alone in his chamber or tent. Pallantides hastened from the pavilion, clanking in the armor he had donned at midnight after a few hours' sleep. He cast a swift glance over the camp, which was beginning to swarm with activity, mail clinking and men moving about dimly in the uncertain light, among the long lines of tents. Stars still glimmered palely in the western sky, but long pink streamers stretched along the eastern horizon, and against them the dragon banner of Nemedia flung out its billowing silken folds.

Pallantides turned toward a smaller tent near by, where slept the royal squires. These were tumbling out already, roused by the trumpets. And as Pallantides called to them to hasten, he was frozen speechless by a deep fierce shout and the impact of a heavy blow inside the king's tent, followed by a heart-stopping crash of a falling body. There sounded a low laugh that turned the general's blood to ice.

Echoing the cry, Pallantides wheeled and rushed back into the pavilion. He cried out again as he saw Conan's powerful frame stretched out on the carpet. The king's great two-handed sword lay near his hand, and a shattered tent-pole seemed to show where his sword had fallen. Pallantides' sword was out, and he glared about the tent, but nothing met his gaze. Save for the king and himself it was empty, as it had been when he left it.

"Your Majesty!" Pallantides threw himself on his knees beside the fallen giant.

Conan's eyes were open; they blazed up at him with full intelligence and recognition. His lips writhed, but no sound came forth. He seemed unable to move.

Voices sounded without. Pallantides rose swiftly and stepped to the door. The royal squires and one of the knights who guarded the tent stood there. "We heard a sound within," said the knight apologetically. "Is all well with the king?"

Pallantides regarded him searchingly.

"None has entered or left the pavilion this night?"

"None save yourself, my lord," answered the knight, and Pallantides could not doubt his honesty.

"The king stumbled and dropped his sword," said Pallantides briefly. "Return to your post."

As the knight turned away, the general covertly motioned to the five royal squires, and when they had followed him in, he drew the flap closely. They turned pale at the sight of the king stretched upon the carpet, but Pallantides' quick gesture checked their exclamations.

The general bent over him again, and again Conan made an effort to speak. The veins in his temples and the cords in his neck swelled with his efforts, and he lifted his head clear off the ground. Voice came at last, mumbling and half intelligible.

"The thing—the thing in the corner!"

Pallantides lifted his head and looked fearfully about him. He saw the pale faces of the squires in the lamplight, the velvet shadows that lurked along the walls of the pavilion. That was all.

"There is nothing here, Your Majesty," he said.

"It was there, in the corner," muttered the king, tossing his lion-maned head from side to side in his efforts to rise. "A man—at least he looked like a man—wrapped in rags like a mummy's bandages, with a moldering cloak drawn about him, and a hood. All I could see was his eyes, as he crouched there in the shadows. I thought he was a shadow himself, until I saw his eyes. They were like black jewels.

"I made at him and swung my sword, but I missed him clean—how, Crom knows—and splintered that pole instead. He caught my wrist as I staggered off balance, and his fingers burned like hot iron. All the strength went out of me, and the floor rose and struck me like a club. Then he was gone, and I was down, and—curse him!—I can't move! I'm paralyzed!"

Pallantides lifted the giant's hand, and his flesh crawled. On the king's wrist showed the blue marks of long, lean fingers. What hand could grip so hard as to leave its print on that thick wrist? Pallantides remembered that low laugh he had heard as he rushed into the tent, and cold perspiration beaded his skin. It had not been Conan who laughed.

"This is a thing diabolical!" whispered a trembling squire. "Men say the children of darkness war for Tarascus!"

"Be silent!" ordered Pallantides sternly.

Outside, the dawn was dimming the stars. A light wind sprang up from the peaks, and brought the fanfare of a thousand trumpets. At the sound a convulsive shudder ran through the king's mighty form. Again the veins in his temples knotted as he strove to break the invisible shackles which crushed him down.

"Put my harness on me and tie me into my saddle," he whispered. "I'll lead the charge yet!"

Pallantides shook his head, and a squire plucked his skirt.

"My lord, we are lost if the host learns the king has been smitten! Only he could have led us to victory this day."

"Help me lift him on the dais," answered the general.

They obeyed, and laid the helpless giant on the furs, and spread a silken cloak over him. Pallantides turned to the five squires and searched their pale faces long before he spoke.

"Our lips must be sealed for ever as to what happens in this tent," he said at last. "The kingdom of Aquilonia depends upon it. One of you go and fetch me the officer Valannus, who is a captain of the Pellian spearmen."

The squire indicated bowed and hastened from the tent, and Pallantides stood staring down at the stricken king, while outside trumpets blared, drums thundered, and the roar of the multitudes rose in the growing dawn. Presently the squire returned with the officer Pallantides had named—a tall man, broad and powerful, built much like the king. Like him, also, he had thick black hair. But his eyes were gray and he did not resemble Conan in his features.

"The king is stricken by a strange malady," said Pallantides briefly. "A great honor is yours; you are to wear his armor and ride at the head of the host today. None must know that it is not the king who rides."

"It is an honor for which a man might gladly give up his life," stammered the captain, overcome by the suggestion. "Mitra grant that I do not fail of this mighty trust!"

And while the fallen king stared with burning eyes that reflected the bitter rage and humiliation that ate his heart, the squires stripped Valannus of mail shirt, burganet and leg-pieces, and clad him in Conan's armor of black plate mail, with the vizored salade, and the dark plumes nodding over the wivern crest. Over all they put the silken surcoat with the royal lion worked in gold upon the breast, and they girt him with a broad gold-buckled belt which supported a jewel-hilted broadsword in a cloth-of-gold scabbard. While they worked, trumpets clamored outside, arms clanged, and across the river rose a deep-throated roar as squadron after squadron swung into place.

Full-armed, Vallanus dropped to his knee and bent his plumes before the figure that lay on the dais.

"Lord king, Mitra grant that I do not dishonor the harness I wear this day!"

"Bring me Tarascus's head and I'll make you a baron!" In the stress of his anguish Conan's veneer of civilization had fallen from him. His eyes flamed, he ground his teeth in fury and blood-lust, as barbaric as any tribesmen in the Cimmerian hills.

3 The Cliffs Reel

The Aquilonian host was drawn up, long serried lines of pikemen and horsemen in gleaming steel, when a giant figure in black armor emerged from the royal pavilion, and as he swung up into the saddle of the black stallion held by four squires, a roar that shook the mountains went up from the host. They shook their blades and thundered forth their acclaim of their warrior king—knights in gold-chased armor, pikemen in mail coats and basinets, archers in their leather jerkins, with their longbows in their left hands.

The host on the opposite side of the valley was in motion, trotting down the long gentle slope toward the river; their steel shone through the mists of morning that swirled about their horses" feet.

The Aquilonian host moved leisurely to meet them. The measured tramp of the armored horses made the ground tremble. Banners flung out long silken folds in the morning wind; lances swayed like a bristling forest, dipped and sank, their pennons fluttering about them.

Ten men-at-arms, grim, taciturn veterans who could hold their tongues, guarded the royal pavilion. One squire stood in the tent, peering out through a slit in the doorway. But for the handful in the secret, no one else in the vast host knew that it was not Conan who rode on the great stallion at the head of the army.

The Aquilonian host had assumed the customary formation:

The strongest part was the center, composed entirely of heavily armed knights; the wings were made up of smaller bodies of horsemen, mounted men-at-arms, mostly, supported by pikemen and archers. The latter were Bossonians from the western marches, strongly built men of medium stature, in leathern jackets and iron head-pieces.

The Nemedian army came on in similar formation and the two hosts moved toward the river, the wings, in advance of the centers. In the center of the Aquilonian host the great lion banner streamed its billowing black folds over the steel-clad figure on the black stallion.

But on his dais in the royal pavilion Conan groaned in anguish of spirit, and cursed with strange heathen oaths.

"The hosts move together," quoth the squire, watching from the door. "Hear the trumpets peal! Ha! The rising sun strikes fire from lance heads and helmets until I am dazzled. It turns the river crimson— aye, it will be truly crimson before this day is done!

"The foe have reached the river. Now arrows fly between the hosts like stinging clouds that hide the sun. Ha! Well loosed, bowman! The Bossonians have the better of it! Hark to them shout!"

Faintly in the ears of the king, above the din of trumpets and clanging steel, came the deep fierce shout of the Bossonians as they drew and loosed in perfect unison.

"Their archers seek to hold ours in play while their knights ride into the river," said the squire. "The banks are not steep; they slope to the water's edge. The knights come on, they crash through the willows. By Mitra, the clothyard shafts find every crevice of their harness! Horses and men go down, struggling and thrashing in the water. It is not deep, nor is the current swift, but men are drowning there, dragged under by their armor, and trampled by the frantic horses. Now the knights of Aquilonia advance. They ride into the water and engage the knights of Nemedia. The water swirls about their horses' bellies and the clang of sword against sword is deafening."

"Crom!" burst in agony from Conan's lip. Life was coursing sluggishly back into his veins, but still he could not lift his mighty frame from the dais.

"The wings close in," said the squire. "Pikemen and swordsmen fight hand to hand in the stream, and behind them the bowmen ply their shafts.

"By Mitra, the Nemedian arbalesters are sorely harried, and the Bossonians arch their arrows to drop amid the rear ranks. Their center gains not a foot, and their wings are pushed back up from the stream again."

"Crom, Ymir, and Mitra!" raged Conan. "Gods and devils, could I but reach the fighting, if but to die at the first blow!"

Outside through the long hot day the battle stormed and thundered. The valley shook to charge and countercharge, to the whistling of shafts, and the crash of rending shields and splintering lances. But the

244 *The Weird Tales of Conan the Barbarian*

hosts of Aquilonia held fast. Once they were forced back from the bank, but a countercharge, with the black banner flowing over the black stallion, regained the lost ground. And like an iron rampart they held the right bank of the stream, and at last the squire gave Conan the news that the Nemedians were falling back from the river.

"Their wings are in confusion!" he cried. "Their knights reel back from the sword play. But what is this? Your banner is in motion—the center sweeps into the stream! By Mitra, Valannus is leading the host across the river!"

"Fool!" groaned Conan. "It may be a trick. He should hold his position; by dawn Prospero will be here with the Poitanian levies."

"The knights ride into a hail of arrows!" cried the squire. "But they do not falter! They sweep on—they have crossed! They charge up the slope! Pallantides has hurled the wings across the river to their support! It is all he can do. The lion banner dips and staggers above the melee.

"The knights of Nemedia make a stand. They are broken! They fall back! Their left wing is in full flight, and our pikemen cut them down as they run! I see Valannus, riding and smiting like a madman. He is carried beyond himself by the fighting-lust. Men no longer look to Pallantides. They follow Valannus, deeming him Conan, as he rides with closed vizor.

"But look! There is method in his madness! He swings wide of the Nemedian front, with five thousand knights, the pick of the army. The main host of the Nemedians is in confusion—and look! Their flank is protected by the cliffs, but there is a defile left unguarded! It is like a great cleft in the wall that opens again behind the Nemedian lines. By Mitra, Valannus sees and seizes the opportunity! He has driven their wing before him, and he leads his knights toward that defile. They swing wide of the main battle; they cut through a line of spearmen, they charge into the defile!"

"An ambush!" cried Conan, striving to struggle upright.

"No!" shouted the squire exultantly. "The whole Nemedian host is in full sight! They have forgotten the defile! They never expected to be pushed back that far. Oh, fool, fool, Tarascus, to make such a blunder! Ah, I see lances and pennons pouring from the farther mouth of the defile, beyond the Nemedian lines. They will smite those ranks from the rear and crumple them. Mitra, what is this?"

He staggered as the walls of the tent swayed drunkenly. Afar over the thunder of the fight rose a deep bellowing roar, indescribably ominous.

"The cliffs reel!" shrieked the squire. "Ah, gods, what is this? The river foams out of its channel, and the peaks are crumbling!"

"The ground shakes and horses and riders in armor are overthrown! The cliffs! The cliffs are falling!"

With his words there came a grinding rumble and a thunderous concussion, and the ground trembled. Over the roar of the battle sounded screams of mad terror.

"The cliffs have crumbled!" cried the livid squire. "They have thundered down into the defile and crushed every living creature in it! I saw the lion banner wave an instant amid the dust and falling stones, and then it vanished! Ha, the Nemedians shout with triumph! Well may they shout, for the fall of the cliffs has wiped out five thousand of our bravest knights—hark!"

To Conan's ears came a vast torrent of sound, rising and rising in frenzy: "The king is dead! The king is dead! Flee! Flee! The king is dead!"

"Liars!" panted Conan. "Dogs! Knaves! Cowards! Oh, Crom, if I could but stand—but crawl to the river with my sword in my teeth! How, boy, do they flee?"

"Aye!" sobbed the squire. "They spur for the river; they are broken, hurled on like spume before a storm. I see Pallantides striving to stem the torrent—he is down, and the horses trample him! They rush into the river, knights, bowmen, pikemen, all mixed and mingled in one mad torrent of destruction. The Nemedians are on their heels, cutting them down like corn."

"But they will make a stand on this side of the river!" cried the king. With an effort that brought the sweat dripping from his temples, he heaved himself up on his elbows.

"Nay!" cried the squire. "They cannot! They are broken! Routed! Oh gods, that I should live to see this day!"

Then he remembered his duty and shouted to the men-at-arms who stood stolidly watching the flight of their comrades. "Get a horse, swiftly, and help me lift the king upon it. We dare not bide here."

But before they could do his bidding, the first drift of the storm was upon them. Knights and spearmen and archers fled among the tents, stumbling over ropes and baggage, and mingled with them were Nemedian riders, who smote right and left at all alien figures. Tent ropes were cut, fire sprang up in a hundred places, and the plundering had already begun. The grim guardsmen about Conan's tent died where they stood, smiting and thrusting, and over their mangled corpses beat the hoofs of the conquerors.

But the squire had drawn the flap close, and in the confused madness of the slaughter none realized that the pavilion held an occupant. So the flight and the pursuit swept past, and roared away up the valley, and the squire looked out presently to see a cluster of men approaching the royal tent with evident purpose.

"Here comes the king of Nemedia with four companions and his squire," quoth he. "He will accept your surrender, my fair lord—"

"Surrender the devil's heart!" gritted the king.

He had forced himself up to a sitting posture. He swung his legs painfully off the dais, and staggered upright, reeling drunkenly. The squire ran to assist him, but Conan pushed him away.

"Give me that bow!" he gritted, indicating a longbow and quiver that hung from a tent-pole.

"But Your Majesty!" cried the squire in great perturbation. "The battle is lost! It were the part of majesty to yield with the dignity becoming one of royal blood!"

"I have no royal blood," ground Conan. "I am a barbarian and the son of a blacksmith."

Wrenching away the bow and an arrow, he staggered toward the opening of the pavilion. So formidable was his appearance, naked but for short leather breeks and sleeveless shirt, open to reveal his great, hairy chest, with his huge limbs and his blue eyes blazing under his tangled black mane, that the squire shrank back, more afraid of his king than of the whole Nemedian host.

Reeling on wide-braced legs Conan drunkenly tore the door-flap open and staggered out under the canopy. The king of Nemedia and his companions had dismounted, and they halted short, staring in wonder at the apparition confronting them.

"Here I am, you jackals!" roared the Cimmerian. "I am the king! Death to you, dog-brothers!"

He jerked the arrow to its head and loosed, and the shaft feathered itself in the breast of the knight who stood beside Tarascus. Conan hurled the bow at the king of Nemedia.

"Curse my shaky hand! Come in and take me if you dare!"

Reeling backward on unsteady legs, he fell with his shoulders against a tent-pole, and propped upright, he lifted his great sword with both hands.

"By Mitra, it is the king!" swore Tarascus. He cast a swift look about him, and laughed. "That other was a jackal in his harness! In, dogs, and take his head!"

The three soldiers—men-at-arms wearing the emblem of the royal guards— rushed at the king, and one felled the squire with a blow of a mace. The other two fared less well. As the first rushed in, lifting his sword, Conan met him with a sweeping stroke that severed mail-links like cloth, and sheared the Nemedian's arm and shoulder clean from his body. His corpse, pitching backward, fell across his companion's legs. The man stumbled, and before he could recover, the great sword was through him.

Conan wrenched out his steel with a racking gasp, and staggered back against the tent-pole. His great limbs trembled, his chest heaved, and sweat poured down his face and neck. But his eyes flamed with exultant savagery and he panted: "Why do you stand afar off, dog of Belverus? I can't reach you; come in and die!" Tarascus hesitated, glanced at the remaining man-at-arms, and his squire, a gaunt, saturnine man in black mail, and took a step forward. He was far inferior in size and strength to the giant Cimmerian, but he was in full armor, and was famed in all the western nations as a swordsman. But his squire caught his arm.

"Nay, Your Majesty, do not throw away your life. I will summon archers to shoot this barbarian, as we shoot lions."

Neither of them had noticed that a chariot had approached while the fight was going on, and now came to a halt before them. But Conan saw, looking over their shoulders, and a queer chill sensation crawled along his spine. There was something vaguely unnatural about the appearance of the black horses that drew the vehicle, but it was the occupant of the chariot that arrested the king's attention.

He was a tall man, superbly built, clad in a long unadorned silk robe. He wore a Shemitish head-dress, and its lower folds hid his features, except for the dark, magnetic eyes. The hands that grasped the reins, pulling the rearing horses back on their haunches, were white but strong. Conan glared at the stranger, all his primitive instincts roused. He sensed an aura of menace and power that exuded from this veiled figure, a menace as definite as the windless waving of tall grass that marks the path of the serpent.

"Hail, Xaltotun!" exclaimed Tarascus. "Here is the king of Aquilonia! He did not die in the landslide as we thought."

"I know," answered the other, without bothering to say how he knew. "What is your present intention?"

"I will summon the archers to slay him," answered the Nemedian. "As long as he lives he will be dangerous to us."

"Yet even a dog has uses," answered Xaltotun. "Take him alive."

Conan laughed raspingly. "Come in and try!" he challenged. "But for my treacherous legs I'd hew you out of that chariot like a woodman hewing a tree. But you'll never take me alive, damn you!"

"He speaks the truth, I fear," said Tarascus. "The man is a barbarian, with the senseless ferocity of a wounded tiger. Let me summon the archers."

"Watch me and learn wisdom," advised Xaltotun.

His hand dipped into his robe and came out with something shining—a glistening sphere. This he threw suddenly at Conan. The Cimmerian contemptuously struck it aside with his sword—at the instant of contact there was a sharp explosion, a flare of white, blinding flame, and Conan pitched senseless to the ground.

"He is dead?" Tarascus' tone was more assertion than inquiry.

"No. He is but senseless. He will recover his senses in a few hours. Bid your men bind his arms and legs and lift him into my chariot."

With a gesture Tarascus did so, and they heaved the senseless king into the chariot, grunting with their burden. Xaltotun threw a velvet cloak over his body, completely covering him from any who might peer in. He gathered the reins in his hands.

"I'm for Belverus," he said. "Tell Amalric that I will be with him if he needs me. But with Conan out of the way, and his army broken, lance and sword should suffice for the rest of the conquest. Prospero cannot be bringing more than ten thousand men to the field, and will doubtless fall back to Tarantia when he hears the news of the battle. Say nothing to Amalric or Valerius or anyone about our capture. Let them think Conan died in the fall of the cliffs."

He looked at the man-at-arms for a long space, until the guardsman moved restlessly, nervous under the scrutiny.

"What is that about your waist?" Xaltotun demanded.

"Why, my girdle, may it please you, my lord!" stuttered the amazed guardsman.

"You lie!" Xaltotun's laugh was merciless as a sword edge. "It is a poisonous serpent! What a fool you are, to wear a reptile about your waist!"

With distended eyes the man looked down; and to his utter horror he saw the buckle of his girdle rear up at him. It was a snake's head! He saw the evil eyes and the dripping fangs, heard the hiss and felt the loathsome contact of the thing about his body. He screamed hideously and struck at it with his naked hand, felt its fangs flesh themselves in that hand—and then he stiffened and fell heavily. Tarascus looked down at him without expression. He saw only the leathern girdle and the buckle, the pointed tongue of which was stuck in the guardsman's palm. Xaltotun turned his hypnotic gaze on Tarascus' squire, and the man turned ashen and began to tremble, but the king interposed: "Nay, we can trust him."

The sorcerer tautened the reins and swung the horses around. "See that this piece of work remains secret. If I am needed, let Altaro, Orastes' servant, summon me as I have taught him. I will be in your palace at Belverus."

Tarascus lifted his hand in salutation, but his expression was not pleasant to see as he looked after the departing mesmerist.

"Why should he spare the Cimmerian?" whispered the frightened squire.

"That I am wondering myself," grunted Tarascus. Behind the rumbling chariot the dull roar of battle and pursuit faded in the distance; the setting sun rimmed the dins with scarlet flame, and the chariot moved into the vast blue shadows floating up out of the east.

4 "From What Hell Have You Crawled?"

Of that long ride in the chariot of Xaltotun, Conan knew nothing. He lay like a dead man while the bronze wheels clashed over the stones of mountain roads and swished through the deep grass of fertile valleys, and finally dropping down from the rugged heights, rumbled rhythmically along the broad white road that winds through the rich meadowlands to the walls of Belverus.

Just before dawn some faint reviving of life touched him. He heard a mumble of voices, the groan of ponderous hinges. Through a slit in the cloak that covered him he saw, faintly in the lurid glare of torches, the great black arch of a gateway, and the bearded faces of men-at-arms, the torches striking fire from their spearheads and helmets.

"How went the battle, my fair lord?" spoke an eager voice, in the Nemedian tongue.

"Well indeed," was the curt reply. "The king of Aquilonia lies slain and his host is broken."

A babble of excited voices rose, drowned the next instant by the whirling wheels of the chariot on the flags. Sparks flashed from under the revolving rims as Xaltotun lashed his steeds through the arch. But Conan heard one of the guardsmen mutter: "From beyond the border to Belverus between sunset and dawn! And the horses scarcely sweating! By Mitra, they—" Then silence drank the voices, and there was only the clatter of hoofs and wheels along the shadowy street.

What he had heard registered itself on Conan's brain but suggested nothing to him. He was like a mindless automaton that hears and sees, but does not understand. Sights and sounds flowed meaninglessly about him. He lapsed again into a deep lethargy, and was only dimly aware when the chariot halted in a deep, high-walled court, and he was lifted from it by many hands and borne up a winding stone stair, and down a long dim corridor. Whispers, stealthy footsteps, unrelated sounds surged or rustled about him, irrelevant and far away.

Yet his ultimate awakening was abrupt and crystal-clear. He possessed full knowledge of the battle in the mountains and its sequences, and he had a good idea of where he was.

He lay on a velvet couch, clad as he was the day before, but with his limbs loaded with chains not even he could break. The room in which he lay was furnished with somber magnificence, the walls covered with black velvet tapestries, the floor with heavy purple carpets. There was no sign of door or window, and one curiously carved gold lamp, swinging from the fretted ceiling, shed a lurid light over all.

In that light the figure seated in a silver, thronelike chair before him seemed unreal and fantastic, with an illusiveness of outline that was heightened by a filmy silken robe. But the features were distinct— unnaturally so in that uncertain light. It was almost as if a weird nimbus played about the man's head, casting the bearded face into bold relief, so that it was the only definite and distinct reality in that mystic, ghostly chamber.

It was a magnificent face, with strongly chiseled features of classical beauty. There was, indeed, something disquieting about the calm tranquility of its aspect, a suggestion of more than human knowledge, of a profound certitude beyond human assurance. Also an uneasy sensation of familiarity twitched at the back of Oman's consciousness. He had never seen this man's face before, he well knew; yet those features reminded him of something or someone. It was like encountering in the flesh some dream-image that had haunted one in nightmares.

"Who are you?" demanded the king belligerently, struggling to a sitting position in spite of his chains.

"Men call me Xaltotun," was the reply, in a strong, golden voice.

"What place is this?" the Cimmerian next demanded.

"A chamber in the palace of King Tarascus, in Belverus."

Conan was not surprized. Belverus, the capital, was at the same time the largest Nemedian city so near the border.

"And where's Tarascus?"

"With the army."

"Well," growled Conan, "if you mean to murder me, why don't you do it and get it over with?"

"I did not save you from the king's archers to murder you in Belverus," answered Xaltotun.

"What the devil did you do to me?" demanded Conan.

"I blasted your consciousness," answered Xaltotun. "How, you would not understand. Call it black magic, if you will."

Conan had already reached that conclusion, and was mulling over something else.

"I think I understand why you spared my life," he rumbled. "Amalric wants to keep me as a check on Valerius, in case the impossible happens and he becomes king of Aquilonia. It's well known that the baron of Tor is behind this move to seat Valerius on my throne. And if I know Amalric, he doesn't intend that Valerius shall be anything more than a figurehead, as Tarascus is now."

"Amalric knows nothing of your capture," answered Xaltotun. "Neither does Valerius. Both think you died at Valkia."

Conan's eyes narrowed as he stared at the man in silence.

"I sensed a brain behind all this," he muttered, "but I thought it was Amalric's. Are Amalric, Tarascus and Valerius all but puppets dancing on your string? Who are you?"

"What does it matter? If I told you, you would not believe me. What if I told you I might set you back on the throne of Aquilonia?"

Conan's eyes burned on him like a wolf.

"What's your price?"

"Obedience to me."

"Go to hell with your offer!" snarled Conan. "I'm no figurehead. I won my crown with my sword. Besides, it's beyond your power to buy and sell the throne of Aquilonia at your will. The kingdom's not con-quered; one battle doesn't decide a war."

"You war against more than swords," answered Xaltotun. "Was it a mortal's sword that felled you in your tent before the fight? Nay, it was a child of the dark, a waif of outer space, whose fingers were afire with the frozen coldness of the black gulfs, which froze the blood in your veins and the marrow of your thews. Coldness so cold it burned your flesh like white-hot iron!"

"Was it chance that led the man who wore your harness to lead his knights into the defile?—chance that brought the cliffs crashing down upon them?"

Conan glared at him unspeaking, feeling a chill along his spine. Wizards and sorcerers abounded in his barbaric mythology, and any fool could tell that this was no common man. Conan sensed an inexplicable something about him that set him apart—an alien aura of Time and Space, a sense of tremendous and sinister antiquity. But his stubborn spirit refused to flinch.

"The fall of the cliffs was chance," he muttered truculently. "The charge into the defile was what any man would have done."

"Not so. You would not have led a charge into it. You would have suspected a trap. You would never have crossed the river in the first place, until you were sure the Nemedian rout was real. Hypnotic suggestions would not have invaded your mind, even in the madness of battle, to make you mad, and rush blindly into the trap laid for you, as it did the lesser man who masqueraded as you."

"Then if this was all planned," Conan grunted skeptically, "all a plot to trap my host, why did not the 'child of darkness' kill me in my tent?"

"Because I wished to take you alive. It took no wizardry to predict that Pallantides would send another man out in your harness. I wanted you alive and unhurt. You may fit into my scheme of things. There is a vital power about you greater than the craft and cunning of my allies. You are a bad enemy, but might make a fine vassal."

Conan spat savagely at the word, and Xaltotun, ignoring his fury, took a crystal globe from a near-by table and placed it before him. He did not support it in any way, nor place it on anything, but it hung motionless in midair, as solidly as if it rested on an iron pedestal. Conan snorted at this bit of necromancy, but he was nevertheless impressed.

"Would you know of what goes on in Aquilonia?" he asked.

Conan did not reply, but the sudden rigidity of his form betrayed his interest.

Xaltotun stared into the cloudy depths, and spoke: "It is now the evening of the day after the battle of Valkia. Last night the main body of the army camped by Valkia, while squadrons of knights harried the fleeing Aquilonians. At dawn the host broke camp and pushed westward through the mountains. Prospero, with ten thousand Poitanians, was miles from the battlefield when he met the fleeing survivors in the early dawn. He had pushed on all night, hoping to reach the field before the battle joined. Unable to rally the remnants of the broken host, he fell back toward Tarantia. Riding hard, replacing his wearied horses with steeds seized from the countryside, he approaches Tarantia.

"I see his weary knights, their armor gray with dust, their pennons drooping as they push their tired horses through the plain. I see, also, the streets of Tarantia. The city is in turmoil. Somehow word has reached the people of the defeat and the death of King Conan. The mob is mad with fear, crying out that the king is dead, and there is none to lead them against the Nemedians. Giant shadows rush on Aquilonia from the east, and the sky is black with vultures."

Conan cursed deeply.

"What are these but words? The raggedest beggar in the street might prophesy as much. If you say you saw all that in the glass ball, then you're a liar as well as a knave, of which last there's no doubt! Prospero will hold Tarantia, and the barons will rally to him. Count Trocero of Poitain commands the kingdom in my absence, and he'll drive these Nemedian dogs howling back to their kennels. What are fifty thousand Nemedians? Aquilonia will swallow them up. They'll never see Belverus again. It's not Aquilonia which was conquered at Valkia; it was only Conan."

"Aquilonia is doomed," answered Xaltotun, unmoved. "Lance and ax and torch shall conquer her; or if they fail, powers from the dark of ages shall march against her. As the cliffs fell at Valkia, so shall walled cities and mountains fall, if the need arise, and rivers roar from their channels to drown whole provinces.

"Better if steel and bowstring prevail without further aid from the arts, for the constant use of mighty spells sometimes sets forces in motion that might rock the universe."

"From what hell have you crawled, you nighted dog?" muttered Conan, staring at the man. The Cimmerian involuntarily shivered; he sensed something incredibly ancient, incredibly evil.

Xaltotun lifted his head, as if listening to whispers across the void. He seemed to have forgotten his prisoner. Then he shook his head impatiently, and glanced impersonally at Conan.

"What? Why, if I told you, you would not believe me. But I am wearied of conversation with you; it is less fatiguing to destroy a walled city than it is to frame my thoughts in words a brainless barbarian can understand."

"If my hands were free," opined Conan, "I'd soon make a brainless corpse out of you."

"I do not doubt it, if I were fool enough to give you the opportunity," answered Xaltotun, clapping his hands. His manner had changed; there was impatience in his tone, and a certain nervousness in his manner, though Conan did not think this attitude was in any way connected with himself.

"Consider what I have told you, barbarian," said Xaltotun.

"You will have plenty of leisure. I have not yet decided what I shall do with you. It depends on circumstances yet unborn. But let this be impressed upon you: that if I decide to use you in my game, it will be better to submit without resistance than to suffer my wrath." Conan spat a curse at him, just as hangings that masked a door swung apart and four giant negroes entered. Each was clad only in a silken breech-clout supported by a girdle, from which hung a great key.

Xaltotun gestured impatiently toward the king and turned away, as if dismissing the matter entirely from his mind. His fingers twitched queerly. From a carven green jade box he took a handful of shimmering black dust, and placed it in a brazier which stood on a golden tripod at his elbow. The crystal globe, which he seemed to have forgotten, fell suddenly to the floor, as if its invisible support had been removed.

Then the blacks had lifted Conan—for so loaded with chains was he that he could not walk—and carried him from the chamber. A glance back, before the heavy, gold-bound teak door was closed, showed him Xaltotun leaning back in his thronelike chair, his arms folded, while a thin wisp of smoke curled up from the brazier. Oman's scalp prickled. In Stygia, that ancient and evil kingdom that lay far to the south, he had seen such black dust before. It was the pollen of the black lotus, which creates deathlike sleep and monstrous dreams; and he knew that only the grisly wizards of the Black Ring, which is the nadir of evil, voluntarily seek the scarlet nightmares of the black lotus, to revive their necromantic powers.

The Black Ring was a fable and a lie to most folk of the western world, but Conan knew of its ghastly reality, and its grim votaries who practise their abominable sorceries amid the black vaults of Stygia and the nighted domes of accursed Sabatea. He glanced back at the cryptic, gold-bound door, shuddering at what it hid.

Whether it was day or night the king could not tell. The palace of King Tarascus seemed a shadowy, nighted place, that shunned natural illumination. The spirit of darkness and shadow hovered over it, and that spirit, Conan felt, was embodied in the stranger Xaltotun. The negroes carried the king along a winding corridor so dimly lighted that they moved through it like black ghosts bearing a dead man, and down a stone stair that wound endlessly. A torch in the hand of one cast the great deformed shadows streaming along the wall; it was like the descent into hell of a corpse borne by dusky demons.

At last they reached the foot of the stair, and then they traversed a long straight corridor, with a blank wall on one hand pierced by an occasional arched doorway with a stair leading up behind it, and on the other hand another wall showing heavy barred doors at regular intervals of a few feet.

Halting before one of these doors, one of the blacks produced the key that hung at his girdle, and turned it in the lock. Then, pushing open the grille, they entered with their captive. They were in a small dungeon with heavy stone walls, floor and ceiling, and in the opposite wall there was another grilled door. What lay beyond that door Conan could not tell, but he did not believe it was another corridor. The glimmering light of the torch, flickering through the bars, hinted at shadowy spaciousness and echoing depths.

In one corner of the dungeon, near the door through which they had entered, a cluster of rusty chains hung from a great iron ring set in the stone. In these chains a skeleton dangled. Conan glared at it with some curiosity, noticing the state of the bare bones, most of which were splintered and broken; the skull which had fallen from the vertebrae, was crushed as if by some savage blow of tremendous force.

Stolidly one of the blacks, not the one who had opened the door, removed the chains from the ring, using his key on the massive lock, and dragged the mass of rusty metal and shattered bones over to one side. Then they fastened Conan's chains to that ring, and the third black turned his key in the lock of the farther door, grunting when he had assured himself that it was properly fastened.

Then they regarded Conan cryptically, slit-eyed ebony giants, the torch striking highlights from their glossy skin.

He who held the key to the nearer door was moved to remark, gutturally: "This your palace now, white dog-king! None but master and we know. All palace sleep. We keep secret. You live and die here, maybe. Like him!" He contemptuously kicked the shattered skull and sent it clattering across the stone floor.

Conan did not deign to reply to the taunt and the black, galled perhaps by his prisoner's silence, muttered a curse, stooped and spat full in the king's face. It was an unfortunate move for the black. Conan was seated on the floor, the chains about his waist; ankles and wrists locked to the ring in the wall. He could neither rise, nor move more than a yard out from the wall. But there was considerable slack in the chains that shackled his wrists, and before the bullet-shaped head could be withdrawn out of reach, the king gathered this slack in his mighty hand and smote the black on the head. The man fell like a butchered ox and his comrades stared to see him lying with his scalp laid open, and blood oozing from his nose and ears.

But they attempted no reprisal, nor did they accept Conan's urgent invitation to approach within reach of the bloody chain in his hand. Presently, grunting in their apelike speech, they lifted the senseless black and bore him out like a sack of wheat, arms and legs dangling. They used his key to lock the door behind them, but did not remove it from the gold chain that fastened it to his girdle. They took the torch with them, and as they moved up the corridor the darkness slunk behind them like an animate thing. Their soft padding footsteps died away, with the glimmer of their torch, and darkness and silence remained unchallenged.

5 The Haunter of the Pits

Conan lay still, enduring the weight of his chains and the despair of his position with the stoicism of the wilds that had bred him. He did not move, because the jangle of his chains, when he shifted his body, sounded startlingly loud in the darkness and stillness, and it was his instinct, born of a thousand wilderness-bred ancestors, not to betray his position in his helplessness. This did not result from a logical reasoning process; he did not lie quiet because he reasoned that the darkness hid lurking dangers that might discover him in his helplessness. Xaltotun had assured him that he was not to be harmed, and Conan believed that it was in the man's interest to preserve him, at least for the time being. But the instincts of the wild were there, that had caused him in his childhood to lie hidden and silent while wild beasts prowled about his covert.

Even his keen eyes could not pierce the solid darkness. Yet after a while, after a period of time he had no way of estimating, a faint glow became apparent, a sort of slanting gray beam, by which Conan could see, vaguely, the bars of the door at his elbow, and even make out the skeleton of the other grille. This puzzled him, until at last he realized the explanation. He was far below ground, in the pits below the palace; yet for some reason a shaft had been constructed from somewhere above. Outside, the moon had risen to a point where its light slanted dimly down the shaft. He reflected that in this manner he could tell the passing of the days and nights. Perhaps the sun, too, would shine down that shaft, though on the other hand it might be closed by day. Perhaps it was a subtle method of torture, allowing a prisoner but a glimpse of daylight or moonlight.

His gaze fell on the broken bones in the farther corner, glimmering dimly. He did not tax his brain with futile speculation as to who the wretch had been and for what reason he had been doomed, but he wondered at the shattered condition of the bones. They had not been broken on a rack. Then, as he looked, another unsavory detail made itself evident. The shin-bones were split lengthwise, and there was but one explanation; they had been broken in that manner in order to obtain the marrow. Yet what creature but man breaks bones for their marrow? Perhaps those remnants were mute evidence of a horrible, cannibalistic feast, of some wretch driven to madness by starvation. Conan wondered if his own bones would be found at some future date, hanging in their rusty chains. He fought down the unreasoning panic of a trapped wolf.

The Cimmerian did not curse, scream, weep or rave as a civilized man might have done. But the pain and turmoil in his bosom were none the less fierce. His great limbs quivered with the intensity of his emotions. Somewhere, far to the westward, the Nemedian host was slashing and burning its way through the heart of his kingdom. The small host of Poitanians could not stand before them. Prospero might be able to hold Tarantia for weeks, or months; but eventually, if not relieved, he must surrender to greater numbers. Surely the barons would rally to him against the invaders. But in the meanwhile he, Conan, must lie helpless in a darkened cell, while others led his spears and fought for his kingdom. The king ground his powerful teeth in red rage.

Then he stiffened as outside the farther door he heard a stealthy step. Straining his eyes he made out a bent, indistinct figure outside the grille. There was a rasp of metal against metal, and he heard the clink of tumblers, as if a key had been turned in the lock. Then the figure moved silently out of his range of vision. Some guard, he supposed, trying the lock. After a while he heard the sound repeated faintly somewhere farther on, and that was followed by the soft opening of a door, and then a swift scurry of softly shod feet retreated in the distance. Then silence fell again.

Conan listened for what seemed a long time, but which could not have been, for the moon still shone down the hidden shaft, but he heard no further sound. He shifted his position at last, and his chains clanked. Then he heard another, lighter footfall—a soft step outside the nearer door, the door though which he had entered the cell. An instant later a slender figure was etched dimly in the gray light.

"King Conan!" a soft voice intoned urgently. "Oh, my lord, are you there?"

"Where else?" he answered guardedly, twisting his head about to stare at the apparition.

It was a girl who stood grasping the bars with her slender fingers. The dim glow behind her outlined her supple figure through the wisp of silk twisted about her loins, and shone vaguely on jeweled breast-plates. Her dark eyes gleamed in the shadows, her white limbs glistened softly, like alabaster. Her hair was a mass of dark foam, at the burnished luster of which the dim light only hinted.

"The keys to your shackles and to the farther door!" she whispered, and a slim white hand came through the bars and dropped three objects with a clink to the flags beside him.

"What game is this?" he demanded. "You speak in the Nemedian tongue, and I have no friends in Nemedia. What deviltry is your master up to now? Has he sent you here to mock me?"

"It is no mockery!" The girl was trembling violently. Her bracelets and breast-plates clinked against the bars she grasped. "I swear by Mitra! I stole the keys from the black jailers. They are the keepers of the pits, and each bears a key which will open only one set of locks. I made them drunk. The one whose head you broke was carried away to a leech, and I could not get his key. But the others I stole. Oh, please do not loiter! Beyond these dungeons lie the pits which are the doors to Hell."

Somewhat impressed, Conan tried the keys dubiously, expecting to meet only failure and a burst of mocking laughter. But he was galvanized to discover that one, indeed, loosed him of his shackles, fitting not only the lock that held them to the ring, but the locks on his limbs as well. A few seconds later he stood upright, exulting fiercely in his comparative freedom. A quick stride carried him to the grille, and his fingers closed about a bar and the slender wrist that was pressed against it, imprisoning the owner, who lifted her face bravely to his fierce gaze.

"Who are you, girl?" he demanded. "Why do you do this?"

"I am only Zenobia," she murmured, with a catch of breathlessness, as if in fright; "only a girl of the king's seraglio."

"Unless this is some cursed trick," muttered Conan, "I cannot see why you bring me these keys."

She bowed her dark head, and then lifted it and looked full into his suspicious eyes. Tears sparkled like jewels on her long dark lashes.

"I am only a girl of the king's seraglio," she said, with a certain humility. "He has never glanced at me, and probably never will. I am less than one of the dogs that gnaw the bones in his banquet hall. "But I am no painted toy; I am of flesh and blood. I breathe, hate, fear, rejoice and love. And I have loved you. King Conan, ever since I saw you riding at the head of your knights along the streets of Belverus when you visited King Nimed, years ago. My heart tugged at its strings to leap from my bosom and fall in the dust of the street under your horse's hoofs."

Color flooded her countenance as she spoke, but her dark eyes did not waver. Conan did not at once reply; wild and passionate and untamed he was, yet any but the most brutish of men must be touched with a certain awe or wonder at the baring of a woman's naked soul.

She bent her head then, and pressed her red lips to the fingers that imprisoned her slim wrist. Then she flung up her head as if in sudden recollection of their position, and terror flared in her dark eyes. "Haste!" she whispered urgently. "It is past midnight. You must be gone."

"But won't they skin you alive for stealing these keys?"

"They'll never know. If the black men remember in the morning who gave them the wine, they will not dare admit the keys were stolen from them while they were drunk. The key that I could not obtain is the one that unlocks this door. You must make your way to freedom through the pits. What awful perils lurk beyond that door I cannot even guess. But greater danger lurks for you if you remain in this cell. "King Tarascus has returned—"

"What? Tarascus?"

"Aye! He has returned, in great secrecy, and not long ago he descended into the pits and then came out again, pale and shaking, like a man who had dared a great hazard. I heard him whisper to his squire, Arideus, that despite Xaltotun you should die."

"What of Xaltotun?" murmured Conan. He felt her shudder.

"Do not speak of him!" she whispered. "Demons are often summoned by the sound of their names. The slaves say that he lies in his chamber, behind a bolted door, dreaming the dreams of the black lotus. I believe that even Tarascus secretly fears him, or he would slay you openly. But he has been in the pits tonight, and what he did here, only Mitra knows."

"I wonder if that could have been Tarascus who fumbled at my cell door awhile ago?" muttered Conan.

"Here is a dagger!" she whispered, pressing something through the bars. His eager fingers closed on an object familiar to their touch. "Go quickly through yonder door, turn to the left and make your way along the cells until you come to a stone stair. On your life do not stray from the line of the cells! Climb the stair and open the door at the top; one of the keys will fit it. If it be the will of Mitra, I will await you there." Then she was gone, with a patter of light slippered feet.

Conan shrugged his shoulders, and turned toward the farther grille. This might be some diabolical trap planned by Tarascus, but plunging headlong into a snare was less abhorrent to Conan's temperament than sitting meekly to await his doom. He inspected the weapon the girl had given him, and smiled grimly. Whatever else she might be, she was proven by that dagger to be a person of practical intelligence. It was no slender stiletto, selected because of a jeweled hilt or gold guard, fitted only for dainty murder in milady's boudoir; it was a forthright poniard, a warrior's weapon, broad-bladed, fifteen inches in length, tapering to a diamond-sharp point.

He grunted with satisfaction. The feel of the hilt cheered him and gave him a glow of confidence. Whatever webs of conspiracy were drawn about him, whatever trickery and treachery ensnared him, this knife was real. The great muscles of his right arm swelled in anticipation of murderous blows.

He tried the farther door, fumbling with the keys as he did so. It was not locked. Yet he remembered the black man locking it. That furtive, bent figure, then, had been no jailer seeing that the bolts were in place. He had unlocked the door, instead. There was a sinister suggestion about that unlocked door. But Conan did not hesitate. He pushed open the grille and stepped from the dungeon into the outer darkness.

As he had thought, the door did not open into another corridor. The flagged floor stretched away under his feet, and the line of cells ran away to right and left behind him, but he could not make out the other limits of the place into which he had come. He could see neither the roof nor any other wall. The moonlight filtered into that vastness only through the grilles of the cells, and was almost lost in the darkness. Less

keen eyes than his could scarcely have discerned the dim gray patches
that floated before each cell door.

Turning to the left, he moved swiftly and noiselessly along the line
of dungeons, his bare feet making no sound on the flags. He glanced
briefly into each dungeon as he passed it. They were all empty, but
locked. In some he caught the glimmer of naked white bones. These
pits were a relic of a grimmer age, constructed long ago when Belverus
was a fortress rather than a city. But evidently their more recent use had
been more extensive than the world guessed.

Ahead of him, presently, he saw the dim outline of a stair sloping
sharply upward, and knew it must be the stair he sought. Then he
whirled suddenly, crouching in the deep shadows at its foot.

Somewhere behind him something was moving—something bulky
and stealthy that padded on feet which were not human feet. He was
looking down the long row of cells, before each one of which lay a
square of dim gray light that was little more than a patch of less dense
darkness. But he saw something moving along these squares. What it
was he could not tell, but it was heavy and huge, and yet it moved with
more than human ease and swiftness. He glimpsed it as it moved across
the squares of gray, then lost it as it merged in the expanses of shadow
between. It was uncanny, in its stealthy advance, appearing and disappearing like a blur of the vision.

He heard the bars rattle as it tried each door in turn. Now it had
reached the cell he had so recently quitted, and the door swung open
as it tugged. He saw a great bulky shape limned faintly and briefly in
the gray doorway, and then the thing had vanished into the dungeon.
Sweat beaded Conan's face and hands. Now he knew why Tarascus
had come so subtly to his door, and later had fled so swiftly. The king
had unlocked his door, and, somewhere in these hellish pits, had
opened a cell or cage that held some grim monstrosity.

Now the thing was emerging from the cell and was again advancing
up the corridor, its misshapen head close to the ground. It paid no
more heed to the locked doors. It was smelling out his trail. He saw it
more plainly now; the gray light limned a giant anthropomorphic
body, but vaster of bulk and girth than any man. It went on two legs,
though it stooped forward, and it was grayish and shaggy, its thick coat
shot with silver. Its head was a grisly travesty of the human, its long
arms hung nearly to the ground.

Conan knew it at last—understood the meaning of those crushed
and broken bones in the dungeon, and recognized the haunter of the

pits. It was a gray ape, one of the grisly man-eaters from the forests that wave on the mountainous eastern shores of the Sea of Vilayet. Half mythical and altogether horrible, these apes were the goblins of Hyborian legendry, and were in reality ogres of the natural world, cannibals and murderers of the nighted forests.

He knew it scented his presence, for it was coming swiftly now, rolling its barrel-like body rapidly along on its short, mighty, bowed legs. He cast a quick glance up the long stair, but knew that the thing would be on his back before he could mount to the distant door. He chose to meet it face to face.

Conan stepped out into the nearest square of moonlight, so as to have all the advantage of illumination that he could; for the beast, he knew, could see better than himself in the dark. Instantly the brute saw him; its great yellow tusks gleamed in the shadows, but it made no sound. Creatures of night and the silence, the gray apes of Vilayet were voiceless. But in its dim, hideous features, which were a bestial travesty of a human face, showed ghastly exultation.

Conan stood poised, watching the oncoming monster without a quiver. He knew he must stake his life on one thrust; there would be no chance for another; nor would there be time to strike and spring away. The first blow must kill, and kill instantly, if he hoped to survive that awful grapple. He swept his gaze over the short, squat throat, the hairy swagbelly, and the mighty breast, swelling in giant arches like twin shields. It must be the heart; better to risk the blade being deflected by the heavy ribs than to strike in where a stroke was not instantly fatal. With full realization of the odds, Conan matched his speed of eye and hand and his muscular power against the brute might and ferocity of the man-eater. He must meet the brute breast to breast, strike a deathblow, and then trust to the ruggedness of his frame to survive the instant of manhandling that was certain to be his.

As the ape came rolling in on him, swinging wide its terrible arms, he plunged in between them and struck with all his desperate power. He felt the blade sink to the hilt in the hairy breast, and instantly, releasing it, he ducked his head and bunched his whole body into one compact mass of knotted muscles, and as he did so he grasped the closing arms and drove his knee fiercely into the monster's belly, bracing himself against that crushing grapple.

For one dizzy instant he felt as if he were being dismembered in the grip of an earthquake; then suddenly he was free, sprawling on the floor, and the monster was gasping out its life beneath him, its red eyes turned upward, the hilt of the poniard quivering in its breast. His desperate stab had gone home.

Conan was panting as if after long conflict, trembling in every limb. Some of his joints felt as if they had been dislocated, and blood dripped from scratches on his side where the monster's talons had ripped; his muscles and tendons had been savagely wrenched and twisted. If the beast had lived a second longer, it would surely have dismembered him. But the Cimmerian's mighty strength had resisted, for the fleeting instant it had endured, the dying convulsion of the ape that would have torn a lesser man limb from limb.

6 The Thrust of a Knife

Conan stooped and tore the knife from the monster's breast. Then he went swiftly up the stair. What other shapes of fear the darkness held he could not guess, but he had no desire to encounter any more. This touch-and-go sort of battling was too strenuous even for the giant Cimmerian. The moonlight was fading from the floor, the darkness closing in, and something like panic pursued him up the stair. He breathed a gusty sigh of relief when he reached the head, and felt the third key turn in the lock. He opened the door slightly, and craned his neck to peer through, half expecting an attack from some human or bestial enemy.

He looked into a bare stone corridor, dimly lighted, and a slender, supple figure stood before the door.

"Your Majesty!" It was a low, vibrant cry, half in relief and half in fear. The girl sprang to his side, then hesitated as if abashed.

"You bleed," she said. "You have been hurt!"

He brushed aside the implication with an impatient hand.

"Scratches that wouldn't hurt a baby. Your skewer came in handy, though. But for it Tarascus's monkey would be cracking my shin bones for the marrow right now. But what now?"

"Follow me," she whispered. "I will lead you outside the city wall. I have a horse concealed there."

She turned to lead the way down the corridor, but he laid a heavy hand on her naked shoulder.

"Walk beside me," he instructed her softly, passing his massive arm about her lithe waist. "You've played me fair so far, and I'm inclined to believe in you; but I've lived this long only because I've trusted no one too far, man or woman. So! Now if you play me false you won't live to enjoy the jest."

She did not flinch at sight of the reddened poniard or the contact of his hard muscles about her supple body.

"Cut me down without mercy if I play you false," she answered. "The very feel of your arm about me, even in menace, is as the fulfillment of a dream."

The vaulted corridor ended at a door, which she opened. Outside lay another black man, a giant in turban and silk loincloth, with a curved sword lying on the flags near his hand. He did not move.

"I drugged his wine," she whispered, swerving to avoid the recumbent figure. "He is the last, and outer, guard of the pits. None ever escaped from them before, and none has ever wished to seek them; so only these black men guard them. Only these of all the servants knew it was King Conan that Xaltotun brought a prisoner in his chariot. I was watching, sleepless, from an upper casement that opened into the court, while the other girls slept; for I knew that a battle was being fought, or had been fought, in the west, and I feared for you.

"I saw the blacks carry you up the stair, and I recognized you in the torchlight. I slipped into this wing of the palace tonight, in time to see them carry you to the pits. I had not dared come here before nightfall. You must have lain in drugged senselessness all day in Xaltotun's chamber.

"Oh, let us be wary! Strange things are afoot in the palace tonight. The slaves said that Xaltotun slept as he often sleeps, drugged by the lotus of Stygia, but Tarascus is in the palace. He entered secretly, through the postern, wrapped in his cloak, which was dusty as with long travel, and attended only by his squire, the lean silent Arideus. I cannot understand, but I am afraid."

They came out at the foot of a narrow, winding stair, and mounting it, passed through a narrow panel which she slid aside. When they had passed through, she slipped it back in place, and it became merely a portion of the ornate wall. They were in a more spacious corridor, carpeted and tapestried, over which hanging lamps shed a golden glow.

Conan listened intently, but he heard no sound throughout the palace. He did not know in what part of the palace he was, or in which direction lay the chamber of Xaltotun. The girl was trembling as she drew him along the corridor, to halt presently beside an alcove masked with satin tapestry. Drawing this aside, she motioned for him to step into the niche, and whispered: "Wait here! Beyond that door at the end of the corridor we are likely to meet slaves or eunuchs at

any time of the day or night. I will go and see if the way is clear, before
we essay it."

Instantly his hair-trigger suspicions were aroused. "Are you leading
me into a trap?"

Tears sprang into her dark eyes. She sank to her knees and seized his
muscular hand. "Oh, my king, do not mistrust me now!" Her voice
shook with desperate urgency. "If you doubt and hesitate, we are lost!
Why should I bring you up out of the pits to betray you now?"

"All right," he muttered. "I'll trust you; though, by Crom, the habits
of a lifetime are not easily put aside. Yet I wouldn't harm you now, if
you brought all the swordsmen in Nemedia upon me. But for you
Tarascus's cursed ape would have come upon me in chains and
unarmed. Do as you wish, girl."

Kissing his hands, she sprang lithely up and ran down the corridor,
to vanish through a heavy double door.

He glanced after her, wondering if he was a fool to trust her; then
he shrugged his mighty shoulders and pulled the satin hangings
together, masking his refuge. It was not strange that a passionate young
beauty should be risking her life to aid him; such things had happened
often enough in his life. Many women had looked on him with favor,
in the days of his wanderings, and in the time of his kingship.

Yet he did not remain motionless in the alcove, waiting for her
return. Following his instincts, he explored the niche for another exit,
and presently found one—the opening of a narrow passage, masked by
the tapestries, that ran to an ornately carved door, barely visible in the
dim light that filtered in from the outer corridor. And as he stared into
it, somewhere beyond that carven door he heard the sound of another
door opening and shutting, and then a low mumble of voices. The
familiar sound of one of those voices caused a sinister expression to
cross his dark face. Without hesitation he glided down the passage, and
crouched like a stalking panther beside the door. It was not locked, and
manipulating it delicately, he pushed it open a crack, with a reckless
disregard for possible consequences that only he could have explained
or defended.

It was masked on the other side by tapestries, but through a thin slit
in the velvet he looked into a chamber lit by a candle on an ebony
table. There were two men in that chamber. One was a scarred, sinis-
ter-looking ruffian in leather breeks and ragged cloak; the other was
Tarascus, king of Nemedia.

Tarascus seemed ill at ease. He was slightly pale, and he kept starting and glancing about him, as if expecting and fearing to hear some sound or footstep.

"Go swiftly and at once," he was saying. "He is deep in drugged slumber, but I know not when he may awaken."

"Strange to hear words of fear issuing from the lips of Tarascus," rumbled the other in a harsh, deep voice.

The king frowned.

"I fear no common man, as you well know. But when I saw the cliffs fall at Valkia I knew that this devil we had resurrected was no charlatan. I fear his powers, because I do not know the full extent of them. But I know that somehow they are connected with this accursed thing which I have stolen from him. It brought him back to life; so it must be the source of his sorcery.

"He had it hidden well; but following my secret order a slave spied on him and saw him place it in a golden chest, and saw where he hid the chest. Even so, I would not have dared steal it had Xaltotun himself not been sunk in lotus slumber.

"I believe it is the secret of his power. With it Orastes brought him back to life. With it he will make us all slaves, if we are not wary. So take it and cast it into the sea as I have bidden you. And be sure you are so far from land that neither tide nor storm can wash it up on the beach. You have been paid."

"So I have," grunted the ruffian. "And I owe more than gold to you, king; I owe you a debt of gratitude. Even thieves can be grateful."

"Whatever debt you may feel you owe me," answered Tarascus, "will be paid when you have hurled this thing into the sea."

"I'll ride for Zingara and take ship from Kordava," promised the other. "I dare not show my head in Argos, because of the matter of a murder or so—"

"I care not, so it is done. Here it is; a horse awaits you in the court. Go, and go swiftly!"

Something passed between them, something that flamed like living fire. Conan had only a brief glimpse of it; and then the ruffian pulled a slouch hat over his eyes, drew his cloak about his shoulder, and hurried from the chamber. And as the door closed behind him, Conan moved with the devastating fury of unchained blood-lust. He had held himself in check as long as he could. The sight of his enemy so near him set his wild blood seething and swept away all caution and restraint.

Tarascus was turning toward an inner door when Conan tore aside the hangings and leaped like a blood-mad panther into the room. Tarascus wheeled, but even before he could recognize his attacker, Conan's poniard ripped into him.

But the blow was not mortal, as Conan knew the instant he struck. His foot had caught in a fold of the curtains and tripped him as he leaped. The point fleshed itself in Tarascus" shoulder and plowed down along his ribs, and the king of Nemedia screamed.

The impact of the blow and Conan's lunging body hurled him back against the table and it toppled and the candle went out. They were both carried to the floor by the violence of Conan's rush, and the foot of the tapestry hampered them both in its folds. Conan was stabbing blindly in the dark, Tarascus screaming in a frenzy of panicky terror. As if fear lent him superhuman energy, Tarascus tore free and blundered away in the darkness, shrieking:

"Help! Guards! Arideus! Orastes! Orastes!"

Conan rose, kicking himself free of the tangling tapestries and the broken table, cursing with the bitterness of his bloodthirsty disappointment. He was confused, and ignorant of the plan of the palace. The yells of Tarascus were still resounding in the distance, and a wild outcry was bursting forth in answer. The Nemedian had escaped him in the darkness, and Conan did not know which way he had gone. The Cimmerian's rash stroke for vengeance had failed, and there remained only the task of saving his own hide if he could.

Swearing luridly, Conan ran back down the passage and into the alcove, glaring out into the lighted corridor, just as Zenobia came running up it, her dark eyes dilated with terror.

"Oh, what has happened?" she cried. "The palace is roused! I swear I have not betrayed you—"

"No, it was I who stirred up the hornet's nest," he grunted. "I tried to pay off a score. What's the shortest way out of this?"

She caught his wrist and ran fleetly down the corridor. But before they reached the heavy door at the other end, muffled shouts arose from behind it and the portals began to shake under an assault from the other side. Zenobia wrung her hands and whimpered.

"We are cut off! I locked that door as I returned through it. But they will burst it in in a moment. The way to the postern gate lies through it."

Conan wheeled. Up the corridor, though still out of sight, he heard a rising clamor that told him his foes were behind as well as before him—

"Quick! Into this door!" the girl cried desperately, running across the corridor and throwing open the door of a chamber.

Conan followed her through, and then threw the gold catch behind them. They stood in an ornately furnished chamber, empty but for themselves, and she drew him to a gold-barred window, through which he saw trees and shrubbery.

"You are strong," she panted. "If you can tear these bars away, you may yet escape. The garden is full of guards, but the shrubs are thick, and you may avoid them. The southern wall is also the outer wall of the city. Once over that, you have a chance to get away. A horse is hidden for you in a thicket beside the road that runs westward, a few hundred paces to the south of the fountain of Thrallos. You know where it is?"

"Aye! But what of you? I had meant to take you with me."

A flood of joy lighted her beautiful face.

"Then my cup of happiness is brimming! But I will not hamper your escape. Burdened with me you would fail. Nay, do not fear for me. They will never suspect that I aided you willingly. Go! What you have just said will glorify my life throughout the long years."

He caught her up in his iron arms, crushed her slim, vibrant figure to him and kissed her fiercely on eyes, cheeks, throat and lips, until she lay panting in his embrace; gusty and tempestuous as a storm-wind, even his lovemaking was violent.

"I'll go," he muttered. "But by Crom, I'll come for you some day!"

Wheeling, he gripped the gold bars and tore them from their sockets with one tremendous wrench; threw a leg over the sill and went down swiftly, clinging to the ornaments on the wall. He hit the ground running and melted like a shadow into the maze of towering rosebushes and spreading trees. The one look he cast back over his shoulder showed him Zenobia leaning over the windowsill, her arms stretched after him in mute farewell and renunciation.

Guards were running through the garden, all converging toward the palace, where the clamor momentarily grew louder—tall men in burnished cuirasses and crested helmets of polished bronze. The starlight struck glints from their gleaming armor, among the trees, betraying their every movement; but the sound of their coming ran far before them. To Conan, wilderness-bred, their rush through the shrubbery was like the blundering stampede of cattle. Some of them passed within a few feet of where he lay flat in a thick cluster of bushes, and never guessed his presence. With the palace as their goal, they were oblivious to all else about them. When they had gone shouting on, he rose and fled through the garden with no more noise than a panther would have made.

So quickly he came to the southern wall, and mounted the steps that led to the parapet. The wall was made to keep people out, not in. No sentry patrolling the battlements was in sight. Crouching by an embrasure he glanced back at the great palace rearing above the cypresses behind him. Lights blazed from every window, and he could see figures flitting back and forth across them like puppets on invisible strings. He grinned hardly, shook his fist in a gesture of farewell and menace, and let himself over the outer rim of the parapet.

A low tree, a few yards below the parapet, received Conan's weight, as he dropped noiselessly into the branches. An instant later he was racing through the shadows with the swinging hillman's stride that eats up long miles.

Gardens and pleasure villas surrounded the walls of Belverus. Drowsy slaves, sleeping by their watchman's pikes, did not see the swift and furtive figure that scaled walls, crossed alleys made by the arching branches of trees, and threaded a noiseless way through orchards and vineyards. Watchdogs woke and lifted their deep-booming clamor at a gliding shadow, half scented, half sensed, and then it was gone.

In a chamber of the palace, Tarascus writhed and cursed on a blood-spattered couch, under the deft, quick fingers of Orastes. The palace was thronged with wide-eyed, trembling servitors, but the chamber where the king lay was empty save for himself and the renegade priest.

"Are you sure he still sleeps?" Tarascus demanded again, setting his teeth against the bite of the herb juices with which Orastes was bandaging the long, ragged gash in his shoulder and ribs. "Ishtar, Mitra and Set! That burns like molten pitch of hell!"

"Which you would be experiencing even now, but for your good fortune," remarked Orastes. "Whoever wielded that knife struck to kill. Yes, I have told you that Xaltotun still sleeps. Why are you so urgent upon that point? What has he to do with this?"

"You know nothing of what has passed in the palace tonight?" Tarascus searched the priest's countenance with burning intensity.

"Nothing. As you know, I have been employed in translating manuscripts for Xaltotun, for some months now, transcribing esoteric volumes written in the younger languages into script he can read. He was well versed in all the tongues and scripts of his day, but he has not yet learned all the newer languages, and to save time he has me translate these works for him, to learn if any new knowledge has been discovered since his time. I did not know that he had returned last night until he sent for me and told me of the battle. Then I returned to my studies, nor did I know that you had returned until the clamor in the palace brought me out of my cell."

"Then you do not know that Xaltotun brought the king of Aquilonia a captive to this palace?"

Orastes shook his head, without particular surprize. "Xaltotun merely said that Conan would oppose us no more. I supposed that he had fallen, but did not ask the details."

"Xaltotun saved his life when I would have slain him," snarled Tarascus. "I saw his purpose instantly. He would hold Conan captive to use as a club against us—against Amalric, against Valerius, and against myself. So long as Conan lives he is a threat, a unifying factor for Aquilonia, that might be used to compel us into courses we would not otherwise follow. I mistrust this undead Pythonian. Of late I have begun to fear him.

"I followed him, some hours after he had departed eastward. I wished to learn what he intended doing with Conan. I found that he had imprisoned him in the pits. I intended to see that the barbarian died, in spite of Xaltotun. And I accomplished—" A cautious knock sounded at the door. "That's Arideus," grunted Tarascus. "Let him in." The saturnine squire entered, his eyes blazing with suppressed excitement. "How, Arideus?" exclaimed Tarascus. "Have you found the man who attacked me?"

"You did not see him, my lord?" asked Arideus, as one who would assure himself of a fact he already knows to exist. "You did not recognize him?"

"No. It happened so quick, and the candle was out—all I could think of was that it was some devil loosed on me by Xaltotun's magic—"

"The Pythonian sleeps in his barred and bolted room. But I have been in the pits." Arideus twitched his lean shoulders excitedly.

"Well, speak, man!" exclaimed Tarascus impatiently. "What did you find there?"

"An empty dungeon," whispered the squire. "The corpse of the great ape!"

"What?" Tarascus started upright, and blood gushed from his opened wound.

"Aye! The man-eater is dead—stabbed through the heart—and Conan is gone!"

Tarascus was gray of face as he mechanically allowed Orastes to force him prostrate again and the priest renewed work upon his mangled flesh.

"Conan!" he repeated. "Not a crushed corpse—escaped! Mitra! He is no man; but a devil himself! I thought Xaltotun was behind this wound. I see now. Gods and devils! It was Conan who stabbed me! Arideus!"

"Aye, Your Majesty!"

"Search every nook in the palace. He may be skulking through the dark corridors now like a hungry tiger. Let no niche escape your scrutiny, and beware. It is not a civilized man you hunt, but a blood-mad barbarian whose strength and ferocity are those of a wild beast. Scour the palace-grounds and the city. Throw a cordon about the walls. If you find he has escaped from the city, as he may well do, take a troop of horsemen and follow him. Once past the walls it will be like hunting a wolf through the hills. But haste, and you may yet catch him."

"This is a matter which requires more than ordinary human wits," said Orastes. "Perhaps we should seek Xaltotun's advice."

"No!" exclaimed Tarascus violently. "Let the troopers pursue Conan and slay him. Xaltotun can hold no grudge against us if we kill a prisoner to prevent his escape."

"Well," said Orastes, "I am no Acheronian, but I am versed in some of the arts, and the control of certain spirits which have cloaked themselves in material substance. Perhaps I can aid you in this matter."

The fountain of Thrallos stood in a clustered ring of oaks beside the road a mile from the walls of the city. Its musical tinkle reached Conan's ears through the silence of the starlight. He drank deep of its icy stream, and then hurried southward toward a small, dense thicket he saw there. Rounding it, he saw a great white horse tied among the bushes. Heaving a deep gusty sigh he reached it with one stride—a mocking laugh brought him about, glaring.

A dully glinting, mail-clad figure moved out of the shadows into the starlight. This was no plumed and burnished palace guardsman. It was a tall man in morion and gray chain mail—one of the Adventurers, a class of warriors peculiar to Nemedia; men who had not attained to the wealth and position of knighthood, or had fallen from that estate; hard-bitten fighters, dedicating their lives to war and adventure. They constituted a class of their own, sometimes commanding troops, but themselves accountable to no man but the king. Conan knew that he could have been discovered by no more dangerous a foeman.

A quick glance among the shadows convinced him that the man was alone, and he expanded his great chest slightly, digging his toes into the turf, as his thews coiled tensely.

"I was riding for Belverus on Amalric's business," said the Adventurer, advancing warily. The starlight was a long sheen on the great two-handed sword he bore naked in his hand. "A horse whinnied to mine from the thicket. I investigated and thought it strange a steed should be tethered here. I waited—and lo, I have caught a rare prize!"

The Adventurers lived by their swords.

"I know you," muttered the Nemedian. "You are Conan, king of Aquilonia. I thought I saw you die in the valley of the Valkia, but—" Conan sprang as a dying tiger springs. Practised fighter though the Adventurer was, he did not realize the desperate quickness that lurks in barbaric sinews. He was caught off guard, his heavy sword half lifted. Before he could either strike or parry, the king's poniard sheathed itself in his throat, above the gorget, slanting downward into his heart. With a choked gurgle he reeled and went down, and Conan ruthlessly tore his blade free as his victim fell. The white horse snorted violently and shied at the sight and scent of blood on the sword.

Glaring down at his lifeless enemy, dripping poniard in hand, sweat glistening on his broad breast, Conan poised like a statue, listening intently. In the woods about there was no sound, save for the sleepy cheep of awakened birds. But in the city, a mile away, he heard the strident blare of a trumpet.

Hastily he bent over the fallen man. A few seconds' search convinced him that whatever message the man might have borne was intended to be conveyed by word of mouth. But he did not pause in his task. It was not many hours until dawn. A few minutes later the white horse was galloping westward along the white road, and the rider wore the gray mail of a Nemedian Adventurer.

7 The Rending of the Veil

Conan knew his only chance of escape lay in speed. He did not even consider hiding somewhere near Belverus until the chase passed on; he was certain that the uncanny ally of Tarascus would be able to ferret him out. Besides, he was not one to skulk and hide; an open fight or an open chase, either suited his temperament better. He had a long start, he knew. He would lead them a grinding race for the border.

Zenobia had chosen well to selecting the white horse. His speed, toughness and endurance were obvious. The girl knew weapons and horses, and, Conan reflected with some satisfaction, she knew men. He rode westward at a gait that ate up the miles.

It was a sleeping land through which he rode, past grove-sheltered villages and white-walled villas amid spacious fields and orchards that grew sparser as he fared westward. As the villages thinned, the land grew more rugged, and the keeps that frowned from eminences told of centuries of border war. But none rode down from those castles to challenge or halt him. The lords of the keeps were following the banner of Amalric; the pennons that were wont to wave over these towers were now floating over the Aquilonian plains.

When the last huddled village fell behind him, Conan left the road, which was beginning to bend toward the northwest, toward the distant passes. To keep to the road would mean to pass by border towers, still garrisoned with armed men who would not allow him to pass unquestioned. He knew there would be no patrols riding the border marches on either side, as to ordinary times, but there were those towers, and with dawn there would probably be cavalcades of returning soldiers with wounded men to ox-carts.

This road from Belverus was the only road that crossed the border for fifty miles from north to south. It followed a series of passes through the hills, and on either hand lay a wide expanse of wild, sparsely inhabited mountains. He maintained his due westerly direction, intending to cross the border deep to the wilds of the hills that lay to the south of the passes. It was a shorter route, more arduous, but safer for a hunted fugitive. One man on a horse could traverse country an army would find impassable.

But at dawn he had not reached the hills; they were a long, low, blue rampart stretching along the horizon ahead of him. Here there were neither farms nor villages, no white-walled villas loomed among clustering trees. The dawn wind stirred the tall stiff grass, and there was nothing but the long rolling swells of brown earth, covered with dry grass, and to the distance the gaunt walls of a stronghold on a low hill. Too many Aquilonian raiders had crossed the mountains to not too-distant days for the countryside to be thickly settled as it was farther to the east.

Dawn ran like a prairie fire across the grasslands, and high overhead sounded a weird crying as a straggling wedge of wild geese winged swiftly southward. In a grassy swale Conan halted and unsaddled his mount. Its sides were heaving, its coat plastered with sweat. He had pushed it unmercifully through the hours before dawn.

While it munched the brittle grass and rolled, he lay at the crest of the low slope, staring eastward. Far away to the northward he could see the road he had left, streaming like a white ribbon over a distant rise. No black dots moved along that glistening ribbon. There was no sign about the castle to the distance to indicate that the keepers had noticed the lone wayfarer.

An hour later the land still stretched bare. The only sign of life was a glint of steel on the far-off battlements, a raven to the sky that wheeled backward and forth, dipping and rising as if seeking something. Conan saddled and rode westward at a more leisurely gait.

As he topped the farther crest of the slope, a raucous screaming burst out over his head, and looking up, he saw the raven flapping high above him, cawing incessantly. As he rode on, it followed him, maintaining its position and making the morning hideous with its strident cries, heedless of his efforts to drive it away.

This kept up for hours, until Conan's teeth were on edge, and he felt that he would give half his kingdom to be allowed to wring that black neck.

"Devils of hell!" he roared to futile rage, shaking his mailed fist at the frantic bird. "Why do you harry me with your squawking? Begone, you black spawn of perdition, and peck for wheat to the farmers' fields!"

He was ascending the first pitch of the hills, and he seemed to hear an echo of the bird's clamor far behind him. Turning to his saddle, he presently made out another black dot against the blue. Beyond that again he caught the glint of the afternoon sun on steel. That could mean only one thing: armed men. And they were not riding along the beaten road, which was out of his sight beyond the horizon. They were following him. His face grew grim and he shivered slightly as he stared at the raven that wheeled high above him.

"So it is more than the whim of a brainless beast?" he muttered. "Those riders cannot see you, spawn of Hell; but the other bird can see you, and they can see him. You follow me, he follows you, and they follow him. Are you only a craftily trained feathered creature, or some devil in the form of a bird? Did Xaltotun set you on my trail? Are you Xaltotun?"

Only a strident screech answered him, a screech vibrating with harsh mockery.

Conan wasted no more breath on his dusky betrayer. Grimly he settled to the long grind of the hills, he dared not push the horse too hard; the rest he had allowed it had not been enough to freshen it. He was still far ahead of his pursuers, but they would cut down that lead steadily. It was almost a certainty that their horses were fresher than his, for they had undoubtedly changed mounts at that castle he had passed. The going grew rougher, the scenery more rugged, steep grassy slopes pitching up to densely timbered mountainsides. Here, he knew, he might elude his hunters, but for that hellish bird that squalled incessantly above him. He could no longer see them in this broken country, but he was certain that they still followed him, guided unerringly by their feathered allies. That black shape became like a demoniac incubus, hounding him through measureless hells. The stones he hurled with a curse went wide or fell harmless, though in his youth he had felled hawks on the wing.

The horse was tiring fast. Conan recognized the grim finality of his position. He sensed an inexorable driving fate behind all this. He could not escape. He was as much a captive as he had been in the pits of Belverus. But he was no son of the Orient to yield passively to what seemed inevitable. If he could not escape, he would at least take some of his foes into eternity with him. He turned into a wide thicket of larches that masked a slope, looking for a place to turn at bay.

Then ahead of him there rang a strange, shrill scream, human yet weirdly timbred. An instant later he had pushed through a screen of branches, and saw the source of that eldritch cry. In a small glade below him four soldiers in Nemedian chain mail were binding a noose about the neck of a gaunt old woman in peasant garb. A heap of fagots, bound with cord on the ground near by, showed what her occupation had been when surprized by these stragglers.

Conan felt slow fury swell his heart as he looked silently down and saw the ruffians dragging her toward a tree whose low-spreading branches were obviously intended to act as a gibbet. He had crossed the frontier an hour ago. He was standing on his own soil, watching the murder of one of his own subjects. The old woman was struggling with surprizing strength and energy, and as he watched, she lifted her head and voiced again the strange, weird, far-carrying call he had heard before. It was echoed as if in mockery by the raven flapping above the trees. The soldiers laughed roughly, and one struck her in the mouth.

Conan swung from his weary steed and dropped down the face of the rocks, landing with a clang of mail on the grass. The four men wheeled at the sound and drew their swords, gaping at the mailed giant who faced them, sword in hand.

Conan laughed harshly. His eyes were bleak as flint.

"Dogs!" he said without passion and without mercy. "Do Nemedian jackals set themselves up as executioners and hang my subjects at will? First you must take the head of their king. Here I stand, awaiting your lordly pleasure!"

The soldiers stared at him uncertainly as he strode toward them.

"Who is this madman?" growled a bearded ruffian. "He wears Nemedian mail, but speaks with an Aquilonian accent."

"No matter," quoth another. "Cut him down, and then we'll hang the old hag."

And so saying he ran at Conan, lifting his sword. But before he could strike, the king's great blade lashed down, splitting helmet and skull. The man fell before him, but the others were hardy rogues. They gave tongue like wolves and surged about the lone figure in the gray mail, and the clamor and din of steel drowned the cries of the circling raven.

Conan did not shout. His eyes coals of blue fire and his lips smiling bleakly, he lashed right and left with his two-handed sword. For all his size he was quick as a cat on his feet, and he was constantly in motion, presenting a moving target so that thrusts and swings cut empty air oftener than not. Yet when he struck he was perfectly balanced, and his blows fell with devastating power. Three of the four were down, dying in their own blood, and the fourth was bleeding from half a dozen wounds, stumbling in headlong retreat as he parried frantically, when Conan's spur caught in the surcoat of one of the fallen men.

The king stumbled, and before he could catch himself the Nemedian, with the frenzy of desperation, rushed him so savagely that Conan staggered and fell sprawling over the corpse. The Nemedian croaked in triumph and sprang forward, lifting his great sword with both hands over his right shoulder, as he braced his legs wide for the stroke—and then, over the prostrate king, something huge and hairy shot like a thunderbolt full on the soldier's breast, and his yelp of triumph changed to a shriek of death.

Conan, scrambling up, saw the man lying dead with his throat torn out, and a great gray wolf stood over him, head sunk as it smelt the blood that formed a pool on the grass.

The king turned as the old woman spoke to him. She stood straight and tall before him, and in spite of her ragged garb, her features, clear-cut and aquiline, and her keen black eyes, were not those of a common peasant woman. She called to the wolf and it trotted to her side like a great dog and rubbed its giant shoulder against her knee, while it gazed at Conan with great green lambent eyes. Absently she laid her hand upon its mighty neck, and so the two stood regarding the king of Aquilonia. He found their steady gaze disquieting, though there was no hostility in it.

"Men say King Conan died beneath the stones and dirt when the cliffs crumbled by Valkia," she said in a deep, strong, resonant voice.

"So they say," he growled. He was in no mood for controversy, and he thought of those armored riders who were pushing nearer every moment. The raven above him cawed stridently, and he cast an involuntary glare upward, grinding his teeth in a spasm of nervous irritation.

Up on the ledge the white horse stood with drooping head. The old woman looked at it, and then at the raven; and then she lifted a strange weird cry as she had before. As if recognizing the call, the raven wheeled, suddenly mute, and raced eastward. But before it had got out of sight, the shadow of mighty wings fell across it. An eagle soared up from the tangle of trees, and rising above it, swooped and struck the black messenger to the earth. The strident voice of betrayal was stilled for ever.

"Crom!" muttered Conan, staring at the old woman. "Are you a magician, too?"

"I am Zeiata," she said. "The people of the valleys call me a witch. Was that child of the night guiding armed men on your trail?"

"Aye." She did not seem to think the answer fantastic. "They cannot be far behind me."

"Lead your horse and follow me, King Conan," she said briefly.

Without comment he mounted the rocks and brought his horse down to the glade by a circuitous path. As he came he saw the eagle reappear, dropping lazily down from the sky, and rest an instant on Zeiata's shoulder, spreading its great wings lightly so as not to crush her with its weight.

Without a word she led the way, the great wolf trotting at her side, the eagle soaring above her. Through deep thickets and along tortuous ledges poised over deep ravines she led him, and finally along a narrow precipice-edged path to a curious dwelling of stone, half hut, half cavern, beneath a cliff hidden among the gorges and crags. The eagle flew to the pinnacle of this cliff, and perched there like a motionless sentinel.

Still silent, Zeiata stabled the horse in a near-by cave, with leaves and grass piled high for provender, and a tiny spring bubbling in the dim recesses.

In the hut she seated the king on a rude, hide-covered bench, and she herself sat upon a low stool before the tiny fireplace, while she made a fire of tamarisk chunks and prepared a frugal meal. The great wolf drowsed beside her, facing the fire, his huge head sunk on his paws, his ears twitching in his dreams.

"You do not fear to sit in the hut of a witch?" she asked, breaking her silence at last.

An impatient shrug of his gray-mailed shoulders was her guest's only reply. She gave into his hands a wooden dish heaped with dried fruits, cheese and barley bread, and a great pot of the heady upland beer, brewed from barley grown in the high valleys.

"I have found the brooding silence of the glens more pleasing than the babble of city streets," she said. "The children of the wild are kinder than the children of men." Her hand briefly stroked the ruff of the sleeping wolf. "My children were afar from me today, or I had not needed your sword, my king. They were coming at my call."

"What grudge had those Nemedian dogs against you?" Conan demanded.

"Skulkers from the invading army straggle all over the countryside, from the frontier to Tarantia," she answered. "The foolish villagers in the valleys told them that I had a store of gold hidden away, so as to divert their attentions from their villages. They demanded treasure from me, and my answers angered them. But neither skulkers nor the men who pursue you, nor any raven will find you here."

He shook his head, eating ravenously.

"I'm for Tarantia."

She shook her head.

"You thrust your head into the dragon's jaws. Best seek refuge abroad. The heart is gone from your kingdom."

"What do you mean?" he demanded. "Battles have been lost before, yet wars won. A kingdom is not lost by a single defeat."

"And you will go to Tarantia?"

"Aye. Prospero will be holding it against Amalric."

"Are you sure?"

"Hell's devils, woman!" he exclaimed wrathfully. "What else?"

She shook her head. "I feel that it is otherwise. Let us see. Not lightly is the veil rent; yet I will rend it a little, and show you your capital city."

Conan did not see what she cast upon the fire, but the wolf whimpered in his dreams, and a green smoke gathered and billowed up into the hut. And as he watched, the walls and ceiling of the hut seemed to widen, to grow remote and vanish, merging with infinite immensities; the smoke rolled about him, blotting out everything. And in it forms moved and faded, and stood out in startling clarity.

He stared at the familiar towers and streets of Tarantia, where a mob seethed and screamed, and at the same time he was somehow able to see the banners of Nemedia moving inexorably westward through the smoke and flame of a pillaged land. In the great square of Tarantia the frantic throng milled and yammered, screaming that the king was dead, that the barons were girding themselves to divide the land between them, and that the rule of a king, even of Valerius, was better than anarchy. Prospero, shining in his armor, rode among them, trying to pacify them, bidding them trust Count Trocero, urging them to man the wall and aid his knights in defending the city. They turned on him, shrieking with fear and unreasoning rage, howling that he was Trocero's butcher, a more evil foe than Amalric himself. Offal and stones were hurled at his knights.

A slight blurring of the picture, that might have denoted a passing of time, and then Conan saw Prospero and his knights filing out of the gates and spurring southward. Behind him the city was in an uproar.

"Fools!" muttered Conan thickly. "Fools! Why could they not trust Prospero? Zeiata, if you are making game of me, with some trickery—"

"This has passed," answered Zeiata imperturbably, though somberly. "It was the evening of the day that has passed, when Prospero rode out of Tarantia, with the hosts of Amalric almost within sight. From the walls men saw the flame of their pillaging. So I read it in the smoke. At sunset the Nemedians rode into Tarantia, unopposed. Look! Even now, in the royal hall of Tarantia—"

Abruptly Conan was looking into the great coronation hall. Valerius stood on the regal dais, clad in ermine robes, and Amalric, still in his dusty, bloodstained armor, placed a rich and gleaming circlet on his yellow locks—the crown of Aquilonia! The people cheered; long lines of steel-clad Nemedian warriors looked grimly on, and nobles long in disfavor at Conan's court strutted and swaggered with the emblem of Valerius on their sleeves.

"Crom!" It was an explosive imprecation from Conan's lips as he started up, his great fists clenched into hammers, his veins on his temples knotting, his features convulsed. "A Nemedian placing the crown of Aquilonia on that renegade—in the royal hall of Tarantia!"

As if dispelled by his violence, the smoke faded, and he saw Zeiata's black eyes gleaming at him through the mist.

"You have seen—the people of your capital have forfeited the freedom you won for them by sweat and blood; they have sold themselves to the slavers and the butchers. They have shown that they do not trust their destiny. Can you rely upon them for the winning back of your kingdom?"

"They thought I was dead," he grunted, recovering some of his poise. "I have no son. Men can't be governed by a memory. What if the Nemedians have taken Tarantia? There still remain the provinces, the barons, and the people of the countrysides. Valerius has won an empty glory."

"You are stubborn, as befits a fighter. I cannot show you the future, I cannot show you all the past. Nay, I show you nothing. I merely make you see windows opened in the veil by powers un-guessed. Would you look into the past for a clue of the present?"

"Aye." He seated himself abruptly.

Again the green smoke rose and billowed. Again images unfolded before him, this time alien and seemingly irrelevant. He saw great towering black walls, pedestals half hidden in the shadows upholding images of hideous, half-bestial gods. Men moved in the shadows, dark, wiry men, clad in red, silken loincloths. They were bearing a green jade sarcophagus along a gigantic black corridor. But before he could tell much about what he saw, the scene shifted. He saw a cavern, dim, shadowy and haunted with a strange intangible horror. On an altar of black stone stood a curious golden vessel, shaped like the shell of a scallop. Into this cavern came some of the same dark, wiry men who had borne the mummy-case. They seized the golden vessel, and then the shadows swirled around them and what happened he could not say. But he saw a glimmer in a whorl of darkness, like a ball of living fire. Then the smoke was only smoke, drifting up from the fire of tamarisk chunks, thinning and fading.

"But what does this portend?" he demanded, bewildered. "What I saw in Tarantia I can understand. But what means this glimpse of Zamorian thieves sneaking through a subterranean temple of Set, in Stygia? And that cavern—I've never seen or heard of anything like it, in all my wanderings. If you can show me that much, these shreds of

vision which mean nothing, disjointed, why can you not show me all
that is to occur?"

Zeiata stirred the fire without replying.

"These things are governed by immutable laws," she said at last. "I
can not make you understand; I do not altogether understand myself,
though I have sought wisdom in the silences of the high places for
more years than I can remember. I cannot save you, though I would if
I might. Man must, at last, work out his own salvation. Yet perhaps
wisdom may come to me in dreams, and in the morn I may be able to
give you the clue to the enigma."

"What enigma?" he demanded.

"The mystery that confronts you, whereby you have lost a kingdom," she answered. And then she spread a sheepskin upon the floor
before the hearth. "Sleep," she said briefly. Without a word he
stretched himself upon it, and sank into restless but deep sleep through
which phantoms moved silently and monstrous shapeless shadows
crept. Once, limned against a purple sunless horizon, he saw the mighty
walls and towers of a great city of such as rose nowhere on the waking
earth he knew. Its colossal pylons and purple minarets lifted toward the
stars, and over it, floating like a giant mirage, hovered the bearded
countenance of the man Xaltotun.

Conan woke in the chill whiteness of early dawn, to see Zeiata
crouched beside the tiny fire. He had not awakened once in the night,
and the sound of the great wolf leaving or entering should have roused
him. Yet the wolf was there, beside the hearth, with its shaggy coat wet
with dew, and with more than dew. Blood glistened wetly amid the
thick fell, and there was a cut upon his shoulder.

Zeiata nodded, without looking around, as if reading the thoughts of
her royal guest.

"He has hunted before dawn, and red was the hunting. I think the
man who hunted a king will hunt no more, neither man nor beast."

Conan stared at the great beast with strange fascination as he moved
to take the food Zeiata offered him.

"When I come to my throne again I won't forget," he said briefly.
"You've befriended me—by Crom, I can't remember when I've lain
down and slept at the mercy of man or woman as I did last night. But
what of the riddle you would read me this morn?"

A long silence ensued, in which the crackle of the tamarisks was loud
on the hearth.

"Find the heart of your kingdom," she said at last. "There lies your defeat and your power. You fight more than mortal man. You will not possess the throne again unless you find the heart of your kingdom."

"Do you mean the city of Tarantia?"

She shook her head. "I am but an oracle, through whose lips the gods speak. My lips are sealed by them lest I speak too much. You must find the heart of your kingdom. I can say no more. My lips are opened and sealed by the gods."

Dawn was still white on the peaks when Conan rode westward. A glance back showed him Zeiata standing in the door of her hut, inscrutable as ever, the great wolf beside her.

A gray sky arched overhead, and a moaning wind was chill with a promise of winter. Brown leaves fluttered slowly down from the bare branches, sifting upon his mailed shoulders.

All day he pushed through the hills, avoiding roads and villages. Toward nightfall he began to drop down from the heights, tier by tier, and saw the broad plains of Aquilonia spread out beneath him.

Villages and farms lay close to the foot of the hills on the western side of the mountains for, for half a century, most of the raiding across the frontier had been done by the Aquilonians. But now only embers and ashes showed where farm huts and villas had stood.

In the gathering darkness Conan rode slowly on. There was little fear of discovery, which he dreaded from friend as well as from foe. The Nemedians had remembered old scores on their westward drive, and Valerius had made no attempt to restrain his allies. He did not count on winning the love of the common people. A vast swath of desolation had been cut through the country from the foothills westward. Conan cursed as he rode over blackened expanses that had been rich fields, and saw the gaunt gable ends of burned houses jutting against the sky. He moved through an empty and deserted land, like a ghost out of a forgotten and outworn past.

The speed with which the army had traversed the land showed what little resistance it had encountered. Yet had Conan been leading his Aquilonians the invading army would have been forced to buy every foot they gained with their blood. The bitter realization permeated his soul; he was not the representative of a dynasty. He was only a lone adventurer. Even the drop of dynastic blood Valerius boasted had more hold on the minds of men than the memory of Conan and the freedom and power he had given the kingdom.

No pursuers followed him down out of the hills. He watched for wandering or returning Nemedian troops, but met none. Skulkers gave him a wide path, supposing him to be one of the conquerors, what of his harness. Groves and rivers were far more plentiful on the western side of the mountains, and coverts for concealment were not lacking.

So he moved across the pillaged land, halting only to rest his horse, eating frugally of the food Zeiata had given him, until, on a dawn when he lay hidden on a river bank where willows and oaks grew thickly, he glimpsed, afar, across the rolling plains dotted with rich groves, the blue and golden towers of Tarantia.

He was no longer in a deserted land, but one teeming with varied life. His progress thenceforth was slow and cautious, through thick woods and unfrequented byways. It was dusk when he reached the plantation of Servius Galannus.

8 Dying Embers

The countryside about Tarantia had escaped the fearful ravaging of the more easterly provinces. There were evidences of the march of a conquering army in broken hedges, plundered fields and looted granaries, but torch and steel had not been loosed wholesale.

There was but one grim splotch on the landscape—a charred expanse of ashes and blackened stone, where, Conan knew, had once stood the stately villa of one of his staunchest supporters.

The king dared not openly approach the Galannus farm, which lay only a few miles from the city. In the twilight he rode through an extensive woodland, until he sighted a keeper's lodge through the trees. Dismounting and tying his horse, he approached the thick, arched door with the intention of sending the keeper after Servius. He did not know what enemies the manor house might be sheltering. He had seen no troops, but they might be quartered all over the countryside. But as he drew near, he saw the door open and a compact figure in silk hose and richly embroidered doublet stride forth and turn up a path that wound away through the woods.

"Servius!"

At the low call the master of the plantation wheeled with a startled exclamation. His hand flew to the short hunting sword at his hip, and he recoiled from the tall gray steel figure standing in the dusk before him.

"Who are you?" he demanded. "What is your—Mitra!"

His breath hissed inward and his ruddy face paled. "Avaunt!" he ejaculated. "Why have you come back from the gray lands of death to terrify me? I was always your true liegeman in your lifetime—"

"As I still expect you to be," answered Conan. "Stop trembling, man; I'm flesh and blood."

Sweating with uncertainty Servius approached and stared into the face of the mail-clad giant, and then, convinced of the reality of what he saw, he dropped to one knee and doffed his plumed cap.

"Your Majesty! Truly, this is a miracle passing belief! The great bell in the citadel has tolled your dirge, days agone. Men said you died at Valkia, crushed under a million tons of earth and broken granite."

"It was another in my harness," grunted Conan. "But let us talk later. If there is such a thing as a joint of beef on your board—"

"Forgive me, my lord!" cried Servius, springing to his feet. "The dust of travel is gray on your mail, and I keep you standing here without rest or sup! Mitra! I see well enough now that you are alive, but I swear, when I turned and saw you standing all gray and dim in the twilight, the marrow of my knees turned to water. It is an ill thing to meet a man you thought dead in the woodland at dusk."

"Bid the keeper see to my steed which is tied behind yonder oak," requested Conan, and Servius nodded, drawing the king up the path. The patrician, recovering from his supernatural fright, had become extremely nervous.

"I will send a servant from the manor," he said. "The keeper is in his lodge—but I dare not trust even my servants in these days. It is better that only I know of your presence."

Approaching the great house that glimmered dimly through the trees, he turned aside into a little-used path that ran between close-set oaks whose intertwining branches formed a vault overhead, shutting out the dim light of the gathering dusk. Servius hurried on through the darkness without speaking, and with something resembling panic in his manner, and presently led Conan through a small side door into a narrow, dimly illuminated corridor. They traversed this in haste and silence, and Servius brought the king into a spacious chamber with a high, oak-beamed ceiling and richly paneled walls. Logs flamed in the wide fireplace, for there was a frosty edge to the air, and a great meat pasty in a stone platter stood smoking on a broad mahogany board. Servius locked the massive door and extinguished the candles that stood in a silver candlestick on the table, leaving the chamber illuminated only by the fire on the hearth.

"Your pardon, Your Majesty," he apologized. "These are perilous times; spies lurk everywhere. It were better that none be able to peer through the windows and recognize you. This pasty, however, is just from the oven, as I intended supping on my return from talk with my keeper. If Your Majesty would deign—"

"The light is sufficient," grunted Conan, seating himself with scant ceremony, and drawing his poniard.

He dug ravenously into the luscious dish, and washed it down with great gulps of wine from grapes grown in Servius's vineyards. He seemed oblivious to any sense of peril, but Servius shifted uneasily on his settle by the fire, nervously fingering the heavy gold chain about his neck. He glanced continually at the diamond panes of the casement, gleaming dimly in the firelight, and cocked his ear toward the door, as if half expecting to hear the pad of furtive feet in the corridor without.

Finishing his meal, Conan rose and seated himself on another settle before the fire.

"I won't jeopardize you long by my presence, Servius," he said abruptly. "Dawn will find me far from your plantation."

"My lord—" Servius lifted his hands in expostulation, but Conan waved his protests aside.

"I know your loyalty and your courage. Both are above reproach. But if Valerius has usurped my throne, it would be death for you to shelter me, if you were discovered."

"I am not strong enough to defy him openly," admitted Servius. "The fifty men-at-arms I could lead to battle would be but a handful of straws. You saw the ruins of Emilius Scavonus' plantation?"

Conan nodded, frowning darkly.

"He was the strongest patrician in this province, as you know. He refused to give his allegiance to Valerius. The Nemedians burned him in the ruins of his own villa. After that the rest of us saw the futility of resistance, especially as the people of Tarantia refused to fight. We submitted and Valerius spared our lives, though he levied a tax upon us that will ruin many. But what could we do? We thought you were dead. Many of the barons had been slain, others taken prisoner. The army was shattered and scattered. You have no heir to take the crown. There was no one to lead us—"

"Was there not Count Trocero of Poitain?" demanded Conan harshly. Servius spread his hands helplessly.

"It is true that his general Prospero was in the field with a small army. Retreating before Amalric, he urged men to rally to his banner. But with Your Majesty dead, men remembered old wars and civil brawls, and how Trocero and his Poitanians once rode through these provinces even as Amalric was riding now, with torch and sword. The barons were jealous of Trocero. Some men—spies of Valerius per-haps—shouted that the Count of Poitain intended seizing the crown for himself. Old sectional hates flared up again. If we had had one man with dynastic blood in his veins, we would have crowned and followed him against Nemedia. But we had none.

"The barons who followed you loyally would not follow one of their own number, each holding himself as good as his neighbor, each fearing the ambitions of the others. You were the cord that held the fagots together. When the cord was cut, the fagots fell apart. If you had had a son, the barons would have rallied loyally to him. But there was no point for their patriotism to focus upon.

"The merchants and commoners, dreading anarchy and a return of feudal days when each baron was his own law, cried out that any king was better than none, even Valerius, who was at least of the blood of the old dynasty. There was no one to oppose him when he rode up at the head of his steel-clad hosts, with the scarlet dragon of Nemedia floating over him, and rang his lance against the gates of Tarantia.

"Nay, the people threw open the gates and knelt in the dust before him. They had refused to aid Prospero in holding the city. They said they had rather be ruled by Valerius than by Trocero. They said—truthfully—that the barons would not rally to Trocero, but that many would accept Valerius. They said that by yielding to Valerius they would escape the devastation of civil war, and the fury of the Nemedians. Prospero rode southward with his ten thousand knights, and the horsemen of the Nemedians entered the city a few hours later. They did not follow him. They remained to see that Valerius was crowned in Tarantia."

"Then the old witch's smoke showed the truth," muttered Conan, feeling a queer chill along his spine. "Amalric crowned Valerius?"

"Aye, in the coronation hall, with the blood of slaughter scarcely dried on his hands."

"And do the people thrive under his benevolent rule?" asked Conan with angry irony.

"He lives like a foreign prince in the midst of a conquered land," answered Servius bitterly. "His court is filled with Nemedians, the palace troops are of the same breed, and a large garrison of them occupy the citadel. Aye, the hour of the Dragon has come at last.

"Nemedians swagger like lords through the streets. Women are outraged and merchants plundered daily, and Valerius either can, or will, make no attempt to curb them. Nay, he is but their puppet, their figurehead. Men of sense knew he would be, and the people are beginning to find it out.

"Amalric has ridden forth with a strong army to reduce the outlying provinces where some of the barons have defied him. But there is no unity among them. Their jealousy of each other is stronger than their fear of Amalric. He will crush them one by one. Many castles and cities, realizing that, have sent in their submission. Those who resist fare miserably. The Nemedians are glutting their long hatred. And their ranks are swelled by Aquilonians whom fear, gold, or necessity of occupation are forcing into their armies. It is a natural consequence."

Conan nodded somberly, staring at the red reflections of the firelight on the richly carved oaken panels.

"Aquilonia has a king instead of the anarchy they feared," said Servius at last. "Valerius does not protect his subjects against his allies. Hundreds who could not pay the ransom imposed upon them have been sold to the Kothic slave-traders."

Conan's head jerked up and a lethal flame lit his blue eyes. He swore gustily, his mighty hands knotting into iron hammers.

"Aye, white men sell white men and white women, as it was in the feudal days. In the palaces of Shem and of Turan, they will live out the lives of slaves. Valerius is king, but the unity for which the people looked, even though of the sword, is not complete.

"Gunderland in the north and Poitain in the south are yet unconquered, and there are unsubdued provinces in the west, where the border barons have the backing of Bossonian bowmen. Yet these outlying provinces are no real menace to Valerius. They must remain on the defensive, and will be lucky if they are able to keep their independence. Here Valerius and his foreign knights are supreme."

"Let him make the best of it then," said Conan grimly. "His time is short. The people will rise when they learn that I'm alive. We'll take Tarantia back before Amalric can return with his army. Then we'll sweep these dogs from the kingdom."

Servius was silent. The crackle of the fire was loud in the stillness.

"Well," exclaimed Conan impatiently, "why do you sit with your head bent, staring at the hearth? Do you doubt what I have said?"

Servius avoided the king's eye.

"What mortal man can do, you will do, Your Majesty," he answered. "I have ridden behind you in battle, and I know that no mortal being can stand before your sword."

"What, then?"

Servius drew his fur-trimmed jupon closer about him, and shivered in spite of the flame.

"Men say your fall was occasioned by sorcery," he said presently.

"What then?"

"What mortal can fight against sorcery? Who is this veiled man who communes at midnight with Valerius and his allies, as men say, who appears and disappears so mysteriously? Men say in whispers that he is a great magician who died thousands of years ago, but has returned from death's gray lands to overthrow the king of Aquilonia and restore the dynasty of which Valerius is heir."

"What matter?" exclaimed Conan angrily. "I escaped from the devil-haunted pits of Belverus, and from diabolism in the mountains. If the people rise—"

Servius shook his head.

"Your staunchest supporters in the eastern and central provinces are dead, fled or imprisoned. Gunderland is far to the north, Poitain far to the south. The Bossonians have retired to their marches far to the west. It would take weeks to gather and concentrate these forces, and before that could be done, each levy would be attacked separately by Amalric and destroyed."

"But an uprising in the central provinces would tip the scales for us!" exclaimed Conan. "We could seize Tarantia and hold it against Amalric until the Gundermen and Poitanians could get here."

Servius hesitated, and his voice sank to a whisper.

"Men say you died accursed. Men say this veiled stranger cast a spell upon you to slay you and break your army. The great bell has tolled your dirge. Men believe you to be dead. And the central provinces would not rise, even if they knew you lived. They would not dare. Sorcery defeated you at Valkia. Sorcery brought the news to Tarantia, for that very night men were shouting of it in the streets.

"A Nemedian priest loosed black magic again in the streets of Tarantia to slay men who still were loyal to your memory. I myself saw it. Armed men dropped like flies and died in the streets in a manner no man could understand. And the lean priest laughed and said: 'I am only Altaro, only an acolyte of Orastes, who is but an acolyte of him who wears the veil; not mine is the power; the power but works through me.' "

"Well," said Conan harshly, "is it not better to die honorably than to live in infamy? Is death worse than oppression, slavery and ultimate destruction?"

"When the fear of sorcery is in, reason is out," replied Servius. "The fear of the central provinces is too great to allow them to rise for you. The outlying provinces would fight for you—but the same sorcery that smote your army at Valkia would smite you again. The Nemedians hold the broadest, richest and most thickly populated sections of Aquilonia, and they cannot be defeated by the forces which might still be at your command. You would be sacrificing your loyal subjects uselessly. In sorrow I say it, but it is true: King Conan, you are a king without a kingdom."

Conan stared into the fire without replying. A smoldering log crashed down among the flames without a bursting shower of sparks. It might have been the crashing ruin of his kingdom.

Again Conan felt the presence of a grim reality behind the veil of material illusion. He sensed again the inexorable drive of a ruthless fate. A feeling of furious panic tugged at his soul, a sense of being trapped, and a red rage that burned to destroy and kill.

"Where are the officials of my court?" he demanded at last.

"Pallantides was sorely wounded at Valkia, was ransomed by his family, and now lies in his castle in Attains. He will be fortunate if he ever rides again. Publius, the chancellor, has fled the kingdom in disguise, no man knows whither. The council has been disbanded. Some were imprisoned, some banished. Many of your loyal subjects have been put to death. Tonight, for instance, the Countess Albiona dies under the headsman's ax."

Conan started and stared at Servius with such anger smoldering in his blue eyes that the patrician shrank back.

"Why?"

"Because she would not become the mistress of Valerius. Her lands are forfeit, her henchmen sold into slavery, and at midnight, in the Iron Tower, her head must fall. Be advised, my king—to me you will ever be my king—and flee before you are discovered. In these days none is safe. Spies and informers creep among us, betraying the slightest deed or word of discontent as treason and rebellion. If you make yourself known to your subjects, it will only end in your capture and death.

"My horses and all the men that I can trust are at your disposal. Before dawn we can be far from Tarantia, and well on our way toward the border. If I cannot aid you to recover your kingdom, I can at least follow you into exile."

Conan shook his head. Servius glanced uneasily at him as he sat staring into the fire, his chin propped on his mighty fist. The firelight gleamed redly on his steel mail, on his baleful eyes. They burned in the firelight like the eyes of a wolf. Servius was again aware, as in the past, and now more strongly than ever, of something alien about the king. That great frame under the mail mesh was too hard and supple for a civilized man; the elemental fire of the primitive burned in those smoldering eyes. Now the barbaric suggestion about the king was more pronounced, as if in his extremity the outward aspects of civilization were stripped away, to reveal the primordial core. Conan was reverting to his pristine type. He did not act as a civilized man would act under the same conditions, nor did his thoughts run in the same channels. He was unpredictable. It was only a stride from the king of Aquilonia to the skin-clad slayer of the Cimmerian hills.

"I'll ride to Poitain, if it may be," Conan said at last. "But I'll ride alone. And I have one last duty to perform as king of Aquilonia."

"What do you mean, your Majesty?" asked Servius, shaken by a premonition.

"I'm going into Tarantia after Albiona tonight," answered the king. "I've failed all my other loyal subjects, it seems—if they take her head, they can have mine too."

"This is madness!" cried Servius, staggering up and clutching his throat, as if he already felt the noose closing about it.

"There are secrets to the Tower which few know," said Conan. "Anyway, I'd be a dog to leave Albiona to die because of her loyalty to me. I may be a king without a kingdom, but I'm not a man without honor."

"It will ruin us all!" whispered Servius.

"It will ruin no one but me if I fail. You've risked enough. I ride alone tonight. This is all I want you to do: procure me a patch for my eye, a staff for my hand, and garments such as travelers wear."

9 "It Is the King or His Ghost!"

Many men passed through the great arched gates of Tarantia between sunset and midnight—belated travelers, merchants from afar with heavily laden mules, free workmen from the surrounding farms and vineyards. Now that Valerius was supreme in the central provinces, there was no rigid scrutiny of the folk who flowed in a steady stream through the wide gates. Discipline had been relaxed. The Nemedian soldiers who stood on guard were half drunk, and much too busy watching for handsome peasant girls and rich merchants who could be bullied to notice workmen or dusty travelers, even one tall wayfarer whose worn cloak could not conceal the hard lines of his powerful frame.

This man carried himself with an erect, aggressive bearing that was too natural for him to realise it himself, much less dissemble it. A great patch covered one eye, and his leather coif, drawn low over his brows, shadowed his features. With a long thick staff in his muscular brown hand, he strode leisurely through the arch where the torches flared and guttered, and, ignored by the tipsy guardsmen, emerged upon the wide streets of Tarantia.

Upon these well-lighted thoroughfares the usual throngs went about their business, and shops and stalls stood open, with their wares displayed. One thread ran a constant theme through the pattern. Nemedian soldiers, singly or in clumps, swaggered through the throngs, shouldering their way with studied arrogance. Women scurried from their path, and men stepped aside with darkened brows and clenched fists. The Aquilonians were a proud race, and these were their hereditary enemies.

The knuckles of the tall traveler knotted on his staff, but, like the others, he stepped aside to let the men in armor have the way. Among the motley and varied crowd he did not attract much attention in his drab, dusty garments. But once, as he passed a sword-seller's stall and the light that streamed from its wide door fell full upon him, he thought he felt an intense stare upon him, and turning quickly, saw a man in the brown jerkin of a free workman regarding him fixedly. This man turned away with undue haste, and vanished in the shifting throng. But Conan turned into a narrow bystreet and quickened his pace. It might have been mere idle curiosity; but he could take no chances.

The grim Iron Tower stood apart from the citadel, amid a maze of narrow streets and crowding houses where the meaner structures, appropriating a space from which the more fastidious shrank, had invaded a portion of the city ordinarily alien to them. The Tower was in reality a castle, an ancient, formidable pile of heavy stone and black iron, which had itself served as the citadel in an earlier, ruder century.

Not a long distance from it, lost in a tangle of partly deserted tenements and warehouses, stood an ancient watchtower, so old and forgotten that it did not appear on the maps of the city for a hundred years back. Its original purpose had been forgotten, and nobody, of such as saw it at all, noticed that the apparently ancient lock which kept it from being appropriated as sleeping-quarters by beggars and thieves, was in reality comparatively new and extremely powerful, cunningly disguised into an appearance of rusty antiquity. Not half a dozen men in the kingdom had ever known the secret of that tower.

No keyhole showed in the massive, green-crusted lock. But Conan's practised fingers, stealing over it, pressed here and there knobs invisible to the casual eye. The door silently opened inward and he entered solid blackness, pushing the door shut behind him. A light would have showed the tower empty, a bare, cylindrical shaft of massive stone.

Groping in a corner with the sureness of familiarity, he found the projections for which he was feeling on a slab of the stone that composed the floor. Quickly he lifted it, and without hesitation lowered himself into the aperture beneath. His feet felt stone steps leading downward into what he knew was a narrow tunnel that ran straight toward the foundations of the Iron Tower, three streets away.

The bell on the citadel, which tolled only at the midnight hour or for the death of a king, boomed suddenly. In a dimly lighted chamber in the Iron Tower a door opened and a form emerged into a corridor. The interior of the Tower was as forbidding as its external appearance. Its massive stone walls were rough, unadorned. The flags of the floor were worn deep by generations of faltering feet, and the vault of the ceiling was gloomy in the dim light of torches set in niches.

The man who trudged down that grim corridor was in appearance in keeping with his surroundings. He was a tall, powerfully-built man, clad in close-fitting black silk. Over his head was drawn a black hood which fell about his shoulders, having two holes for his eyes. From his shoulders hung a loose black cloak, and over one shoulder he bore a heavy ax, the shape of which was that of neither tool nor weapon.

As he went down the corridor, a figure came hobbling up it, a bent, surly old man, stooping under the weight of his pike and a lantern he bore in one hand.

"You are not as prompt as your predecessor, master headsman," he grumbled. "Midnight has just struck, and masked men have gone to milady's cell. They await you."

"The tones of the bell still echo among the towers," answered the executioner. "If I am not so quick to leap and run at the beck of Aquilonians as was the dog who held this office before me, they shall find my arm no less ready. Get you to your duties, old watchman, and leave me to mine. I think mine is the sweeter trade, by Mitra, for you tramp cold corridors and peer at rusty dungeon doors, while I lop off the fairest head in Tarantia this night."

The watchman limped on down the corridor, still grumbling, and the headsman resumed his leisurely way. A few strides carried him around a turn in the corridor, and he absently noted that at his left a door stood partly open. If he had thought, he would have known that that door had been opened since the watchman passed; but thinking was not his trade. He was passing the unlocked door before he realized that aught was amiss, and then it was too late.

A soft tigerish step and the rustle of a cloak warned him, but before he could turn, a heavy arm hooked about his throat from behind, crushing the cry before it could reach his lips. In the brief instant that was allowed him he realized with a surge of panic the strength of his attacker, against which his own brawny thews were helpless. He sensed without seeing the poised dagger.

"Nemedian dog!" muttered a voice thick with passion in his ear. "You've cut off your last Aquilonian head!"

And that was the last thing he ever heard.

In a dank dungeon, lighted only by a guttering torch, three men stood about a young woman who knelt on the rush-strewn flags staring wildly up at them. She was clad only in a scanty shift; her golden hair fell in lustrous ripples about her white shoulders, and her wrists were bound behind her. Even in the uncertain torchlight, and in spite of her disheveled condition and pallor of fear, her beauty was striking. She knelt mutely, staring with wide eyes up at her tormentors. The men were closely masked and cloaked. Such a deed as this needed masks, even in a conquered land. She knew them all nevertheless; but what she knew would harm no one—after that night.

"Our merciful sovereign offers you one more chance, Countess," said the tallest of the three, and he spoke Aquilonian without an accent. "He bids me say that if you soften your proud, rebellious spirit, he will still open his arms to you. If not—" he gestured toward a grim wooden block in the center of the cell. It was blackly stained, and showed many deep nicks as if a keen edge, cutting through some yielding substance, had sunk into the wood.

Albiona shuddered and turned pale, shrinking back. Every fiber in her vigorous young body quivered with the urge of life. Valerius was young, too, and handsome. Many women loved him, she told herself, fighting with herself for life. But she could not speak the word that would ransom her soft young body from the block and the dripping ax. She could not reason the matter. She only knew that when she thought of the clasp of Valerius' arms, her flesh crawled with an abhorrence greater than the fear of death. She shook her head helplessly, compelled by an impulsion more irresistible than the instinct to live.

"Then there is no more to be said!" exclaimed one of the others impatiently, and he spoke with a Nemedian accent. "Where is the headsman?"

As if summoned by the word, the dungeon door opened silently, and a great figure stood framed in it, like a black shadow from the underworld.

Albiona voiced a low, involuntary cry at the sight of that grim shape, and the others stared silently for a moment, perhaps themselves daunted with superstitious awe at the silent, hooded figure. Through the coif the eyes blazed like coals of blue fire, and as these eyes rested on each man in turn, he felt a curious chill travel down his spine.

Then the tall Aquilonian roughly seized the girl and dragged her to the block. She screamed uncontrollably and fought hopelessly against him, frantic with terror, but he ruthlessly forced her to her knees, and bent her yellow head down to the bloody block.

"Why do you delay, headsman?" he exclaimed angrily. "Perform your task!"

He was answered by a short, gusty boom of laughter that was indescribably menacing. All in the dungeon froze in their places, staring at the hooded shape—the two cloaked figures, the masked man bending over the girl, the girl herself on her knees, twisting her imprisoned head to look upward.

"What means this unseemly mirth, dog?" demanded the Aquilonian uneasily.

The man in the black garb tore his hood from his head and flung it to the ground; he set his back to the closed door and lifted the headsman's ax.

"Do you know me, dogs?" he rumbled. "Do you know me?"

The breathless silence was broken by a scream.

"The king!" shrieked Albiona, wrenching herself free from the slackened grasp of her captor. "Oh, Mitra, the king!"

The three men stood like statues, and then the Aquilonian started and spoke, like a man who doubts his own senses.

"Conan!" he ejaculated. "It is the king, or his ghost! What devil's work is this?"

"Devil's work to match devils!" mocked Conan, his lips laughing but Hell flaming in his eyes. "Come, fall to, my gentlemen. You have your swords, and I this cleaver. Nay, I think this butcher's tool fits the work at hand, my fair lords!"

"At him!" muttered the Aquilonian, drawing his sword. "It is Conan and we must kill or be killed!"

And like men waking from a trance, the Nemedians drew their blades and rushed on the king.

The headsman's ax was not made for such work, but the king wielded the heavy, clumsy weapon as lightly as a hatchet, and his quickness of foot, as he constantly shifted his position, defeated their purpose of engaging him all three at once.

He caught the sword of the first man on his ax-head and crushed in the wielder's breast with a murderous counterstroke before he could step back or parry. The remaining Nemedian, missing a savage swipe, had his brains dashed out before he could recover his balance, and an instant later the Aquilonian was backed into a corner, desperately parrying the crashing strokes that rained about him, lacking opportunity even to scream for help.

Suddenly Conan's long left arm shot out and ripped the mask from the man's head, disclosing the pallid features.

"Dog!" grated the king. "I thought I knew you. Traitor! Damned renegade! Even this base steel is too honorable for your foul head. Nay, die as thieves die!"

The ax fell in a devastating arc, and the Aquilonian cried out and went to his knees, grasping the severed stump of his right arm from which blood spouted. It had been shorn away at the elbow, and the ax, unchecked in its descent, had gashed deeply into his side, so that his entrails bulged out.

"Lie there and bleed to death," grunted Conan, casting the ax away disgustedly. "Come, Countess!"

Stooping, he slashed the cords that bound her wrists and lifting her as if she had been a child, strode from the dungeon. She was sobbing hysterically, with her arms thrown about his corded neck in a frenzied embrace.

"Easy all," he muttered. "We're not out of this yet. If we can reach the dungeon where the secret door opens on stairs that lead to the tunnel—devil take it, they've heard that noise, even through these walls."

Down the corridor arms clanged and the tramp and shouting of men echoed under the vaulted roof. A bent figure came hobbling swiftly along, lantern held high, and its light shone full on Conan and the girl. With a curse the Cimmerian sprang toward him, but the old watchman, abandoning both lantern and pike, scuttled away down the corridor, screeching for help at the top of his cracked voice. Deeper shouts answered him.

Conan turned swiftly and ran the other way. He was cut off from the dungeon with the secret lock and the hidden door through which he had entered the Tower, and by which he had hoped to leave, but he knew this grim building well. Before he was king he had been imprisoned in it.

He turned off into a side passage and quickly emerged into another, broader corridor, which ran parallel to the one down which he had come, and which was at the moment deserted. He followed this only a few yards, when he again turned back, down another side passage. This brought him back into the corridor he had left, but at a strategic point. A few feet farther up the corridor there was a heavy bolted door, and before it stood a bearded Nemedian in corselet and helmet his back to Conan as he peered up the corridor in the direction of the growing tumult and wildly waving lanterns.

Conan did not hesitate. Slipping the girl to the ground, he ran at the guard swiftly and silently, sword in hand. The man turned just as the king reached him, bawled in surprize and fright and lifted his pike; but before he could bring the clumsy weapon into play, Conan brought down his sword on the fellow's helmet with a force that would have felled an ox. Helmet and skull gave way together and the guard crumpled to the floor.

In an instant Conan had drawn the massive bolt that barred the door—too heavy for one ordinary man to have manipulated—and called hastily to Albiona, who ran staggering to him. Catching her up unceremoniously with one arm, he bore her through the door and into the outer darkness.

They had come into a narrow alley, black as pitch, walled by the side of the Tower on one hand, and the sheer stone back of a row of buildings on the other. Conan, hurrying through the darkness as swiftly as he dared, felt the latter wall for doors or windows, but found none.

The great door clanged open behind them, and men poured out, with torches gleaming on breastplates and naked swords. They glared about, bellowing, unable to penetrate the darkness which their torches served to illuminate for only a few feet in any direction, and then rushed down the alley at random—heading in the direction opposite to that taken by Conan and Albiona.

"They'll learn their mistake quick enough," he muttered, increasing his pace. "If we ever find a crack in this infernal wall—damn! The street watch!"

Ahead of them a faint glow became apparent, where the alley opened into a narrow street, and he saw dim figures looming against it with a glimmer of steel. It was indeed the street watch, investigating the noise they had heard echoing down the alley.

"Who goes here?" they shouted, and Conan grit his teeth at the hated Nemedian accent.

"Keep behind me," he ordered the girl. "We've got to cut our way through before the prison guards come back and pin us between them."

And grasping his sword, he ran straight at the oncoming figures.

The advantage of surprize was his. He could see them, limned against the distant glow, and they could not see him coming at them out of the black depths of the alley. He was among them before they knew it, smiting with the silent fury of a wounded lion.

His one chance lay in hacking through before they could gather their wits. But there were half a score of them, in full mail, hard-bitten veterans of the border wars, in whom the instinct for battle could take the place of bemused wits. Three of them were down before they realized that it was only one man who was attacking them, but even so their reaction was instantaneous. The clangor of steel rose deafeningly, and sparks flew as Conan's sword crashed on basinet and hauberk. He could see better than they, and in the dim light his swiftly moving figure was an uncertain mark. Flailing swords cut empty air or glanced from his blade, and when he struck, it was with the fury and certainty of a hurricane.

But behind him sounded the shouts of the prison guards, returning up the alley at a run, and still the mailed figures before him barred his way with a bristling wall of steel. In an instant the guards would be on his back—in desperation he redoubled his strokes, flailing like a smith on an anvil, and then was suddenly aware of a diversion. Out of nowhere behind the watchmen rose a score of black figures and there was a sound of blows, murderously driven. Steel glinted in the gloom, and men cried out, struck mortally from behind. In an instant the alley was littered with writhing forms. A dark, cloaked shape sprang toward Conan, who heaved up his sword, catching a gleam of steel in the right hand. But the other was extended to him empty and a voice hissed urgently: "This way, Your Majesty! Quickly!"

With a muttered oath of surprize, Conan caught up Albiona in one massive arm, and followed his unknown befriender. He was not inclined to hesitate, with thirty prison guardsmen closing in behind him.

Surrounded by mysterious figures he hurried down the alley, carrying the countess as if she had been a child. He could tell nothing of his rescuers except that they wore dark cloaks and hoods. Doubt and suspicion crossed his mind, but at least they had struck down his enemies, and he saw no better course than to follow them.

As if sensing his doubt, the leader touched his arm lightly and said: "Fear not, King Conan; we are your loyal subjects." The voice was not familiar, but the accent was Aquilonian of the central provinces.

Behind them the guards were yelling as they stumbled over the shambles in the mud, and they came pelting vengefully down the alley, seeing the vague dark mass moving between them and the light of the distant street. But the hooded men turned suddenly toward the seemingly blank wall, and Conan saw a door gape there. He muttered a curse. He had traversed that alley by day, in times past, and had never noticed a door there. But through it they went, and the door closed behind them with the click of a lock. The sound was not reassuring, but his guides were hurrying him on, moving with the precision of familiarity, guiding Conan with a hand at either elbow. It was like traversing a tunnel, and Conan felt Albiona's lithe limbs trembling in his arms. Then somewhere ahead of them an opening was faintly visible, merely a somewhat less black arch in the blackness, and through this they filed.

After that there was a bewildering succession of dim courts and shadowy alleys and winding corridors, all traversed in utter silence, until at last they emerged into a broad lighted chamber, the location of which Conan could not even guess, for their devious route had confused even his primitive sense of direction.

10 A Coin from Acheron

Not all his guides entered the chamber. When the door closed, Conan saw only one man standing before him—a slim figure, masked in a black cloak with a hood. This the man threw back, disclosing a pale oval of a face, with calm, delicately chiseled features.

The king set Albiona on her feet, but she still clung to him and stared apprehensively about her. The chamber was a large one, with marble walls partly covered with black velvet hangings and thick rich carpets on the mosaic floor, laved in the soft golden glow of bronze lamps.

Conan instinctively laid a hand on his hilt. There was blood on his hand, blood clotted about the mouth of his scabbard, for he had sheathed his blade without cleansing it.

"Where are we?" he demanded.

The stranger answered with a low, profound bow in which the suspicious king could detect no trace of irony.

"In the temple of Asura, Your Majesty."

Albiona cried out faintly and clung closer to Conan, staring fearfully at the black, arched doors, as if expecting the entry of some grisly shape of darkness.

"Fear not, my lady," said their guide. "There is nothing here to harm you, vulgar superstition to the contrary. If your monarch was sufficiently convinced of the innocence of our religion to protect us from the persecution of the ignorant, then certainly one of his subjects need have no apprehensions."

"Who are you?" demanded Conan.

"I am Hadrathus, priest of Asura. One of my followers recognized you when you entered the city, and brought the word to me."

Conan grunted profanely.

"Do not fear that others discovered your identity," Hadrathus assured him. "Your disguise would have deceived any but a follower of Asura, whose cult it is to seek below the aspect of illusion. You were followed to the watchtower, and some of my people went into the tunnel to aid you if you returned by that route. Others, myself among them, surrounded the tower. And now, King Conan, it is yours to command. Here in the temple of Asura you are still king."

"Why should you risk your lives for me?" asked the king.

"You were our friend when you sat upon your throne," answered Hadrathus. "You protected us when the priests of Mitra sought to scourge us out of the land."

Conan looked about him curiously. He had never before visited the temple of Asura, had not certainly known that there was such a temple in Tarantia. The priests of the religion had a habit of hiding their temples in a remarkable fashion. The worship of Mitra was overwhelmingly predominant in the Hyborian nations, but the cult of Asura persisted, in spite of official ban and popular antagonism. Conan had been told dark tales of hidden temples where intense smoke drifted up incessantly from black altars where kidnaped humans were sacrificed before a great coiled serpent, whose fearsome head swayed for ever in the haunted shadows.

Persecution caused the followers of Asura to hide their temples with cunning art, and to veil their rituals in obscurity; and this secrecy, in turn, evoked more monstrous suspicions and tales of evil.

But Conan's was the broad tolerance of the barbarian, and he had refused to persecute the followers of Asura or to allow the people to do so on no better evidence than was presented against them, rumors and accusations that could not be proven. "If they are black magicians," he had said, "how will they suffer you to harry them? If they are not, there is no evil in them. Crom's devils! Let men worship what gods they will."

At a respectful invitation from Hadrathus, he seated himself on an ivory chair, and motioned Albiona to another, but she preferred to sit on a golden stool at his feet, pressing close against his thigh, as if seeking security in the contact. Like most orthodox followers of Mitra, she had an intuitive horror of the followers and cult of Asura, instilled in her infancy and childhood by wild tales of human sacrifice and anthropomorphic gods shambling through shadowy temples.

Hadrathus stood before them, his uncovered head bowed.

"What is your wish, Your Majesty? "

"Food first," he grunted, and the priest smote a golden gong with a silver wand.

Scarcely had the mellow notes ceased echoing when four hooded figures came through a curtained doorway bearing a great four-legged silver platter of smoking dishes and crystal vessels.

This they set before Conan, bowing low, and the king wiped his hands on the damask, and smacked his lips with unconcealed relish.

"Beware, Your Majesty!" whispered Albiona. "These folk eat human flesh!"

"I'll stake my kingdom that this is nothing but honest roast beef," answered Conan. "Come, lass, fall to! You must be hungry after the prison fare."

Thus advised, and with the example before her of one whose word was the ultimate law to her, the countess complied, and ate ravenously though daintily, while her liege lord tore into the meat joints and guzzled the wine with as much gusto as if he had not already eaten once that night.

"You priests are shrewd, Hadrathus," he said, with a great beef bone in his hands and his mouth full of meat. "I'd welcome your service in my campaign to regain my kingdom."

Slowly Hadrathus shook his head, and Conan slammed the beef bone down on the table in a gust of impatient wrath.

"Crom's devils! What ails the men of Aquilonia? First Servius—now you! Can you do nothing but wag your idiotic heads when I speak of ousting these dogs?"

Hadrathus sighed and answered slowly: "My lord, it is ill to say, and I fain would say otherwise. But the freedom of Aquilonia is at an end! Nay, the freedom of the whole world may be at an end! Age follows age in the history of the world, and now we enter an age of horror and slavery, as it was long ago."

"What do you mean?" demanded the king uneasily.

Hadrathus dropped into a chair and rested his elbows on his thighs, staring at the floor.

"It is not alone the rebellious lords of Aquilonia and the armies of Nemedia which are arrayed against you," answered Hadrathus. "It is sorcery—grisly black magic from the grim youth of the world. An awful shape has risen out of the shades of the Past, and none can stand before it."

"What do you mean?" Conan repeated.

"I speak of Xaltotun of Acheron, who died three thousand years ago, yet walks the earth today."

Conan was silent, while in his mind floated an image—the image of a bearded face of calm inhuman beauty. Again he was haunted by a sense of uneasy familiarity. Acheron—the sound of the word roused instinctive vibrations of memory and associations in his mind.

"Acheron," he repeated. "Xaltotun of Acheron—man, are you mad? Acheron has been a myth for more centuries than I can remember. I've often wondered if it ever existed at all."

"It was a black reality," answered Hadrathus, "an empire of black magicians, steeped in evil now long forgotten. It was finally overthrown by the Hyborian tribes of the west. The wizards of Acheron practised foul necromancy, thaumaturgy of the most evil kind, grisly magic taught them by devils. And of all the sorcerers of that accursed kingdom, none was so great as Xaltotun of Python."

"Then how was he ever overthrown?" asked Conan skeptically.

"By some means a source of cosmic power which he jealously guarded was stolen and turned against him. That source has been returned to him, and he is invincible."

Albiona, hugging the headsman's black cloak about her, stared from the priest to the king, not understanding the conversation. Conan shook his head angrily.

"You are making game of me," he growled. "If Xaltotun has been dead three thousand years, how can this man be he? It's some rogue who's taken the old one's name."

Hadrathus leaned to an ivory table and opened a small gold chest which stood there. From it he took something which glinted dully in the mellow light—a broad gold coin of antique minting.

"You have seen Xaltotun unveiled? Then look upon this. It is a coin which was stamped in ancient Acheron, before its fall. So pervaded with sorcery was that black empire, that even this coin has its uses in making magic."

Conan took it and scowled down at it. There was no mistaking its great antiquity. Conan had handled many coins in the years of his plunderings, and had a good practical knowledge of them. The edges were worn and the inscription almost obliterated. But the countenance stamped on one side was still clear-cut and distinct. And Conan's breath sucked in between his clenched teeth. It was not cool in the chamber, but he felt a prickling of his scalp, an icy contraction of his flesh. The countenance was that of a bearded man, inscrutable, with a calm inhuman beauty.

"By Crom! It's he!" muttered Conan. He understood, now, the sense of familiarity that the sight of the bearded man had roused in him from the first. He had seen a coin like this once before, long ago in a far land.

With a shake of his shoulders he growled: "The likeness is only a coincidence—or if he's shrewd enough to assume a forgotten wizard's name, he's shrewd enough to assume his likeness." But he spoke without conviction. The sight of that coin had shaken the foundations of his universe. He felt that reality and stability were crumbling into an abyss of illusion and sorcery. A wizard was understandable; but this was diabolism beyond sanity.

"We cannot doubt that it is indeed Xaltotun of Python," said Hadrathus. "He it was who shook down the cliffs at Valkia, by his spells that enthrall the elementals of the earth—he it was who sent the creature of darkness into your tent before dawn."

Conan scowled at him. "How did you know that?"

"The followers of Asura have secret channels of knowledge. That does not matter. But do you realize the futility of sacrificing your subjects in a vain attempt to regain your crown?"

Conan rested his chin on his fist, and stared grimly into nothing. Albiona watched him anxiously, her mind groping bewildered in the mazes of the problem that confronted him.

"Is there no wizard in the world who could make magic to fight Xaltotun's magic?" he asked at last.

Hadrathus shook his head. "If there were, we of Asura would know of him. Men say our cult is a survival of the ancient Stygian serpent-worship. That is a lie. Our ancestors came from Vendhya, beyond the Sea of Vilayet and the blue Himelian mountains. We are sons of the East, not the South, and we have knowledge of all the wizards of the East, who are greater than the wizards of the West. And not one of them but would be a straw in the wind before the black might of Xaltotun."

"But he was conquered once," persisted Conan.

"Aye; a cosmic source was turned against him. But now that source is again in his hands, and he will see that it is not stolen again."

"And what is this damnable source?" demanded Conan irritably.

"It is called the Heart of Ahriman. When Acheron was overthrown, the primitive priest who had stolen it and turned it against Xaltotun hid it in a haunted cavern and built a small temple over the cavern. Thrice thereafter the temple was rebuilt, each time greater and more elaborately than before, but always on the site of the original shrine, though men forgot the reason therefor. Memory of the hidden symbol faded from the minds of common men, and was preserved only in priestly books and esoteric volumes. Whence it came no one knows. Some say it is the veritable heart of a god, others that it is a star that fell from the skies long ago. Until it was stolen, none had looked upon it for three thousand years.

"When the magic of the Mitran priests failed against the magic of Xaltotun's acolyte, Altaro, they remembered the ancient legend of the Heart, and the high priest and an acolyte went down into the dark and terrible crypt below the temple into which no priest had descended for three thousand years. In the ancient iron-bound volumes which speak of the Heart in their cryptic symbolism, it is also told of a creature of darkness left by the ancient priest to guard it."

"Far down in a square chamber with arched doorways leading off into immeasurable blackness, the priest and his acolytes found a black stone altar that glowed dimly with inexplicable radiance.

"On that altar lay a curious gold vessel like a double-valved seashell, which clung to the stone like a barnacle. But it gaped open and empty. The Heart of Ahriman was gone. While they stared in horror, the keeper of the crypt, the creature of darkness, came upon them and mangled the high priest so that he died. But the acolyte fought off the being—a mindless, soulless waif of the pits brought long ago to guard the Heart—and escaped up the long black narrow stairs carrying the dying priest, who before he died, gasped out the news to his followers, bade them submit to a power they could not overcome, and commanded secrecy. But the word has been whispered about among the priests, and we of Asura learned of it."

"And Xaltotun draws his power from this symbol?" asked Conan, still skeptical.

"No. His power is drawn from the black gulf. But the Heart of Ahriman came from some far universe of flaming light, and against it the powers of darkness cannot stand, when it is in the hands of an adept. It is like a sword that might smite at him, not a sword with which he can smite. It restores life, and can destroy life. He has stolen it, not to use it against his enemies, but to keep them from using it against him."

"A shell-shaped bowl of gold on a black altar in a deep cavern," Conan muttered, frowning as he sought to capture the illusive image. "That reminds me of something I have heard or seen. But what, in Crom's name, is this notable Heart?"

"It is in the form of a great jewel, like a ruby, but pulsing with blinding fire with which no ruby ever burned. It glows like living flame—"

But Conan sprang suddenly up and smote his right fist into his left palm like a thunderclap.

"Crom!" he roared. "What a fool I've been! The Heart of Ahriman! The heart of my kingdom! Find the heart of my kingdom, Zeiata said. By Ymir, it was the jewel I saw in the green smoke, the jewel which Tarascus stole from Xaltotun while he lay in the sleep of the black lotus!"

Hadrathus was also on his feet, his calm dropped from him like a garment.

"What are you saying? The Heart stolen from Xaltotun?"

"Aye!" Conan boomed. "Tarascus feared Xaltotun and wanted to cripple his power, which he thought resided in the Heart. Maybe he thought the wizard would die if the Heart was lost. By Crom—ahhh!" With a savage grimace of disappointment and disgust he dropped his clenched hand to his side.

"I forgot. Tarascus gave it to a thief to throw into the sea. By this time the fellow must be almost to Kordava. Before I can follow him he'll take ship and consign the Heart to the bottom of the ocean."

"The sea will not hold it!" exclaimed Hadrathus, quivering with excitement. "Xaltotun would himself have cast it into the ocean long ago, had he not known that the first storm would carry it ashore. But on what unknown beach might it not land!"

"Well," Conan was recovering some of his resilient confidence, "there's no assurance that the thief will throw it away. If I know thieves—and I should, for I was a thief in Zamora in my early youth—he won't throw it away. He'll sell it to some rich trader. By Crom!" He strode back and forth in his growing excitement. "It's worth looking for! Zeiata bade me find the heart of my kingdom, and all else she showed me proved to be truth. Can it be that the power to conquer Xaltotun lurks in that crimson bauble?"

"Aye! My head upon it!" cried Hadrathus, his face lightened with fervor, his eyes blazing, his fists clenched. "With it in our hands we can dare the powers of Xaltotun! I swear it! If we can recover it, we have an even chance of recovering your crown and driving the invaders from our portals. It is not the swords of Nemedia that Aquilonia fears, but the black arts of Xaltotun."

Conan looked at him for a space, impressed by the priest's fire.

"It's like a quest in a nightmare," he said at last. "Yet your words echo the thought of Zeiata, and all else she said was truth. I'll seek for this jewel."

"It holds the destiny of Aquilonia," said Hadrathus with conviction. "I will send men with you—"

"Nay!" exclaimed the king impatiently, not caring to be hampered by priests on his quest, however skilled in esoteric arts. "This is a task for a fighting-man. I go alone. First to Poitain, where I'll leave Albiona with Trocero. Then to Kordava, and to the sea beyond, if necessary. It may be that, even if the thief intends carrying out Tarascus' order, he'll have some difficulty finding an outbound ship at this time of the year."

"And if you find the Heart," cried Hadrathus, "I will prepare the way for your conquest. Before you return to Aquilonia I will spread the word through secret channels that you live and are returning with a magic stronger than Xaltotun's. I will have men ready to rise on your return. They will rise, if they have assurance that they will be protected from the black arts of Xaltotun.

"And I will aid you on your journey."

He rose and struck the gong.

"A secret tunnel leads from beneath this temple to a place outside the city wall. You shall go to Poitain on a pilgrim's boat. None will dare molest you."

"As you will." With a definite purpose in mind Conan was afire with impatience and dynamic energy. "Only let it be done swiftly."

In the meantime events were moving not slowly elsewhere in the city. A breathless messenger had burst into the palace where Valerius was amusing himself with his dancing girls, and throwing himself on his knee, gasped out a garbled story of a bloody prison break and the escape of a lovely captive. He bore also the news that Count Thespius, to whom the execution of Albiona's sentence had been entrusted, was dying and begging for a word with Valerius before he passed. Hurriedly cloaking himself, Valerius accompanied the man through various winding ways, and came to a chamber where Thespius lay. There was no doubt that the count was dying; bloody froth bubbled from his lips at each shuddering gasp. His severed arm had been bound to stop the flow of blood, but even without that, the gash in his side was mortal.

Alone in the chamber with the dying man, Valerius swore softly.

"By Mitra, I had believed that only one man ever lived who could strike such a blow."

"Valerius!" gasped the dying man. "He lives! Conan lives!"

"What are you saying?" ejaculated the other.

"I swear by Mitra!" gurgled Thespius, gagging on the blood that gushed to his lips. "It was he who carried off Albiona! He is not dead— no phantom come back from hell to haunt us. He is flesh and blood, and more terrible than ever. The alley behind the tower is full of dead men. Beware, Valerius—he has come back—to slay us all—"

A strong shudder shook the blood-smeared figure, and Count Thespius went limp.

Valerius frowned down at the dead man, cast a swift glance about the empty chamber, and stepping swiftly to the door, cast it open suddenly. The messenger and a group of Nemedian guardsmen stood several paces down the corridor. Valerius muttered something that might have indicated satisfaction.

"Have all the gates been closed?" he demanded.

"Yes, Your Majesty."

"Triple the guards at each. Let no one enter or leave the city without strictest investigation. Set men scouring the streets and searching the quarters. A very valuable prisoner has escaped, with the aid of an Aquilonian rebel. Did any of you recognize the man?"

"No, Your Majesty. The old watchman had a glimpse of him, but could only say that he was a giant, clad in the black garb of the executioner, whose naked body we found in an empty cell."

"He is a dangerous man," said Valerius. "Take no chances with him. You all know the Countess Albiona. Search for her, and if you find her, kill her and her companion instantly. Do not try to take them alive."

Returning to his palace chamber, Valerius summoned before him four men of curious and alien aspect. They were tall, gaunt, of yellowish skin, and immobile countenances. They were very similar in appearance, clad alike in long black robes beneath which their sandaled feet were just visible. Their features were shadowed by their hoods. They stood before Valerius with their hands in their wide sleeves; their arms folded. Valerius looked at them without pleasure. In his far journeyings he had encountered many strange races.

"When I found you starving in the Khitan jungles," he said abruptly, "exiles from your kingdom, you swore to serve me. You have served me well enough, in your abominable way. One more service I require, and then I set you free of your oath."

"Conan the Cimmerian, king of Aquilonia, still lives, in spite of Xaltotun's sorcery—or perhaps because of it. I know not. The dark mind of that resurrected devil is too devious and subtle for a mortal man to fathom. But while Conan lives I am not safe. The people accepted me as the lesser of two evils, when they thought he was dead. Let him reappear and the throne will be rocking under my feet in revolution before I can lift my hand.

"Perhaps my allies mean to use him to replace me, if they decide I have served my purpose. I do not know. I do know that this planet is too small for two kings of Aquilonia. Seek the Cimmerian. Use your uncanny talents to ferret him out wherever he hides or runs. He has many friends in Tarantia. He had aid when he carried off Albiona. It took more than one man, even such a man as Conan, to wreak all that slaughter in the alley outside the tower. But no more. Take your staffs and strike his trail. Where that trail will lead you, I know not. But find him! And when you find him, slay him!"

The four Khitans bowed together, and still unspeaking, turned and padded noiselessly from the chamber.

11 Swords of the South

Dawn that rose over the distant hills shone on the sails of a small craft that dropped down the river which curves to within a mile of the walls of Tarantia, and loops southward like a great shining serpent. This boat differed from the ordinary craft plying the broad Khorotas—fishermen and merchant barges loaded with rich goods. It was long and slender, with a high, curving prow, and was black as ebony, with white skulls painted along the gunwales. Amidships rose a small cabin, the windows closely masked. Other craft gave the ominously painted boat a wide berth; for it was obviously one of those "pilgrim boats" that carried a lifeless follower of Asura on his last mysterious pilgrimage southward to where, far beyond the Poitanian mountains, a river flowed at last into the blue ocean. In that cabin undoubtedly lay the corpse of the departed worshipper. All men were familiar with the sight of those gloomy craft; and the most fanatical votary of Mitra would not dare touch or interfere with their somber voyages.

Where the ultimate destination lay, men did not know. Some said Stygia; some a nameless island lying beyond the horizon; others said it was in the glamorous and mysterious land of Vendhya where the dead came home at last. But none knew certainly. They only knew that when a follower of Asura died, the corpse went southward down the great river, in a black boat rowed by a giant slave, and neither boat nor corpse nor slave was ever seen again; unless, indeed, certain dark tales were true, and it was always the same slave who rowed the boats southward.

The man who propelled this particular boat was as huge and brown as the others, though closer scrutiny might have revealed the fact that the hue was the result of carefully applied pigments. He was clad in leather loin-clout and sandals, and he handled the long sweep and oars with unusual skill and power. But none approached the grim boat closely, for it was well known that the followers of Asura were accursed, and that these pilgrim boats were loaded with dark magic. So men swung their boats wide and muttered an incantation as the dark craft slid past, and they never dreamed that they were thus assisting in the flight of their king and the Countess Albiona.

It was a strange journey, in that black, slim craft down the great river for nearly two hundred miles to where the Khorotas swings eastward, skirting the Poitanian mountains. Like a dream the ever-changing panorama glided past. During the day Albiona lay patiently in the little cabin, as quietly as the corpse she pretended to be. Only late at night, after the pleasure boats with their fair occupants lounging on silken cushions in the flare of torches held by slaves had left the river, before dawn brought the hurrying fisher-boats, did the girl venture out. Then she held the long sweep, cunningly bound in place by ropes to aid her, while Conan snatched a few hours of sleep. But the king needed little rest. The ardor of his desire drove him relentlessly; and his powerful frame was equal to the grinding test. Without halt or pause they drove southward.

So down the river they fled, through nights when the flowing current mirrored the million stars, and through days of golden sunlight, leaving winter behind them as they sped southward. They passed cities in the night, above which throbbed and pulsed; the reflection of the myriad lights, lordly river villas and fertile fruit groves. So at last the blue mountains of Poitain rose above them, tier above tier, like ramparts of the gods, and the great river, swerving from those turreted cliffs, swept thunderously through the marching hills with many a rapid and foaming cataract.

Conan scanned the shoreline closely, and finally swung the long sweep and headed inshore at a point where a neck of land jutted into the water, and fir trees grew in a curiously symmetrical ring about a gray, strangely shaped rock.

"How these boats ride those falls we hear roaring ahead of us is more than I can see," he grunted. "Hadrathus said they did—but there's where we halt. He said a man would be waiting for us with horses, but I don't see anyone. How word of our coming could have preceded us I don't know anyway."

He drove inshore and bound the prow to an arching root in the low bank, and then, plunging into the water, washed the brown paint from his skin and emerged dripping, and in his natural color. From the cabin he brought forth a suit of Aquilonian ring mail which Hadrathus had procured for him, and his sword. These he donned while Albiona put on garments suitable for mountain travel. And when Conan was fully armed, and turned to look toward the shore, he started and his hand went to his sword. For on the shore, under the trees, stood a black-cloaked figure holding the reins of a white palfrey and a bay war-horse.

"Who are you?" demanded the king.

The other bowed low.

"A follower of Asura. A command came. I obeyed."

"How, 'came'?" inquired Conan, but the other merely bowed again.

"I have come to guide you through the mountains to the first Poitanian stronghold."

"I don't need a guide," answered Conan. "I know these hills well. I thank you for the horses, but the countess and I will attract less attention alone than if we were accompanied by an acolyte of Asura."

The man bowed profoundly, and giving the reins into Conan's hands, stepped into the boat. Casting off, he floated down the swift current, toward the distant roar of the unseen rapids. With a baffled shake of his head, Conan lifted the countess into the palfrey's saddle, and then mounted the war-horse and reined toward the summits that castellated the sky.

The rolling country at the foot of the towering mountains were now a borderland, in a state of turmoil, where the barons reverted to feudal practises, and bands of outlaws roamed unhindered. Poitain had not formally declared her separation from Aquilonia, but she was now, to all intents, a self-contained kingdom, ruled by her hereditary count, Trocero. The rolling south country had submitted nominally to Valerius, but he had not attempted to force the passes guarded by strongholds where the crimson leopard banner of Poitain waved defiantly.

The king and his fair companion rode up the long blue slopes in the soft evening. As they mounted higher, the rolling country spread out like a vast purple mantle far beneath them, shot with the shine of rivers and lakes, the yellow glint of broad fields, and the white gleam of distant towers. Ahead of them and far above, they glimpsed the first of the Poitanian holds—a strong fortress dominating a narrow pass, the crimson banner streaming against the clear blue sky.

Before they reached it, a band of knights in burnished armor rode from among the trees, and their leader sternly ordered the travelers to halt. They were tall men, with the dark eyes and raven locks of the south.

"Halt, sir, and state your business, and why you ride toward Poitain."

"Is Poitain in revolt then," asked Conan, watching the other closely, "that a man in Aquilonian harness is halted and questioned like a foreigner?"

"Many rogues ride out of Aquilonia these days," answered the other coldly. "As for revolt, if you mean the repudiation of a usurper, then Poitain is in revolt. We had rather serve the memory of a dead man than the scepter of a living dog."

Conan swept off his helmet, and shaking back his black mane stared full at the speaker. The Poitanian stared violently and went livid.

"Saints of heaven!" he gasped. "It is the king—alive!"

The others stared wildly, then a roar of wonder and joy burst from them. They swarmed about Conan, shouting their war-cries and brandishing their swords in their extreme emotion. The acclaim of Poitanian warriors was a thing to terrify a timid man.

"Oh, but Trocero will weep tears of joy to see you, sire!" cried one.

"Aye, and Prospero!" shouted another. "The general has been like one wrapped in a mantle of melancholy, and curses himself night and day that he did not reach the Valkia in time to die beside his king!"

"Now we will strike for empery!" yelled another, whirling his great sword about his head. "Hail, Conan king of Poitain!"

The clangor of bright steel about him and the thunder of their acclaim frightened the birds that rose in gay-hued clouds from the surrounding trees. The hot southern blood was afire, and they desired nothing but for their new-found sovereign to lead them to battle and pillage.

"What is your command, sire?" they cried. "Let one of us ride ahead and bear the news of your coming into Poitain! Banners will wave from every tower, roses will carpet the road before your horse's feet, and all the beauty and chivalry of the south will give you the honor due you—"

Conan shook his head.

"Who could doubt your loyalty? But winds blow over these mountains into the countries of my enemies, and I would rather these didn't know that I lived—yet. Take me to Trocero, and keep my identity a secret."

So what the knights would have made a triumphal procession was more in the nature of a secret flight. They traveled in haste, speaking to no one, except for a whisper to the captain on duty at each pass; and Conan rode among them with his vizor lowered.

The mountains were uninhabited save by outlaws and garrisons of soldiers who guarded the passes. The pleasure-loving Poitanians had no need nor desire to wrest a hard and scanty living from their stern breasts. South of the ranges the rich and beautiful plains of Poitain stretched to the river Alimane; but beyond the river lay the land of Zingara.

Even now, when winter was crisping the leaves beyond the mountains, the tall rich grass waved upon the plains where grazed the horses and cattle for which Poitain was famed. Palm trees and orange groves smiled in the sun, and the gorgeous purple and gold and crimson towers of castles and cities reflected the golden light. It was a land of warmth and plenty, of beautiful men and ferocious warriors. It is not only the hard lands that breed hard men. Poitain was surrounded by covetous neighbors and her sons learned hardihood in incessant wars. To the north the land was guarded by the mountains, but to the south only the Alimane separated the plains of Poitain from the plains of Zingara, and not once but a thousand times had that river run red. To the east lay Argos and beyond that Ophir, proud kingdoms and avaricious. The knights of Poitain held their lands by the weight and edge of their swords, and little of ease and idleness they knew.

So Conan came presently to the castle of Count Trocero.

Conan sat on a silken divan in a rich chamber whose filmy curtains the warm breeze billowed. Trocero paced the floor like a panther, a lithe, restless man with the waist of a woman and the shoulders of a swordsman, who carried his years lightly.

"Let us proclaim you king of Poitain!" urged the count. "Let those northern pigs wear the yoke to which they have bent their necks. The south is still yours. Dwell here and rule us, amid the flowers and the palms."

But Conan shook his head. "There is no nobler land on earth than Poitain. But it cannot stand alone, bold as are its sons."

"It did stand alone for generations," retorted Trocero, with the quick jealous pride of his breed. "We were not always a part of Aquilonia."

"I know. But conditions are not as they were then, when all kingdoms were broken into principalities which warred with each other. The days of dukedoms and free cities are past, the days of empires are upon us. Rulers are dreaming imperial dreams, and only in unity is there strength."

"Then let us unite Zingara with Poitain," argued Trocero. "Half a dozen princes strive against each other, and the country is torn asunder by civil wars. We will conquer it, province by province, and add it to your dominions. Then with the aid of the Zingarans we will conquer Argos and Ophir. We will build an empire—"

Again Conan shook his head. "Let others dream imperial dreams. I but wish to hold what is mine. I have no desire to rule an empire welded together by blood and fire. It's one thing to seize a throne with the aid of its subjects and rule them with their consent. It's another to subjugate a foreign realm and rule it by fear. I don't wish to be another Valerius. No, Trocero, I'll rule all Aquilonia and no more, or I'll rule nothing."

"Then lead us over the mountains and we will smite the Nemedians."

Conan's fierce eyes glowed with appreciation. "No, Trocero. It would be a vain sacrifice. I've told you what I must do to regain my kingdom. I must find the Heart of Ahriman."

"But this is madness!" protested Trocero. "The maunderings of a heretical priest, the mumblings of a mad witch-woman."

"You were not in my tent before Valkia," answered Conan grimly, involuntarily glancing at his right wrist, on which blue marks still showed faintly. "You didn't see the cliffs thunder down to crush the flower of my army. No, Trocero, I've been convinced. Xaltotun's no mortal man, and only with the Heart of Ahriman can I stand against him. So I'm riding to Kordava, alone."

"But that is dangerous," protested Trocero.

"Life is dangerous," rumbled the king. "I won't go as king of Aquilonia, or even as a knight of Poitain, but as a wandering mercenary, as I rode in Zingara in the old days. Oh, I have enemies enough south of the Alimane, in the lands and the waters of the south. Many who won't know me as king of Aquilonia will remember me as Conan of the Barachan pirates, or Amra of the black corsairs. But I have friends, too, and men who'll aid me for their own private reasons." A faint reminiscent grin touched his lips.

Trocero dropped his hands helplessly and glanced at Albiona, who sat on a near-by divan.

"I understand your doubts, my lord," said she. "But I too saw the coin in the temple of Asura, and look you, Hadrathus said it was dated five hundred years before the fall of Acheron. If Xaltotun, then, is the man pictured on the coin, as his Majesty swears he is, that means he was no common wizard, even in his other life, for the years of his life were numbered by centuries, not as the lives of other men are numbered."

Before Trocero could reply, a respectful rap was heard on the door and a voice called: "My lord, we have caught a man skulking about the castle, who says he wishes to speak with your guest. I await your orders."

"A spy from Aquilonia!" hissed Trocero, catching at his dagger, but Conan lifted his voice and called: "Open the door and let me see him."

The door was opened and a man was framed in it, grasped on either hand by stern-looking men-at-arms. He was a slender man, clad in a dark hooded robe.

"Are you a follower of Asura?" asked Conan.

The man nodded, and the stalwart men-at-arms looked shocked and glanced hesitantly at Trocero.

"The word came southward," said the man. "Beyond the Alimane we cannot aid you, for our sect goes no farther southward, but stretches eastward with the Khorotas. But this I have learned: the thief who took the Heart of Ahriman from Tarascus never reached Kordava. In the mountains of Poitain he was slain by robbers. The jewel fell into the hands of their chief, who, not knowing its true nature, and being harried after the destruction of his band by Poitanian knights, sold it to the Kothic merchant Zorathus."

"Ha!" Conan was on his feet, galvanized. "And what of Zorathus?"

"Four days ago he crossed the Alimane, headed for Argos, with a small band of armed servants."

"He's a fool to cross Zingara in such times," said Trocero.

"Aye, times are troublous across the river. But Zorathus is a bold man, and reckless in his way. He is in great haste to reach Messantia, where he hopes to find a buyer for the jewel. Perhaps he hopes to sell it finally in Stygia. Perhaps he guesses at its true nature. At any rate, instead of following the long road that winds along the borders of Poitain and so at last comes into Argos far from Messantia, he has struck straight across eastern Zingara, following the shorter and more direct route."

Conan smote the table with his clenched fist so that the great board quivered.

"Then, by Crom, fortune has at last thrown the dice for me! A horse, Trocero, and the harness of a Free Companion! Zorathus has a long start, but not too long for me to overtake him, if I follow him to the end of the world!"

12 The Fang of the Dragon

At dawn Conan waded his horse across the shallows of the Alimane and struck the wide caravan trail which ran southeastward, and behind him, on the farther bank, Trocero sat his horse silently at the head of his steel-clad knights, with the crimson leopard of Poitain floating its long folds over him in the morning breeze. Silently they sat, those dark-haired men in shining steel, until the figure of their king had vanished in the blue of distance that whitened toward sunrise.

Conan rode a great black stallion, the gift of Trocero. He no longer wore the armor of Aquilonia. His harness proclaimed him a veteran of the Free Companies, who were of all races. His head piece was a plain morion, dented and battered. The leather and mail mesh of his hauberk were worn and shiny as if by many campaigns, and the scarlet cloak flowing carelessly from his mailed shoulders was tattered and stained. He looked the part of the hired fighting-man, who had known all vicissitudes of fortune, plunder and wealth one day, an empty purse and a close-drawn belt the next.

And more than looking the part, he felt the part; the awakening of old memories, the resurge of the wild, mad, glorious days of old before his feet were set on the imperial path when he was a wandering mercenary, roistering, brawling, guzzling, adventuring, with no thought for the morrow, and no desire save sparkling ale, red lips, and a keen sword to swing on all the battlefields of the world.

Unconsciously he reverted to the old ways; a new swagger became evident in his bearing, in the way he sat his horse; half-forgotten oaths rose naturally to his lips, and as he rode he hummed old songs that he had roared in chorus with his reckless companions in many a tavern and on many a dusty road or bloody field.

It was an unquiet land through which he rode. The companies of cavalry which usually patrolled the river, alert for raids out of Poitain, were nowhere in evidence. Internal strife had left the borders unguarded: The long white road stretched bare from horizon to horizon. No laden camel trains or rumbling wagons or lowing herds moved along it now; only occasional groups of horsemen in leather and steel, hawk-faced, hard-eyed men, who kept together and rode warily. These swept Conan with their searching gaze but rode on, for the solitary rider's harness promised no plunder, but only hard strokes.

Villages lay in ashes and deserted, the fields and meadows idle. Only the boldest would ride the roads these days, and the native population had been decimated in the civil wars, and by raids from across the river. In more peaceful times the road was thronged with merchants riding to Messantia in Argos, or back. But now these found it wiser to follow the road that led east through Poitain, and then turned south down across Argos. It was longer, but safer. Only an extremely reckless man would risk his life and goods on this road through Zingara.

The southern horizon was fringed with flame by night, and in the day straggling pillars of smoke drifted upward; in the cities and plains to the south men were dying, thrones were toppling and castles going up in flames. Conan felt the old tug of the professional fighting-man, to turn his horse and plunge into the fighting, the pillaging and the looting as in the days of old. Why should he toil to regain the rule of a people which had already forgotten him? why chase a will-o'-the-wisp, why pursue a crown that was lost for ever? Why should he not seek forgetfulness, lose himself in the red tides of war and rapine that had engulfed him so often before? Could he not, indeed, carve out another kingdom for himself? The world was entering an age of iron, an age of war and imperialistic ambition; some strong man might well rise above the ruins of nations as a supreme conqueror. Why should it not be himself? So his familiar devil whispered in his ear, and the phantoms of his lawless and bloody past crowded upon him. But he did not turn aside; he rode onward, following a quest that grew dimmer and dimmer as he advanced, until sometimes it seemed that he pursued a dream that never was.

He pushed the black stallion as hard as he dared, but the long white road lay before him, from horizon to horizon. It was a long start Zorathus had, but Conan rode steadily on, knowing that he was traveling faster than the burdened merchants could travel. And so he came to the castle of Count Valbroso, perched like a vulture's eyrie on a bare hill overlooking the road.

Valbroso rode down with his men-at-arms, a lean, dark man with glittering eyes and a predatory beak of a nose. He wore black plate armor and was followed by thirty spearmen, black-mustached hawks of the border wars, as avaricious and ruthless as himself. Of late the toll of the caravans had been slim, and Valbroso cursed the civil wars that stripped the roads of their fat traffic, even while he blessed them for the free hand they allowed him with his neighbors.

He had not hoped much from the solitary rider he had glimpsed from his tower, but all was grist that came to his mill. With a practised eye he took in Conan's worn mail and dark, scarred face, and his conclusions were the same as those of the riders who had passed the Cimmerian on the road—an empty purse and a ready blade.

"Who are you, knave?" he demanded.

"A mercenary, riding for Argos," answered Conan. "What matter names?"

"You are riding in the wrong direction for a Free Companion," grunted Valbroso. "Southward the fighting is good and also the plundering. Join my company. You won't go hungry. The road remains bare of fat merchants to strip, but I mean to take my rogues and fare southward to sell our swords to whichever side seems strongest."

Conan did not at once reply, knowing that if he refused outright, he might be instantly attacked by Valbroso's men-at-arms. Before he could make up his mind, the Zingaran spoke again:

"You rogues of the Free Companies always know tricks to make men talk. I have a prisoner—the last merchant I caught, by Mitra, and the only one I've seen for a week—and the knave is stubborn. He has an iron box, the secret of which defies us, and I've been unable to persuade him to open it. By Ishtar, I thought I knew all the modes of persuasion there are, but perhaps you, as a veteran Free Companion, know some that I do not. At any rate come with me and see what you may do."

Valbroso's words instantly decided Conan. That sounded a great deal like Zorathus. Conan did not know the merchant, but any man who was stubborn enough to try to traverse the Zingaran road in times like these would very probably be stubborn enough to defy torture.

He fell in beside Valbroso and rode up the straggling road to the top of the hill where the gaunt castle stood. As a man-at-arms he should have ridden behind the count, but force of habit made him careless and Valbroso paid no heed. Years of life on the border had taught the count that the frontier is not the royal court. He was aware of the independence of the mercenaries, behind whose swords many a king had trodden the throne-path.

There was a dry moat, half filled with debris in some places. They clattered across the drawbridge and through the arch of the gate. Behind them the portcullis fell with a sullen clang. They came into a bare courtyard, grown with straggling grass, and with a well in the middle. Shacks for the men-at-arms straggled about the bailey wall, and women, slatternly or decked in gaudy finery, looked from the doors. Fighting-men in rusty mail tossed dice on the flags under the arches. It was more like a bandit's hold than the castle of a nobleman.

Valbroso dismounted and motioned Conan to follow him. They went through a doorway and along a vaulted corridor, where they were met by a scarred, hard-looking man in mail descending a stone staircase— evidently the captain of the guard.

"How, Beloso," quoth Valbroso; "has he spoken?"

"He is stubborn," muttered Beloso, shooting a glance of suspicion at Conan.

Valbroso ripped out an oath and stamped furiously up the winding stair, followed by Conan and the captain. As they mounted, the groans of a man in mortal agony became audible. Valbroso's torture-room was high above the court, instead of in a dungeon below. In that chamber, where a gaunt, hairy beast of a man in leather breeks squatted gnawing a beef bone voraciously, stood the machines of torture—racks, boots, hooks and all the implements that the human mind devises to tear flesh, break bones and rend and rupture veins and ligaments.

On a rack a man was stretched naked, and a glance told Conan that he was dying. The unnatural elongation of his limbs and body told of unhinged joints and unnamable ruptures. He was a dark man, with an intelligent, aquiline face and quick dark eyes. They were glazed and bloodshot now with pain, and the dew of agony glistened on his face. His lips were drawn back from blackened gums.

"There is the box." Viciously Valbroso kicked a small but heavy iron chest that stood on the floor near by. It was intricately carved, with tiny skulls and writhing dragons curiously intertwined, but Conan saw no catch or hasp that might serve to unlock the lid. The marks of fire, of ax and sledge and chisel showed on it but as scratches.

"This is the dog's treasure box," said Valbroso angrily. "All men of the south know of Zorathus and his iron chest. Mitra knows what is in it. But he will not give up its secret."

Zorathus! It was true, then; the man he sought lay before him. Conan's heart beat suffocatingly as he leaned over the writhing form, though he exhibited no evidence of his painful eagerness.

"Ease those ropes, knave!" he ordered the torturer harshly, and Valbroso and his captain stared. In the forgetfulness of the moment Conan had used his imperial tone, and the brute in leather instinctively obeyed the knife edge of command in that voice. He eased away gradually, for else the slackening of the ropes had been as great a torment to the torn joints as further stretching.

Catching up a vessel of wine that stood near by, Conan placed the rim to the wretch's lips. Zorathus gulped spasmodically, the liquid slopping over on his heaving breast.

Into the bloodshot eyes came a gleam of recognition, and the froth-smeared lips parted. From them issued a racking whimper in the Kothic tongue.

"Is this death, then? Is the long agony ended? For this is King Conan who died at Valkia, and I am among the dead."

"You're not dead," said Conan. "But you're dying. You'll be tortured no more. I'll see to that. But I can't help you further. Yet before you die, tell me how to open your iron box!"

"My iron box," mumbled Zorathus in delirious disjointed phrases. "The chest forged in unholy fires among the flaming mountains of Khrosha; the metal no chisel can cut. How many treasures has it borne, across the width and the breadth of the world! But no such treasure as it now holds."

"Tell me how to open it," urged Conan. "It can do you no good, and it may aid me."

"Aye, you are Conan," muttered the Kothian. "I have seen you sitting on your throne in the great public hall of Tarantia, with your crown on your head and the scepter in your hand. But you are dead; you died at Valkia. And so I know my own end is at hand."

"What does the dog say?" demanded Valbroso impatiently, not understanding Kothic. "Will he tell us how to open the box?"

As if the voice roused a spark of life in the twisted breast, Zorathus rolled his bloodshot eyes toward the speaker.

"Only Valbroso will I tell," he gasped in Zingaran. "Death is upon me. Lean close to me, Valbroso!"

The count did so, his dark face lit with avarice; behind him his saturnine captain, Beloso, crowded closer.

"Press the seven skulls on the rim, one after another," gasped Zorathus. "Press then the head of the dragon that writhes across the lid. Then press the sphere in the dragon's claws. That will release the secret catch."

"Quick, the box!" cried Valbroso with an oath.

Conan lifted it and set it on a dais, and Valbroso shouldered him aside.

"Let me open it!" cried Beloso, starting forward.

Valbroso cursed him back, his greed blazing in his black eyes.

"None but me shall open it!" he cried.

Conan, whose hand had instinctively gone to his hilt, glanced at Zorathus. The man's eyes were glazed and bloodshot, but they were fixed on Valbroso with burning intensity; and was there the shadow of a grim twisted smile on the dying man's lips? Not until the merchant knew he was dying had he given up the secret. Conan turned to watch Valbroso, even as the dying man watched him.

Along the rim of the lid seven skulls were carved among intertwining branches of strange trees. An inlaid dragon writhed its way across the top of the lid, amid ornate arabesques. Valbroso pressed the skulls in rumbling haste, and as he jammed his thumb down on the carved head of the dragon he swore sharply and snatched his hand away, shaking it in irritation.

"A sharp point on the carvings," he snarled. "I've pricked my thumb."

He pressed the gold ball clutched in the dragon's talons, and the lid flew abruptly open. Their eyes were dazzled by a golden flame. It seemed to their dazed minds that the carven box was full of glowing fire that spilled over the rim and dripped through the air in quivering flakes. Beloso cried out and Valbroso sucked in his breath. Conan stood speechless, his brain snared by the blaze.

"Mitra, what a jewel!" Valbroso's hand dived into the chest, came out with a great pulsing crimson sphere that filled the room with a lambent glow. In its glare Valbroso looked like a corpse. And the dying man on the loosened rack laughed wildly and suddenly.

"Fool!" he screamed. "The jewel is yours! I give you death with it! The scratch on your thumb—look at the dragon's head, Valbroso!"

They all wheeled, stared. Something tiny and dully gleaming stood up from the gaping, carved mouth.

"The dragon's fang!" shrieked Zorathus. "Steeped in the venom of the black Stygian scorpion! Fool, fool to open the box of Zorathus with your naked hand! Death! You are a dead man now!"

And with bloody foam on his lips he died.

Valbroso staggered, crying out. "Ah, Mitra, I burn!" he shrieked. "My veins race with liquid fire! My joints are bursting asunder! Death! Death!" And he reeled and crashed headlong. There was an instant of awful convulsions, in which the limbs were twisted into hideous and unnatural positions, and then in that posture the man froze, his glassy eyes staring sightlessly upward, his lips drawn back from blackened gums.

"Dead!" muttered Conan, stooping to pick up the jewel where it rolled on the floor from Valbroso's rigid hand. It lay on the floor like a quivering pool of sunset fire.

"Dead!" muttered Beloso, with madness in his eyes. And then he moved.

Conan was caught off guard, his eyes dazzled, his brain dazed by the blaze of the great gem. He did not realize Beloso's intention until something crashed with terrible force upon his helmet. The glow of the jewel was splashed with redder flame, and he went to his knees under the blow.

He heard a rush of feet, a bellow of oxlike agony. He was stunned but not wholly senseless, and realized that Beloso had caught up the iron box and crashed it down on his head as he stooped. Only his basinet had saved his skull. He staggered up, drawing his sword, trying to shake the dimness out of his eyes. The room swam to his dizzy gaze. But the door was open and fleet footsteps were dwindling down the winding stair. On the floor the brutish torturer was gasping out his life with a great gash under his breast. And the Heart of Ahriman was gone.

Conan reeled out of the chamber, sword in hand, blood streaming down his face from under his burganet. He ran drunkenly down the steps, hearing a clang of steel in the courtyard below, shouts, then the frantic drum of hoofs. Rushing into the bailey he saw the men-at-arms milling about confusedly, while women screeched. The postern gate stood open and a soldier lay across his pike with his head split. Horses, still bridled and saddled, ran neighing about the court, Conan's black stallion among them.

"He's mad!" howled a woman, wringing her hands as she rushed brainlessly about. "He came out of the castle like a mad dog, hewing right and left! Beloso's mad! Where's Lord Valbroso?"

"Which way did he go?" roared Conan. All turned and stared at the stranger's bloodstained face and naked sword. "Through the postern!" shrilled a woman, pointing eastward, and another bawled: "Who is this rogue?"

"Beloso has killed Valbroso!" yelled Conan, leaping and seizing the stallion's mane, as the men-at-arms advanced uncertainly on him. A wild outcry burst forth at his news, but their reaction was exactly as he had anticipated. Instead of closing the gates to take him prisoner, or pursuing the fleeing slayer to avenge their lord, they were thrown into even greater confusion by his words. Wolves bound together only by fear of Valbroso, they owed no allegiance to the castle or to each other. Swords began to clash in the courtyard, and women screamed. And in the midst of it all, none noticed Conan as he shot through the postern gate and thundered down the hill. The wide plain spread before him, and beyond the hill the caravan road divided: one branch ran south, the other east. And on the eastern road he saw another rider, bending low and spurring hard. The plain swam to Conan's gaze, the sunlight was a thick red haze and he reeled in his saddle, grasping the flowing mane with his hand. Blood rained on his mail, but grimly he urged the stallion on.

Behind him smoke began to pour out of the castle on the hill where the count's body lay forgotten and unheeded beside that of his prisoner. The sun was setting; against a lurid red sky the two black figures fled. The stallion was not fresh, but neither was the horse ridden by Beloso. But the great beast responded mightily, calling on deep reservoirs of reserve vitality.

Why the Zingaran fled from one pursuer, Conan did not tax his bruised brain to guess. Perhaps unreasoning panic rode Beloso, born of the madness that lurked in that blazing jewel. The sun was gone; the white road was a dim glimmer through a ghostly twilight fading into purple gloom far ahead of him. The stallion panted, laboring hard. The country was changing, in the gathering dusk. Bare plains gave way to clumps of oaks and alders. Low hills mounted up in the distance. Stars began to blink out. The stallion gasped and reeled in his course. But ahead rose a dense wood that stretched to the hills on the horizon, and between it and himself Conan glimpsed the dim form of the fugitive. He urged on the distressed stallion, for he saw that he was overtaking his prey, yard by yard. Above the pounding of the hoofs a strange cry rose from the shadows, but neither pursuer nor pursued gave heed.

As they swept in under the branches that overhung the road, they were almost side by side. A fierce cry rose from Conan's lips as his sword went up; a pale oval of a face was turned toward him, a sword gleamed in a half-seen hand, and Beloso echoed the cry—and then the weary stallion, with a lurch and a groan, missed his footing in the shadows and went heels over head, hurling his dazed rider from the saddle. Conan's throbbing head crashed against a stone, and the stars were blotted out in a thicker night.

How long Conan lay senseless he never knew. His first sensation of returning consciousness was that of being dragged by one arm over rough and stony ground, and through dense underbrush. Then he was thrown carelessly down, and perhaps the jolt brought back his senses.

His helmet was gone, his head ached abominably, he felt a qualm of nausea, and blood was clotted thickly among his black locks. But with the vitality of a wild thing, life and consciousness surged back into him, and he became aware of his surroundings.

A broad red moon was shining through the trees, by which he knew that it was long after midnight. He had lain senseless for hours, long enough to have recovered from that terrible blow Beloso had dealt him, as well as the fall which had rendered him senseless. His brain felt clearer than it had felt during that mad ride after the fugitive.

He was not lying beside the white road, he noticed with a start of surprize, as his surroundings began to record themselves on his perceptions. The road was nowhere in sight. He lay on the grassy earth, in a small glade hemmed in by a black wall of tree stems and tangled branches. His face and hands were scratched and lacerated as if he had been dragged through brambles. Shifting his body he looked about him. And then he started violently—something was squatting over him.

At first Conan doubted his consciousness, thought it was but a figment of delirium. Surely it could not be real, that strange, motionless gray being that squatted on its haunches and stared down at him with unblinking soulless eyes.

Conan lay and stared, half expecting it to vanish like a figure of a dream, and then a chill of recollection crept along his spine. Half-forgotten memories surged back, of grisly tales whispered of the shapes that haunted these uninhabited forests at the foot of the hills that mark the Zingaran-Argossean border. Ghouls, men called them, eaters of human flesh, spawn of darkness, children of unholy matings of a lost and forgotten race with the demons of the underworld. Somewhere in these primitive forests were the ruins of an ancient, accursed city, men whispered, and among its tombs slunk gray, anthropomorphic shadows—Conan shuddered strongly.

He lay staring at the malformed head that rose dimly above him, and cautiously he extended a hand toward the sword at his hip. With a horrible cry that the man involuntarily echoed, the monster was at his throat.

Conan threw up his right arm, and the doglike jaws closed on it, driving the mail links into the hard flesh. The misshapen yet manlike hands clutched for his throat, but he evaded them with a heave and roll of his whole body, at the same time drawing his dagger with his left hand.

They tumbled over and over on the grass, smiting and tearing. The muscles coiling under that gray corpselike skin were stringy and hard as steel wires, exceeding the strength of a man. But Conan's thews were iron too, and his mail saved him from the gnashing fangs and ripping claws long enough for him to drive home his dagger, again and again and again. The horrible vitality of the semihuman monstrosity seemed inexhaustible, and the king's skin crawled at the feel of that slick, clammy flesh. He put all his loathing and savage revulsion behind the plunging blade, and suddenly the monster heaved up convulsively beneath him as the point found its grisly heart, and then lay still.

Conan rose, shaken with nausea. He stood in the center of the glade uncertainly, sword in one hand and dagger in the other. He had not lost his instinctive sense of direction, as far as the points of the compass were concerned, but he did not know in which direction the road lay. He had no way of knowing in which direction the ghoul had dragged him. Conan glared at the silent, black, moon-dappled woods which ringed him, and felt cold moisture bead his flesh. He was without a horse and lost in these haunted woods, and that staring, deformed thing at his feet was a mute evidence of the horrors that lurked in the forest. He stood almost holding his breath in his painful intensity, straining his ears for some crack of twig or rustle of grass.

When a sound did come he started violently. Suddenly out on the night air broke the scream of a terrified horse. His stallion! There were panthers in the wood-or-ghouls ate beasts as well as men.

He broke savagely through the brush in the direction of the sound, whistling shrilly as he ran, his fear drowned in berserk rage. If his horse was killed, there went his last chance of following Beloso and recovering the jewel. Again the stallion screamed with fear and fury, somewhere nearer. There was a sound of lashing heels, and something that was struck heavily and gave way.

Conan burst out into the wide white road without warning, and saw the stallion plunging and rearing in the moonlight, his ears laid back, his eyes and teeth flashing wickedly. He lashed out with his heels at a slinking shadow that ducked and bobbed about him—and then about Conan other shadows moved: gray, furtive shadows that closed in on all sides. A hideous charnel-house scent reeked up in the night air.

With a curse the king hewed right and left with his broadsword, thrust and ripped with his dagger. Dripping fangs flashed in the moonlight, foul paws caught at him, but he hacked his way through to the stallion, caught the rein, leaped into the saddle. His sword rose and fell, a frosty arc in the moon, showering blood as it split misshapen heads, clove shambling bodies. The stallion reared, biting and kicking. They burst through and thundered down the road. On either hand, for a short space, flitted gray abhorrent shadows. Then these fell behind, and Conan, topping a wooded crest, saw a vast expanse of bare slopes sweeping up and away before him.

13 "A Ghost Out of the Past"

Soon after sunrise Conan crossed the Argossean border. Of Beloso he had seen no trace. Either the captain had made good his escape while the king lay senseless, or had fallen prey to the grim man-eaters of the Zingaran forest. But Conan had seen no signs to indicate the latter possibility. The fact that he had lain unmolested for so long seemed to indicate that the monsters had been engrossed in futile pursuit of the captain. And if the man lived, Conan felt certain that he was riding along the road somewhere ahead of him. Unless he had intended going into Argos he would never have taken the eastward road in the first place.

The helmeted guards at the frontier did not question the Cimmerian. A single wandering mercenary required no passport nor safe-conduct, especially when his unadorned mail showed him to be in the service of no lord. Through the low, grassy hills where streams murmured and oak groves dappled the sward with lights and shadows he rode, following the long road that rose and fell away ahead of him over dales and rises in the blue distance. It was an old, old road, this highway from Poitain to the sea.

Argos was at peace; laden ox-wains rumbled along the road, and men with bare, brown, brawny arms toiled in orchards and fields that smiled away under the branches of the roadside trees. Old men on settles before inns under spreading oak branches called greetings to the wayfarer.

From the men that worked the fields, from the garrulous old men in the inns where he slaked his thirst with great leathern jacks of foaming ale, from the sharp-eyed silk-clad merchants he met upon the road, Conan sought for news of Beloso.

Stories were conflicting, but this much Conan learned: that a lean, wiry Zingaran with the dangerous black eyes and mustaches of the western folk was somewhere on the road ahead of him, and apparently making for Messantia. It was a logical destination; all the seaports of Argos were cosmopolitan, in strong contrast with the inland provinces, and Messantia was the most polyglot of all. Craft of all the maritime nations rode in its harbor, and refugees and fugitives from many lands gathered there. Laws were lax; for Messantia thrived on the trade of the sea, and her citizens found it profitable to be somewhat blind in their dealings with seamen. It was not only legitimate trade that flowed into Messantia; smugglers and buccaneers played their part. All this Conan knew well, for had he not, in the days of old when he was a Barachan pirate, sailed by night into the harbor of Messantia to discharge strange cargoes? Most of the pirates of the Barachan Isles—small islands on the southwestern coast of Zingara—were Argossean sailors, and as long as they confined their attentions to the shipping of other nations, the authorities of Argos were not too strict in their interpretation of sea-laws.

But Conan had not limited his activities to those of the Barachans. He had also sailed with the Zingaran buccaneers, and even with those wild black corsairs that swept up from the far south to harry the northern coasts, and this put him beyond the pale of any law. If he were recognized in any of the ports of Argos it would cost him his head. But without hesitation he rode on to Messantia, halting day or night only to rest the stallion and to snatch a few winks of sleep for himself.

He entered the city unquestioned, merging himself with the throngs that poured continually in and out of this great commercial center. No walls surrounded Messantia. The sea and the ships of the sea guarded the great southern trading city.

It was evening when Conan rode leisurely through the streets that marched down to the waterfront. At the ends of these streets he saw the wharves and the masts and sails of ships. He smelled salt water for the first time in years, heard the thrum of cordage and the creak of spars in the breeze that was kicking up whitecaps out beyond the headlands. Again the urge of far wandering tugged at his heart.

But he did not go on to the wharves. He reined aside and rode up a steep flight of wide, worn stone steps, to a broad street where ornate white mansions overlooked the waterfront and the harbor below. Here dwelt the men who had grown rich from the hard-won fat of the seas-a few old sea-captains who had found treasure afar, many traders and merchants who never trod the naked decks nor knew the roar of tempest of sea-fight.

Conan turned in his horse at a certain gold-worked gate, and rode into a court where a fountain tinkled and pigeons fluttered from marble coping to marble flagging. A page in jagged silken jupon and hose came forward inquiringly. The merchants of Messantia dealt with many strange and rough characters but most of these smacked of the sea. It was strange that a mercenary trooper should so freely ride into the court of a lord of commerce.

"The merchant Publio dwells here?" It was more statement than question, and something in the timbre of the voice caused the page to doff his feathered chaperon as he bowed and replied:

"Aye, so he does, my captain."

Conan dismounted and the page called a servitor, who came running to receive the stallion's rein.

"Your master is within?" Conan drew off his gauntlets and slapped the dust of the road from cloak and mail.

"Aye, my captain. Whom shall I announce?"

"I'll announce myself," grunted Conan. "I know the way well enough. Bide you here."

And obeying that peremptory command the page stood still, staring after Conan as the latter climbed a short flight of marble steps, and wondering what connection his master might have with this giant fighting-man who had the aspect of a northern barbarian.

Menials at their tasks halted and gaped open-mouthed as Conan crossed a wide, cool balcony overlooking the court and entered a broad corridor through which the sea-breeze swept. Half-way down this he heard a quill scratching, and turned into a broad room whose many wide casements overlooked the harbor.

Publio sat at a carved teakwood desk writing on rich parchment with a golden quill. He was a short man, with a massive head and quick dark eyes. His blue robe was of the finest watered silk, trimmed with cloth-of-gold, and from his thick white throat hung a heavy gold chain.

As the Cimmerian entered, the merchant looked up with a gesture of annoyance. He froze in the midst of his gesture. His mouth opened; he stared as at a ghost out of the past. Unbelief and fear glimmered in his wide eyes. "Well," said Conan, "have you no word of greeting, Publio?"

Publio moistened his lips.

"Conan!" he whispered incredulously. "Mitra! Conan! Amra!"

"Who else?"

The Cimmerian unclasped his cloak and threw it with his gauntlets down upon the desk. "How, man?" he exclaimed irritably. "Can't you at least offer me a beaker of wine? My throat's caked with the dust of the highway."

"Aye, wine!" echoed Publio mechanically. Instinctively his hand reached for a gong, then recoiled as from a hot coal, and he shuddered.

While Conan watched him with a flicker of grim amusement in his eyes, the merchant rose and hurriedly shut the door, first craning his neck up and down the corridor to be sure that no slave was loitering about. Then, returning, he took a gold vessel of wine from a near-by table and was about to fill a slender goblet when Conan impatiently took the vessel from him and lifting it with both hands, drank deep and with gusto.

"Aye, it's Conan, right enough," muttered Publio. "Man, are you mad?"

"By Crom, Publio," said Conan, lowering the vessel but retaining it in his hands, "you dwell in different quarters than of old. It takes an Argossean merchant to wring wealth out of a little waterfront shop that stank of rotten fish and cheap wine."

"The old days are past," muttered Publio, drawing his robe about him with a slight involuntary shudder. "I have put off the past like a worn-out cloak."

"Well," retorted Conan, "you can't put me off like an old cloak. It isn't much I want of you, but that much I do want. And you can't refuse me. We had too many dealings in the old days. Am I such a fool that I'm not aware that this fine mansion was built on my sweat and blood? How many cargoes from my galleys passed through your shop?"

"All merchants of Messantia have dealt with the sea-rovers at one time or another," mumbled Publio nervously.

"But not with the black corsairs," answered Conan grimly.

"For Mitra's sake, be silent!" ejaculated Publio, sweat starting out on his brow. His fingers jerked at the gilt-worked edge of his robe.

"Well, I only wished to recall it to your mind," answered Conan. "Don't be so fearful. You took plenty of risks in the past, when you were struggling for life and wealth in that lousy little shop down by the wharves, and were hand-and-glove with every buccaneer and smuggler and pirate from here to the Barachan Isles. Prosperity must have softened you."

"I am respectable," began Publio.

"Meaning you're rich as hell," snorted Conan. "Why? Why did you grow wealthy so much quicker than your competitors? Was it because you did a big business in ivory and ostrich feathers, copper and skins and pearls and hammered gold ornaments, and other things from the coast of Kush? And where did you get them so cheaply, while other merchants were paying their weight in silver to the Stygians for them? I'll tell you, in case you've forgotten: you bought them from me, at considerably less than their value, and I took them from the tribes of the Black Coast, and from the ships of the Stygians—I, and the black corsairs."

"In Mitra's name, cease!" begged Publio. "I have not forgotten. But what are you doing here? I am the only man in Argos who knew that the king of Aquilonia was once Conan the buccaneer, in the old days. But word has come southward of the overthrow of Aquilonia and the death of the king."

"My enemies have killed me a hundred times by rumors," grunted Conan. "Yet here I sit and guzzle wine of Kyros." And he suited the action to the word.

Lowering the vessel, which was now nearly empty, he said: "It's but a small thing I ask of you, Publio. I know that you're aware of everything that goes on in Messantia. I want to know if a Zingaran named Beloso, or he might call himself anything, is in this city. He's tall and lean and dark like all his race, and it's likely he'll seek to sell a very rare jewel." Publio shook his head.

"I have not heard of such a man. But thousands come and go in Messantia. If he is here my agents will discover him."

"Good. Send them to look for him. And in the meantime have my horse cared for, and food served me here in this room."

Publio assented volubly, and Conan emptied the wine vessel, tossed it carelessly into a corner, and strode to a near-by casement, involuntarily expanding his chest as he breathed deep of the salt air. He was looking down upon the meandering waterfront streets. He swept the ships in the harbor with an appreciative glance, then lifted his head and stared beyond the bay, far into the blue haze of the distance where sea met sky. And his memory sped beyond that horizon, to the golden seas of the south, under flaming suns, where laws were not and life ran hotly. Some vagrant scent of spice or palm woke clear-etched images of strange coasts where mangroves grew and drums thundered, of ships locked in battle and decks running blood, of smoke and flame and the crying of slaughter. Lost in his thoughts he scarcely noticed when Publio stole from the chamber.

Gathering up his robe, the merchant hurried along the corridors until he came to a certain chamber where a tall, gaunt man with a scar upon his temple wrote continually upon parchment. There was something about this man which made his clerkly occupation seem incongruous. To him Publio spoke abruptly:

"Conan has returned!"

"Conan?" The gaunt man started up and the quill fell from his fingers. "The corsair?"

"Aye!"

The gaunt man went livid. "Is he mad? If he is discovered here we are ruined! They will hang a man who shelters or trades with a corsair as quickly as they'll hang the corsair himself! What if the governor should learn of our past connections with him?"

"He will not learn," answered Publio grimly. "Send your men into the markets and wharfside dives and learn if one Beloso, a Zingaran, is in Messantia. Conan said he had a gem, which he will probably seek to dispose of. The jewel merchants should know of him, if any do. And here is another task for you: pick up a dozen or so desperate villains who can be trusted to do away with a man and hold their tongues afterward. You understand me?"

"I understand." The other nodded slowly and somberly.

"I have not stolen, cheated, lied and fought my way up from the gutter to be undone now by a ghost out of my past," muttered Publio, and the sinister darkness of his countenance at that moment would have surprized the wealthy nobles and ladies, who bought their silks and pearls from his many stalls. But when he returned to Conan a short time later, bearing in his own hands a platter of fruit and meats, he presented a placid face to his unwelcome guest.

Conan still stood at the casement, staring down into the harbor at the purple and crimson and vermilion and scarlet sails of galleons and carracks and galleys and dromonds.

"There's a Stygian galley, if I'm not blind," he remarked, pointing to a long, low, slim black ship lying apart from the others, anchored off the low broad sandy beach that curved round to the distant headland. "Is there peace, then, between Stygia and Argos?"

"The same sort that has existed before," answered Publio, setting the platter on the table with a sigh of relief, for it was heavily laden; he knew his guest of old. "Stygian ports are temporarily open to our ships, as ours to theirs. But may no craft of mine meet their cursed galleys out of sight of land! That galley crept into the bay last night. What its masters wish I do not know. So far they have neither bought nor sold. I distrust those dark-skinned devils. Treachery had its birth in that dusky land."

"I've made them howl," said Conan carelessly, turning from the window. "In my galley manned by black corsairs I crept to the very bastions of the sea-washed castles of black-walled Khemi by night, and burned the galleons anchored there. And speaking of treachery, mine host, suppose you taste these viands and sip a bit of this wine, just to show me that your heart is on the right side."

Publio complied so readily that Conan's suspicions were lulled, and without further hesitation he sat down and devoured enough for three men.

And while he ate, men moved through the markets and along the waterfront, searching for a Zingaran who had a jewel to sell or—who sought for a ship to carry him to foreign ports. And a tall gaunt man with a scar on his temple sat with his elbows on a wine-stained table in a squalid cellar with a brass lantern hanging from a smoke-blackened beam overhead, and held converse with the desperate rogues whose sinister countenances and ragged garments proclaimed their profession.

And as the first stars blinked out, they shone on a strange band spurring their mounts along the white road that led to Messantia from the west. They were four men, tall, gaunt, clad in black, hooded robes, and they did not speak. They forced their steeds mercilessly onward, and those steeds were gaunt as themselves, and sweat-stained and weary as if from long travel and far wandering.

14 The Black Hand of Set

Conan woke from a sound sleep as quickly and instantly as a cat. And like a cat he was on his feet with his sword out before the man who had touched him could so much as draw back.

"What word, Publio?" demanded Conan, recognizing his host. The gold lamp burned low, casting a mellow glow over the thick tapestries and the rich coverings of the couch whereon he had been reposing.

Publio, recovering from the start given him by the sudden action of his awakening guest, replied: "The Zingaran has been located. He arrived yesterday, at dawn. Only a few hours ago he sought to sell a huge, strange jewel to a Shemitish merchant, but the Shemite would have naught to do with it. Men say he turned pale beneath his black beard at the sight of it, and closing his stall, fled as from a thing accursed."

"It must be Beloso," muttered Conan, feeling the pulse in his temples pounding with impatient eagerness. "Where is he now?"

"He sleeps in the house of Servio."

"I know that dive of old," grunted Conan. "I'd better hasten before some of these waterfront thieves cut his throat for the jewel."

He took up his cloak and flung it over his shoulders, then donned a helmet Publio had procured for him.

"Have my steed saddled and ready in the court," said he. "I may return in haste. I shall not forget this night's work, Publio."

A few moments later Publio, standing at a small outer door, watched the king's tall figure receding down the shadowy street.

"Farewell to you, corsair," muttered the merchant. "This must be a notable jewel, to be sought by a man who has just lost a kingdom. I wish I had told my knaves to let him secure it before they did their work. But then, something might have gone awry. Let Argos forget Amra, and let my dealings with him be lost in the dust of the past. In the alley behind the house of Servio—that is where Conan will cease to be a peril to me."

Servio's house, a dingy, ill-famed den, was located close to the wharves, facing the waterfront. It was a shambling building of stone and heavy ship-beams, and a long narrow alley wandered up alongside it. Conan made his way along the alley, and as he reached the house he had an uneasy feeling that he was being spied upon. He stared hard into the shadows of the squalid buildings, but saw nothing, though once he caught the faint rasp of cloth or leather against flesh. But that was nothing unusual. Thieves and beggars prowled these alleys all night, and they were not likely to attack him, after one look at his size and harness.

But suddenly a door opened in the wall ahead of him, and he slipped into the shadow of an arch. A figure emerged from the open door and moved along the alley, not furtively, but with a natural noiselessness, like that of a jungle beast. Enough starlight filtered into the alley to silhouette the man's profile dimly as he passed the doorway where Conan lurked. The stranger was a Stygian. There was no mistaking that hawk-faced, shaven head, even in the starlight, nor the mantle over the broad shoulders. He passed on down the alley in the direction of the beach, and once Conan thought he must be carrying a lantern among his garments, for he caught a flash of lambent light, just as the man vanished.

But the Cimmerian forgot the stranger as he noticed that the door through which he had emerged still stood open. Conan had intended entering by the main entrance and forcing Servio to show him the room where the Zingaran slept. But if he could get into the house without attracting anyone's attention, so much the better.

A few long strides brought him to the door, and as his hands fell on the lock he stifled an involuntary grunt. His practised fingers, skilled among the thieves of Zamora long ago, told him that the lock had been forced, apparently by some terrific pressure from the outside that had twisted and bent the heavy iron bolts, tearing the very sockets loose from the jambs. How such damage could have been wrought so violently without awakening everyone in the neighborhood Conan could not imagine, but he felt sure that it had been done that night. A broken lock, if discovered, would not go unmended in the house of Servio, in this neighborhood of thieves and cutthroats.

Conan entered stealthily, poniard in hand, wondering how he was to find the chamber of the Zingaran. Groping in total darkness he halted suddenly. He sensed death in that room, as a wild beast senses it—not as peril threatening him, but a dead thing, something freshly slain. In the darkness his foot hit and recoiled from something heavy and yielding. With a sudden premonition he groped along the wall until he found the shelf that supported the brass lamp, with its flint, steel and tinder beside it. A few seconds later a flickering, uncertain light sprang up, and he stared narrowly about him.

A bunk built against the rough stone wall, a bare table and a bench completed the furnishings of the squalid chamber. An inner door stood closed and bolted. And on the hard-beaten dirt floor lay Beloso. On his back he lay, with his head drawn back between his shoulders so that he seemed to stare with his wide glassy eyes at the sooty beams of the cobwebbed ceiling. His lips were drawn back from his teeth in a frozen grin of agony. His sword lay near him, still in its scabbard. His shirt was torn open, and on his brown, muscular breast was the print of a black hand, thumb and four fingers plainly distinct.

Conan glared in silence, feeling the short hairs bristle at the back of his neck.

"Crom!" he muttered. "The black hand of Set!"

He had seen that mark of old, the death-mark of the black priests of Set, the grim cult that ruled in dark Stygia. And suddenly he remembered that curious flash he had seen emanating from the mysterious Stygian who had emerged from this chamber.

"The Heart, by Crom!" he muttered. "He was carrying it under his mantle. He stole it. He burst that door by his magic, and slew Beloso. He was a priest of Set."

A quick investigation confirmed at least part of his suspicions. The jewel was not on the Zingaran's body. An uneasy feeling rose in Conan that this had not happened by chance, or without design; a conviction that the mysterious Stygian galley had come into the harbor of Messantia on a definite mission. How could the priests of Set know that the Heart had come southward? Yet the thought was no more fantastic than the necromancy that could slay an armed man by the touch of an open, empty hand.

A stealthy footfall outside the door brought him round like a great cat. With one motion he extinguished the lamp and drew his sword. His ears told him that men were out there in the darkness, were closing in on the doorway. As his eyes became accustomed to the sudden darkness, he could make out dim figures ringing the entrance. He could not guess their identity, but as always he took the initiative—leaping suddenly forth from the doorway without awaiting the attack.

His unexpected movement took the skulkers by surprise. He sensed and heard men close about him, saw a dim masked figure in the starlight before him; then his sword crunched home, and he was fleeting away down the alley before the slower-thinking and slower-acting attackers could intercept him.

As he ran he heard, somewhere ahead of him, a faint creak of oarlocks, and he forgot the men behind him. A boat was moving out into the bay! Gritting his teeth he increased his speed, but before he reached the beach he heard the rasp and creak of ropes, and the grind of the great sweep in its socket.

Thick clouds, rolling up from the sea, obscured the stars. In thick darkness Conan came upon the strand, straining his eyes out across the black restless water. Something was moving out there—a long, low, black shape that receded in the darkness, gathering momentum as it went. To his ears came the rhythmical clack of long oars. He ground his teeth in helpless fury. It was the Stygian galley and she was racing out to sea, bearing with her the jewel that meant to him the throne of Aquilonia.

With a savage curse he took a step toward the waves that lapped against the sands, catching at his hauberk and intending to rip it off and swim after the vanishing ship. Then the crunch of a heel in the sand brought him about. He had forgotten his pursuers.

Dark figures closed in on him with a rush of feet through the sands. The first went down beneath the Cimmerian's flailing sword, but the others did not falter. Blades whickered dimly about him in the darkness or rasped on his mail. Blood and entrails spilled over his hand and someone screamed as he ripped murderously upward. A muttered voice spurred on the attack, and that voice sounded vaguely familiar. Conan plowed through the clinging, hacking shapes toward the voice. A faint light gleaming momentarily through the drifting clouds showed him a tall gaunt man with a great livid scar on his temple. Conan's sword sheared through his skull as through a ripe melon.

Then an ax, swung blindly in the dark, crashed on the king's basinet, filling his eyes with sparks of fire. He lurched and lunged, felt his sword sink deep and heard a shriek of agony. Then he stumbled over a corpse, and a bludgeon knocked the dented helmet from his head; the next instant the club fell full on his unprotected skull.

The king of Aquilonia crumpled into the wet sands. Over him wolfish figures panted in the gloom.

"Strike off his head," muttered one.

"Let him be," grunted another. "Help me tie up my wounds before I bleed to death. The tide will wash him into the bay. See, he fell at the water's edge. His skull's split; no man could live after such blows."

"Help me strip him," urged another. "His harness will fetch a few pieces of silver. And haste. Tiberio is dead, and I hear seamen singing as they reel along the strand. Let us be gone."

There followed hurried activity in the darkness, and then the sound of quickly receding footsteps. The tipsy singing of the seamen grew louder.

In his chamber Publio, nervously pacing back and forth before a window that overlooked the shadowed bay, whirled suddenly, his nerves tingling. To the best of his knowledge the door had been bolted from within; but now it stood open and four men filed into the chamber. At the sight of them his flesh crawled. Many strange beings Publio had seen in his lifetime, but none before like these. They were tall and gaunt, black-robed, and their faces were dim yellow ovals in the shadows of their coifs. He could not tell much about their features and was unreasoningly glad that he could not. Each bore a long, curiously molded staff.

"Who are you?" he demanded, and his voice sounded brittle and hollow. "What do you wish here?"

"Where is Conan, he who was king of Aquilonia?" demanded the tallest of the four in a passionless monotone that made Publio shudder. It was like the hollow tone of a Khitan temple bell.

"I do not know what you mean," stammered the merchant, his customary poise shaken by the uncanny aspect of his visitors. "I know no such man."

"He has been here," returned the other with no change of inflection. "His horse is in the courtyard. Tell us where he is before we do you an injury."

"Gebal!" shouted Publio frantically, recoiling until he crouched against the wall. "Gebal!"

The four Khitans watched him without emotion or change of expression.

"If you summon your slave, he will die," warned one of them, which only served to terrify Publio more than ever.

"Gebal!" he screamed. "Where are you, curse you? Thieves are murdering your master!"

Swift footsteps in the corridor outside, and Gebal burst into the chamber—a Shemite, of medium height and mightily muscled build, his curled blue-black beard bristling, and a short leaf-shaped sword in his hand.

He stared in stupid amazement at the four invaders, unable to understand their presence; dimly remembering that he had drowsed unexplainably on the stair he was guarding and up which they must have come. He had never slept on duty before. But his master was shrieking with a note of hysteria in his voice, and the Shemite drove like a bull at the strangers, his thickly muscled arm drawing back for the disemboweling thrust. But the stroke was never dealt.

A black-sleeved arm shot out, extending the long staff. Its end but touched the Shemite's brawny breast and was instantly withdrawn. The stroke was horribly like the dart and recovery of a serpent's head.

Gebal halted short in his headlong plunge, as if he had encountered a solid barrier. His bull head toppled forward on his breast, the sword slipped from his fingers, and then he melted slowly to the floor. It was as if all the bones of his frame had suddenly become flabby. Publio turned sick.

"Do not shout again," advised the tallest Khitan. "Your servants sleep soundly, but if you awaken them they will die, and you with them. Where is Conan?"

"He is gone to the house of Servio, near the waterfront, to search for the Zingaran Beloso," gasped Publio, all his power of resistance gone out of him. The merchant did not lack courage; but these uncanny visitants turned his marrow to water. He started convulsively at a sudden noise of footsteps hurrying up the stair outside, loud in the ominous stillness.

"Your servant?" asked the Khitan.

Publio shook his head mutely, his tongue frozen to his palate. He could not speak.

One of the Khitans caught up a silken cover from a couch and threw it over the corpse. Then they melted behind the tapestry, but before the tallest man disappeared, he murmured: "Talk to this man who comes, and send him away quickly. If you betray us, neither he nor you will live to reach that door. Make no sign to show him that you are not alone." And lifting his staff suggestively, the yellow man faded behind the hangings.

Publio shuddered and choked down a desire to retch. It might have been a trick of the light, but it seemed to him that occasionally those staffs moved slightly of their own accord, as if possessed of an unspeakable life of their own.

He pulled himself together with a mighty effort, and presented a composed aspect to the ragged ruffian who burst into the chamber.

"We have done as you wished, my lord," this man exclaimed. "The barbarian lies dead on the sands at the water's edge."

Publio felt a movement in the arras behind him, and almost burst from fright. The man swept heedlessly on.

"Your secretary, Tiberio, is dead. The barbarian slew him, and four of my companions. We bore their bodies to the rendezvous. There was nothing of value on the barbarian except a few silver coins. Are there any further orders?"

"None!" gasped Publio, white about the lips. "Go!"

The desperado bowed and hurried out, with a vague feeling that Publio was both a man of weak stomach and few words.

The four Khitans came from behind the arras.

"Of whom did this man speak?" the taller demanded.

"Of a wandering stranger who did me an injury," panted Publio.

"You lie," said the Khitan calmly. "He spoke of the king of Aquilonia. I read it in your expression. Sit upon that divan and do not move or speak. I will remain with you while my three companions go search for the body."

So Publio sat and shook with terror of the silent, inscrutable figure which watched him, until the three Khitans filed back into the room, with the news that Conan's body did not lie upon the sands. Publio did not know whether to be glad or sorry.

"We found the spot where the fight was fought," they said. "Blood was on the sand. But the king was gone."

The fourth Khitan drew imaginary symbols upon the carpet with his staff, which glistened scalily in the lamplight.

"Did you read naught from the sands?" he asked.

"Aye," they answered. "The king lives, and he has gone southward in a ship."

The tall Khitan lifted his head and gazed at Publio, so that the merchant broke into a profuse sweat.

"What do you wish of me?" he stuttered.

"A ship," answered the Khitan. "A ship well manned for a very long voyage."

"For how long a voyage?" stammered Publio, never thinking of refusing.

"To the ends of the world, perhaps," answered the Khitan, "or to the molten seas of hell that lie beyond the sunrise."

15 The Return of the Corsair

Conan's first sensation of returning consciousness was that of motion; under him was no solidity, but a ceaseless heaving and plunging. Then he heard wind humming through cords and spars, and knew he was aboard a ship even before his blurred sight cleared. He heard a mutter of voices and then a dash of water deluged him, jerking him sharply into full animation. He heaved up with a sulfurous curse, braced his legs and glared about him, with a burst of coarse guffaws in his ears and the reek of unwashed bodies in his nostrils.

He was standing on the poop-deck of a long galley, which was running before the wind that whipped down from the north, her striped sail bellying against the taut sheets. The sun was just rising, in a dazzling blaze of gold and blue and green. To the left of the shoreline was a dim purple shadow. To the right stretched the open ocean. This much Conan saw at a glance that likewise included the ship itself.

It was long and narrow, a typical trading ship of the southern coasts, high of poop and stern, with cabins at either extremity. Conan looked down into the open waist, whence wafted that sickening abominable odor. He knew it of old. It was the body scent of the oarsmen, chained to their benches. They were all negroes, forty men to each side, each confined by a chain locked about his waist, with the other end welded to a heavy ring set deep in the solid runway beam that ran between the benches from stem to stern. The life of a slave aboard an Argossean galley was a hell unfathomable. Most of these were Kushites, but some thirty of the blacks who now rested on their idle oars and stared up at the stranger with dull curiosity were from the far southern isles, the homelands of the corsairs. Conan recognized them by their straighter features and hair, their rangier, cleaner-limbed build. And he saw among them men who had followed him of old.

But all this he saw and recognized in one swift, all-embracing glance as he rose, before he turned his attention to the figures about him. Reeling momentarily on braced legs, his fists clenched wrathfully, he glared at the figures clustered about him. The sailor who had drenched him stood grinning, the empty bucket still poised in his hand, and Conan cursed him with venom, instinctively reaching for his hilt. Then he discovered that he was weaponless and naked except for his short leather breeks.

"What lousy tub is this?" he roared. "How did I come aboard here?"

The sailors laughed jeeringly—stocky, bearded Argosseans to a man—and one, whose richer dress and air of command proclaimed him captain, folded his arms and said domineeringly:

"We found you lying on the sands. Somebody had rapped you on the pate and taken your clothes. Needing an extra man, we brought you aboard."

"What ship is this?" Conan demanded.

"The *Venturer*, out of Messantia, with a cargo of mirrors, scarlet silk cloaks, shields, gilded helmets and swords to trade to the Shemites for copper and gold ore. I am Demetrio, captain of this vessel and your master henceforward."

"Then I'm headed in the direction I wanted to go, after all," muttered Conan, heedless of that last remark. They were racing southeastward, following the long curve of the Argossean coast. These trading ships never ventured far from the shoreline. Somewhere ahead of him he knew that low dark Stygian galley was speeding southward.

"Have you sighted a Stygian galley—" began Conan, but the beard of the burly, brutal-faced captain bristled. He was not in the least interested in any question his prisoner might wish to ask, and felt it high time he reduced this independent wastrel to his proper place.

"Get for'ard!" he roared. "I've wasted time enough with you! I've done you the honor of having you brought to the poop to be revived, and answered enough of your infernal questions. Get off this poop! You'll work your way aboard this galley—"

"I'll buy your ship—" began Conan, before he remembered that he was a penniless wanderer.

A roar of rough mirth greeted these words, and the captain turned purple, thinking he sensed ridicule.

"You mutinous swine!" he bellowed, taking a threatening step forward, while he closed on his knife at his belt. "Get for'ard before I have you flogged! You'll keep a civil tongue in your jaws, or by Mitra, I'll have you chained among the blacks to tug an oar!"

Conan's volcanic temper, never long at best, burst into explosion. Not in years, even before he was king, had a man spoken to him thus and lived.

"Don't lift your voice to me, you tar-breeched dog!" he roared in a voice as gusty as the sea-wind, while the sailors gaped dumbfounded. "Draw that toy and I'll feed you to the fishes!"

"Who do you think you are?" gasped the captain.

"I'll show you!" roared the maddened Cimmerian, and he wheeled and bounded toward the rail, where weapons hung in their brackets.

The captain drew his knife and ran at him bellowing, but before he could strike, Conan gripped his wrist with a wrench that tore the arm clean out of the socket. The captain bellowed like an ox in agony, and then rolled clear across the deck as he was hurled contemptuously from his attacker. Conan ripped a heavy ax from the rail and wheeled catlike to meet the rush of the sailors. They ran in, giving tongue like hounds, clumsy-footed and awkward in comparison to the pantherish Cimmerian. Before they could reach him with their knives he sprang among them, striking right and left too quickly for the eye to follow, and blood and brains spattered as two corpses struck the deck.

Knives flailed the air wildly as Conan broke through the stumbling, gasping mob and bounded to the narrow bridge that spanned the waist from poop to forecastle, just out of reach of the slaves below. Behind him the handful of sailors on the poop were floundering after him, daunted by the destruction of their fellows, and the rest of the crew—some thirty in all—came running across the bridge toward him, with weapons in their hands.

Conan bounded out on the bridge and stood poised above the upturned black faces, ax lifted, black mane blown in the wind.

"Who am I?" he yelled. "Look, you dogs! Look, Ajonga, Yasunga, Laranga! Who am I?"

And from the waist rose a shout that swelled to a mighty roar:

"Amra! It is Amra! The Lion has returned!"

The sailors who caught and understood the burden of that awesome shout paled and shrank back, staring in sudden fear at the wild figure on the bridge. Was this in truth that bloodthirsty ogre of the southern seas who had so mysteriously vanished years ago, but who still lived in gory legends? The blacks were frothing crazy now, shaking and tearing at their chains and shrieking the name of Amra like an invocation. Kushites who had never seen Conan before took up the yell. The slaves in the pen under the after-cabin began to batter at the walls, shrieking like the damned.

Demetrio, hitching himself along the deck on one hand and his knees, livid with the agony of his dislocated arm, screamed: "In and kill him, dogs, before the slaves break loose!"

Fired to desperation by that word, the most dread to all galleymen, the sailors charged on to the bridge from both ends. But with a lionlike bound Conan left the bridge and hit like a cat on his feet on the runway between the benches.

"Death to the masters!" he thundered, and his ax rose and fell crashingly full on a shackle-chain, severing it like matchwood. In an instant a shrieking slave was free, splintering his oar for a bludgeon. Men were racing frantically along the bridge above, and all hell and bedlam broke loose on the *Venturer*. Conan's ax rose and fell without pause, and with every stroke a frothing, screaming black giant broke free, mad with hate and the fury of freedom and vengeance.

Sailors, leaping down into the waist to grapple or smite at the naked white giant hewing like one possessed at the shackles, found themselves dragged down by hands of slaves yet unfreed, while others, their broken chains whipping and snapping about their limbs, came up out of the waist like a blind, black torrent, screaming like fiends, smiting with broken oars and pieces of iron, tearing and rending with talons and teeth. In the midst of the melee the slaves in the pen broke down the walls and came surging up on the decks, and with fifty blacks freed of their benches Conan abandoned his iron-hewing and bounded up on the bridge to add his notched ax to the bludgeons of his partizans.

Then it was massacre. The Argosseans were strong, sturdy, fearless like all their race, trained in the brutal school of the sea. But they could not stand against these maddened giants, led by the tigerish barbarian. Blows and abuse and hellish suffering were avenged in one red gust of fury that raged like a typhoon from one end of the ship to the other, and when it had blown itself out, but one white man lived aboard the *Venturer*, and that was the bloodstained giant about whom the chanting blacks thronged to cast themselves prostrate on the bloody deck and beat their heads against the boards in an ecstasy of hero worship.

Conan, his mighty chest heaving and glistening with sweat, the red ax gripped in his blood-smeared hand, glared about him as the first of men might have glared in some primordial dawn, and shook back his black mane. In that moment he was not king of Aquilonia; he was again lord of the black corsairs, who had hacked his way to lordship through flame and blood.

"Amra! Amra!" chanted the delirious blacks, those who were left to chant. "The Lion has returned! Now will the Stygians howl like dogs in the night, and the black dogs of Kush will howl! Now will villages burst in flames and ships founder! Aie, there will be wailing of women and the thunder of the spears!"

"Cease this yammering, dogs!" Conan roared in a voice that drowned the clap of the sail in the wind. "Ten of you go below and free the oarsmen who are yet chained. The rest of you man the sweeps and bend to oars and halyards. Crom's devils, don't you see we've drifted inshore during the fight? Do you want to run aground and be retaken by the Argosseans? Throw these carcasses overboard. Jump to it, you rogues, or I'll notch your hides for you!"

With shouts and laughter and wild singing they leaped to do his commands. The corpses, white and black, were hurled overboard, where triangular fins were already cutting the water.

Conan stood on the poop, frowning down at the black men who watched him expectantly. His heavy brown arms were folded, his black hair, grown long in his wanderings, blew in the wind. A wilder and more barbaric figure never trod the bridge of a ship, and in this ferocious corsair few of the courtiers of Aquilonia would have recognized their king.

"There's food in the hold!" he roared. "Weapons in plenty for you, for this ship carried blades and harness to the Shemites who dwell along the coast. There are enough of us to work ship, aye, and to fight! You rowed in chains for the Argossean dogs: will you row as free men for Amra?"

"Aye!" they roared. "We are thy children! Lead us where you will!"

"Then fall to and clean out that waste," he commanded. "Free men don't labor in such filth. Three of you come with me and break out food from the after-cabin. By Crom, I'll pad out your ribs before this cruise is done!"

Another yell of approbation answered him, as the half-starved blacks scurried to do his bidding. The sail bellied as the wind swept over the waves with renewed force, and the white crests danced along the sweep of the wind. Conan planted his feet to the heave of the deck, breathed deep and spread his mighty arms.

King of Aquilonia he might no longer be; king of the blue ocean he was still.

16 Black-Walled Khemi

The *Venturer* swept southward like a living thing, her oars pulled now by free and willing hands. She had been transformed from a peaceful trader into a war-galley, insofar as the transformation was possible. Men sat at the benches now with swords at their sides and gilded helmets on their kinky heads. Shields were hung along the rails, and sheafs of spears, bows and arrows adorned the mast. Even the elements seemed to work for Conan now; the broad purple sail bellied to a stiff breeze that held day by day, needing little aid from the oars.

But though Conan kept a man on the masthead day and night, they did not sight a long, low, black galley fleeing southward ahead of them. Day by day the blue waters rolled empty to their view, broken only by fishing-craft which fled like frightened birds before them, at sight of the shields hung along the rail. The season for trading was practically over for the year, and they sighted no other ships.

When the lookout did sight a sail, it was to the north, not the south. Far on the skyline behind them appeared a racing-galley, with full spread of purple sail. The blacks urged Conan to turn and plunder it, but he shook his head. Somewhere south of him a slim black galley was racing toward the ports of Stygia. That night, before darkness shut down, the lookout's last glimpse showed him the racing-galley on the horizon, and at dawn it was still hanging on their tail, afar off, tiny in the distance. Conan wondered if it was following him, though he could think of no logical reason for such a supposition. But he paid little heed. Each day that carried him farther southward filled him with fiercer impatience. Doubts never assailed him. As he believed in the rise and set of the sun he believed that a priest of Set had stolen the Heart of Ahriman. And where would a priest of Set carry it but to Stygia? The blacks sensed his eagerness, and toiled as they had never toiled under the lash, though ignorant of his goal. They anticipated a red career of pillage and plunder and were content. The men of the southern isles knew no other trade; and the Kushites of the crew joined whole-heartedly in the prospect of looting their own people, with the callousness of their race. Blood-ties meant little; a victorious chieftain and personal gain everything.

Soon the character of the coastline changed. No longer they sailed past steep cliffs with blue hills marching behind them. Now the shore was the edge of broad meadowlands, which barely rose above the water's edge and swept away and away into the hazy distance. Here were few harbors and fewer ports, but the green plain was dotted with the cities of the Shemites; green sea, lapping the rim of the green plains, and the zikkurats of the cities gleaming whitely in the sun, some small in the distance.

Through the grazing-lands moved the herds of cattle, and squat, broad riders with cylindrical helmets and curled blue-black beards, with bows in their hands. This was the shore of the lands of Shem, where there was no law save as each city-state could enforce its own. Far to the eastward, Conan knew, the meadowlands gave way to desert, where there were no cities and the nomadic tribes roamed unhindered.

Still as they plied southward, past the changeless panorama of city-dotted meadowland, at last the scenery again began to alter. Clumps of tamarind appeared, the palm groves grew denser. The shoreline became more broken, a marching rampart of green fronds and trees, and behind them rose bare, sandy hills. Streams poured into the sea, and along their moist banks vegetation grew thick and of vast variety.

So at last they passed the mouth of a broad river that mingled its flow with the ocean, and saw the great black walls and towers of Khemi rise against the southern horizon.

The river was the Styx, the real border of Stygia. Khemi was Stygia's greatest port, and at the time her most important city. The king dwelt at more ancient Luxur, but in Khemi reigned the priestcraft; though men said the center of their dark religion lay far inland, in a mysterious, deserted city near the bank of the Styx. This river, springing from some nameless source far in the unknown lands south of Stygia, ran northward for a thousand miles before it turned and flowed westward for some hundreds of miles, to empty at last into the ocean.

The *Venturer*, showing no lights, stole past the port in the night, and before dawn discovered her, anchored in a small bay a few miles south of the city. It was surrounded by marsh, a green tangle of mangroves, palms and lianas, swarming with crocodiles and serpents. Discovery was extremely unlikely. Conan knew the place of old; he had hidden there before, in his corsair days.

As they slid silently past the city whose great black bastions rose on the jutting prongs of land, which locked the harbor, torches gleamed and smoldered luridly, and to their ears came the low thunder of drums. The port was not crowded with ships, as were the harbors of Argos. The Stygians did not base their glory and power upon ships and fleets. Trading-vessels and war-galleys, indeed, they had, but not in proportion to their inland strength. Many of their craft plied up and down the great river, rather than along the seacoasts.

The Stygians were an ancient race, a dark, inscrutable people, powerful and merciless. Long ago their rule had stretched far north of the Styx, beyond the meadowlands of Shem, and into the fertile uplands now inhabited by the peoples of Koth and Ophir and Argos. Their borders had marched with those of ancient Acheron. But Acheron had fallen, and the barbaric ancestors of the Hyborians had swept southward in wolfskins and horned helmets, driving the ancient rulers of the land before them. The Stygians had not forgotten.

All day the *Venturer* lay at anchor in the tiny bay, walled in with green branches and tangled vines through which flitted gay-plumed, harsh-voiced birds, and among which glided bright-scaled, silent reptiles. Toward sundown a small boat crept out and down along the shore, seeking and finding that which Conan desired—a Stygian fisherman in his shallow, flat-prowed boat.

They brought him to the deck of the *Venturer*—a tall, dark, rangily built man, ashy with fear of his captors, who were ogres of that coast. He was naked except for his silken breeks, for, like the Hyrkanians, even the commoners and slaves of Stygia wore silk; and in his boat was a wide mantle such as these fishermen flung about their shoulders against the chill of the night.

He fell to his knees before Conan, expecting torture and death. "Stand on your legs, man, and quit trembling," said the Cimmerian impatiently, who found it difficult to understand abject terror, "You won't be harmed. Tell me but this: has a galley, a black racing-galley returning from Argos, put into Khemi within the last few days?"

"Aye, my lord," answered the fisherman. "Only yesterday at dawn the priest Thutothmes returned from a voyage far to the north. Men say he has been to Messantia."

"What did he bring from Messantia?"

"Alas, my lord, I know not."

"Why did he go to Messantia?" demanded Conan.

"Nay, my lord, I am but a common man. Who am I to know the minds of the priests of Set? I can only speak what I have seen and what I have heard men whisper along the wharves. Men say that news of great import came southward, though of what none knows; and it is well known that the lord Thutothmes put off in his black galley in great haste. Now he is returned, but what he did in Argos, or what cargo he brought back, none knows, not even the seamen who manned his galley. Men say that he has opposed Thoth-Amon, who is the master of all priests of Set, and dwells in Luxur, and that Thutothmes seeks hidden power to overthrow the Great One. But who am I to say? When priests war with one another a common man can but lie on his belly and hope neither treads upon him."

Conan snarled in nervous exasperation at this servile philosophy, and turned to his men. "I'm going alone into Khemi to find this thief Thutothmes. Keep this man prisoner, but see that you do him no hurt. Crom's devils, stop your yowling! Do you think we can sail into the harbor and take the city by storm? I must go alone."

Silencing the clamor of protests, he doffed his own garments and donned the prisoner's silk breeches and sandals, and the band from the man's hair, but scorned the short fisherman's knife. The common men of Stygia were not allowed to wear swords, and the mantle was not voluminous enough to hide the Cimmerian's long blade, but Conan buckled to his hip a Ghanta knife, a weapon borne by the fierce desert men who dwelt to the south of the Stygians, a broad, heavy, slightly curved blade of fine steel, edged like a razor and long enough to dismember a man.

Then, leaving the Stygian guarded by the corsairs, Conan climbed into the fisherman's boat.

"Wait for me until dawn," he said. "If I haven't come then, I'll never come, so hasten southward to your own homes."

As he clambered over the rail, they set up a doleful wail at his going, until he thrust his head back into sight to curse them into silence. Then, dropping into the boat, he grasped the oars and sent the tiny craft shooting over the waves more swiftly than its owner had ever propelled it.

17 "He Has Slain the Sacred Son of Set!"

The harbor of Khemi lay between two great jutting points of land that ran into the ocean. He rounded the southern point, where the great black castles rose like a man-made hill, and entered the harbor just at dusk, when there was still enough light for the watchers to recognize the fisherman's boat and mantle, but not enough to permit recognition of betraying details. Unchallenged he threaded his way among the great black war-galleys lying silent and unlighted at anchor, and drew up to a flight of wide stone steps which mounted up from the water's edge. There he made his boat fast to an iron ring set in the stone, as numerous similar craft were tied. There was nothing strange in a fisherman leaving his boat there. None but a fisherman could find a use for such a craft, and they did not steal from one another.

No one cast him more than a casual glance as he mounted the long steps, unobtrusively avoiding the torches that flared at intervals above the lapping black water. He seemed but an ordinary, empty-handed fisherman, returning after a fruitless day along the coast. If one had observed him closely, it might have seemed that his step was somewhat too springy and sure, his carriage somewhat too erect and confident for a lowly fisherman. But he passed quickly, keeping in the shadows, and the commoners of Stygia were no more given to analysis than were the commoners of the less exotic races.

In build he was not unlike the warrior castes of the Stygians, who were a tall, muscular race. Bronzed by the sun, he was nearly as dark as many of them. His black hair, square-cut and confined by a copper band, increased the resemblance. The characteristics which set him apart from them were the subtle difference in his walk, and his alien features and blue eyes.

But the mantle was a good disguise, and he kept as much in the shadow as possible, turning away his head when a native passed him too closely.

But it was a desperate game, and he knew he could not long keep up the deception. Khemi was not like the seaports of the Hyborians, where types of every race swarmed. The only aliens here were negro and Shemite slaves; and he resembled neither even as much as he resembled the Stygians themselves. Strangers were not welcome in the cities of Stygia; tolerated only when they came as ambassadors or licensed traders. But even then the latter were not allowed ashore after dark. And now there were no Hyborian ships in the harbor at all. A strange restlessness ran through the city, a stirring of ancient ambitions, a whispering none could define except those who whispered. This Conan felt rather than knew, his whetted primitive instincts sensing unrest about him.

If he were discovered his fate would be ghastly. They would slay him merely for being a stranger; if he were recognized as Amra, the corsair chief who had swept their coasts with steel and flame—an involuntary shudder twitched Conan's broad shoulders. Human foes he did not fear, nor any death by steel or fire. But this was a black land of sorcery and nameless horror. Set the Old Serpent, men said, banished long ago from the Hyborian races, yet lurked in the shadows of the cryptic temples, and awful and mysterious were the deeds done in the nighted shrines.

He had drawn away from the waterfront streets with their broad steps leading down to the water, and was entering the long shadowy streets of the main part of the city. There was no such scene as was offered by any Hyborian city—no blaze of lamps and cressets, with gay-clad people laughing and strolling along the pavements, and shops and stalls wide open and displaying their wares.

Here the stalls were closed at dusk. The only lights along the streets were torches, flaring smokily at wide intervals. People walking the streets were comparatively few; they went hurriedly and unspeaking, and their numbers decreased with the lateness of the hour. Conan found the scene gloomy and unreal; the silence of the people, their furtive haste, the great black stone walls that rose on each side of the streets. There was a grim massiveness about Stygian architecture that was overpowering and oppressive.

Few lights showed anywhere except in the upper parts of the buildings. Conan knew that most of the people lay on the flat roofs, among the palms of artificial gardens under the stars. There was a murmur of weird music from somewhere. Occasionally a bronze chariot rumbled along the flags, and there was a brief glimpse of a tall, hawk-faced noble, with a silk cloak wrapped about him, and a gold band with a rearing serpent-head emblem confining his black mane; of the ebon, naked charioteer bracing his knotty legs against the straining of the fierce Stygian horses.

But the people who yet traversed the streets on foot were commoners, slaves, tradesmen, harlots, toilers, and they became fewer as he progressed. He was making toward the temple of Set, where he knew he would be likely to find the priest he sought. He believed he would know Thutothmes if he saw him, though his one glance had been in the semidarkness of the Messantian alley. That the man he had seen there had been the priest he was certain. Only occultists high in the mazes of the hideous Black Ring possessed the power of the black hand that dealt death by its touch; and only such a man would dare defy

Thoth-Amon, whom the western world knew only as a figure of terror and myth.

The street broadened, and Conan was aware that he was getting into the part of the city dedicated to the temples. The great structures reared their black bulks against the dim stars, grim, indescribably menacing in the flare of the few torches. And suddenly he heard a low scream from—a woman on the other side of the street and somewhat ahead of him—a naked courtezan wearing the tall plumed head-dress of her class. She was shrinking back against the wall, staring across at something he could not yet see. At her cry the few people on the street halted suddenly as if frozen. At the same instant Conan was aware of a sinister slithering ahead of him. Then about the dark corner of the building he was approaching poked a hideous, wedge-shaped head, and after it flowed coil after coil of rippling, darkly glistening trunk.

The Cimmerian recoiled, remembering tales he had heard—serpents were sacred to Set, god of Stygia, who, men said, was himself a serpent. Monsters such as this were kept in the temples of Set, and when they hungered, were allowed to crawl forth into the streets to take what prey they wished. Their ghastly feasts were considered a sacrifice to the scaly god.

The Stygians within Conan's sight fell to their knees, men and women, and passively awaited their fate. One the great serpent would select, would lap in scaly coils, crush to a red pulp and swallow as a rat-snake swallows a mouse. The others would live. That was the will of the gods.

But it was not Conan's will. The python glided toward him, its attention probably attracted by the fact that he was the only human in sight still standing erect. Gripping his great knife under his mantle, Conan hoped the slimy brute would pass him by. But it halted before him and reared up horrifically in the flickering torchlight, its forked tongue flickering in and out, its cold eyes glittering with the ancient cruelty of the serpent-folk. Its neck arched, but before it could dart, Conan whipped his knife from under his mantle and struck like a flicker of lightning. The broad blade split that wedge-shaped head and sheared deep into the thick neck.

Conan wrenched his knife free and sprang clear as the great body knotted and looped and whipped terrifically in its death throes. In the moment that he stood staring in morbid fascination, the only sound was the thud and swish of the snake's tail against the stones.

Then from the shocked votaries burst a terrible cry: "Blasphemer! He has slain the sacred son of Set! Slay him! Slay! Slay!"

Stones whizzed about him and the crazed Stygians rushed at him, shrieking hysterically, while from all sides others emerged from their houses and took up the cry. With a curse Conan wheeled and darted into the black mouth of an alley. He heard the patter of bare feet on the flags behind him as he ran more by feel than by sight, and the walls resounded to the vengeful yells of the pursuers. Then his left hand found a break in the wall, and he turned sharply into another, narrower alley. On both sides rose sheer black stone walls. High above him he could see a thin line of stars. These giant walls, he knew, were the walls of temples. He heard, behind him, the pack sweep past the dark mouth in full cry. Their shouts grew distant, faded away. They had missed the smaller alley and run straight on in the blackness. He too kept straight ahead, though the thought of encountering another of Set's "sons" in the darkness brought a shudder from him.

Then somewhere ahead of him he caught a moving glow, like that of a crawling glow-worm. He halted, flattened himself against the wall and gripped his knife. He knew what it was: a man approaching with a torch. Now it was so close he could make out the dark hand that gripped it, and the dim oval of a dark face. A few more steps and the man would certainly see him. He sank into a tigerish crouch—the torch halted. A door was briefly etched in the glow, while the torch-bearer fumbled with it. Then it opened, the tall figure vanished through it, and darkness closed again on the alley. There was a sinister suggestion of furtiveness about that slinking figure, entering the alley door in darkness; a priest, perhaps returning from some dark errand.

But Conan groped toward the door. If one man came up that alley with a torch, others might come at any time. To retreat the way he had come might mean to run full into the mob from which he was fleeing. At any moment they might return, find the narrower alley and come howling down it. He felt hemmed in by those sheer, unscalable walls, desirous of escape, even if escape meant invading some unknown building.

The heavy bronze door was not locked. It opened under his fingers and he peered through the crack. He was looking into a great square chamber of massive black stone. A torch smoldered in a niche in the wall. The chamber was empty. He glided through the lacquered door and closed it behind him.

His sandaled feet made no sound as he crossed the black marble floor. A teak door stood partly open, and gliding through this, knife in hand, he came out into a great, dim, shadowy place whose lofty ceiling was only a hint of darkness high above him, toward which the black walls swept upward. On all sides black-arched doorways opened into the great still hall. It was lit by curious bronze lamps that gave a dim weird light. On the other side of the great hall a broad black marble stairway, without a railing, marched upward to lose itself in gloom, and above him on all sides dun galleries hung like black stone ledges.

Conan shivered; he was in a temple of some Stygian god, if not Set himself, then someone only less grim. And the shrine did not lack an occupant. In the midst of the great hall stood a black stone altar, massive, somber, without carvings or ornament, and upon it coiled one of the great sacred serpents, its iridescent scales shimmering in the lamplight. It did not move, and Conan remembered stories that the priests kept these creatures drugged part of the time. The Cimmerian took an uncertain step out from the door, then shrank back suddenly, not into the room he had just quitted, but into a velvet-curtained recess. He had heard a soft step somewhere near by.

From one of the black arches emerged a tall, powerful figure in sandals and silken loincloth, with a wide mantle trailing from his shoulders. But face and head were hidden by a monstrous mask, a half-bestial, half-human countenance, from the crest of which floated a mass of ostrich plumes.

In certain ceremonies the Stygian priests went masked. Conan hoped the man would not discover him, but some instinct warned the Stygian. He turned abruptly from his destination, which apparently was the stair, and stepped straight to the recess. As he jerked aside the velvet hanging, a hand darted from the shadows, crushed the cry in his throat and jerked him headlong into the alcove, and the knife impaled him.

Conan's next move was the obvious one suggested by logic. He lifted off the grinning mask and drew it over his own head. The fisherman's mantle he flung over the body of the priest, which he concealed behind the hangings, and drew the priestly mantle about his own brawny shoulders. Fate had given him a disguise. All Khemi might well be searching now for the blasphemer who dared defend himself against a sacred snake; but who would dream of looking for him under the mask of a priest?

He strode boldly from the alcove and headed for one of the arched doorways at random; but he had not taken a dozen strides when he wheeled again, all his senses edged for peril.

A band of masked figures filed down the stair, appareled exactly as he was. He hesitated, caught in the open, and stood still, trusting to his disguise, though cold sweat gathered on his forehead and the backs of his hands. No word was spoken. Like phantoms they descended into the great hall and moved past him toward a black arch. The leader carried an ebon staff which supported a grinning white skull, and Conan knew it was one of the ritualistic processions so inexplicable to a foreigner, but which played a strong—and often sinister— part in the Stygian religion. The last figure turned his head slightly toward the motionless Cimmerian, as if expecting him to follow. Not to do what was obviously expected of him would rouse instant suspicion. Conan fell in behind the last man and suited his gait to their measured pace.

They traversed a long, dark, vaulted corridor in which, Conan noticed uneasily, the skull on the staff glowed phosphorescently. He felt a surge of unreasoning, wild animal panic that urged him to rip out his knife and slash right and left at these uncanny figures, to flee madly from this grim, dark temple. But he held himself in check, fighting down the dim monstrous intuitions that rose in the back of his mind and peopled the gloom with shadowy shapes of horror; and presently he barely stifled a sigh of relief as they filed through a great double-valved door which was three times higher than a man, and emerged into the starlight.

Conan wondered if he dared fade into some dark alley; but hesitated, uncertain, and down the long dark street they padded silently, while such folk as they met turned their heads away and fled from them. The procession kept far out from the walls; to turn and bolt into any of the alleys they passed would be too conspicuous. While he mentally fumed and cursed, they came to a low-arched gateway in the southern wall, and through this they filed. Ahead of them and about them lay clusters of low, flat-topped mud houses, and palm groves, shadowy in the starlight. Now if ever, thought Conan, was his time to escape his silent companions.

But the moment the gate was left behind them those companions were no longer silent. They began to mutter excitedly among themselves. The measured, ritualistic gait was abandoned, the staff with its skull was tucked unceremoniously under the leader's arm, and the whole group broke ranks and hurried onward. And Conan hurried with them. For in the low murmur of speech he had caught a word that galvanized him. The word was: "Thutothmes!"

18 "I Am the Woman Who Never Died"

Conan stared with burning interest at his masked companions. One of them was Thutothmes, or else the destination of the band was a rendezvous with the man he sought. And he knew what the destination was, when beyond the palms he glimpsed a black triangular bulk looming against the shadowy sky.

They passed through the belt of huts and groves, and if any man saw them he was careful not to show himself. The huts were dark. Behind them the black towers of Khemi rose gloomily against the stars that were mirrored in the waters of the harbor; ahead of them the desert stretched away in dim darkness; somewhere a jackal yapped. The quick-passing sandals of the silent neophytes made no noise in the sand. They might have been ghosts, moving toward that colossal pyramid that rose out of the murk of the desert. There was no sound over all the sleeping land.

Conan's heart beat quicker as he gazed at the grim black wedge that stood etched against the stars, and his impatience to close with Thutothmes in whatever conflict the meeting might mean was not unmixed with a fear of the unknown. No man could approach one of those somber piles of black stone without apprehension. The very name was a symbol of repellent horror among the northern nations, and legends hinted that the Stygians did not build them; that they were in the land at whatever immeasurably ancient date the dark-skinned people came into the land of the great river.

As they approached the pyramid he glimpsed a dim glow near the base which presently resolved itself into a doorway, on either side of which brooded stone lions with the heads of women, cryptic, inscrutable, nightmares crystallized in stone. The leader of the band made straight for the doorway, in the deep well of which Conan saw a shadowy figure.

The leader paused an instant beside this dim figure, and then vanished into the dark interior, and one by one the others followed. As each masked priest passed through the gloomy portal he was halted briefly by the mysterious guardian and something passed between them, some word or gesture Conan could not make out. Seeing this, the Cimmerian purposely lagged behind, and stooping, pretended to be fumbling with the fastening of his sandal. Not until the last of the masked figures had disappeared did he straighten and approach the portal.

He was uneasily wondering if the guardian of the temple were human, remembering some tales he had heard. But his doubts were set at rest. A dim bronze cresset glowing just within the door lighted a long narrow corridor that ran away into blackness, and a man standing silent in the mouth of it, wrapped in a wide black cloak. No one else was in sight. Obviously the masked priests had disappeared down the corridor. Over the cloak that was drawn about his lower features, the Stygian's piercing eyes regarded Conan sharply. With his left hand he made a curious gesture. On a venture Conan imitated it. But evidently another gesture was expected; the Stygian's right hand came from under his cloak with a gleam of steel and his murderous stab would have pierced the heart of an ordinary man. But he was dealing with one whose thews were nerved to the quickness of a jungle cat. Even as the dagger flashed in the dim light, Conan caught the dusky wrist and smashed his clenched right fist against the Stygian's jaw. The man's head went back against the stone wall with a dull crunch that told of a fractured skull. Standing for an instant above him, Conan listened intently. The cresset burned low, casting vague shadows about the door. Nothing stirred in the blackness about the door. Nothing stirred in the blackness beyond, though far away and below him, as it seemed, he caught the faint, muffled note of a gong.

He stooped and dragged the body behind the great bronze door which stood wide, opened inward, and then the Cimmerian went warily but swiftly down the corridor, toward what doom he did not even try to guess. He had not gone far when he halted, baffled. The corridor split in two branches, and he had no way of knowing which the masked priests had taken. At a venture he chose the left. The floor slanted slightly downward and worn smooth as by many feet. Here and there a dim cresset cast a faint nightmarish twilight. Conan wondered uneasily for what purpose these colossal piles had been reared, in what forgotten age. This was an ancient, ancient land. No man knew how many ages the black temples of Stygia looked.

Against the stars, narrow black arches opened occasionally to right and left, but he kept to the main corridor, although a conviction that he had taken the wrong branch was growing in him. Even with their start on him, he should have overtaken the priests by this time. He was growing nervous. The silence was like a tangible thing, and yet he had a feeling that he was not alone. More than once, passing a nighted arch he seemed to feel the glare of unseen eyes fixed upon him. He paused, half minded to turn back to where the corridor had first branched. He wheeled abruptly, knife lifted, every nerve tingling.

A girl stood at the mouth of a smaller tunnel, staring fixedly at him. Her ivory skin showed her to be Stygian of some ancient noble family, and like all such women she was tall, lithe, voluptuously figured, her hair a great pile of black foam, among which gleamed a sparkling ruby. But for her velvet sandals and broad jewel-crusted girdle about her supple waist she was quite nude.

"What do you here?" she demanded.

To answer would betray his alien origin. He remained motionless, a grim, somber figure in the hideous mask with the plumes floating over him. His alert gaze sought the shadows behind her and found them empty. But there might be hordes of fighting-men within her call.

She advanced toward him, apparently without apprehension though with suspicion.

"You are not a priest," she said. "You are a fighting-man. Even with that mask that is plain. There is as much difference between you and a priest as there is between a man and a woman. By Set!" she exclaimed, halting suddenly, her eyes flaring wide. "I do not believe you are even a Stygian!"

With a movement too quick for the eye to follow, his hand closed about her round throat, lightly as a caress.

"Not a sound out of you!" he muttered.

Her smooth ivory flesh was cold as marble, yet there was no fear in the wide, dark, marvelous eyes which regarded him.

"Do not fear," she answered calmly. "I will not betray you. But you are mad to come, a stranger and a foreigner, to the forbidden temple of Set."

"I'm looking for the priest Thutothmes," he answered. "Is he in this temple?"

"Why do you seek him?" she parried.

"He has something of mine which was stolen."

"I will lead you to him," she volunteered, so promptly that his suspicions were instantly aroused.

"Don't play with me, girl," he growled.

"I do not play with you. I have no love for Thutothmes." He hesitated, then made up his mind; after all, he was in her power as she was in his.

"Walk beside me," he commanded, shifting his grasp from her throat to her wrist. "But walk with care. If you make a move—"

She led him down the slanting corridor, down and down, until there were no more cressets, and he groped his way in darkness, aware less by sight than by feel and sense of the woman at his side. Once when he spoke to her, she turned her head toward him and he was startled to see her eyes glowing like golden fire in the dark. Dim doubts and vague monstrous suspicions haunted his mind, but he followed her, through a labyrinthine maze of black corridors that confused even his primitive sense of direction. He mentally cursed himself for a fool, allowing himself to be led into that black abode of mystery; but it was too late to turn back now. Again he felt life and movement in the darkness about him, sensed peril and hunger burning impatiently in the blackness. Unless his ears deceived him he caught a faint sliding noise that ceased and receded at a muttered command from the girl.

She led him at last into a chamber lighted by a curious seven-branched candelabrum in which black candles burned weirdly. He knew they were far below the earth. The chamber was square, with walls and ceilings of polished black marble and furnished after the manner of the ancient Stygians; there was a couch of ebony, covered with black velvet, and on a black stone dais lay a carven mummy-case.

Conan stood waiting expectantly, staring at the various black arches which opened into the chamber. But the girl made no move to go farther. Stretching herself on the couch with feline suppleness, she intertwined her fingers behind her sleek head and regarded him from under long, drooping lashes.

"Well?" he demanded impatiently. "What are you doing?" Where's Thutothmes?"

"There is no haste," she answered lazily. "What is an hour—or a day, or a year, or a century, for that matter? Take off your mask. Let me see your features."

With a grunt of annoyance Conan dragged on the bulky head-piece, and the girl nodded as if in approval as she scanned his dark, scarred face and blazing eyes.

"There is strength in you—great strength; you could strangle a bullock."

He moved restlessly, his suspicion growing. With his hand on his hilt he peered into the gloomy arches.

"If you've brought me into a trap," he said, "you won't live to enjoy your handiwork. Are you going to get off that couch and do as you promised, or do I have to—"

His voice trailed away. He was staring at the mummy-case, on which the countenance of the occupant was carved in ivory with the startling vividness of a forgotten art. There was a disquieting familiarity about that carven mask, and with something of a shock he realized what it was; there was a startling resemblance between it and the face of the girl lolling on the ebon couch. She might have been the model from which it was carved, but he knew the portrait was at least centuries old. Archaic hieroglyphics were scrawled across the lacquered lid, and, seeking back into his mind for tag-ends of learning, picked up here and there as incidentals of an adventurous life, he spelled them out, and said aloud: "Akivasha!"

"You have heard of Princess Akivasha?" inquired the girl on the couch.

"Who hasn't?" he grunted. The name of that ancient, evil, beautiful princess still lived the world over in song and legend, though ten thousand years had rolled their cycles since the daughter of Tuthamon had reveled in purple feasts amid the black halls of ancient Luxur.

"Her only sin was that she loved life and all the meanings of life," said the Stygian girl. "To win life she courted death. She could not bear to think of growing old and shriveled and worn, and dying at last as hags die. She wooed Darkness like a lover and his gift was life— life that, not being life as mortals know it, can never grow old and fade. She went into the shadows to cheat age and death—"

Conan glared at her with eyes that were suddenly burning slits. And he wheeled and tore the lid from the sarcophagus. It was empty. Behind him the girl was laughing and the sound froze the blood in his veins. He whirled back to her, the short hairs on his neck bristling.

"You are Akivasha!" he grated.

She laughed and shook back her burnished locks, spread her arms sensuously.

"I am Akivasha! I am the woman who never died, who never grew old! Who fools say was lifted from the earth by the gods, in the full bloom of her youth and beauty, to queen it for ever in some celestial clime! Nay, it is in the shadows that mortals find immortality! Ten thousand years ago I died to live for ever! Give me your lips, strong man!"

Rising lithely she came to him, rose on tiptoe and flung her arms about his massive neck. Scowling down into her upturned, beautiful countenance he was aware of a fearful fascination and an icy fear.

"Love me!" she whispered, her head thrown back, eyes closed and lips parted. "Give me of your blood to renew my youth and perpetuate my everlasting life! I will make you, too, immortal! I will teach you the wisdom of all the ages, all the secrets that have lasted out the eons in the blackness beneath these dark temples. I will make you king of that shadowy horde which revel among the tombs of the ancients when night veils the desert and bats flit across the moon. I am weary of priests and magicians, and captive girls dragged screaming through the portals of death. I desire a man. Love me, barbarian!"

She pressed her dark head down against his mighty breast, and he felt a sharp pang at the base of his throat. With a curse he tore her away and flung her sprawling across the couch.

"Damned vampire!" Blood was trickling from a tiny wound in his throat. She reared up on the couch like a serpent poised to strike, all the golden fires of Hell blazing in her wide eyes. Her lips drew back, revealing white pointed teeth.

"Fool!" she shrieked. "Do you think to escape me? You will live and die in darkness! I have brought you far below the temple. You can never find your way out alone. You can never cut your way through those which guard the tunnels. But for my protection the sons of Set would long ago have taken you into their bellies.

"Fool, I shall yet drink your blood!"

"Keep away from me or I'll slash you asunder," he grunted, his flesh crawling with revulsion. "You may be immortal, but steel will dismember you."

As he backed toward the arch through which he had entered, the light went out suddenly. All the candles were extinguished at once, though he did not know how; for Akivasha had not touched them. But the vampire's laugh rose mockingly behind him, poison-sweet as the viols of hell, and he sweated as he groped in the darkness for the arch in a near-panic. His fingers encountered an opening and he plunged through it. Whether it was the arch through which he had entered he did not know, nor did he very much care. His one thought was to get out of the haunted chamber which had housed that beautiful, hideous, undead fiend for so many centuries.

His wanderings through those black, winding tunnels, were a sweating nightmare. Behind him and about him he heard faint slitherings and glidings, and once the echo of that sweet, hellish laughter he had heard in the chamber of Akivasha. He slashed ferociously at sounds and movements he heard or imagined he heard in the darkness near him, and once his sword cut through some yielding tenuous substance that might have been cobwebs. He had a desperate feeling that he was being played with, lured deeper and deeper into ultimate night, before being set upon by demoniac talon and fang.

And through his fear ran the sickening revulsion of his discovery. The legend of Akivasha was so old, and among the evil tales told of her ran a thread of beauty and idealism, of everlasting youth. To so many dreamers and poets and lovers she was not alone the evil princess of Stygian legend, but the symbol of eternal youth and beauty, shining for ever in some far realm of the gods. And this was the hideous reality. This foul perversion was the truth of that everlasting life. Through his physical revulsion ran the sense of a shattered dream of man's idolatry, its glittering gold proved slime and cosmic filth. A wave of futility swept over him, a dim fear of the falseness of all men's dreams and idolatries.

And now he knew that his ears were not playing him tricks. He was being followed, and his pursuers were closing in on him. In the darkness sounded shufflings and slidings that were never made by human feet; no, nor by the feet of any normal animal. The underworld had its bestial life too, perhaps. They were behind him. He turned to face them, though he could see nothing, and slowly backed away. Then the sounds eased, even before he turned his head and saw, somewhere down the long corridor, a glow of light.

19 In the Hall of the Dead

Conan moved cautiously in the direction of the light he had seen, his ear cocked over his shoulder, but there was no further sound of pursuit, though he felt the darkness pregnant with sentient life.

The glow was not stationary; it moved, bobbing grotesquely along. Then he saw the source. The tunnel he was traversing crossed another, wider corridor some distance ahead of him. And along this latter tunnel filed a bizarre procession—four tall, gaunt men in black, hooded robes, leaning on staffs. The leader held a torch above his head—a torch that burned with a curious steady glow. Like phantoms they passed across his limited range of vision and vanished, with only a fading glow to tell of their passing. Their appearance was indescribably eldritch. They were not Stygians, not anything Conan had ever seen. He doubted if they were even humans. They were like black ghosts, stalking ghoulishly along the haunted tunnels.

But his position could be no more desperate than it was. Before the inhuman feet behind him could resume their slithering advance at the fading of the distant illumination, Conan was running down the corridor. He plunged into the other tunnel and saw, far down it, small in the distance, the weird procession moving in the glowing sphere. He stole noiselessly after them, then shrank suddenly back against the wall as he saw them halt and cluster together as if conferring on some matter. They turned as if to retrace their steps, and he slipped into the nearest archway. Groping in the darkness to which he had become so accustomed that he could all but see through it, he discovered that the tunnel did not run straight, but meandered, and he fell back beyond the first turn, so that the light of the strangers should not fall on him as they passed.

But as he stood there, he was aware of a low hum of sound from somewhere behind him, like the murmur of human voices. Moving down the corridor in that direction, he confirmed his first suspicion. Abandoning his original intention of following the ghoulish travelers to whatever destination might be theirs, he set out in the direction of the voices.

Presently he saw a glint of light ahead of him, and turning into the corridor from which it issued, saw a broad arch filled with a dim glow at the other end. On his left a narrow stone stair went upward, and instinctive caution prompted him to turn and mount the stair. The voices he heard were coming from beyond that flame-filled arch.

The sounds fell away beneath him as he climbed, and presently he came out through a low arched door into a vast open space glowing with a weird radiance.

He was standing on a shadowy gallery from which he looked down into a broad dim-lit hall of colossal proportions. It was a hall of the dead, which few ever see but the silent priests of Stygia. Along the black walls rose tier above tier of carven, painted sarcophagi. Each stood in a niche in the dusky stone, and the tiers mounted up and up to be lost in the gloom above. Thousands of carven masks stared impassively down upon the group in the midst of the hall, rendered futile and insignificant by that vast array of the dead.

Of this group ten were priests, and though they had discarded their masks Conan knew they were the priests he had accompanied to the pyramid. They stood before a tall, hawk-faced man beside a black altar on which lay a mummy in rotting swathings. And the altar seemed to stand in the heart of a living fire which pulsed and shimmered, dripping flakes of quivering golden flame on the black stone about it. This dazzling glow emanated from a great red jewel which lay upon the altar, and in the reflection of which the faces of the priests looked ashy and corpselike. As he looked, Conan felt the pressure of all the weary leagues and the weary nights and days of his long quest, and he trembled with the mad urge to rush among those silent priests, clear his way with mighty blows of naked steel, and grasp the red gem with passion-taut fingers. But he gripped himself with iron control, and crouched down in the shadow of the stone balustrade. A glance showed him that a stair led down into the hall from the gallery, hugging the wall and half hidden in the shadows. He glared into the dimness of the vast place, seeking other priests or votaries, but saw only the group about the altar.

In that great emptiness the voice of the man beside the altar sounded hollow and ghostly:

"And so the word came southward. The night wind whispered it, the ravens croaked of it as they flew, and the grim bats told it to the owls and the serpents that lurk in hoary ruins. Were-wolf and vampire knew, and the ebon-bodied demons that prowl by night. The sleeping Night of the World stirred and shook its heavy mane, and there began a throbbing of drums in deep darkness, and the echoes of far weird cries frightened men who walked by dusk. For the Heart of Ahriman had come again into the world to fulfill its cryptic destiny. "Ask me not how I, Thutothmes of Khemi and the Night, heard the word before Thoth-Amon, who calls himself prince of all wizards. There are secrets not meet for such ears even as yours, and Thoth-Amon is not the only lord of the Black Ring."

"I knew, and I went to meet the Heart which came southward. It was like a magnet which drew me, unerringly. From death to death it came, riding on a river of human blood. Blood feeds it, blood draws it. Its power is greatest when there is blood on the hands that grasp it, when it is wrested by slaughter from its holder. Wherever it gleams, blood is spilt and kingdoms totter, and the forces of nature are put in turmoil.

"And here I stand, the master of the Heart, and have summoned you to come secretly, who are faithful to me, to share in the black kingdom that shall be. Tonight you shall witness the breaking of Thoth-Amon's chains which enslave us, and the birth of empire. Who am I, even I, Thutothmes, to know what powers lurk and dream in those crimson deeps? It holds secrets forgotten for three thousand years. But I shall learn. These shall tell me!" He waved his hand toward the silent shapes that lined the hall. "See how they sleep, staring through their carven masks! Kings, queens, generals, priests, wizards, the dynasties and the nobility of Stygia for ten thousand years! The touch of the Heart will awaken them from their long slumber. Long, long the Heart throbbed and pulsed in ancient Stygia. Here was its home in the centuries before it journeyed to Acheron. The ancients knew its full power, and they will tell me when by its magic I restore them to life to labor for me. "I will rouse them, will waken them, will learn their forgotten wisdom, the knowledge locked in those withered skulls. By the lore of the dead we shall enslave the living! Aye, kings, and generals and wizards of old shall be our helpers and our slaves. Who shall stand before us? "Look! This dried, shriveled thing on the altar was once Thoth-mekri, a high priest of Set, who died three thousand years ago."

"He was an adept of the Black Ring. He knew of the Heart. He will tell us of its powers."

Lifting the great jewel, the speaker laid it on the withered breast of the mummy, and lifted his hand as he began an incantation. But the incantation was never finished. With his hand lilted and his lips parted he froze, glaring past his acolytes, and they wheeled to stare in the direction in which he was looking.

Through the black arch of a door four gaunt, black-robed shapes had filed into the great hall. Their faces were dim yellow ovals in the shadows of their hoods.

"Who are you?" ejaculated Thutothmes in a voice as pregnant with danger as the hiss of a cobra. "Are you mad, to invade the holy shrine of Set?"

The tallest of the strangers spoke, and his voice was toneless as a Khitan temple bell.

"We follow Conan of Aquilonia."

"He is not here," answered Thutothmes, shaking back his mantle from his right hand with a curious menacing gesture, like a panther unsheathing his talons.

"You lie. He is in this temple. We tracked him from a corpse behind the bronze door of the outer portal through a maze of corridors. We were following his devious trail when we became aware of this conclave. We go now to take it up again. But first give us the Heart of Ahriman."

"Death is the portion of madmen," murmured Thutothmes, moving nearer the speaker. His priests closed in on catlike feet, but the strangers did not appear to heed.

"Who can look upon it without desire?" said the Khitan. "In Khitai we have heard of it. It will give us power over the people which cast us out. Glory and wonder dream in its crimson deeps. Give it to us, before we slay you."

A fierce cry rang out as a priest leaped with a flicker of steel. Before he could strike, a scaly staff licked out and touched his breast, and he fell as a dead man falls. In an instant the mummies were staring down on a scene of blood and horror. Curved knives flashed and crimsoned, snaky staffs licked in and out, and whenever they touched a man, that man screamed and died.

At the first stroke Conan had bounded up and was racing down the stairs. He caught only glimpses of that brief, fiendish fight—saw men swaying, locked in battle and streaming blood; saw one Khitan, fairly hacked to pieces, yet still on his feet and dealing death, when Thutothmes smote him on the breast with his open empty hand, and he dropped dead, though naked steel had not been enough to destroy his uncanny vitality.

By the time Conan's hurtling feet left the stair, the fight was all but over. Three of the Khitans were down, and slashed and cut to ribbons and disemboweled, but of the Stygians only Thutothmes remained on his feet.

He rushed at the remaining Khitan, his empty hand lifted like a weapon, and that hand was black as that of a negro. But before he could strike, the staff in the tall Khitan's hand licked out, seeming to elongate itself as the yellow man thrust. The point touched the bosom of Thutothmes and he staggered; again and yet again the staff licked out, and Thutothmes reeled and fell dead, his features blotted out in a rush of blackness that made the whole of him the same hue as his enchanted hand.

The Khitan turned toward the jewel that burned on the breast of the mummy, but Conan was before him.

In a tense stillness the two faced each other, amid that shambles, with the carven mummies staring down upon them.

"Far have I followed you, oh king of Aquilonia," said the Khitan calmly. "Down the long river, and over the mountains, across Poitain and Zingara and through the hills of Argos and down the coast. Not easily did we pick up on your trail from Tarantia, for the priests of Asura are crafty. We lost it in Zingara, but we found your helmet in the forest below the border hills, where you had fought with the ghouls of the forests. Almost we lost the trail tonight among these labyrinths."

Conan reflected that he had been fortunate in returning from the vampire's chamber by another route than that by which he had been led to it. Otherwise he would have run full into these yellow fiends instead of sighting them from afar as they smelled out his spoor like human bloodhounds, with whatever uncanny gift was theirs.

The Khitan shook his head slightly, as if reading his mind.

"That is meaningless; the long trail ends here."

"Why have you hounded me?" demanded Conan, poised to move in any direction with the celerity of a hair-trigger.

"It was a debt to pay," answered the Khitan. "To you who are about to die, I will not withhold knowledge. We were vassals of the king of Aquilonia, Valerius. Long we served him, but of that service we are free now—my brothers by death, and I by the fulfilment of obligation. I shall return to Aquilonia with two hearts; for myself the Heart of Ahriman; for Valerius the heart of Conan. A kiss of the staff that was cut from the living Tree of Death—"

The staff licked out like the dart of a viper, but the slash of Conan's knife was quicker. The staff fell in writhing halves, there was another flicker of the keen steel like a jet of lightning, and the head of the Khitan rolled to the floor.

Conan wheeled and extended his hand toward the jewel—then he shrank back, his hair bristling, his blood congealing idly.

For no longer a withered brown thing lay on the altar. The jewel shimmered on the full, arching breast of a naked, living man who lay among the moldering bandages. Living? Conan could not decide. The eyes were like dark murky glass under which shone inhuman somber fires.

Slowly the man rose, taking the jewel in his hand. He towered beside the altar, dusky, naked, with a face like a carven image. Mutely he extended his hand toward Conan, with the jewel throbbing like a living heart within it. Conan took it, with an eery sensation of receiving gifts from the hand of the dead. He somehow realized that the proper incantations had not been made—the conjurement had not been completed— life had not been fully restored to his corpse.

"Who are you?" demanded the Cimmerian.

The answer came in a toneless monotone, like the dripping of water from stalactites in subterranean caverns. "I was Thoth-mekri; I am dead."

"Well, lead me out of this accursed temple, will you?" Conan requested, his flesh crawling.

With measured, mechanical steps the dead man moved toward a black arch. Conan followed him. A glance back showed him once again the vast, shadowy hall with its tiers of sarcophagi, the dead men sprawled about the altar; the head of the Khitan he had slain stared sightless up at the sweeping shadows.

The glow of the jewel illuminated the black tunnels like an ensorcelled lamp, dripping golden fire. Once Conan caught a glimpse of ivory flesh in the shadows, believed he saw the vampire that was Akivasha shrinking back from the glow of the jewel; and with her, other less-human shapes scuttled or shambled into the darkness.

The dead man strode straight on, looking neither to right nor left, his pace as changeless as the tramp of doom. Cold sweat gathered thick on Conan's flesh. Icy doubts assailed him. How could he know that this terrible figure out of the past was leading him to freedom? But he knew that, left to himself, he could never untangle this bewitched maze of corridors and tunnels. He followed his awful guide through blackness that loomed before and behind them and was filled with skulking shapes of horror and lunacy that cringed from the blinding glow of the Heart.

Then the bronze doorway was before him, and Conan felt the night wind blowing across the desert, and saw the stars, and the starlit desert across which streamed the great black shadow of the pyramid. Thothmekri pointed silently into the desert, and then turned and stalked soundlessly back in the darkness. Conan stared after that silent figure that receded into the blackness on soundless, inexorable feet as one that moves to a known and inevitable doom, or returns to everlasting sleep.

With a curse the Cimmerian leaped from the doorway and fled into the desert as if pursued by demons. He did not look back toward the pyramid, or toward the black towers of Khemi looming dimly across the sands. He headed southward toward the coast, and he ran as a man runs in ungovernable panic. The violent exertion shook his brain free of black cobwebs; the clean desert wind blew the nightmares from his soul and his revulsion changed to a wild tide of exultation before the desert gave way to a tangle of swampy growth through which he saw the black water lying before him, and the *Venturer* at anchor.

He plunged through the undergrowth, hip-deep in the marshes; dived headlong into the deep water, heedless of sharks or crocodiles, and swam to the galley and was clambering up the chain on to the deck, dripping and exultant, before the watch saw him.

"Awake, you dogs!" roared Conan, knocking aside the spear the startled lookout thrust at his breast. "Heave up the anchor! Lay to the doors! Give that fisherman a helmet full of gold and put him ashore!

Dawn will soon be breaking, and before sunrise we must be racing for the nearest port of Zingara!"

He whirled about his head the great jewel, which threw off splashes of light that spotted the deck with golden fire.

20 Out of the Dust Shall Acheron Arise

Winter had passed from Aquilonia. Leaves sprang out on the limbs of trees, and the fresh grass smiled to the touch of the warm southern breezes. But many a field lay idle and empty, many a charred heap of ashes marked the spot where proud villas or prosperous towns had stood. Wolves prowled openly along the grass-grown highways, and bands of gaunt, masterless men slunk through the forests. Only in Tarantia was feasting and wealth and pageantry.

Valerius ruled like one touched with madness. Even many of the barons who had welcomed his return cried out at last against him. His tax-gatherers crushed rich and poor alike; the wealth of a looted kingdom poured into Tarantia, which became less like the capital of a realm than the garrison of conquerors in a conquered land. Its merchants waxed rich, but it was a precarious prosperity; for none knew when he might be accused of treason on a trumped-up charge, and his property confiscated, himself cast into prison or brought to the bloody block.

Valerius made no attempt to conciliate his subjects. He maintained himself by means of the Nemedian soldiery and by desperate mercenaries. He knew himself to be a puppet of Amalric. He knew that he ruled only on the sufferance of the Nemedian. He knew that he could never hope to unite Aquilonia under his rule and cast off the yoke of his masters, for the outland provinces would resist him to the last drop of blood. And for that matter the Nemedians would cast him from his throne if he made attempt to consolidate his kingdom. He was caught in his own vise. The gall of defeated pride corroded his soul, and he threw himself into a reign of debauchery, as one who lives from day to day, without thought or care for tomorrow.

Yet there was subtlety in his madness, so deep that not even Amalric guessed it. Perhaps the wild, chaotic years of wandering as an exile had bred in him a bitterness beyond common conception. Perhaps his loathing of his present position increased this bitterness to a kind of madness. At any event he lived with one desire: to cause the ruin of all who associated with him.

He knew that his rule would be over the instant he had served Amalric's purpose; he knew, too, that so long as he continued to oppress his native kingdom the Nemedian would suffer him to reign, for Amalric wished to crush Aquilonia into ultimate submission, to destroy its last shred of independence, and then at last to seize it himself, rebuild it after his own fashion with his vast wealth, and use its men and natural resources to wrest the crown of Nemedia from Tarascus. For the throne of an emperor was Amalric's ultimate ambition, and Valerius knew it. Valerius did not know whether Tarascus suspected this, but he knew that the king of Nemedia approved of his ruthless course. Tarascus hated Aquilonia, with a hate born of old wars. He desired only the destruction of the western kingdom.

And Valerius intended to ruin the country so utterly that not even Amalric's wealth could ever rebuild it. He hated the baron quite as much as he hated the Aquilonians, and hoped only to live to see the day when Aquilonia lay in utter ruin, and Tarascus and Amalric were locked in hopeless civil war that would as completely destroy Nemedia.

He believed that the conquest of the still defiant provinces of Gunderland and Poitain and the Bossonian marches would mark his end as king. He would then have served Amalric's purpose, and could be discarded. So he delayed the conquest of these provinces, confining his activities to objectless raids and forays, meeting Amalric's urges for action with all sorts of plausible objections and postponements.

His life was a series of feasts and wild debauches. He filled his palace with the fairest girls of the kingdom, willing or unwilling. He blasphemed the gods and sprawled drunken on the floor of the banquet hall wearing the golden crown, and staining his royal purple robes with the wine he spilled. In gusts of blood-lust he festooned the gallows in the market square with dangling corpses, glutted the axes of the headsmen and sent his Nemedian horsemen thundering through the land pillaging and burning. Driven to madness, the land was in a constant upheaval of frantic revolt, savagely suppressed. Valerius plundered and raped and looted and destroyed until even Amalric protested, warning him that he would beggar the kingdom beyond repair, not knowing that such was his fixed determination.

But while in both Aquilonia and Nemedia men talked of the madness of the king, in Nemedia men talked much of Xaltotun, the masked one. Yet few saw him on the streets of Belverus. Men said he spent much time in the hills, in curious conclaves with surviving remnants of an old race: dark, silent folk who claimed descent from an ancient kingdom. Men whispered of drums beating far up in the dreaming hills, of fires glowing in the darkness, and strange chantings borne on the winds, chantings and rituals forgotten centuries ago except as meaningless formulas mumbled beside mountain hearths in villages whose inhabitants differed strangely from the people of the valleys.

The reason for these conclaves none knew, unless it was Orastes, who frequently accompanied the Pythonian, and on whose countenance a haggard shadow was growing.

But in the full flood of spring a sudden whisper passed over the sinking kingdom that woke the land to eager life. It came like a murmurous wind drifting up from the south, waking men sunk in the apathy of despair. Yet how it first came none could truly say. Some spoke of a strange, grim old woman who came down from the mountains with her hair flowing in the wind, and a great gray wolf following her like a dog. Others whispered of the priests of Asura who stole like furtive phantoms from Gunderland to the marches of Poitain, and to the forest villages of the Bossonians.

However the word came, revolt ran like a flame along the borders. Outlying Nemedian garrisons were stormed and put to the sword, foraging parties were cut to pieces; the west was up in arms, and there was a different air about the rising, a fierce resolution and inspired wrath rather than the frantic despair that had motivated the preceding revolts. It was not only the common people; barons were fortifying their castles and hurling defiance at the governors of the provinces. Bands of Bossonians were seen moving along the edges of the marches: stocky, resolute men in brigandines and steel caps, with longbows in their hands. From the inert stagnation of dissolution and ruin the realm was suddenly alive, vibrant and dangerous. So Amalric sent in haste for Tarascus, who came with an army.

In the royal palace in Tarantia, the two kings and Amalric discussed the rising. They had not sent for Xaltotun, immersed in his cryptic studies in the Nemedian hills. Not since that bloody day in the valley of the Valkia had they called upon him for aid of his magic, and he had drawn apart, communing but little with them, apparently indifferent to their intrigues.

Nor had they sent for Orastes, but he came, and he was white as spume blown before the storm. He stood in the gold-domed chamber where the kings held conclave and they beheld in amazement his haggard stare, the fear they had never guessed the mind of Orastes could hold.

"You are weary, Orastes," said Amalric. "Sit upon this divan and I will have a slave fetch you wine. You have ridden hard—"

Orastes waved aside the invitation.

"I have killed three horses on the road from Belverus. I cannot drink wine, I cannot rest, until I have said what I have to say."

He paced back and forth as if some inner fire would not let him stand motionless, and halting before his wondering companions:

"When we employed the Heart of Ahriman to bring a dead man back to life," Orastes said abruptly, "we did not weigh the consequences of tampering in the black dust of the past. The fault is mine, and the sin. We thought only of our four ambitions, forgetting what ambitions this man might himself have. And we have loosed a demon upon the earth, a fiend inexplicable to common humanity. I have plumbed deep in evil, but there is a limit to which I, or any man of my race and age, can go. My ancestors were clean men, without any demoniacal taint; it is only I who have sunk into the pits, and I can sin only to the extent of my personal individuality. Out behind Xaltotun lie a thousand centuries of black magic and diabolism, an ancient tradition of evil. He is beyond our conception not only because he is a wizard himself, but also because he is the son of a race of wizards.

"I have seen things that have blasted my soul. In the heart of the slumbering hills I have watched Xaltotun commune with the souls of the damned, and invoke the ancient demons of forgotten Acheron. I have seen the accursed descendants of that accursed empire worship him and hail him as their archpriest. I have seen what he plots—and I tell you it is no less than the restoration of the ancient, black, grisly kingdom of Acheron!"

"What do you mean?" demanded Amalric. "Acheron is dust. There are not enough survivals to make an empire. Not even Xaltotun can reshape the dust of three thousand years."

"You know little of his black powers," answered Orastes grimly. "I have seen the very hills take on an alien and ancient aspect under the spell of his incantations. I have glimpsed, like shadows behind the realities, the dim shapes and outlines of valleys, forests, mountains and lakes that are not as they are today, but as they were in that dim yesterday— have even sensed, rather than glimpsed, the purple towers of forgotten Python shimmering like figures of mist in the dusk.

"And in the last conclave to which I accompanied him, understanding of his sorcery came to me at last, while the drums beat and the beastlike worshippers howled with their heads in the dust. I tell you he would restore Acheron by his magic, by the sorcery of a gigantic blood-sacrifice such as the world has never seen. He would enslave the world, and with a deluge of blood wash away the present and restore the past!"

"You are mad!" exclaimed Tarascus.

"Mad?" Orastes turned a haggard stare upon him. "Can any man see what I have seen and remain wholly sane? Yet I speak the truth. He plots the return of Acheron, with its towers and wizards and kings and horrors, as it was in the long ago. The descendants of Acheron will serve him as a nucleus upon which to build, but it is the blood and the bodies of the people of the world today that will furnish the mortar and the stones for the rebuilding. I cannot tell you how. My own brain reels when I try to understand. But I have seen! Acheron will be Acheron again, and even the hills, the forests and the rivers will resume their ancient aspect. Why not? If I, with my tiny store of knowledge, could bring to life a man dead three thousand years, why cannot the greatest wizard of the world bring back to life a kingdom dead three thousand years? Out of the dust shall Acheron arise at his bidding."

"How can we thwart him?" asked Tarascus, impressed.

"There is but one way," answered Orastes. "We must steal the Heart of Ahriman!"

"But I—" began Tarascus involuntarily, then closed his mouth quickly.

None had noticed him, and Orastes was continuing.

"It is a power that can be used against him. With it in my hands I might defy him. But how shall we steal it? He has it hidden in some secret place, from which not even a Zamorian thief might filch it. I cannot learn its hiding-place. If he would only sleep again the sleep of the black lotus—but the last time he slept thus was after the battle of the Valkia, when he was weary because of the great magic he had performed, and—"

The door was locked and bolted, but it swung silently open and Xaltotun stood before them, calm, tranquil, stroking his patriarchal beard; but the lambent lights of Hell flickered in his eyes.

"I have taught you too much," he said calmly, pointing a finger like an index of doom at Orastes. And before any could move, he had cast a handful of dust on the floor near the feet of the priest, who stood like a man turned to marble. It flamed, smoldered; a blue serpentine of smoke rose and swayed upward about Orastes in a slender spiral. And when it had risen above his shoulders it curled about his neck with a whipping suddenness like the stroke of a snake. Orastes' scream was choked to a gurgle. His hands flew to his neck, his eyes were distended, his tongue protruded. The smoke was like a blue rope about his neck; then it faded and was gone, and Orastes slumped to the floor a dead man.

Xaltotun smote his hands together and two men entered, men often observed accompanying him—small, repulsively dark, with red, oblique eyes and pointed, ratlike teeth. They did not speak. Lifting the corpse, they bore it away.

Dismissing the matter with a wave of his hand, Xaltotun seated himself at the ivory table about which sat the pale kings. "Why are you in conclave?" he demanded. "The Aquilonians have risen in the west," answered Amalric, recovering from the grisly jolt the death of Orastes had given him. "The fools believe that Conan is alive, and coming at the head of a Poitanian army to reclaim his kingdom. If he had reappeared immediately after Valkia, or if a rumor had been circulated that he lived, the central provinces would not have risen under him, they feared your powers so. But they have become so desperate under Valerius's misrule that they are ready to follow any man who can unite them against us, and prefer sudden death to torture and continual misery.

"Of course the tale has lingered stubbornly in the land that Conan was not really slain at Valkia, but not until recently have the masses accepted it. But Pallantides is back from exile in Ophir, swearing that the king was ill in his tent that day, and that a man-at-arms wore his harness, and a squire who but recently recovered from the stroke of a mace received at Valkia confirms his tale—or pretends to.

"An old woman with a pet wolf has wandered up and down the land, proclaiming that King Conan yet lives, and will return some day to reclaim the crown. And of late the cursed priests of Asura sing the same song. They claim that word has come to them by some mysterious means that Conan is returning to reconquer his domain. I cannot catch either her or them. This is, of course, a trick of Trocero's. My spies tell me there is indisputable evidence that the Poitanians are gathering to invade Aquilonia. I believe that Trocero will bring forward some pretender who he will claim is King Conan."

Tarascus laughed, but there was no conviction in his laughter. He surreptitiously felt a scar beneath his jupon, and remembered ravens that cawed on the trail of a fugitive; remembered the body of his squire, Arideus, brought back from the border mountains horribly mangled, by a great gray wolf, his terrified soldiers said. But he also remembered a red jewel stolen from a golden chest while a wizard slept, and he said nothing.

And Valerius remembered a dying nobleman who gasped out a tale of fear, and he remembered four Khitans who disappeared into the mazes of the south and never returned. But he held his tongue, for hatred and suspicions of his allies ate at him like a worm, and he desired nothing so much as to see both rebels and Nemedians go down locked in the death grip.

But Amalric exclaimed, "It is absurd to dream that Conan lives!"

For answer Xaltotun cast a roll of parchment on the table.

Amalric caught it up, glared at it. From his lips burst a furious, incoherent cry. He read:

To Xaltotun, grand fakir of Nemedia: Dog of Acheron, I am returning to my kingdom, and I mean to hang your hide on a bramble.

CONAN.

"A forgery!" exclaimed Amalric.

Xaltotun shook his head.

"It is genuine. I have compared it with the signature on the royal documents in the libraries of the court. None could imitate that bold scrawl."

"Then if Conan lives," muttered Amalric, "this uprising will not be like the others, for he is the only man living who can unite the Aquilonians. But," he protested, "this is not like Conan. Why should he put us on guard with his boasting? One would think that he would strike without warning, after the fashion of the barbarians."

"We are already warned," pointed out Xaltotun. "Our spies have told us of preparations for war in Poitain. He could not cross the mountains without our knowledge; so he sends his defiance in characteristic manner."

"Why to you?" demanded Valerius. "Why not to me, or to Tarascus?"

Xaltotun turned his inscrutable gaze upon the king. "Conan is wiser than you," he said at last. "He already knows what you kings have yet to learn—that it is not Tarascus, nor Valerius, no, nor Amalric, but Xaltotun who is the real master of the western nations."

They did not reply; they sat staring at him, assailed by a numbing realization of the truth of his assertion.

"There is no road for me but the imperial highway," said Xaltotun. "But first we must crush Conan. I do not know how he escaped me at Belverus, for knowledge of what happened while I lay in the slumber of the black lotus is denied me. But he is in the south, gathering an army. It is his last, desperate blow, made possible only by the desperation of the people who have suffered under Valerius. Let them rise; I hold them all in the palm of my hand. We will wait until he moves against us, and then we will crush him once and for all.

"Then we shall crush Poitain and Gunderland and the stupid Bossonians. After them Ophir, Argos, Zingara, Koth—all the nations of the world we shall weld into one vast empire. You shall rule as my satraps, and as my captains shall be greater than kings are now. I am unconquerable, for the Heart of Ahriman is hidden where no man can ever wield it against me again."

Tarascus averted his gaze, lest Xaltotun read his thoughts. He knew the wizard had not looked into the golden chest with its carven serpents that had seemed to sleep, since he laid the Heart therein. Strange as it seemed, Xaltotun did not know that the Heart had been stolen; the strange jewel was beyond or outside the ring of his dark wisdom; his uncanny talents did not warn him that the chest was empty. Tarascus did not believe that Xaltotun knew the full extent of Orastes' revelations, for the Pythonian had not mentioned the restoration of Acheron, but only the building of a new, earthly empire. Tarascus did not believe that Xaltotun was yet quite sure of his power; if they needed his aid in their ambitions, no less he needed theirs. Magic depended, to a certain extent after all, on sword strokes and lance thrusts. The king read meaning in Amalric's furtive glance; let the wizard use his arts to help them defeat their most dangerous enemy. Time enough then to turn against him. There might yet be a way to cheat this dark power they had raised.

21 Drums of Peril

Confirmation of the war came when the army of Poitain, ten thousand strong, marched through the southern passes with waving banners and shimmer of steel. And at their head, the spies swore, rode a giant figure in black armor, with the royal lion of Aquilonia worked in gold upon the breast of his rich silken surcoat. Conan lived! The king lived! There was no doubt of it in men's minds now, whether friend or foe.

With the news of the invasion from the south there also came word, brought by hard-riding couriers, that a host of Gundermen was moving southward, reinforced by the barons of the northwest and the northern Bossonians. Tarascus marched with thirty-one thousand men to Galparan, on the river Shirki, which the Gundermen must cross to strike at the towns still held by the Nemedians. The Shirki was a swift, turbulent river rushing south-westward through rocky gorges and canyons, and there were few places where an army could cross at that time of the year, when the stream was almost bank-full with the melting of the snows. All the country east of the Shirki was in the hands of the Nemedians, and it was logical to assume that the Gundermen would attempt to cross either at Galparan, or at Tanasul, which lay to the south of Galparan. Reinforcements were daily expected from Nemedia, until word came that the king of Ophir was making hostile demonstrations on Nemedia's southern border, and to spare any more troops would be to expose Nemedia to the risk of an invasion from the south.

Amalric and Valerius moved out from Tarantia with twenty-five thousand men, leaving as large a garrison as they dared to discourage revolts in the cities during their absence. They wished to meet and crush Conan before he could be joined by the rebellious forces of the kingdom.

The king and his Poitanians had crossed the mountains, but there had been no actual clash of arms, no attack on towns or fortresses. Conan had appeared and disappeared. Apparently he had turned westward through the wild, thinly settled hill country, and entered the Bossonian marches, gathering recruits as he went. Amalric and Valerius with their host, Nemedians, Aquilonian renegades, and ferocious mercenaries, moved through the land in baffled wrath, looking for a foe which did not appear.

Amalric found it impossible to obtain more than vague general tidings about Conan's movements. Scouting-parties had a way of riding out and never returning, and it was not uncommon to find a spy crucified to an oak. The countryside was up and striking as peasants and country-folk strike-savagely, murderously and secretly. All that Amalric knew certainly was that a large force of Gundermen and northern Bossonians was somewhere to the north of him, beyond the Shirki, and that Conan with a smaller force of Poitanians and southern Bossonians was somewhere to the south-west of him.

He began to grow fearful that if he and Valerius advanced farther into the wild country, Conan might elude them entirely, march around

them and invade the central provinces behind them. Amalric fell back
from the Shirki valley and camped in a plain a day's ride from Tanasul.
There he waited. Tarascus maintained his position at Galparan, for he
feared that Conan's maneuvers were intended to draw him southward,
and so let the Gundermen into the kingdom at the northern crossing.

To Amalric's camp came Xaltotun in his chariot drawn by the
uncanny horses that never tired, and he entered Amalric's tent where
the baron conferred with Valerius over a map spread on an ivory camp
table.

This map Xaltotun crumpled and flung aside.

"What your scouts cannot learn for you," quoth he, "my spies tell
me, though their information is strangely blurred and imperfect, as if
unseen forces were working against me."

"Conan is advancing the Shirki river with ten thousand Poitanians,
three thousand southern Bossonians, and barons of the west and south
with the retainers to the number of five thousand. An army of thirty
thousand Gundermen and northern Bossonians is pushing southward to
join him. They have established contact by means of secret communi-
cations used by the cursed priests of Asura, who seem to be opposing
me, and whom I will feed to a serpent when the battle is over—I swear
it by Set!

"Both armies are headed for the crossing at Tanasul, but I do not
believe that the Gundermen will cross the river. I believe that Conan
will cross, instead, and join them."

"Why should Conan cross the river?"

"Because it is to his advantage to delay the battle. The longer he
waits, the stronger he will become, the more precarious our position.
The hills on the other side of the river swarm with people passionately
loyal to his cause—broken men, refugees, fugitives from Valerius's
cruelty. From all over the kingdom men are hurrying to join his army,
singly and by companies. Daily, parties from our armies are ambushed
and cut to pieces by the country-folk. Revolt grows in the central
provinces, and will soon burst into open rebellion. The garrisons we
left there are not sufficient, and we can hope for no reinforcements
from Nemedia for the time being. I see the hand of Pallantides in this
brawling on the Ophirean frontier. He has kin in Ophir.

"If we do not catch and crush Conan quickly the provinces will be
in blaze of revolt behind us. We shall have to fall back to Tarantia to
defend what we have taken; and we may have to fight our way through
a country in rebellion, with Conan's whole force at our heels, and then

stand siege in the city itself, with enemies within as well as without. No, we cannot wait. We must crush Conan before his army grows too great, before the central provinces rise. With his head hanging above the gate at Tarantia you will see how quickly the rebellion will fall apart."

"Why do you not put a spell on his army to slay them all?" asked Valerius, half in mockery.

Xaltotun stared at the Aquilonian as if he read the full extent of the mocking madness that lurked in those wayward eyes.

"Do not worry," he said at last. "My arts shall crush Conan finally like a lizard under the heel. But even sorcery is aided by pikes and swords."

"If he crosses the river and takes up his position in the Goralian hills he may be hard to dislodge," said Amalric. "But if we catch him in the valley on this side of the river we can wipe him out. How far is Conan from Tanasul?"

"At the rate he is marching he should reach the crossing sometime tomorrow night. His men are rugged and he is pushing them hard. He should arrive there at least a day before the Gundermen."

"Good!" Amalric smote the table with his clenched fist. "I can reach Tanasul before he can. I'll send a rider to Tarascus, bidding him follow me to Tanasul. By the time he arrives I will have cut Conan off from the crossing and destroyed him. Then our combined force can cross the river and deal with the Gundermen."

Xaltotun shook his head impatiently.

"A good enough plan if you were dealing with anyone but Conan. But your twenty-five thousand men are not enough to destroy his eighteen thousand before the Gundermen come up. They will fight with the desperation of wounded panthers. And suppose the Gundermen come up while the hosts are locked in battle? You will be caught between two fires and destroyed before Tarascus can arrive. He will reach Tanasul too late to aid you."

"What then?" demanded Amalric.

"Move with your whole strength against Conan," answered the man from Acheron. "Send a rider bidding Tarascus join us here. We will wait his coming. Then we will march together to Tanasul."

"But while we wait," protested Amalric, "Conan will cross the river and join the Gundermen."

"Conan will not cross the river," answered Xaltotun.

Amalric's head jerked up and he stared into the cryptic dark eyes.

"What do you mean?"

"Suppose there were torrential rains far to the north, at the head of the Shirki? Suppose the river came down in such flood as to render the crossing at Tanasul impassable? Could we not then bring up our entire force at our leisure, catch Conan on this side of the river and crush him, and then, when the flood subsided, which I think it would do the next day, could we not cross the river and destroy the Gundermen? Thus we could use our full strength against each of these smaller forces in turn."

Valerius laughed as he always laughed at the prospect of the ruin of either friend or foe, and drew a restless hand jerkily through his unruly yellow locks. Amalric stared at the man from Acheron with mingled fear and admiration.

"If we caught Conan in Shirki valley with the hill ridges to his right and the river in flood to his left," he admitted, "without whole force we could annihilate him. Do you think—are you sure—do you believe such rains will fall?"

"I go to my tent," answered Xaltotun, rising. "Necromancy is not accomplished by the waving of a wand. Send a rider to Tarascus. And let none approach my tent."

That last command was unnecessary. No man in that host could have been bribed to approach that mysterious black silken pavilion, the door flaps of which were always closely drawn. None but Xaltotun ever entered it, yet voices were often heard issuing from it; its walls billowed sometimes without a wind, and weird music came from it. Sometimes, deep in midnight, its silken walls were lit red by flames flickering within, limning misshapen silhouettes that passed to and fro.

Lying in his own tent that night, Amalric heard the steady rumble of a drum in Xaltotun's tent; through the darkness it boomed steadily, and occasionally the Nemedian could have sworn that a deep, croaking voice mingled with the pulse of the drum. And he shuddered, for he knew that voice was not the voice of Xaltotun. The drum rustled and muttered on like deep thunder, heard afar off, and before dawn Amalric, glancing from his tent, caught the red flicker of lightning afar on the northern horizon. In all other parts of the sky the great stars blazed whitely. But the distant lightning flickered incessantly, like the crimson glint of firelight on a tiny, turning blade.

At sunset of the next day Tarascus came up with his host, dusty and weary from hard marching, the footmen straggling hours behind the horsemen. They camped in the plain near Amalric's camp, and at dawn the combined army moved westward.

Ahead of him roved a swarm of scouts, and Amalric waited impatiently for them to return and tell of the Poitanians trapped beside a furious flood. But when the scouts met the column it was with the news that Conan had crossed the river!

"What?" exclaimed Amalric. "Did he cross before the flood?"

"There was no flood," answered the scouts, puzzled. "Late last night he came up to Tanasul and flung his army across."

"No flood?" exclaimed Xaltotun, taken aback for the first time in Amalric's knowledge. "Impossible! There were mighty rains upon the headwaters of the Shirki last night and the night before that!"

"That may be, your lordship," answered the scout. "It is true the water was muddy, and the people of Tanasul said that the river rose perhaps a foot yesterday; but that was not enough to prevent Conan's crossing."

Xaltotun's sorcery had failed! The thought hammered in Amalric's brain. His horror of this strange man out of the past had grown steadily since that night in Belverus when he had seen a brown, shriveled mummy swell and grow into a living man. And the death of Orastes had changed lurking horror into active fear. In his heart was a grisly conviction that the man—or devil—was invincible. Yet now he had undeniable proof of his failure.

Yet even the greatest of necromancers might fail occasionally, thought the baron. At any rate, he dared not oppose the man from Acheron—yet. Orastes was dead, writhing in Mitra only knew what nameless hell, and Amalric knew his sword would scarcely prevail where the black wisdom of the renegade priest had failed. What grisly abomination Xaltotun plotted lay in the unpredictable future. Conan and his host were a present menace against which Xaltotun's wizardry might well be needed before the play was all played.

They came to Tanasul, a small fortified village at the spot where a reef of rocks made a natural bridge across the river, passable always except in times of greatest flood. Scouts brought in the news that Conan had taken up his position in the Goralian hills, which began to rise a few miles beyond the river. And just before sundown the Gundermen had arrived in his camp.

Amalric looked at Xaltotun, inscrutable and alien in the light of the flaring torches. Night had fallen.

"What now? Your magic has failed. Conan confronts us with an army nearly as strong as our own, and he has the advantage of position. We have a choice of two evils: to camp here and await his attack, or to fall back toward Tarantia and await reinforcements."

"We are ruined if we wait," answered Xaltotun. "Cross the river and camp on the plain. We will attack at dawn."

"But his position is too strong!" exclaimed Amalric.

"Fool!" A gust of passion broke the veneer of the wizard's calm. "Have you forgotten Valkia? Because some obscure elemental principle prevented the flood do you deem me helpless? I had intended that your spears should exterminate our enemies; but do not fear: it is my arts shall crush their host. Conan is in a trap. He will never see another sunset. Cross the river!"

They crossed by the flare of torches. The hoofs of the horses clinked on the rocky bridge, splashed through the shallows. The glint of the torches on shields and breastplates was reflected redly in the black water. The rock bridge was broad on which they crossed, but even so it was past midnight before the host was camped in the plain beyond. Above them they could see fires winking redly in the distance. Conan had tamed a bay in the Goralian hills, which had more than once before served as the last stand of an Aquilonian king. Amalric left his pavilion and strode restlessly through the camp.

A weird glow flickered in Xaltotun's tent, and from time to time a demoniacal cry slashed the silence, and there was a low sinister muttering of a drum that rustled rather than rumbled.

Amalric, his instincts whetted by the night and the circumstances, felt that Xaltotun was opposed by more than physical force. Doubts of the wizard's power assailed him. He glanced at the fires high above him, and his face set in grim lines. He and his army were deep in the midst of a hostile country. Up there among those hills lurked thousands of wolfish figures out of whose hearts and souls all emotion and hope had been scourged except a frenzied hate for their conquerors, a mad lust for vengeance. Defeat meant annihilation, retreat through a land swarming with blood-mad enemies. And on the morrow he must hurl his host against the grimmest fighter in the western nations, and his desperate horde. If Xaltotun failed them now—

Half a dozen men-at-arms strode out of the shadows. The firelight glinted on their breastplates and helmet crests. Among them they half led, half dragged a gaunt figure in tattered rags. Saluting, they spoke:

"My lord, this man came to the outposts and said he desired word with King Valerius. He is an Aquilonian."

He looked more like a wolf—a wolf the traps had scarred. Old sores that only fetters make showed on his wrists and ankles. A great brand, the mark of hot iron, disfigured his face. His eyes glared through the tangle of his matted hair as he half crouched before the baron.

"Who are you, you filthy dog?" demanded the Nemedian. "Call me Tiberias," answered the man, and his teeth clicked in an involuntary spasm. "I have come to tell you how to trap Conan."

"A traitor, eh?" rumbled the baron.

"Men say you have gold," mouthed the man, shivering under his rags. "Give some to me! Give me gold and I will show you how to defeat the king!" His eyes glazed widely, his outstretched, upturned hands were spread like quivering claws.

Amalric shrugged his shoulders in distaste. But no tool was too base for his use.

"If you speak the truth you shall have more gold than you can carry," he said. "If you are a liar and a spy I will have you crucified head-down. Bring him along."

In the tent of Valerius, the baron pointed to the man who crouched shivering before them, huddling his rags about him.

"He says he knows a way to aid us on the morrow. We will need aid, if Xaltotun's plan is no better than it has proved so far. Speak on, dog."

The man's body writhed in strange convulsions. Words came in a stumbling rush:

"Conan camps at the head of the Valley of Lions. It is shaped like a fan, with steep hills on either side. If you attack him tomorrow you will have to march straight up the valley. You cannot climb the hills on either side. But if King Valerius will deign to accept my service, I will guide him through the hills and show him how he can come upon King Conan from behind. But if it is to be done at all, we must start soon. It is many hours' riding, for one must go miles to the west, then miles to the north, then turn eastward and so come into the Valley of Lions from behind, as the Gundermen came."

Amalric hesitated, tugging his chin. In these chaotic times it was not rare to find men willing to sell their souls for a few gold pieces.

"If you lead me astray you will die," said Valerius. "You are aware of that, are you not?"

The man shivered, but his wide eyes did not waver.

"If I betray you, slay me!"

"Conan will not divide his force," mused Amalric. "He will need all his men to repel our attack. He cannot spare any to lay ambushes in the hills. Besides, this fellow knows his hide depends on his leading you as he promised. Would a dog like him sacrifice himself? Nonsense! No, Valerius, I believe the man is honest."

"Or a greater thief than most, for he would sell his liberator," laughed Valerius. "Very well. I will follow the dog. How many men can you spare me?"

"Five thousand should be enough," answered Amalric. "A surprize attack on their rear will throw them into confusion, and that will be enough. I shall expect your attack about noon."

"You will know when I strike," answered Valerius. As Amalric returned to his pavilion he noted with gratification that Xaltotun was still in his tent, to judge from the blood-freezing cries that shuddered forth into the night air from time to time. When presently he heard the clink of steel and the jingle of bridles in the outer darkness, he smiled grimly. Valerius had about served his purpose. The baron knew that Conan was like a wounded lion that rends and tears even in his death throes. When Valerius struck from the rear, the desperate strokes of the Cimmerian might well wipe his rival out of existence before he himself succumbed. So much the better. Amalric felt he could well dispense with Valerius, once he had paved the way for a Nemedian victory.

The five thousand horsemen who accompanied Valerius were hard-bitten Aquilonian renegades for the most part. In the still starlight they moved out of the sleeping camp, following the westward trend of the great black masses that rose against the stars ahead of them. Valerius rode at their head, and beside him rode Tiberias, a leather thong about his wrist gripped by a man-at-arms who rode on the other side of him. Others kept close behind with drawn swords.

"Play us false and you die instantly," Valerius pointed out. "I do not know every sheep-path in these hills, but I know enough about the general configuration of the country to know the directions we must take to come in behind the Valley of Lions. See that you do not lead us astray."

The man ducked his head and his teeth chattered as he volubly assured his captor of his loyalty, staring up stupidly at the banner that floated over him, the golden serpent of the old dynasty.

Skirting the extremities of the hills that locked the Valley of Lions, they swung wide to the west. An hour's ride and they turned north, forging through wild and rugged hills, following dim trails and tortuous paths. Sunrise found them some miles northwest of Conan's position, and here the guide turned eastward and led them through a maze of labyrinths and crags. Valerius nodded, judging their position by various peaks thrusting up above the others. He had kept his bearings in a general way, and he knew they were still headed in the right direction.

But now, without warning, a gray fleecy mass came billowing down from the north, veiling the slopes, spreading out through the valleys. It blotted out the sun; the world became a blind gray void in which visibility was limited to a matter of yards. Advance became a stumbling, groping muddle. Valerius cursed. He could no longer see the peaks that had served him as guideposts. He must depend wholly upon the traitorous guide. The golden serpent drooped in the windless air.

Presently Tiberias seemed himself confused; he halted, stared about uncertainly.

"Are you lost, dog?" demanded Valerius harshly.

"Listen!"

Somewhere ahead of them a faint vibration began, the rhythmic rumble of a drum.

"Conan's drum!" exclaimed the Aquilonian.

"If we are close enough to hear the drum," said Valerius, "why do we not hear the shouts and the clang of arms? Surely battle has joined."

"The gorges and the winds play strange tricks," answered Tiberias, his teeth chattering with the ague that is frequently the lot of men who have spent much time in damp underground dungeons. "Listen!"

"They are fighting down in the valley!" cried Tiberias. "The drum is beating on the heights. Let us hasten!"

He rode straight on toward the sound of the distant drum as one who knows his ground at last. Valerius followed, cursing the fog. Then it occurred to him that it would mask his advance. Conan could not see him coming. He could be at the Cimmerian's back before the noonday sun dispelled the mists.

Just now he could not tell what lay on either hand, whether cliffs, thickets or gorges. The drum throbbed unceasingly, growing louder as they advanced, but they heard no more of the battle. Valerius had no idea toward what point of the compass they were headed. He started as he saw gray rock walls looming through the smoky drifts on either hand, and realized that they were riding through a narrow defile. But the guide showed no sign of nervousness, and Valerius hove a sigh of relief when the walls widened out and became invisible in the fog. They were through the defile; if an ambush had been planned, it would have been made in that pass.

But now Tiberias halted again. The drum was rumbling louder, and Valerius could not determine from what direction the sound was coming. Now it seemed ahead of him, now behind, now on one hand or the other. Valerius glared about him impatiently, sitting on his warhorse with wisps of mist curling about him and the moisture gleaming on his armor. Behind him the long lines of steel-clad riders faded away and away like phantoms into the mist. "Why do you tarry, dog?" he demanded. The man seemed to be listening to the ghostly drum. Slowly he straightened in his saddle, turned his head and faced Valerius, and the smile on his lips was terrible to see.

"The fog is thinning, Valerius," he said in a new voice, pointing a bony finger. "Look!"

The drum was silent. The fog was fading away. First the crests of cliffs came in sight above the gray clouds, tall and spectral. Lower and lower crawled the mists, shrinking, fading. Valerius started up in his stirrups with a cry that the horsemen echoed behind him. On all sides of them the cliffs towered. They were not in a wide, open valley as he had supposed. They were in a blind gorge walled by sheer cliffs hundreds of feet high. The only entrance or exit was the narrow defile through which they had ridden.

"Dog!" Valerius struck Tiberias full in the mouth with his clenched mailed hand. "What devil's trick is this?" Tiberias spat out a mouthful of blood and shook with fearful laughter.

"A trick that shall rid the world of a beast! Look, dog!" Again Valerius cried out, more in fury than in fear. The defile was blocked by a wild and terrible band of men who stood silent as images—ragged, shock-headed men with spears in their hands—hundreds of them. And up on the cliffs appeared other faces—thousands of faces—wild, gaunt, ferocious faces, marked by fire and steel and starvation. "A trick of Conan's!" raged Valerius.

"Conan knows nothing of it," laughed Tiberias. "It was the plot of broken men, of men you ruined and turned to beasts. Amalric was right. Conan has not divided his army. We are the rabble who followed him, the wolves who skulked in these hills, the homeless men, the hopeless men. This was our plan, and the priests of Asura aided us with their mist. Look at them, Valerius! Each bears the mark of your hand, on his body or on his heart!

"Look at me! You do not know me, do you, what of this scar your hangman burned upon me? Once you knew me. Once I was lord of Amilius, the man whose sons you murdered, whose daughter your mercenaries ravished and slew. You said I would not sacrifice myself to trap you? Almighty gods, if I had a thousand lives I would give them all to buy your doom!

"And I have bought it! Look on the men you broke, dead man who once played the king! Their hour has come! This gorge is your tomb. Try to climb the cliffs: they are steep, they are high. Try to fight your way back through the defile: spears will block your path, boulders will crush you from above! Dog! I will be waiting for you in Hell!"

Throwing back his head he laughed until the rocks rang. Valerius leaned from his saddle and slashed down with his great sword, severing shoulder bone and breast. Tiberias sank to the earth, still laughing ghastlily through a gurgle of gushing blood.

The drums had begun again, encircling the gorge with guttural thunder; boulders came crushing down; above the screams of dying men shrilled the arrows in blinding clouds from the cliffs.

22 The Road to Acheron

Dawn was just whitening the east when Amalric drew up his hosts in the mouth of the Valley of Lions. This valley was flanked by low, rolling but steep hills, and the floor pitched upward in a series of irregular natural terraces. On the uppermost of these terraces Conan's army held its position, awaiting the attack. The host that had joined him, marching down from Gunderman, had not been composed exclusively of spearmen. With them had come seven thousand Bossonian archers, and four thousand barons and their retainers of the north and west, swelling the ranks of his cavalry.

The pikemen were drawn up in a compact wedge-shaped formation at the narrow head of the valley. There were nineteen thousand of them, mostly Gundermen, though some four thousand were Aquilonians of the other provinces. They were flanked on either hand by five thousand Bossonian archers. Behind the ranks of the pikemen the knights sat, their steeds motionless, lances raised: ten thousand knights of Poitain, nine thousand Aquilonians, barons and their retainers.

It was a strong position. His flanks could not be turned, for that would mean climbing the steep, wooded hills in the teeth of the arrows and swords of the Bossonians. His camp lay directly behind him, in a narrow, steep-walled valley which was indeed merely a continuation of the Valley of Lions, pitching up at a higher level. He did not fear a surprize from the rear, because the hills behind him were full of refugees and broken men whose loyalty to him was beyond question.

But if his position was hard to shake, it was equally hard to escape from. It was a trap as well as a fortress for the defenders, a desperate last stand of men who did not expect to survive unless they were victorious. The only line of retreat possible was through the narrow valley at their rear.

Xaltotun mounted a hill on the left side of the valley, near the wide mouth. This hill rose higher than the others, and was known as the King's Altar, for a reason long forgotten. Only Xaltotun knew, and his memory dated back three thousand years.

He was not alone. His two familiars, silent, hairy, furtive and dark, were with him, and they bore a young Aquilonian girl, bound hand and foot. They laid her on an ancient stone, which was curiously like an altar, and which crowned the summit of the hill. For long centuries it had stood there, worn by the elements until many doubted that it was anything but a curiously shapen natural rock. But what it was, and why it stood there, Xaltotun remembered from of old. The familiars went away, with their bent backs like silent gnomes, and Xaltotun stood alone beside the stone altar, his dark beard blown in the wind, overlooking the valley.

He could see clear back to the winding Shirki, and up into the hills beyond the head of the valley. He could see the gleaming wedge of steel drawn up at the head of the terraces, the burganets of the archers glinting among the rocks and bushes, the silent knights motionless on their steeds, their pennons flowing above their helmets, their lances rising in a bristling thicket.

Looking in the other direction he could see the long serried lines of the Nemedians moving in ranks of shining steel into the mouth of the valley. Behind them the gay pavilions of the lords and knights and the drab tents of the common soldiers stretched back almost to the river.

Like a river of a molten steel the Nemedian host flowed into the valley, the great scarlet dragon rippling over it. First marched the bowmen, in even ranks, arbalests half raised, bolts nocked, fingers on triggers. After them came the pikemen, and behind them the real strength of the army—the mounted knights, their banners unfurled to the wind, their lances lifted, walking their great steeds forward as if they rode to a banquet.

And higher up on the slopes the smaller Aquilonian host stood grimly silent.

There were thirty thousand Nemedian knights, and, as in most Hyborian nations, it was the chivalry which was the sword of the army. The footmen were used only to clear the way for a charge of the armored knights. There were twenty-one thousand of these, pikemen and archers.

The bowmen began loosing as they advanced, without breaking ranks, launching their quarrels with a whir and tang. But the bolts fell short or rattled harmlessly from the overlapping shields of the Gundermen. And before the arbalesters could come within killing range, the arching shafts of the Bossonians were wreaking havoc in their ranks.

A little of this, a futile attempt at exchanging fire, and the Nemedian bowmen began falling back in disorder. Their armor was light, their weapons no match for the Bossonian longbows. The western archers were sheltered by bushes and rocks. Moreover, the Nemedian footmen lacked something of the morale of the horsemen, knowing as they did that they were being used merely to clear the way for the knights.

The crossbowmen fell back, and between their opening lines the pikemen advanced. These were largely mercenaries, and their masters had no compunction about sacrificing them. They were intended to mask the advance of the knights until the latter were within smiting distance. So while the arbalesters plied their bolts from either flank at long range, the pikemen marched into the teeth of the blast from above, and behind them the knights came on.

When the pikemen began to falter beneath the savage hail of death that whistled down the slopes among them, a trumpet blew, their companies divided to right and left, and through them the mailed knights thundered.

They ran full into a cloud of stinging death. The clothyard shafts found every crevice in their armor and the housings of the steeds. Horses scrambling up the grassy terraces reared and plunged backward, bearing their riders with them. Steel-clad forms littered the slopes. The charge wavered and ebbed back.

Back down in the valley Amalric re-formed his ranks. Tarascus was fighting with drawn sword under the scarlet dragon, but it was the baron of Tor who commanded that day. Amalric swore as he glanced at the forest of lance tips visible above and beyond the head-pieces of the Gundermen. He had hoped his retirement would draw the knights out in a charge down the slopes after him, to be raked from either flank by his bowmen and swamped by the numbers of his horsemen. But they had not moved. Camp servants brought skins of water from the river. Knights doffed their helmets and drenched their sweating heads. The wounded on the slopes screamed vainly for water. In the upper valley, springs supplied the defenders. They did not thirst that long, hot spring day.

On the King's Altar, beside the ancient, carven stone, Xaltotun watched the steel tide ebb and flow. On came the knights, with waving plumes and dipping lances. Through a whistling cloud of arrows they plowed to break like a thundering wave on the bristling wall of spears and shields. Axes rose and fell above the plumed helmets, spears thrust upward, bringing down horses and riders. The pride of the Gundermen was no less fierce than that of the knights. They were not spear-fodder, to be sacrificed for the glory of better men. They were the finest infantry in the world, with a tradition that made their morale unshakable. The kings of Aquilonia had long learned the worth of unbreakable infantry. They held their formation unshaken; over their gleaming ranks flowed the great lion banner, and at the tip of the wedge a giant figure in black armor roared and smote like a hurricane, with a dripping ax that split steel and bone alike.

The Nemedians fought as gallantly as their traditions of high courage demanded. But they could not break the iron wedge, and from the wooded knolls on either hand arrows raked their close-packed ranks mercilessly. Their own bowmen were useless, their pikemen unable to climb the heights and come to grips with the Bossonians. Slowly, stubbornly, sullenly, the grim knights fell back, counting their empty saddles. Above them the Gundermen made no outcry of triumph. They closed their ranks, locking up the gaps made by the fallen. Sweat ran into their eyes from under their steel caps. They gripped their spears and waited, their fierce hearts swelling with pride that a king should fight on foot with them. Behind them the Aquilonian knights had not moved. They sat their steeds, grimly immobile.

A knight spurred a sweating horse up the hill called the King's Altar, and glared at Xaltotun with bitter eyes.

"Amalric bids me say that it is time to use your magic, wizard," he said. "We are dying like flies down there in the valley. We cannot break their ranks."

Xaltotun seemed to expand, to grow tall and awesome and terrible.

"Return to Amalric," he said. "Tell him to re-form his ranks for a charge, but to await my signal. Before that signal is given he will see a sight that he will remember until he lies dying!"

The knight saluted as if compelled against his will, and thundered down the hill at breakneck pace.

Xaltotun stood beside the dark altarstone and stared across the valley, at the dead and wounded men on the terraces, at the grim, blood-stained band at the head of the slopes, at the dusty, steel-clad ranks re-forming in the vale below. He glanced up at the sky, and he glanced down at the slim white figure on the dark stone. And lifting a dagger inlaid with archaic hieroglyphs, he intoned an immemorial invocation:

"Set, god of darkness, scaly lord of the shadows, by the blood of a virgin and the sevenfold symbol I call to your sons below the black earth! Children of the deeps, below the red earth, under the black earth, awaken and shake your awful manes! Let the hills rock and the stones topple upon my enemies! Let the sky grow dark above them, the earth unstable beneath their feet! Let a wind from the deep black earth curl up beneath their feet, and blacken and shrivel them——"

He halted short, dagger lifted. In the tense silence the roar of the hosts rose beneath him, borne on the wind.

On the other side of the altar stood a man in a black, hooded robe, whose coif shadowed pale delicate features and dark eyes calm and meditative.

"Dog of Asura!" whispered Xaltotun, his voice was like the hiss of an angered serpent. "Are you mad, that you seek your doom? Ho, Baal! Chiron!"

"Call again, dog of Acheron!" said the other, and laughed. "Summon them loudly. They will not hear, unless your shouts reverberate in Hell."

From a thicket on the edge of the crest came a somber old woman in a peasant garb, her hair flowing over her shoulders, a great gray wolf following at her heels.

"Witch, priest and wolf," muttered Xaltotun grimly, and laughed. "Fools, to pit your charlatan's mummery against my arts! With a wave of my hand I brush you from my path!"

"Your arts are straws in the wind, dog of Python," answered the Asurian. "Have you wondered why the Shirki did not come down in flood and trap Conan on the other bank? When I saw the lightning in the night I guessed your plan, and my spells dispersed the clouds you had summoned before they could empty their torrents. You did not even know that your rain-making wizardry had failed."

"You lie!" cried Xaltotun, but the confidence in his voice was shaken. "I have felt the impact of a powerful sorcery against mine—but no man on earth could undo the rain-magic, once made, unless he possessed the very heart of sorcery."

"But the flood you plotted did not come to pass," answered the priest. "Look at your allies in the valley, Pythonian! You have led them to the slaughter! They are caught in the fangs of the trap, and you cannot aid them. Look!"

He pointed. Out of the narrow gorge of the upper valley, behind the Poitanians, a horseman came flying, whirling something about his head that flashed in the sun. Recklessly he hurled down the slopes, through the ranks of the Gundermen, who sent up a deep-throated roar and clashed their spears and shields like thunder in the hills. On the terraces between the hosts the sweat-soaked horse reared and plunged, and his wild rider yelled and brandished the thing in his hands like one demented. It was the torn remnant of a scarlet banner, and the sun struck dazzlingly on the golden scales of a serpent that writhed thereon.

"Valerius is dead!" cried Hadrathus ringingly. "A fog and a drum lured him to his doom! I gathered that fog, dog of Python, and I dispersed it! I, with my magic, which is greater than your magic!"

"What matters it?" roared Xaltotun, a terrible sight, his eyes blazing, his features convulsed. "Valerius was a fool. I do not need him. I can crush Conan without human aid!"

"Why have you delayed?" mocked Hadrathus. "Why have you allowed so many of your allies to fall pierced by arrows and spitted on spears?"

"Because blood aids great sorcery!" thundered Xaltotun, in a voice that made the rocks quiver. A lurid nimbus played about his awful head. "Because no wizard wastes his strength thoughtlessly. Because I would conserve my powers for the great days to be, rather than employ them in a hill-country brawl. But now, by Set, I shall loose them to the uttermost! Watch, dog of Asura, false priest of an outworn god, and see a sight that shall blast your reason forevermore!"

Hadrathus threw back his head and laughed, and hell was in his laughter.

"Look, black devil of Python!"

His hand came from under his robe holding something that flamed and burned in the sun, changing the light to a pulsing golden glow in which the flesh of Xaltotun looked like the flesh of a corpse.

Xaltotun cried out as if he had been stabbed.

"The Heart! The Heart of Ahriman!"

"Aye! The one power that is greater than your power!"

Xaltotun seemed to shrivel, to grow old. Suddenly his beard was shot with snow, his locks flecked with gray.

"The Heart!" he mumbled. "You stole it! Dog! Thief!"

"Not I! It has been on a long journey far to the southward. But now it is in my hands, and your black arts cannot stand against it. As it resurrected you, so shall it hurl you back into the night whence it drew you. You shall go down the dark road to Acheron, which is the road of silence and the night. The dark empire, unreborn, shall remain a legend and a black memory. Conan shall reign again. And the Heart of Ahriman shall go back into the cavern below the temple of Mitra, to burn as a symbol of the power of Aquilonia for a thousand years!"

Xaltotun screamed inhumanly and rushed around the altar, dagger lifted; but from somewhere—out of the sky, perhaps, or the great jewel that blazed in the hand of Hadrathus—shot a jetting beam of blinding blue light. Full against the breast of Xaltotun it flashed, and the hills re-echoed the concussion. The wizard of Acheron went down as though struck by a thunderbolt, and before he touched the ground he was fearfully altered. Beside the altarstone lay no fresh-slain corpse, but a shriveled mummy, a brown, dry, unrecognizable carcass sprawling among moldering swathings.

Somberly old Zeiata looked down.

"He was not a living man," she said. "The Heart lent him a false aspect of life, that deceived even himself. I never saw him as other than a mummy."

Hadrathus bent to unbind the swooning girl on the altar, when from among the trees appeared a strange apparition—Xaltotun's chariot drawn by the weird horses. Silently they advanced to the altar and halted, with the chariot wheel almost touching the brown withered thing on the grass. Hadrathus lifted the body of the wizard and placed it in the chariot. And without hesitation the uncanny steeds turned and moved off southward, down the hill. And Hadrathus and Zeiata and the gray wolf watched them go—down the long road to Acheron, which is beyond the ken of men.

Down in the valley Amalric had stiffened in his saddle when he saw that wild horseman curvetting and caracoling on the slopes while he brandished that bloodstained serpent banner. Then some instinct jerked his head about, toward the hill known as the King's Altar. And his lips parted. Every man in the valley saw it—an arching shaft of dazzling light that towered up from the summit of the hill, showering golden fire. High above the hosts it burst in a blinding blaze that momentarily paled the sun.

"That's not Xaltotun's signal!" roared the baron.

"No!" shouted Tarascus. "It's a signal to the Aquilonians!

"Look!" Above them the immobile ranks were moving at last, and a deep-throated roar thundered across the vale.

"Xaltotun has failed us!" bellowed Amalric furiously. "Valerius has failed us! We have been led into a trap! Mitra's curse on Xaltotun who led us here! Sound the retreat!"

"Too late!" yelled Tarascus. "Look!"

Up on the slopes the forest of lances dipped, leveled. The ranks of the Gundermen rolled back to right and left like a parting curtain. And with a thunder like the rising roar of a hurricane, the knights of Aquilonia crashed down the slopes.

The impetus of that charge was irresistible. Bolts driven by the demoralized arbalesters glanced from their shields, their bent helmets. Their plumes and pennons streaming out behind them, their lances lowered, they swept over the wavering lines of pikemen and roared down the slopes like a wave.

Amalric yelled an order to charge, and the Nemedians with desperate courage spurred their horses at the slopes. They still outnumbered the attackers.

But they were weary men on tired horses, charging uphill. The onrushing knights had not struck a blow that day. Their horses were fresh. They were coming downhill and they came like a thunderbolt. And like a thunderbolt they smote the struggling ranks of the Nemedians—smote them, split them apart, ripped them asunder and dashed the remnants headlong down the slopes.

After them on foot came the Gundermen, blood-mad, and the Bossonians were swarming down the hills, loosing as they ran at every foe that still moved.

Down the slopes washed the tide of battle, the dazed Nemedians swept on the crest of the wave. Their archers had thrown down their arbalests and were fleeing. Such pikemen as had survived the blasting charge of the knights were cut to pieces by the ruthless Gundermen.

In a wild confusion the battle swept through the wide mouth of the valley and into the plain beyond. All over the plain swarmed the warriors, fleeing and pursuing, broken into single combat and clumps of smiting, hacking knights on rearing, wheeling horses. But the Nemedians were smashed, broken, unable to re-form or make a stand. By the hundreds they broke away, spurring for the river. Many reached it, rushed across and rode eastward. The countryside was up behind them; the people hunted them like wolves. Few ever reached Tarantia.

The final break did not come until the fall of Amalric. The baron, striving in vain to rally his men, rode straight at the clump of knights that followed the giant in black armor whose surcoat bore the royal lion, and over whose head floated the golden lion banner with the scarlet leopard of Poitain beside it. A tall warrior in gleaming armor couched his lance and charged to meet the lord of Tor. They met like a thunderclap. The Nemedian's lance, striking his foe's helmet, snapped bolts and rivets and tore off the casque, revealing the features of Pallantides. But the Aquilonian's lance head crashed through shield and breastplate to transfix the baron's heart.

A roar went up as Amalric was hurled from his saddle, snapping the lance that impaled him, and the Nemedians gave way as a barrier bursts under the surging impact of a tidal wave. They rode for the river in a blind stampede that swept the plain like a whirlwind. The hour of the Dragon had passed.

Tarascus did not flee. Amalric was dead, the color-bearer slain, and the royal Nemedian banner trampled in the blood and dust. Most of his knights were fleeing and the Aquilonians were riding them down; Tarascus knew the day was lost, but with a handful of faithful followers he raged through the melee, conscious of but one desire—to meet Conan, the Cimmerian. And at last he met him.

Formations had been destroyed utterly, close-knit bands broken asunder and swept apart. The crest of Trocero gleamed in one part of the plain, those of Prospero and Pallantides in others. Conan was alone. The house-troops of Tarascus had fallen one by one. The two kings met man to man.

Even as they rode at each other, the horse of Tarascus sobbed and sank under him. Conan leaped from his own steed and ran at him, as the king of Nemedia disengaged himself and rose. Steel flashed blindingly in the sun, clashed loudly, and blue sparks flew; then a clang of armor as Tarascus measured his full length on the earth beneath a thunderous stroke of Conan's broadsword.

The Cimmerian paced a mail-shod foot on his enemy's breast, and lifted his sword. His helmet was gone; he shook back his black mane and his blue eyes blazed with their old fire.

"Do you yield?"

"Will you give me quarter?" demanded the Nemedian.

"Aye. Better than you'd have given me, you dog. Life for you and all your men who throw down their arms. Though I ought to split your head for an infernal thief," the Cimmerian added.

Tarascus twisted his neck and glared over the plain. The remnants of the Nemedian host were flying across the stone bridge with swarms of victorious Aquilonians at their heels, smiting with the fury of glutted vengeance. Bossonians and Gundermen were swarming through the camp of their enemies, tearing the tents to pieces in search of plunder, seizing prisoners, ripping open the baggage and upsetting the wagons.

Tarascus cursed fervently, and then shrugged his shoulders, as well as he could, under the circumstances.

"Very well. I have no choice. What are your demands?"

"Surrender to me all your present holdings in Aquilonia. Order your garrisons to march out of the castles and towns they hold, without their arms, and get your infernal armies out of Aquilonia as quickly as possible. In addition you shall return all Aquilonians sold as slaves, and pay an indemnity to be designated later, when the damage your occupation of the country has caused has been properly estimated. You will remain as hostage until these terms have been carried out."

"Very well," surrendered Tarascus. "I will surrender all the castles and towns now held by my garrisons without resistance, and all the other things shall be done. What ransom for my body?"

Conan laughed and removed his foot from his foe's steel-clad breast, grasped his shoulder and heaved him to his feet. He started to speak, then turned to see Hadrathus approaching him. The priest was as calm and self-possessed as ever, picking his way between rows of dead men and horses.

Conan wiped the sweat-smeared dust from his face with blood-stained hand. He had fought all through the day, first on foot with the pikemen, then in the saddle, leading the charge. His surcoat was gone, his armor splashed with blood and battered with strokes of sword, mace and ax. He loomed gigantically against a background of blood and slaughter, like some grim pagan hero of mythology.

"Well done, Hadrathus!" quoth he gustily. "By Crom, I am glad to see your signal! My knights were almost mad with impatience and eating their hearts out to be at sword strokes. I could not have held them much longer. What of the wizard?"

"He has gone down the dim road to Acheron," answered Hadrathus. "And I—I am for Tarantia. My work is done here, and I have a task to perform at the temple of Mitra. All our work is done here. On this field we have saved Aquilonia—and more than Aquilonia. Your ride to your capital will be a triumphal procession through a kingdom mad with joy. All Aquilonia will be cheering the return of their king. And so, until we meet again in the great royal hall—farewell!"

Conan stood silently watching the priest as he went. From various parts of the field knights were hurrying toward him. He saw Pallantides, Trocero, Prospero, Servius, Gallannus, their armor splashed with crimson. The thunder of battle was giving way to a roar of triumph and acclaim. All eyes, hot with strife and shining with exultation, were turned toward the great black figure of the king; mailed arms brandished red-stained swords. A confused torrent of sound rose, deep and thunderous as the sea-surf: "Hail, Conan, king of Aquilonia!"

Tarascus spoke.

"You have not yet named my ransom."

Conan laughed and slapped his sword home in its scabbard. He flexed his mighty arms, and ran his bloodstained fingers through his thick black locks, as if feeling there his rewon crown.

"There is a girl in your seraglio named Zenobia."

"Why, yes, so there is."

"Very well." The king smiled as at an exceedingly pleasant memory. "She shall be your ransom, and naught else. I will come to Belverus for her as I promised. She was a slave in Nemedia, but I will make her queen of Aquilonia!"

THE END